The Man Who Solved Mysteries

More Short Fiction by William Brittain

The Man Who Solved Mysteries

More Short Fiction by William Brittain

Edited and Introduced by
JOSH PACHTER

Crippen & Landru Publishers
Cincinnati, Ohio
2022

This book is a work of fiction. Names, characters, businesses, organizations, places, events and incidents either are the product of the author's imagination or are used fictitiously. Any resemblance to actual persons, living or dead, events, or locales is entirely coincidental.

For information contact:

Crippen & Landru, Publishers
P. O. Box 532057
Cincinnati, OH 45253 USA
Web: www.crippenlandru.com
E-mail: Info@crippenlandru.com

ISBN (softcover): 978-1-936363-61-2

ISBN (clothbound): 978-1-936363-60-5

First Edition: January 2022

10 9 8 7 6 5 4 3 2 1

TABLE OF CONTENTS

INTRODUCTION
STRANG BREW

Between 1964 and 1983, William E. Brittain published a total of seventy-two short crime stories, all but one of them in the pages of either *Ellery Queen's Mystery Magazine* or *Alfred Hitchcock's Mystery Magazine*. Eleven of the seventy-two, known collectively as the "Man Who Read" series—although in one case it was a *woman* who read, in one a boy, in one a *group* of men, and in one a man who *didn't* read—originally appeared in EQMM, as did thirty-two tales featuring high-school science teacher Leonard Strang. The remaining twenty-nine were non-series stories; an even score of those debuted in AHMM, eight were in EQMM, and one anomalously showed up in a literary journal called *Antaeus*.

In 1979, Brittain wrote his first children's book, *All the Money in the World* (which four years later was adapted as an episode of the *Adventures of Teddy Ruxpin* television series). He followed it up with a baker's dozen more books for younger readers, including several set in the fictional New England village of Coven Tree (the second of which, *The Wish Giver*, won a Newbery Honor Award in 1983), continuing to produce new volumes through 1994, eleven years after he "retired" from writing short stories.

In addition to being a talented writer for both adult and younger readers and an English teacher who devoted more than three decades to the students at Lawrence Junior High School on Long Island (NY), Bill Brittain was also my friend.

I met him and his wife Ginny at a Mystery Writers of America function in the late 1960s, when I was just a year or two older than Bill's students and had recently sold a story of my own to EQMM. The Brittains took me under their wing and made me feel, not like the punk kid I was, but like a colleague, a full-fledged member of the crime-writing community.

Bill died in Weaverville, North Carolina, on December 16, 2011—his eighty-first birthday. In 2018, Crippen & Landru published *The Man Who Read Mysteries: The Short Fiction of William Brittain,* which I edited and introduced. That volume included all eleven of the "Man Who Read" stories and seven of the Mr. Strangs.

The book turned out to be one of C&L's all-time best-sellers, and, soon after it came out, publishers in China and South Korea licensed editions for their countries. COVID-19 slowed down both of those volumes, and Chinese government censors deleted "The Man Who Read John Dickson Carr" ("because the plot of the crime is inspired by the detective story; the solution of the crime is inspired by the detection story is OK, but the detective story couldn't inspire a crime"), "Mr. Strang Performs an Experiment" ("because of the suspectable sexual harassment between the teacher and the girl student"), and "Mr. Strang Takes a Hand" ("because of the drug issues among students; drug topic is OK, but it couldn't involve the student"). Different strokes for different folks, amiright?

Anyway, due to popular demand in *this* country, Jeff Marks and Doug Greene have asked me to put together this second volume, in which you will find all twenty-five of the Mr. Strang stories that weren't included in *The Man Who Read Mysteries.*

I have left them largely as they were originally published in EQMM, but—full disclosure here—I *have* made occasional editorial changes. In some cases, I tightened up sentences that I suspect EQMM editor Fred Dannay or someone else made a bit longer than they needed to be in order to fit them into the magazine's two-narrow-columns format.

Occasionally, I fixed a typo or corrected a larger error. In "Mr. Strang Takes a Partner," for example, Maude Wiggins refers to Shakespeare's *Anthony and Cleopatra,* which she—being Aldershot High School's librarian—really *must* have known is in fact titled *Antony and Cleopatra,* not *Anthony.* So I have given her the benefit of the doubt and corrected the name of the play. And, speaking of plays, in "Mr. Strang Sees a Play," Russian chemist D.I. Mendeleev is referred to twice, once correctly but once as "E.I. Mendeleev," and there's a moment when Mr. Strang shrugs out of an overcoat that we last saw him carrying draped over one arm. So I changed "E.I." to "D.I." and had the teacher wearing his coat instead of carrying it. In some of the stories, Mr. Strang's friend Paul Roberts of the Aldershot Police Department is referred to as "Detective Roberts," while in others he appears as either "Detective Sergeant Roberts" or just "Sergeant Roberts." For the sake of consistency, I have identified him as "Detective Roberts" in these pages.

On the other hand, Ralph Waldo Emerson once wrote that "[a] foolish consistency is the hobgoblin of little minds," and so, to avoid being foolish, I have in some cases made the decision not to meddle. In both "Mr. Strang Finds the Answers" and "Mr. Strang Follows Through," for example, the gnomelike science teacher has a telephone next to his bed, while in "Mr. Strang Finds an Angle" he skitters downstairs to *make* a call. So be it. Even Lawrence Block's Matt Scudder makes some phone calls from his room and others from the booth in the lobby of his West 57ᵗʰ Street hotel.

The Mr. Strang stories were written half a century ago, and their language is at times dated—in "Mr. Strang Follows Through," for one example, a woman in her twenties is referred to as a "girl," a usage that in 2021 makes me cringe but that I probably would have been guilty of myself in the early 1970s—and there are occasional instances of stereotyping, especially of teenagers. Despite these infelicities, many of the tales offer lessons that are still relevant. Like my friend Bill, I am a teacher, and I am deeply touched when, in "Mr. Strang Unlocks a Door," our wizened educator protagonist marvels that "in this day and age, to find a young person who values the good opinion of others—remarkable!" Similarly, I wish the parents of some of my students would read "Mr. Strang Pulls a Switch" and take its message to heart. And the relevance of the Strang series isn't limited to the schoolyard: the tragic revelations at the end of "Mr. Strang Checks a Record" and "Mr. Strang and the Cat Lady," for example, remain sad realities in the lives of many of today's young and elderly Americans, respectively.

The plotting of the Strang tales is occasionally simple but more often intricate, and the resolutions are generally surprising and almost always satisfying. Every once in a while— as in "Mr. Strang Accepts a Challenge"—the solution as presented by the little science teacher stretches the reader's credulity pretty thin, but those cases are the exceptions. As a rule, Mr. Strang cuts right to the heart of the matter by logical and in retrospect inevitable reasoning, often stimulated by a serendipitous observation of the world around him.

As I prepared this volume, I noted that Brittain never once mentions the name of the state in which his fictional village of Aldershot is located.

Curious, I consulted Google Maps, and learned that there's an Aldershot in England and two of them in Canada, but the Strang stories are distinctively American, and enough of the names of the secondary characters who populate the series are of Swedish or Norwegian origin to suggest the possibility of a Minnesota setting....

... except there's no Aldershot in the Land of Ten Thousand Lakes, or anywhere else in the Midwest. In fact, there doesn't seem to be a municipality by that name *anywhere* in the US—although, oddly, there *is* an Aldershot Drive in Henrico, Virginia, only twenty-three miles from my home!

I asked Brittain's daughter, Sue Brittain Gawley, if her

father ever identified a particular small town after which he'd modeled Mr. Strang's Aldershot—and, laughing, she told me that she's always wondered the same thing. "It occurs to me that dad may have chosen the name Aldershot precisely to *avoid* its being confused with an actual place," she said. "Aldershot sounds sufficiently academic and generic. One thing I *can* tell you is that it's definitely *not* Freeport, New York, where I grew up."

The only substantive hint within the stories appears in "Mr. Strang and the Lost Ship," where we learn (a) that Edward Hotchkiss, Mr. Strang's former college classmate, has invited the teacher to spend a long weekend in Pixley's Cove, a fishing village somewhere in New England, (b) that, in extending the invitation, Hotchkiss urged his old friend to "c'mon up," (c) that Mr. Strang made the journey not in his little purple car but by bus, and (d) that on arrival the teacher was so exhausted that he "collapsed on the bed as if poleaxed and slept for ten hours."

From these snippets, I deduce that Aldershot must be too far south of New England for the old teacher to have made the drive himself, but close enough to have made it worth his while to visit for a long weekend. Google Maps tells me that it's about eight hours by car from Philadelphia to Portland, Maine—so I'm going to conclude that Aldershot might perhaps be a suburb of the City of Brotherly Love.

I'm probably wrong, though, which leaves one Strangian mystery yet to be solved....

If this collection turns out to be as popular as was its predecessor, we intend to do a third volume, in which we'll collect the twenty-nine standalone stories ... and anyone who owns all three books will thus own the complete short fiction of my friend Bill Brittain.

For now, though, allow me to polish my black-rimmed glasses on my acid-stained necktie, wave them around to indicate that a lecture is about to begin, and invite you to turn the page and step into the classroom of that remarkable man who solved mysteries, Leonard Strang....

Josh Pachter
Midlothian, Virginia
October 2021

MR. STRANG FINDS THE ANSWERS

Mr. Strang walked up the steps through a haze that might have been fog and onto the flag-draped platform. Three men wearing high silk hats and cutaway coats smiled at him. He wondered if his old tweed jacket with the leather patches at the elbows was suitable for the occasion, but there really hadn't been time to change. Amid thunderous applause, he was awarded the Nobel Prize in Chemistry, and then the main speaker rose and approached the microphone that would carry his words of praise for Leonard Strang, Aldershot High School's veteran science teacher, all over the planet....

"Mr. Strang, waddaya use lime water for?"

With an almost audible *pop*, Mr. Strang's dream of glory faded into the reality of the classroom. He raised his head and considered his lilies of the field.

Guy Oringer, Ward Hilditch, and Alan Speed—in mentally dubbing them "lilies of the field," Mr. Strang was only half correct. For while it was certain that, in the academic sense, they toiled not, their ability to spin was amply proven by their fantastic yarns concerning undone homework and late entrances to class. In fact, it was their unique ability to procrastinate that accounted for their presence in Mr. Strang's classroom at a time when all other students and teachers had long since left the building.

"Carbon dioxide bubbled through lime water will turn it a milky white, Guy," Mr. Strang replied wearily, "and if it doesn't work, you get an incomplete in chemistry. That experiment should have been done two weeks ago."

The teacher wrinkled his nose at the musky odor of hair oil as Guy Oringer slicked his locks into place with a pocket comb. "Well, you see, Mr. Strang," he said, "I was sick when you assigned it, and—"

"—and in about five minutes I'm going home, whether you're finished or not. I hate to hurry you, boys, but it's after five o'clock, and you've been here since three-thirty. Now either finish your experiments or take the consequences."

Each boy bent to his assigned task with a diligence that would have guaranteed a listing on the Honor Roll—if the diligence could have been maintained for more than ten minutes at a time.

Finally the three approached Mr. Strang's desk. Ward

Hilditch held out a flask of Benedict's solution with one hand while he nervously inspected the fingers of the other in a fruitless search for a fingernail that hadn't already been gnawed to the quick. Guy Oringer presented a beaker of lime water of a satisfactorily whitish color with the élan of one who has discovered a cure for an incurable disease. And with a cackle that any mad scientist in a horror movie would have been proud to utter, Alan Speed exhibited a lump of black, spongy carbon as proof that he had been able to separate table sugar into its component elements.

"Gentlemen, I'd like to say I'm proud of you," sighed Mr. Strang. "Unfortunately, the words would stick in my throat. However, you *will* be allowed to take the final examination next week."

"Will you tell my mom and dad I can take the test?" asked Ward, still nibbling on a nonexistent fingernail. "They were real sore when they found out I might have to go to summer school."

"I've already written letters to your families, telling them the good news," Mr. Strang replied, "but up to now it's been questionable whether they'd ever be sent. I'll mail them on my way home. Now wait until I get my briefcase, and I'll walk you as far as the school exit."

He went to a door at the rear of the classroom, which led to the chemistry storage closet where he had left his briefcase. He opened the door, took a deep breath, and stepped back, coughing and gasping.

"What's the matter, Mr. Strang?" asked Alan, finding it hard to keep from laughing.

Pulling off his black-rimmed glasses, Mr. Strang rubbed his eyes with his handkerchief. "Ether!" he gasped, when he could catch his breath. "The whole closet reeks of ether! Is this your idea of a joke, Mr. Speed?"

Alan's smile faded as he understood what the teacher was implying. "Oh, gee, Mr. Strang," he wailed. "I didn't do anything. It's just that you were hopping around rubbing at your eyes and—well, you looked so funny that—oh, gee!"

Holding the handkerchief firmly over his nose, Mr. Strang entered the closet. It was deep enough that he was out of the boys' sight for several seconds. When he came back through the door, his mouth was set in a grim line and his eyes glittered menacingly. "Ward Hilditch, Guy Oringer, Alan Speed—sit down!" he said, slowly and distinctly, pointing to each of them in turn with a rigid index finger.

Mr. Strang usually called students by their first names. On rare occasions, when formality was necessary, he used last names—but he always preceded them with "Mr." or

"Miss." The last time he had addressed a student by both first and last names, that student had been expelled. The three boys knew that, whatever was the matter, it involved something more serious than spilled ether.

"I've cleaned up the ether," said the teacher thickly, "and almost asphyxiated myself in the process. The fumes should dissipate in a few minutes. Then I have something I'd like you to see."

The classroom clock ticked off three minutes, while Mr. Strang fanned the closet door back and forth vigorously to force fresh air into the storage room. Then he beckoned to the boys.

Most of the wall space in the closet was lined with shelves containing a variety of scientific supplies and apparatus. An empty ether can lay in the tiny sink, along with several cleaning rags. In one corner of the room was a coat rack, on which hung Mr. Strang's overcoat and battered felt hat.

"Look!" said the teacher, pointing a slender finger at the floor below the coat rack, where his briefcase lay on its side. And then the boys knew the reason for his anger.

Although the briefcase was still locked, one side gaped wide open. It had been cut through with a knife or some other sharp instrument.

"Now, who did that?" barked Mr. Strang. For one of the few times in his teaching career, he was dangerously close to losing his temper.

Silence. The boys looked at one another. Even Alan Speed, who normally had a quip for every occasion, knew better than to open his mouth.

Finally, Guy Oringer asked, "Why would *anyone* do a thing like that?"

"Correction, Mr. Oringer," said Mr. Strang. "The question is, 'Why would one of *you* three do a thing like that?' I didn't put my briefcase in here until after you were in the classroom, and no one else has come in after you.

"For the benefit of the two innocent parties, let me elucidate. Inside that briefcase is—was—a copy of the final exam in chemistry that you will take next week. As senior member of the chem department, I was going to take it home this evening to check it for possible typographical errors, a fact that was not unknown to my students. Attached to the examination was an answer key—a single sheet of paper containing the answers to all the questions except the essays. I'd be very much surprised if one of those items isn't missing—or both of them!"

Quickly, the teacher leafed through the contents of the mutilated case. A set of essays, still uncorrected, was in order. A packet of letters still had its rubber band around it. Privately, Mr. Strang hoped that the letter to the parents of one of the three boys might be missing, but no such luck. Even the final exam was there. The answer key, however, was gone.

"Well, at least whichever one of you took it was intelligent enough not to try to get out with the exam itself," said the teacher. "Ten pages would have been quite a wad to try to slip past me. I suppose the guilty one expected to be well away from here before I discovered my damaged briefcase."

"Does—does this mean we can't take the final after all?" asked Alan, now almost in tears.

"That exam took more than six weeks to prepare," replied Mr. Strang. "It would be impossible to replace it at this late date. And if there's a chance of the answers having been exposed, it may be that *nobody* will take the test. Now, which of you has the answer key?"

Mr. Strang suspected that he would get nowhere by appealing to the boys' sense of honor. In his years of teaching, he had tried that strategy too many times with only negative results, and he was no longer shocked by the idea that teenagers are not wholly honest.

"May I suggest," he said, "that each of you submit to a search?"

The boys gave frightened nods. A few minutes later, they were dressed in only their shorts, and all their clothing had been examined. The contents of their pockets were on Mr. Strang's desk, and the answer key was still missing. Guy Oringer and Alan Speed laughed nervously at their near-naked condition, while Ward Hilditch munched at the end of one finger and stared at the floor.

"*Protozoa, Mesozoa, Porifera, Coelenterata,*" muttered Mr. Strang. This recitation of animal phyla made him feel no better. He had lost the answers, and he had ordered three of his students to strip in his classroom. There would be telephone calls from irate parents. And Marvin W. Guthrey, Aldershot High School's principal, was not known for taking a firm stand in times of adversity. He would call Mr. Strang to his office the following morning, and the teacher winced at the thought of Guthrey's sarcasm, which could cut like a knife.

A knife—that was it! Whoever had cut open the briefcase must have used a knife. All he had to do was search the three piles of belongings on his desk.

As he did this, Mr. Strang smiled broadly at his own cleverness. Ward Hilditch had a folding knife. It was tiny, but—when the teacher got it open at the cost of a broken thumbnail—he found that its scratched and battered blade would easily have been able to cut through the leather of the briefcase.

When he had sorted through the second pile, Mr. Strang's smile slipped a bit. For Guy Oringer also carried a knife. It was bulky and had enough gadgets to equip a machine shop. Guy insisted on displaying each of them and explaining its use. There were no less than six different tools that might have been used to slit the case.

By the time Mr. Strang examined Alan Speed's belongings, he was right back where he had started. By pressing a catch on Alan's knife, the teacher almost succeeded in amputating one of his fingers. Switchblades were forbidden at Aldershot, but this did not concern Mr. Strang at the moment. The fact was that each of the three boys carried equipment capable of having cut open the case.

Mr. Strang looked at the boys. The room still reeked of ether, and his head had begun to ache. The ether bothered him in another way, too. What had been the point of it? The can was kept on the highest shelf in the closet, so it certainly hadn't been spilled accidentally. Whoever had slit open the case must have used the ether for something. But what? Was it supposed to put the teacher to sleep?

Mr. Strang shook his head in annoyance and spoke to the boys. "I don't suppose any of you remember who was the last one to go into the storeroom before me?" he drawled, his voice dripping with irony.

They didn't.

"Well, at least I know the answer key won't be going out with you," he continued. "I'll go on with the search after you leave. Get dressed."

After he had escorted the boys—fully clothed—out of the school, Mr. Strang checked the classroom and the storage closet with a thoroughness that would have turned a customs inspector green with envy. He scrutinized the desks, opened and peered into the bottles of chemicals, probed the cracks in the woodwork, and pulled down the window shades to see if the missing sheet of paper had been rolled up in one of them. He even searched his own pockets on the off chance that he himself had forgotten having taking the answers from his briefcase.

At the end of a frustrating hour, he reluctantly came to two inescapable conclusions:

First, none of the boys could possibly have taken the answer key away with him when he left the classroom.

Second, the missing answers were no longer in either

the classroom or the storage closet.

For a moment, Mr. Strang seriously considered the possibility that one of the boys had chewed and swallowed the key. But there would have been no point in doing that *before* the teacher found his damaged briefcase, and there had been no opportunity afterward. Marching into the closet, he jammed his arms into the sleeves of his coat, crushed his hat onto his head, and then in a burst of irritation kicked viciously at the briefcase. It skittered across the tile floor, and Mr. Strang saw the glint of a metal object that had remained hidden beneath it throughout his search.

His stiff joints cracking, he knelt and picked up the object. It was a dime. And Mr. Strang was sure it hadn't been there when he had first placed the briefcase on the floor. He put the coin on the briefcase and shoved it with a finger, listening to the sharp *clink* it made when it hit the floor.

"Funny," he muttered. "It seems to me that, if it was dropped, anybody in here would have heard it." Thoughtfully, he put the dime in his pocket.

Mr. Strang consigned the three boys, the answer key, and Mr. Guthrey's temper to the devil and prepared to leave. He absentmindedly grasped the briefcase by its handle and lifted—and was rewarded by a cascade of papers that poured through the gaping hole in its side. Unmarked assignments, the bundle of letters, and the final examination lay strewn across the floor of the closet.

"*Sipunculoidea!*" he cried at this last outrage against his dignity. He retrieved the final exam, put it in a cupboard, and snapped the lock. Then he gathered the uncorrected papers into a pile, folded the pile in half, and stuffed it into a coat pocket. He debated whether or not to mail the letters on his way home, decided that—since he had to go to the drugstore anyway—he might as well, and crammed them into his pocket on top of the other papers. "With my luck," he growled, "I'll drop the wrong stack through the mail slot, and tomorrow morning there'll be twenty-eight essays delivered to homes all over town."

He walked out of the building to his battered automobile. Roaring angrily out of the parking lot, he yanked at the steering wheel and headed towards Aldershot's business district. There he stole a parking space from under the headlights of a waiting taxi. Then, still fuming over the loss of the answers, he completed his errands, treating the druggist with lofty disdain and leaving the man behind the stamp window at the post office an amazed and innocent victim of one of Mr. Strang's rare temper tantrums.

When he reached his rooming house, he rocketed into

the driveway, narrowly missing the yellow cat that belonged to his landlady, Mrs. Mackey, and stopped the car with a screech of brakes. He entered the house prepared to oppose any views Mrs. Mackey might make about the weather, only to find her on her hands and knees, fumbling in the pile of the living-room rug.

Mrs. Mackey knew better than to ask what the trouble was: she could almost see the steam coming out from under Mr. Strang's collar. She limited herself to a noncommittal hello and continued prowling over the rug, an envelope clutched in one fist.

"Picking daisies, Mrs. Mackey?" asked Mr. Strang sarcastically, and was immediately ashamed of himself.

Mrs. Mackey stopped, picked up something from the rug, and placed it in the envelope. "Not daisies," she answered. "Pearls."

"What?"

"*Pearls*. The string on my necklace broke, and the pearls went all over the rug. I just found the last one." She held up the envelope triumphantly.

Mr. Strang nodded and headed for the stairway. He was halfway up when he turned his head to where Mrs. Mackey, in the living room below, was pouring the pearls into the palm of her left hand. A wide smile crossed the teacher's face.

Of course, he said to himself. *That must have been the way it was done.*

He climbed the rest of the stairs, did a little dance step at the top in what he hoped was a fair imitation of Vernon Castle—or perhaps of Fred Astaire—and said happily, "Leonard Strang, you are a fat-headed idiot."

In his room, he took a copy of his class list from a bureau, looked up Ward Hilditch's telephone number, and began to dial the instrument next to his bed. "Mr. Hilditch, please," he said a moment later. "This is Mr. Strang, Ward's chemistry teacher."

He made two more phone calls—to the other two fathers—and then sat back to await his visitors.

It was past eight o'clock when Mrs. Mackey called Mr. Strang to meet the first of his guests. "Mr. Oringer," he said to the scowling man, who was removing his overcoat. "Good of you to come."

"Good, my foot!" rumbled Paul Oringer. "What did you expect me to do? The idea: threatening to fail Guy without even letting him take the final examination!" Removing from his pocket a comb that might have been a twin of the one his son carried, Oringer began to draw his hair over an incipient bald spot. "I heard about what happened at school today," he said as he combed. "You should be ashamed of yourself, making Guy take his clothes off in the classroom. As a lawyer, Mr. Strang, I ought to—"

Whatever Mr. Oringer ought to was interrupted by the arrival of Benjamin Hilditch. His hands shook visibly as he unbuttoned his coat, and he had a habit of clutching at one ear, much as a drowning man might grab for a life preserver. Mr. Strang remembered Ward's almost nonexistent fingernails and wondered if his father's ear was the adult equivalent of a security blanket.

Before Hilditch could do more than mumble a polite greeting, Winslow Speed entered the living room. More reasonable than Oringer and more vocal than Hilditch, he admitted that his boy might be capable of stealing the exam answers, but he wanted to know what proof the teacher had of his son's guilt.

Mr. Strang led the three men up to his room. Warning them not to trip on the threadbare spot in his rug, he offered them seats, while he himself perched on the edge of the bed.

"Now I'm willing to keep an open mind about this, Mr. Strang," began Oringer. "Only tell me, where in hell do you get off, acting like a—"

"Paul Oringer, close your mouth," said Mr. Strang. "You always were too talkative, even when I taught you physics in high school. I see maturity hasn't changed you much."

"That's one on you, Paul," chortled Hilditch, still holding his ear.

"Look, Mr. Strang, you called us here, so let's get down to business," said Speed. "I'm not too happy about the way you handled things with our boys today—at least from the way Alan tells it. But I'd like to hear your side of the story."

"For the benefit of anyone whose son may have given a slightly biased view of the day's events, let me review what exactly *did* happen," said the teacher. He swiftly described what went on in the classroom before and after the disappearance of the answer key. "So you see," he concluded, "it's obvious not only that one of the boys made arrangements to get the answers, but that those arrangements were successful."

"You made my boy strip," said Oringer. "Right there in the classroom."

"Oh, come off it, Paul," said Speed. "This thing involves every kid who's taking chemistry. What did you expect the man to do, just let someone leave with all the answers?

What about it, Hilditch? If you caught three guys in your store, and you knew one of 'em was a shoplifter, what would *you* do? Just let 'em walk out on you?"

"No, I suppose not," said Hilditch nervously. Mr. Strang was afraid the ear would come away in his hand.

"That's different!" shouted Oringer. "Mr. Strang is—"

"How is it different?" asked Mr. Strang softly. "The stolen answer key represents, I'd say, a great deal more work on the part of the various individuals who prepared it than, say, one of the keys Mr. Hilditch sells in his hardware store."

"Look," said Oringer, "kids are going to cheat, right? You did it, I did it, we all do it. Can it really be that wrong?"

"Yes," said Mr. Strang simply.

"Oh, come on!" Oringer shook his head impatiently. "Everything today is test, test, test. Schools, jobs, the Army—everything. And if a kid fails, the doors start closing. All he gets are the dirty jobs."

"I'm inclined to agree that testing is overdone," said Mr. Strang. "But does that mean we should do away with it entirely? Mr. Oringer, if you took on a partner in your legal work, wouldn't you like to know what kind of job he was doing, just out of curiosity if for no other reason? Most businesses have quality checks on the products they manufacture, don't they? And the product that—hopefully—our schools produce is educated citizens."

"Oh, for Pete's sake, be reasonable. Do you mean to tell me, Mr. Strang, that you never sneaked a look at an answer while you were taking an exam? *Never*?"

"What we're talking about," said the teacher, "is not a weak-willed individual suddenly giving in to temptation. We're talking about a deliberate plan to steal—"

"I still don't think it's stealing," said Oringer.

"What *would* you call it, Paul?" Winslow Speed asked grimly.

"Why—why—"

"It *is* stealing, and nothing less," said Mr. Strang. "It was the theft of a year's work in chemistry from those students who may now not be allowed to take their final exam."

"All right," said Oringer in his best cross-examination manner, "let's say it was, ah, stealing and get down to cases. I'm even willing to overlook, under the circumstances, the impromptu striptease in the classroom. But I'd like to ask a question: why should all three boys be punished for what only one of them did?"

"A good point," said Mr. Strang. "So if one of us should be on hand when the thief picks up the stolen answer key from its hiding place, then we'd all know who the guilty boy was, wouldn't we?"

The three men sat forward in their chairs. "You mean you know where the answers are?" asked Speed.

"Yes, I know."

"Then why don't you get them?"

"Impossible. The men guarding them—"

"What!" Paul Oringer stood up and looked down at the teacher. "You mean whoever stole the answers had a gang working for him?"

"In a sense, yes."

"I think you're cracking up, Mr. Strang," said Oringer, sitting down again.

Benjamin Hilditch detached his hand from his ear and drummed his fingers nervously on the arm of his chair. "This is more serious than I thought," he said. "A gang. I had no idea.... You can prove what you're saying, of course?"

"Certainly." Mr. Strang stood up, jerked his black-rimmed glasses from his nose, polished them on his neck-tie, and held them tightly between the thumb and forefinger of his right hand. Thrusting his left hand deep into his jacket pocket, he looked from one to another of the men in front of him. Oringer vaguely remembered Mr. Strang performing these rites before giving a lecture in the classroom.

"Fact one," began the teacher, holding up the glasses dramatically. "The missing answers did not leave the room when the boys left. Even a single sheet of paper has a certain amount of bulk to it, no matter how tightly it is folded. And I went over the clothing and possessions of the boys with a fine-tooth comb. No, the answer key was still in school when I searched the classroom and the storage closet."

"Then why didn't the key turn up?" asked Speed.

"Because there was one place I didn't search."

"All right, Mr. Strang, I'll bite. First you say you looked all over the classroom and the closet. Now you say you *didn't* look everywhere. If that's the case, why don't you go back right now and get it?"

"Because it's no longer there."

There was a murmuring of voices. Then Oringer quieted the others. "You mean the guilty boy sneaked back and—"

"Of course not. Even if he'd been able to get into the school and unlock my classroom door, one of the custodians would have been sure to see him."

"Then who took the answers out of the room?" shouted Oringer.

Mr. Strang looked ruefully at the men. "I did," he said softly.

"You? Oh, come on, Mr. Strang, make sense. You took

the answer key, but now a gang has it, and you know where it is, but you can't find it? What's going on?"

"I didn't find the key in the classroom," said Mr. Strang, "because it never left my briefcase—at least not until I myself took it out."

"But you said you *looked* in your briefcase!"

"I did. But not in the right place."

After a short silence, Hilditch snapped his fingers. "The letters!" he cried.

"Go to the head of the class, Mr. Hilditch," said Mr. Strang. "Of course: the answer key was in one of those sealed envelopes I had prepared to mail to you three."

"Then the 'gang' is—"

"—our faithful postmen," replied Mr. Strang. "Neither sleet, nor storm, nor hail, and so on. It was a beautiful plan, really. Once the thief put the answer key in the envelope addressed to his own parents, I myself would carry it out and mail it, and the next day it would be delivered right to his door. All he had to do was be the first one to get to the mail. He would be able to take the final exam—if it were given—and I would have no reason to suspect him more than the other two. It would have worked, too, if I hadn't seen my landlady earlier this evening putting some pearls into an envelope. That got me thinking about what else might have been stuffed into an envelope—and suddenly the whole scheme was crystal clear."

"Wait a minute," said Oringer. "You said the envelopes were sealed. How could the answer-key envelope have been opened without tearing the paper, to say nothing about re-sealing it?"

"Ether," said Mr. Strang. "What do you think of when I mention ether?"

"Why, putting people to sleep."

"Unfortunately, that was my first reaction, too. But ether is also an excellent solvent. A very small amount applied to the outside of the envelope flap would have softened the glue to the point where the envelope could be opened. It would have been easy for the thief to insert the answer key and then reseal the letter. As soon as the ether dried, the glue would harden again, and there would be nothing to show what had been done."

It was Winslow Speed who finally asked the question in the minds of the three fathers. "Who did it, Mr. Strang? Which one of our boys—?"

"I don't know, Mr. Speed."

"What?"

"I don't know. But it shouldn't be hard to find out. I

suggest that all three of you make a point of being on hand when your mail is delivered for the next day or so. There will be a letter from me addressed to each of you. But in the case of the guilty boy, the parent will get something additional. Finding the answer key in your envelope should be convincing enough proof for any of you. From then on, whatever action you wish to take will be up to you."

When the men had left, Mr. Strang sat at his desk, idly flipping the dime he had found under the briefcase. As proof, the dime wouldn't hold up in a court of law for thirty seconds. After all, it might have been dropped in the closet accidentally. But the science teacher was sure the thief had taken the dime out of his pocket deliberately.

It was because of the knife, of course. Two of the knives had opened easily—one of them much *too* easily, thought Mr. Strang, remembering the near miss with the switchblade. But one knife had been hard to open. It was tiny, and the blade was difficult to grip in its closed position. It would have been difficult to open it, he thought, especially if its owner had bitten his fingernails to the point where they were too short to hook under the notch in the tiny blade. He would have needed a tool—and a dime was thin enough to insert in the notch and use to flick the blade open.

But Mr. Strang had not had the heart to mention it and break a father's heart in front of the other men. "I must be getting old," he whispered to himself. "Now, what do I do about the final exam?"

It was two days later when he found the package on his desk. Tearing open the wrapping paper, he found a new and expensive leather briefcase with the initials "L.S." stamped in gold on one side.

There were two pieces of paper in the case.

One of them had printed at the top:

CHEMISTRY — FINAL EXAMINATION
— ALDERSHOT HIGH SCHOOL.

The other was a handwritten letter that read:

Mr. Strang,

My father told me what you said the other night. But I saw the postman a block before he got to our house, and he gave me the mail with your letter in it. I didn't have any more ether to get it open, but the steam from a teakettle worked just as well, so my father was pretty happy when he opened the envelope and there was nothing inside but your letter. As for me, I haven't been too happy about anything since I took the answers out of your briefcase.

Honest, I didn't look at any of the answers, but if you don't want me to take the final exam, I won't squawk. And I'll accept any punishment the school feels I've got coming. But is there any way to keep my folks from finding out who took the answers? I'm not afraid of what they'll do to me, but it would just about kill my father and mother to find out what I did.

The letter was signed Ward Hilditch.

Mr. Strang looked at the letter again, remembering a scared little man tugging nervously at one ear. Maybe something *could* be worked out....
He decided that he would have to drastically alter his dim views concerning honor among teenagers.

MR. STRANG SEES A PLAY

The three figures—each wearing a long, tattered robe—stood in almost complete darkness, with only their outlines visible. In front of them, a large cauldron was suspended from a rude tripod over what appeared to be the glowing coals of a fire. Out of the cauldron issued a sickly white vapor that dribbled down the outside edges and swirled like small satanic lizards about the feet of the dimly seen figures.

A greenish light sprang up, giving a ghastly illumination to the scene. The three wraithlike forms looked at one another and cackled evilly. The stringy wisps of white hair hanging limply over their shoulders and the pale, wrinkled faces looking strangely like skulls in the dim light made it clear that they could be nothing but witches.

One of the three weird sisters took a long spoon from a hidden pocket of her robe and came forward to the cauldron. She held the spoon high, as if making some devilish incantation, and then plunged it deep into whatever vile brew was being concocted. She began to speak in a high, cracked voice:

"When shall we three meet again? In thunder, lightning, or in rain?"

The second witch grasped the spoon, waved her hand through the mist above the cauldron, and continued:

"When the hurlyburly's done, when the battle's lost and won!"

The two looked expectantly at the third figure, who took up the chant:

"That will be ere the set of sun."

Standing near an exit door at the rear of the Aldershot High School auditorium, Mr. Strang softly clapped his gloved hands in approval. The high school's Drama Club production of *Macbeth* was off to a flying start, and there was a large audience in spite of the cold, wet weather that Aldershot had been having for almost a week.

The thin science teacher reminded himself that he would have to find Frank Tabor, the Drama Club's faculty advisor and director, and offer his congratulations. The makeup on the witches—none of whom was more than sixteen years old—was superb, and Mr. Strang marveled at the way in which a few cardboard cartons, a bit of gray paint, and some dried twigs had been transformed into the blasted heath called for in the play's stage directions.

The witches disappeared into darkness again, and there was a squeaking of pulleys as a backdrop was lowered for the next scene. Mr. Strang put on his overcoat and bent down to pick up a gallon Thermos jug from the floor beside him. Then he walked out into the lobby, just as the stage lights behind him came up on what the program described as "A Camp Near Forres," and Duncan, King of Scotland, began to examine the wounds of a bloodstained soldier.

"Not walking out on us already, are you, Mr. Strang? Is the play that bad?"

Mr. Strang set down the Thermos, ran slender fingers through his fast-disappearing gray hair, and looked around the lobby. In one corner, the doorway leading to the office of assistant principal Dan Wilstater had been converted into a temporary box office by latching the door in its open position and placing a wooden table across the opening.

The old science teacher pulled from a pocket of his jacket a pair of black-rimmed glasses and put them on, peering at the figure in the doorway. "No, I was about to start looking for you, Frank," he said finally. "What are you doing out here? I thought you'd be backstage, directing traffic—or whatever it is a director does."

Frank Tabor shrugged and continued to count money as he talked. "Over the last five weeks, I've seen enough of *Macbeth* to last me the next five years," he said. "From now on, the kids are on their own. Besides, they won't make any mistakes. With all the rehearsals we've had, they could do this play blindfolded. I thought I'd come out here and see how much money we took in."

"Your cast certainly started out in fine style," said Mr. Strang. "That opening scene with the three witches is one of the spookiest things I've seen in years."

"Yeah, we spent a lot of time on that," replied Tabor. "It kind of gets the audience in the mood for what's coming next. Incidentally, I want to thank you for your help. It added a lot to the play."

"Think nothing of it. Glad to be of service. Besides, it was one of the boys in the Science Club who came up with the idea. I just passed it along to you." Mr. Strang looked at the growing stack of money on the table in front of Tabor. "How are the receipts coming?" he asked.

"I'm not sure," Tabor said with a wink. "I'll have to ask my business manager." He turned to the desk behind him, where a girl about seventeen years old was stacking coins in neat piles. "What's our grand total, Barbara?" he called.

"With the advance sale plus the tickets we sold tonight, I think it'll come to a little over six hundred dollars." Barbara Priott looked up from her work and smiled. "Hi, Mr. Strang!"

The science teacher raised his battered felt hat in reply. "That's a lot of money to be responsible for, Barbara," he said. "Don't let Mr. Tabor here make off with it."

Barbara smiled shyly and continued counting coins. Tabor placed his stack of bills in a metal box and put it in a drawer of the table. "Keep an eye on things, Barbara," he said. "I'm going to stretch my legs. Call me when you've finished counting, and we'll put the money in the safe."

The girl nodded. "Would you like to leave your coat in here, Mr. Strang?" she asked, as Tabor moved the table and stepped out into the lobby.

"Thank you, Barbara, I think I will. And would you stash this jug, too? It's getting a bit heavy to carry around."

As Barbara nodded, the science teacher removed his gloves and put them in one pocket of his coat. Shucking off the coat, he placed it on the table in the doorway, setting his hat carefully on top of it. Then he picked up the Thermos jug and set it on the table with a thump.

"Leave them there, Mr. Strang," said Barbara. "I'll bring them in here as soon as I'm finished."

As Mr. Strang and Frank Tabor walked through the lobby past the open door of the auditorium, they could hear Lady Macbeth summoning up her courage for the murder of Duncan:

> *Come, you spirits*
> *That tend on mortal thoughts,*
> *Unsex me here,*
> *And fill me from the crown to the toe, top-full*
> *Of direst cruelty!*

"Poor Barbara," Tabor mused, lighting a cigarette. "She wanted desperately to play Lady Macbeth. She might have made a good one, too."

"Then why didn't you use her?" asked Mr. Strang. "Learning the lines wouldn't have given her any trouble. I have her in one of my chemistry classes, and her memory's excellent."

Tabor nodded. "She did well during the first readings, too. But apparently she chokes under pressure. The first time I had tryouts in front of an audience, she froze completely. It's too bad. Next April, I'm planning to put on *Pygmalion,* and she'd have made a wonderful Eliza Doolittle."

"Any chance of her conquering her stage fright?"

"I don't know," answered Tabor. "If she'd just give *some*

indication that she could perform under pressure, I'd use her in a minute. As it is, I can't take the chance. It wouldn't be fair to the other kids."

"I see." Mr. Strang jammed tobacco from his pouch into a massive briar pipe and applied a match. "I wouldn't give up on Barbara yet, Frank," he said. "She might surprise you."

"I hope so. She wanted to be in a play this year more than anything else in the world. She's a good business manager, but I'd like to see her on stage. Look, you came to see the play, not gab with me, so why don't you go back inside? I'll help Barbara finish counting the money."

"No hurry," replied Mr. Strang. "The murders don't start coming until Act Two, and I'm a necrophile from way back. Now that the witches have had their big scene, I'm just marking time until Macbeth gets ready to skewer Duncan and Banquo's ghost starts waltzing around the stage. And later on, of course, I'll want to see the return of the witches."

Act II found Mr. Strang standing again at the rear of the auditorium. Macbeth—as portrayed by the captain of the debate team—was suitably horrified at seeing the phantom dagger, and the science teacher felt a prickling along his spine as the lights dimmed onstage and the clanging of a bell broke the hushed silence as Macbeth made ready to murder his king:

> *I go, and it is done; the bell invites me.*
> *Hear it not, Duncan, for it is a knell*
> *That summons thee to heaven or to hell.*

Mr. Strang remained long enough to watch the play's drunken porter reel across the stage, finally managing to open the gates of the castle to Macduff and Lennox before staggering off to oblivion to the accompaniment of laughter and applause from the audience. Then the science teacher went back to the lobby to await the murder of Banquo in Act III.

Behind the table in the temporary box office, Barbara Priott was busy stuffing packets of bills into a manila envelope. As Mr. Strang walked toward the open door, the girl dropped a quarter, and the coin rolled out onto the marble floor of the lobby. The teacher stopped it with his foot, picked it up, and placed it on the table.

It was then that he saw the boy standing inside the office. A tall, heavy-set teenager, he wore a thick wool jacket that had droplets of water on the shoulders.

"Who are you?" asked the teacher bluntly. Mr. Strang was certain he knew the faces of all of the students at Aldershot High, and this boy was a complete stranger to him.

The boy mumbled something that sounded like "fine."

"I didn't ask *how* you are but *who* you are," said Mr. Strang.

"Huh? Oh, that's my name—Fein. Johnny Fein, that's me."

"Well, Johnny, nobody's supposed to be behind that table who doesn't belong there. What are you doing here? And where's Mr. Tabor, Barbara?"

"He went backstage to see how the play's going, Mr. Strang," said the girl coolly, "and Johnny's a friend of mine. He stopped by to pick me up. He's going to take me home after the money's all counted. There's nothing wrong with that, is there?"

Mr. Strang shook his head. "Not so long as your parents know about it," he said. "Just be sure he takes you right home. It's a bit cold outside for any—er—side trips. Besides, I was rather hoping you might find time tonight to put in a little work on that chemistry assignment you owe me. I'm afraid your work with the Drama Club has had a rather bad effect on your studies."

Barbara stared wide-eyed at Mr. Strang for a moment and then glanced at the boy standing next to her. "About that assignment, Mr. Strang, I had an idea for something I want to put in my report, and I was wondering if you'd approve it for me before I go ahead."

"I don't want to take you away from your work—or from young Mr. Fein here," replied the teacher. "Could it wait until tomorrow?"

"I have a study hall first period, and I'd like to work on it then," said the girl. "I'll just jot down what I had in mind—it'll only take a second."

"*Chaetognatha!*" said the teacher vehemently. "I shouldn't do that, Barbara. Wait until we've both got more time."

But by now the girl had taken a scrap of paper from her purse and was scribbling something on it with a ballpoint pen. When she was finished writing, but before she could hand the paper to Mr. Strang, Johnny Fein plucked it from the table and read it carefully.

"I never took much science myself," said the boy when he had finished. "I hope you can make something out of this, Mr. Strong."

"The name is *Strang*," replied the teacher. "S-T-R—oh, forget it." He picked up the paper and glanced at what the girl had written:

> Iron + Indium
> Hydrogen + Arsenic
> Silver + Uranium + Nitrogen
> Reference: D.I. Mendeleev

Mr. Strang shook his head, puzzling over the list. "I'm afraid you've misinterpreted the assignment, Barbara," he said. "We were dealing with chemical compounds. These are elements. Perhaps—"

"Well, *really*, Mr. Strang!" Barbara looked daggers at the teacher. "You suggested that reference yourself. It was during Monday's chemistry period."

Mr. Strang frowned. Perhaps it was his imagination, but it seemed to him that Barbara had put more stress on her last word than was really necessary.

"Wait a minute, let me see that again!" Johnny Fein snatched the paper from Mr. Strang's fingers with his left hand. His right slipped inside the opening of his jacket, giving him a vaguely Napoleonic appearance. After reading the note for the second time, the boy shrugged and dropped it on the table.

The teacher opened his mouth to protest such patent rudeness. But suddenly he paused, looking strangely at the girl. "I—I think I see what you're getting at, Barbara," he said slowly, picking up the list. "Maybe I can think of some way in which the connections could be made."

"I hope so, Mr. Strang," replied the girl. "I could sure use some help."

"By the way, how much did the Drama Club take in tonight?"

"Six hundred and eighteen dollars," said Barbara slowly, "and seventy-five cents."

"Look, Mr. Strang, why don't you go back in and see the rest of the show?" asked Johnny. "Barb and me, we'd kind of like to get going, if you know what I mean."

"Yes, I'm sure you would," the teacher mused, "but I think I've had enough of *Macbeth* for one evening. I'm going home myself. Would you give me my coat, Barbara?"

The girl passed Mr. Strang's coat and hat across the table, and the teacher put them on. Then, drawing his leather gloves from a pocket, he slipped his hands into them. He turned away from the table and began to shuffle toward the door leading outside.

Then he shook his head, as if disgusted with himself.

"The original absent-minded professor, that's me," he said ruefully. Turning back to where the two teenagers were peering after him, he smiled with disarming innocence. "I've forgotten my Thermos, Barbara," he said. "Would you let me have it, please?"

Barbara lifted the wide-mouthed jug onto the table, and Mr. Strang rested one gloved hand on its top. "Say, I've got something in here that might interest you two," he said. He raised the jug and, with his back to the doorway, unscrewed the top and reached inside. Then he spun around quickly and dropped something onto the table with a click. "Look!" he cried.

The object on the table was almost round, and about as large as a golf ball. Its crystalline whiteness made it appear like some rare jewel. Instinctively, Johnny Fein reached for it with his right hand.

"What in the blazes—?" he began.

Mr. Strang grabbed Johnny's wrist. Pushing downward with all his strength, the teacher forced the boy's open palm onto the white sphere.

A scream echoed through the lobby. "My hand!" cried Johnny. "It's on fire! It's burning up!"

Moving quickly but surely, Barbara Priott pulled open the drawer in the table that served as a shelf for the box office. Grasping the metal cash box in both hands, she raised it high and brought it down with a crash of jingling coins on top of the boy's head. He crumpled to the floor as a group of people, attracted by the yells of pain, stampeded from the auditorium into the lobby.

Barbara leaned over the boy's unconscious body and unbuttoned his jacket. From the waistband of his trousers, she took the .22 caliber pistol he had been concealing and passed it gingerly to Mr. Strang.

It took almost fifteen minutes to calm the anxious parents in the lobby and herd them back into the auditorium for the start of Act III. In the assistant principal's office, a police doctor had finished treating the bump on Frank Tabor's head and was applying a salve to Johnny Fein's hand, on the palm of which a mean-looking blister had formed.

Detective Paul Roberts, who had sped to the school in answer to Mr. Strang's telephone call, stood with notebook in hand, questioning the teacher and Barbara Priott.

"You know, Mr. Strang," Roberts was saying, "I always thought teaching was a nice, quiet, peaceful job. That was before I met you. Now, every time I come to this school, I feel like bringing the riot squad with me."

Mr. Strang grinned.

"Okay," continued the detective, "the boy showed up while the lobby was empty and pulled a gun. I've got all that. Then he hit Mr. Tabor on the head and dragged him behind the desk back there. He told you, Barbara, to get the money together for him, and you were in the middle of doing that when Mr. Strang came into the lobby. Then what?"

"He put the gun back under his jacket and ducked behind the door," answered Barbara. "But I deliberately dropped a quarter, and when Mr. Strang returned it to me he saw him hiding there. So Johnny Fein decided to pretend he was my date." The girl grimaced. "I thought he'd shoot us if I didn't go along with the act."

"Pretty smart," said Roberts. "If he could get you out of the way, though, Mr. Strang, then he'd only have Barbara to deal with."

The teacher nodded. "Fortunately, I was able to stop him before he added kidnapping to his other crimes."

"But what did you do to him, Mr. Strang?" asked the detective. "That hand of his looks like you worked him over with a red-hot poker. What were you carrying that was hot enough to—?"

"Not hot," interrupted Mr. Strang. "Cold. That 'crystal' I took from my Thermos was a piece of dry ice."

"Dry ice?"

"Yes—or, to be more scientific, carbon dioxide gas cooled to a temperature of more than a hundred degrees below zero, at which point it becomes a solid. Because of its extreme cold, dry ice produces an effect on human tissue much the same as a burn. And I assure you, I held the boy's hand against that chunk of dry ice for several seconds. I wanted to make sure he wouldn't be able to reach for his gun when I released him. Fortunately, by the time I let go, Barbara had knocked him out with the cash box."

"Wait a minute," said Roberts. "Are you trying to tell me you always carry around a hunk of dry ice, just for emergencies?"

"Not always—just tonight. My dry ice has a fairly important role in the play."

"Huh?"

"Come over here," said Mr. Strang, motioning to the auditorium door. "I think it's just about time for one of the scenes I'm talking about."

Roberts followed the teacher inside. On the stage, the three witches again stood around their cauldron, dropping small objects into its seething depths.

> *Fillet of a fenny snake,*
> *In the cauldron boil and bake;*
> *Eye of newt and toe of frog,*
> *Wool of bat and tongue of dog,*
> *Adder's fork, and blind-worm's sting*
> *Lizard's leg, and owlet's wing—*

And again the thick steam came from the pot, flowing over its sides and down to the floor like something alive.

Roberts wrinkled his nose. "What's really in that kettle?" he whispered.

"The rest of my dry ice, plus a little water," replied Mr. Strang. "As the water warms the dry ice, carbon dioxide is given off. That's the white 'steam' you see. And since carbon dioxide is heavier than air, it falls to the floor instead of rising, as ordinary steam would do. That gimmick is the mainstay of every mad scientist's laboratory in B movies. And when Mr. Tabor asked for such an effect, one of the boys in the Science Club came up with this idea. I brought the dry ice myself, because it's dangerous to handle—especially without gloves. I planned to get rid of the extra pieces where there'd be no chance of anyone touching them."

As Mr. Strang walked ahead of him out into the lobby, Roberts chuckled softly. "You might say Johnny Fein really got burned tonight—in more ways than one. But tell me, Mr. Strang, what tipped you off to what the kid was really up to? I mean, with him standing right there, Barbara Priott couldn't signal you or—"

"It was her note, of course," said the teacher, taking it from his pocket. "Barbara kept her wits about her and managed to give me this, right in front of the boy's nose."

Roberts looked at the note carefully, examining it front and back and even trying to read it upside down. "Iron and Indium," he said, almost to himself. "Hydrogen and Arsenic. I don't get it, Mr. Strang. Is this a code or something?"

"In a way, yes. Look at the reference."

"D.I. Mendeleev?"

"Yes. He was a Russian who found out that certain groups of elements have almost identical characteristics. Barbara's chemistry class has studied about him. He grouped the elements into what's called the Periodic Table. Barbara, incidentally, stressed the word 'period' when she spoke to me."

"I still don't understand how—"

"In most versions of the Periodic Table, each element is referred to by a chemical symbol, a sort of shorthand way of writing its name. I insist that the students in my chemistry class memorize those symbols. I've been told that rote memorization is bad pedagogy, but I'm sure that, after this evening, Barbara will agree that it does have its uses. Watch."

The teacher took the scrap of paper and began printing letters over each of the elements listed: "Fe" over Iron, "In" over Indium, "H" over Hydrogen, "As" over Arsenic, "Ag" over Silver, "U" over Uranium, and "N" over Nitrogen.

"I was pretty dense there for a while," said the teacher. "What Barbara had written seemed like nonsense to me. But I finally got it."

Roberts looked at the paper, focusing on the symbols printed over the names of the elements. The symbols read:

Fe In
H As
Ag U N

"Fein has a gun!" cried the detective.

"Exactly," replied Mr. Strang. "It was no secret there'd be a lot of money here at school tonight—Mr. Tabor's productions are always well attended. Johnny Fein intended to scoop up the loot and get away before anyone besides Mr. Tabor and Barbara knew he'd been in the building. Once I was alerted that the boy was armed, my problem was to help Barbara without getting either or both of us shot. I relied on his curiosity about what I had in my Thermos, and—well, you know the rest."

"Barbara was still pretty lucky," said Roberts. "The name Fein just happens to fit the Periodic Table. But let's suppose you'd been the one with the gun, Mr. Strang. Could she have spelled out *your* name that way?"

"No," said Mr. Strang after a moment's thought. "But the symbols for Tellurium, Actinium, Hydrogen, and Erbium would have spelled 'teacher,' which I suppose would have been sufficient under the circumstances. Still, if the boy had introduced himself as Pipsissewa Frackenbush or some equally long and involved name—"

But a snort of laughter from the detective made Mr. Strang stop and grin.

Later, as Roberts left with his prisoner, Mr. Strang walked back to the small office, where Frank Tabor was sitting with the cash box on his lap and talking with Barbara.

"Frank," said the science teacher, "a while ago you said you were afraid to put Barbara in a play because she froze under pressure. But tonight, at the point of a gun, she put on a better performance than anyone on the auditorium stage. Nearly every other student would probably have screamed for help the moment I came into view. Barbara could have been killed, but she was as cool as—well, ice—when she outwitted that boy and wrote her message. How about giving her a crack at that Eliza Doolittle part?"

Frank Tabor considered the idea and nodded.

There was a shrill girlish shriek of joy from behind the science teacher, and he felt Barbara's arms tug at the sleeve of his coat.

"Now cut that out, young lady," yelped Mr. Strang. "I don't want you to—it's undignified, that's what it is!"

But as the girl left the office, walking on air, Mr. Strang smiled to himself and passed his fingers across his cheek, trying to remember the last time he'd been kissed.

MR. STRANG PULLS A SWITCH

It was nearly six-thirty when Mr. Strang trudged up the steps of Mrs. Mackey's rooming house.

He was tired. His day at Aldershot High School had seemed infinitely long. In addition to his usual schedule of five classes and a study hall, the old teacher had spent a bad forty-five minutes with Mr. Guthrey, explaining to the irate principal why a science experiment had gone wrong, permeating the entire third floor with a stench unequaled since Hercules had cleaned the Augean stables.

Then, after school, he had kept an appointment with Mike Trowbridge, trying patiently to explain to that upset, nervous student why it was highly unlikely that he would receive a passing midyear mark in general science.

Now Mr. Strang wanted nothing more than to have a bowl of hot soup and then ease his frail body into his overstuffed armchair and read for an hour or so before going to bed.

As the teacher stepped through the front door, he heard the telephone ringing in the kitchen.

"Mr. Strang! Mr. Strang, it's for you!" The strident voice of Mrs. Mackey, his landlady, grated on his eardrums with a sound like that of a fingernail dragged across a blackboard.

Mr. Strang shuffled to the kitchen and took the phone reluctantly, favoring Mrs. Mackey with a glare that would have etched glass. "Leonard Strang speaking," he said into the mouthpiece.

"This is Walter Trowbridge, Mike's father," said a quavering voice. "The reason I called—well, it's about Mike."

"He got home all right, didn't he?" asked the teacher. "He left school two hours ago."

"Yes, he got home," continued the worried voice, "but would it be possible for you to come over here, Mr. Strang? Right away?"

"*Phoronidae!*" exploded the teacher. "I just got in. I haven't even eaten yet. What seems to be the trouble?"

"Mike went up to his room a little while ago, Mr. Strang. And then he—well, he just disappeared."

"Disappeared? Then look for him, Mr. Trowbridge. He must be around somewhere. Surely you can look for him without outside help. Or are you trying to tell me that he simply vanished in a puff of smoke?"

"Oh, there wasn't any smoke. Still..."

There was a silence at the other end of the line. Then:

"Do you believe in magic, Mr. Strang?"

"Magic? You mean real magic? Of course not!"

"I don't, either. But one minute Mike was in his room with the door locked, and the next minute he was gone. I'm really not sure whether I should call the police, and I thought that you, as a science teacher, might—"

"Mr. Trowbridge, I've had a hard day. Are you sure this isn't a joke of some kind?"

"Mr. Strang," replied Trowbridge, his voice edged with hysteria, "Mike is gone, I tell you. That's not the sort of thing I joke about."

"I'll be right over," said the teacher quietly. He placed the receiver back in its cradle and turned to Mrs. Mackey. "He just disappeared," he said in amazement. "Out of a locked room."

And with that astonishing remark, the gnome-like teacher walked out the door, leaving his landlady wondering if her boarder had taken leave of his senses.

Ten minutes later, Mr. Strang's battered purple car pulled to the curb in front of the Trowbridge home, a rambling fieldstone-and-clapboard house. The teacher jabbed at the doorbell impatiently and listened to several bars of "Home, Sweet Home" as they chimed beyond the thick door.

The door opened. "Come in, Mr. Strang," said the same voice the teacher had heard over the telephone.

Walter Trowbridge almost filled the doorway. Looking up at his face, Mr. Strang was reminded of a picture of a bulldog he had seen recently. Clearly here was a man who stood for no nonsense. But judging from the terror in his voice and the nervousness with which he mopped his face with a handkerchief, here was a man who was scared, perhaps terrified.

After taking the teacher's coat, Trowbridge ushered him into a spacious living room. A slender woman in a plain black dress was seated on the sofa.

"This is my wife, Alice, Mr. Strang," said Trowbridge.

The teacher shook her offered hand and noticed it was trembling.

"Alice was seated right where she is now, facing those stairs, when Mike—when Mike vanished," said Trowbridge, pointing to the steps at the far end of the room. "So you see, he couldn't have come down here, even if—"

"Just a moment, please," said the teacher. "If the boy's simply missing, it may be a matter for the police. But you said something about his having been in a locked room."

"That's right," said Mrs. Trowbridge. "Upstairs."

"I see," said Mr. Strang. "Or rather I don't see. Suppose you start at the beginning."

"It was just—"

"I was the one who—"

"Wait a minute." The teacher held up his hands like a referee at a football game. "You first, Mr. Trowbridge. Tell me what happened, from the time Mike returned home."

"I met him at the front door and asked him where he'd been. He said he'd stayed after school to talk to you about his work."

"That checks," said Mr. Strang.

"I got after him about his marks—just as I have to do nearly every day," Trowbridge went on. "Finally, he yanked himself away from me and said he was going up to his room to run his trains."

"Trains?"

"Yes, he's got an electric-train layout in his room. They're the old three-rail kind, and he's put in about a mile of track, with little houses and everything. It always surprises us that he still has room for his bed."

"I see," nodded the teacher. "You said that Mike 'yanked' himself away from you?"

"Just like that, while I was still talking to him. That's a hell of a way for a boy to act toward his own father, isn't it?"

"Walter!" cried Mrs. Trowbridge. "We asked Mr. Strang here to help us find Mike, not involve him in a family argument."

"Sure, Alice. Anyway, I went upstairs right after Mike, but he slammed into his room and locked the door. I shouted for him to open up, but he just yelled at me to go away. Then I heard him start the trains. For about five minutes, I could hear him in there, starting an engine, stopping it, switching—things like that. He still wouldn't open the door, so I asked Alice what she thought we ought to do. She was outside, trimming some rosebushes directly below the window of Mike's room."

"What did you decide?" asked Mr. Strang.

"We agreed that Walter should just sit outside that door until Mike opened it," said Mrs. Trowbridge. "I knew that, sooner or later, Mike would get hungry and come out. We came back into the house, and I sat right here where I could see the stairs when the two of them finally came down."

"Was Mike still in his room when you got back to his door?" Mr. Strang asked Trowbridge.

"Yes, I could hear him running the trains, just like before. He did a lot of starting and stopping, so I knew he must be angry. When things are going all right for him, he just lets the trains run round and round without working the controls much. I must have stood out there for fifteen or twenty minutes."

"Then what?"

"I heard something crash inside Mike's room," said Trowbridge. "I wasn't about to let him wreck the house just because he didn't like me talking to him about his marks, so I ordered him to open the door. He didn't answer. I noticed that the trains had stopped, too. I guess that's when I lost my temper."

"And—?"

"I started kicking the door," said Trowbridge. "It's made of light wood. I kept banging away at it until the lock broke. Then I went inside." Trowbridge took a deep breath. "There was nobody in the room, Mr. Strang! Mike was gone. In the time it took me to break down the door, Mike had just—just disappeared!"

Mr. Strang ran slender fingers through his sparse crop of gray hair. "I don't suppose the window—"

"It was locked," said Trowbridge, "from the inside. And besides, there's a twenty-foot drop to the ground."

"Any other exits?" asked the teacher.

Trowbridge shook his head.

"Walter, wouldn't it be better if Mr. Strang saw the room?" asked Mrs. Trowbridge.

Trowbridge nodded and led the way to the stairs, followed by his wife and the teacher. When they reached the top step, he indicated an open door at one end of the hallway. "That's Mike's room," he said.

As they entered the room, Mr. Strang noticed that the spring lock on the inside of the door had been torn away from the wood, leaving splinters on the floor. As Trowbridge had said, the room was filled with electric-train apparatus mounted on large sheets of plywood raised about three feet above the floor. In a roundhouse at one end, two miniature diesel locomotives were waiting to be sent on their way. Farther on, a tiny village looked exceedingly lifelike, right down to the figure of a postman having his ankle nipped by a plastic dog not more than half an inch long. There were houses and shops, a rustic station, crossings and tunnels and turnpikes. Plaster had been laid over chicken wire and then painted to look like rugged mountains.

"Why, it's superb!" marveled the teacher, looking at an outcropping of "rock" that indicated a certain familiarity with geological formations. "Did Mike do all this himself?"

"Yes, Alice and I don't have much time to play with trains," replied Trowbridge. "We always say that, if the time he wastes just wiring those trains was spent on studying, he'd be on the honor roll. I even had to have a special electrical circuit put in, just for this room."

Mrs. Trowbridge pointed at some pieces of broken pottery on the floor, under the corner of one of the tables. "That mess used to be a bust of George Washington," she said. "Mike won it at a shooting gallery when we went to a carnival last year."

"I figure that must have been the crash I heard," explained Trowbridge. "What do you think, Mr. Strang?"

But the teacher seemed more interested in what was on the table above the clay fragments. At that point, the tracks came near the edge and then made a tight turn, almost doubling back on themselves. Next to the track, on the inside of the turn, a train lay on its side. It was made up primarily of freight cars; their contents—carloads of lead fishing sinkers—had spilled out, overturning several tiny trees. A derrick was mounted on one of the cars, and its arm stuck straight out.

Mr. Strang crossed the room, sat on the bed, and considered the control system. He reached out and touched one of the twin transformers. "*Arthropoda!*" he yipped, snatching his hand away. "This thing is still hot!"

"I guess I never thought to turn it off," said Trowbridge sheepishly.

"Umm." The teacher tapped the side of his nose slowly with an index finger. Then he peered at the Trowbridges over the top of his black-rimmed glasses.

"Mind if I run the trains?" he asked, grinning shyly.

"Now, look, Mr. Strang, I asked you here to help find Mike, not to—"

"Walter, don't be rude."

"Ah!" Trowbridge threw up his hands. "I told you we should have called the police first thing."

"You may be glad you didn't," said the teacher, waving an admonishing finger. "But if it'll make you feel any better, Mr. Trowbridge, I'm not playing. I intend to perform a controlled scientific experiment."

Trowbridge shrugged helplessly.

Mr. Strang returned to the train table, detached the engine from the rest of the derailed train, and placed it on the track. There was a click as the contacts underneath the engine touched the rails, and a tiny light glowed in the cab. The engine was motionless, but it gave off a slight hum.

Mr. Strang went back to the controls and touched a button on one transformer. As he pressed down, the humming stopped and the cab light went out.

"Did you break it?" asked Trowbridge.

"No, this button cuts off the electricity to the track. There's a control inside the engine that operates every time that happens. Watch."

He released the button. The light went on again, and the engine moved slowly—in reverse.

Again the teacher pushed the button. The lights went off and the engine stopped, as if awaiting further instructions. This time when Mr. Strang took his finger off the button, the engine remained motionless.

When the button was pushed and released a third time, the engine finally started forward. It crawled along the outermost rim of the web of tracks, taking a full minute to return to where Mr. Strang had originally placed it.

"Interesting," said the teacher.

"What's interesting?" demanded Mr. Trowbridge.

"There are eight switches in this setup. They're easy to operate. See?" Mr. Strang touched several other buttons, and, as he did, switches snapped into new positions all along the track. The train started again, but this time it took a shortcut through the miniature town.

"Eight switches had to be set exactly right to send the train the longest possible way," said the teacher. "Doesn't it make you wonder why that particular route was selected? Mike had an almost infinite variety of other routes he could have used."

"Just coincidence," scoffed Trowbridge. "Look, we're getting nowhere, Mr. Strang. I'm going to call the police, as I should have done in the first place. It's easy enough to figure out what happened here."

"What?" asked the teacher innocently.

"Someone must have gotten into this room," replied Trowbridge. "Whoever it was grabbed Mike, and the bust of Washington fell to the floor while they struggled. The train was still running, but when it reached the curve it went off the track. That's why the transformer was still on. Whoever it was took Mike out—somehow—before I could get in to help him."

"You were outside the door of the room," said Mr. Strang calmly, "and the window was shut and locked on the inside. How do you suggest this mysterious someone got in here? Or got out?"

"I don't know. That's for the police to determine."

"And what do you say, Mrs. Trowbridge?"

"I—I'm afraid I must agree with my husband, Mr. Strang. I can't explain how it happened, but it had to have been the way Walter said."

"Uh-huh." Mr. Strang nodded. "Well, if you must, you must. But before you rush off to make complete idiots of yourselves—"

"Now just a minute!"

"I repeat: complete idiots of yourselves. Before you do that, might I point out just one fallacy in your reconstruction?"

"What's that?"

"You imply that the train was thrown off its track because it probably came into the curve too fast. If that were the case, though, centrifugal force would have thrown it to the outside of the curve. Correct?"

Trowbridge nodded—and then turned to look at the engineless train lying on its side on the inside edge of the curve.

"Well, then," Trowbridge said slowly, "how did Mike disappear? Have you got any idea, Mr. Strang?"

"How? Oh, that's easy. It's the why that bothers me. But I think I know that, too. Suppose we go downstairs and discuss it."

"But what about Mike?" asked Mr. Trowbridge. "How do we know he's safe—wherever he is?"

"Oh, Mike's safe enough," chuckled the teacher. "A bit uncomfortable, perhaps, but safe."

The Trowbridges followed Mr. Strang back downstairs to the living room. They sat, and the teacher stoked up his massive briar pipe, sending clouds of foul fumes into the air.

"I suppose this whole thing is partly my fault," he began. "You see, when Mike stopped in to see me after school, I told him his chances of passing science were poor."

"What's that got to do with it?"

"I was rather hard on him," Mr. Strang went on. "I never saw a person so dejected. But after he left, I went over his record. It was quite revealing."

"Revealing? How?" asked Mr. Trowbridge.

"This year," said the teacher, "Mike had the choice of one elective class, and he signed up for art. But there was a note at the bottom of his schedule card that said you refused to give him permission to take that class, Mr. Trowbridge."

"Of course I refused! If he's going to study law, the way we planned, he doesn't need—"

"The second time around, Mike chose mechanical drawing, and again you withheld permission. He finally took a foreign language—and his marks there are well below passing."

"Now hold on a minute," said Trowbridge. "Let's understand one thing, Mr. Strang: I want Mike to go to college. I never had the chance, myself. And a language will give him a better chance of getting accepted than just learning to draw pictures. If he wasn't so lazy—"

"Yes, I'm sure your motives were good ones," replied the teacher, "but he won't even graduate from high school with the marks he's been getting. And lazy? Mike? *Platyhelminthes*, that boy of yours tries harder than any other student at Aldershot High. He simply can't cope with the work, Mr. Trowbridge."

Mr. Strang paused for breath. "I did notice one interesting thing, however," he went on. "Mike's taking a required shop class—and in that course his average is ninety-five out of a hundred."

"This is all very fine, Mr. Strang," said Mrs. Trowbridge anxiously, "but what does it have to do with Mike's disappearance?"

"It tells me why it happened," said the teacher. "You see, Mrs. Trowbridge, I don't believe that Mike was abducted, as your husband thinks. I think he arranged his 'disappearance' himself."

"But why?" asked Trowbridge.

"Think about it," said the teacher. "Obviously Mike has little academic ability. He takes the prescribed college entrance courses because you, his parents, force him to—and in spite of his striving he gets low marks. And yet this same boy has great aptitude and interest in mechanical and artistic things. That model-train setup in his room is ample proof of that—it's one of the most remarkable things I've ever seen.

"Mike was not allowed to take the courses he was really interested in. And it was constantly drummed into him that he had to study harder—that he was a failure because he couldn't accomplish what you wanted him to. According to your own admission, Mr. Trowbridge, the last time you actually saw Mike you were berating him because of his low marks. I think he'd finally had enough, and he decided to do something quite typical of children—even children in their teens."

"What did he decide to do?" asked Mrs. Trowbridge.

"Run away from home."

"Run away?" said Trowbridge in astonishment. "Don't be ridiculous!"

"Mike was old enough to know you'd take precisely that attitude if he simply packed up and left," said the teacher. "Furthermore, he knew that sooner or later he'd have to return—and then you'd merely laugh at him, and the quarreling and bickering over marks would start all over again. So he had to do something to frighten you. I'd say," Mr. Strang concluded with a smile, "that he succeeded admirably."

Trowbridge turned to his wife. "I guess I have been pretty hard on the boy," he agreed. "Maybe you're right, Mr. Strang. Maybe college isn't for him."

"And is that such a bad thing? Is it worth making the boy miserable—perhaps for the rest of his life—to prepare him for a career in which he has neither interest nor ability?"

"Okay, so Mike ran away," said Trowbridge. "That I can understand, even if I don't approve of it. Now tell me, Mr. Strang, how did he get out of his room? I heard him in there, running his trains. A few seconds later, he was gone—and the window was locked on the inside."

"The trains. We always come back to the trains, don't we? Let's begin by reviewing what actually happened. Mike entered his room. You went outside to consult with your wife, and when you got back you heard—what?"

"I heard Mike putting the trains through their paces—stopping and starting—for at least fifteen minutes. Then there was a crash, and—"

"Did your son say anything to you after you returned from outside?"

"No, we were both angry, and both of us tend to clam up when we feel that way."

Mr. Strang reached into a jacket pocket and produced his black-rimmed glasses. He polished the lenses on his necktie and then waved the glasses dramatically.

"I'm sure, Mr. Trowbridge," he began, in his best classroom manner, "that when you returned to the door of his room, Mike couldn't have spoken to you, not if you had suddenly become the most sympathetic and understanding father in the world—for the simple reason that he was no longer in the room!"

"What do you mean?"

"The only opportunity he had to leave," said the teacher, "was while you were talking with your wife. He undoubtedly set the spring lock on the door to snap into place after he'd left. Your 'locked room' is as simple as that."

"But I heard—"

"You heard the train," said Mr. Strang. "There's no denying that. But Mike wasn't in the room to operate it."

"But the starting and stopping—and the crash?"

"Yes, the crash. The idea of a mysterious disappearance must have occurred to Mike the moment he entered his room—if he hadn't planned it all out beforehand. He had plenty of time to set things up before you left to talk to his mother. What did he need to convince you that he was still inside the room? Only the sound of a train running and, after about fifteen minutes, a crash to startle you into forcing your way into the room."

"That's quite a bit—if, as you say, he wasn't even in the room."

"The crash was easy to accomplish. The curve in the track, remember, came almost to the edge of the table. Now suppose the bust of Washington were balanced precariously at that point. What would happen?"

"Nothing. Not unless the bust was actually on the track. And then it would only stop the train. And even though the curve comes close to the edge, the bust couldn't have been both on the track and balanced on the edge of the table."

"True. But picture the wrecked train in your mind, Mr. Trowbridge. Among the cars was one rather special one."

"The derrick car?"

"Exactly. The arm of the derrick was sticking out, and the car was weighted with lead. It went into the curve, the derrick's arm swept the Father of His Country off the table, and the bust fell to the floor and smashed. At the same time, the weight of the bust pushed the car in the opposite direction, and the train came off the track—on the inside of the curve."

"But that was fifteen minutes after I got back to the door," said Trowbridge. "How could Mike have been running the train that long and kept it away from the curve, if he wasn't even in the room?"

"I remarked earlier," said the teacher, "on the fact that the track switches were set to make the train go the longest possible route."

"Yes, but the train still took only a minute to go around."

"True. Do you remember, though, how the train's direction is controlled?"

"Sure. You push the button on the transformer. Each time you push it, the train does a different thing: back up, stop, go forward, stop."

"Remember that cycle," said Mr. Strang. "It never varies. If the train is going forward and you want to reverse it, for example, you have to push the button twice. It's quite predictable."

"Spare me the lecture, Mr. Strang," said Trowbridge. "Just tell me how Mike was able to control the train from outside the room. After all, I did hear it stop and start many times. I suppose Mike just reached through a solid wall and pushed the button, huh?"

"All pushing the button accomplishes is to cut off the electricity to the track; a solenoid switch inside the engine does the rest. One could just as easily change the direction of the train by unplugging the transformer and then plugging it in again."

"But the transformer plug is inside the room, too," objected Trowbridge.

"I was just giving an example," said the teacher impatiently. "Think of the rest of the house, not just Mike's room. Where is the one other place from which the electricity can be switched off and on?"

"Why, there isn't another—wait a minute! The fusebox in the basement!"

"Bravo!" said Mr. Strang. "Mike set up the bust of Washington and then crept down to the basement while you were outside. After you returned, he kept the train moving backward and forward along that outside track by screwing and unscrewing the fuse. He could keep that up for quite some time without sending the train into the curve; the long outer track gave him plenty of leeway. And since the room has its own circuit, his disconnecting and reconnecting its fuse wouldn't be noticed in the rest of the house. Incidentally, if you go down to the basement now, I think you'll find your son hiding there."

There was a long pause. Then Alice Trowbridge began to giggle. "He's probably gorging himself on the ginger ale and potato chips we keep down there," she said. "He won't want a thing for supper."

"The fuse—that's the third one," murmured her husband thoughtfully.

"The third what?" asked the teacher.

"Switch. There are the ones on the track and the solenoid in the engine. And then there was the fuse screwed in and out to switch the electricity on and off." He walked purposely toward the basement door. "And now there's going to be a fourth."

"A fourth switch? Surely you're not going to beat the boy," said Mr. Strang.

"No, of course not. But I've been thinking. Maybe a kid who can plan something like this fuse gimmick would benefit from mechanical drawing. Or even from art. The fourth switch is the one we'll be making in Mike's academic program."

MR. STRANG TAKES A HAND

"No, no, I haven't forgotten, Miss Ansell. But you have to understand that, under the circumstances—"

Marvin W. Guthrey, the principal of Aldershot High School, ground his teeth and looked daggers at the telephone receiver in his hand as a voice from the other end of the line chattered in his ear. "I don't know what else you expect me to do about it," he finally blurted. "Goodbye, Miss Ansell!"

Guthrey slammed the receiver into its cradle and ran a hand nervously though his dense growth of snow-white hair, which, in its present condition, gave the appearance of a mop set carelessly atop his head. His eyes almost flashing sparks, he glanced at Leonard Strang, who stood on the other side of his desk.

"At a time like this," Guthrey groaned, "I have to tell the custodians to inspect the students' lockers for overdue library books? Sit down, Mr. Strang, use the sense you were born with. There's no reason for you to stand there like an idiot!"

There was no reason, of course, for Guthrey to be angry with Mr. Strang. The wizened science teacher had been asked to report to the principal's office, and here he was. It was just that the whole situation was so unfair. With Aldershot High facing a tense situation that might at any time erupt into violence, what right did the school librarian have to trouble Guthrey with something as trivial as her damn— as a few overdue books?

"Sit down, Leonard," Guthrey repeated, more gently now.

Mr. Strang eased himself into the chair at the corner of the desk and peered over the tops of his black-rimmed glasses at the harried principal.

"You did promise you'd have the custodians check the lockers after school today," Mr. Strang said softly. "You announced it on the public-address system during homeroom this morning."

"Yes, but that was before—"

"Before what?"

"Leonard, I've been hearing rumors all day about a student protest that's to be held on the front lawn after school."

"A protest?" The teacher dragged out his battered briar pipe, filled it, and applied a match. Clouds of foul smoke filled the room as he puffed away. "What kind of protest?"

"Last Friday, Sid Lewis was declared ineligible for the basketball team because of his low marks. Some of his friends—plus a few others—have planned to stage a demonstration. Apparently today's the day."

"Ah." Mr. Strang leaned back in his chair and considered the ceiling. "So the student-protest movement has finally reached us. Signs, chanting, marching..."

"If it was limited to signs and chanting and marching," said Guthrey, "I wouldn't be worried. But I understand this group—the kids who've organized the protest—are going to try to re-enter the building and break into some of the classrooms. They feel that a display of force will give their cause publicity."

"I wouldn't be surprised if they're right," replied the teacher.

Guthrey shook his head in dismay. "High-school students. They're *children*, Leonard. What's *happening* to the younger generation nowadays?"

Mr. Strang looked quizzically at his principal. "How many students do you expect to stay after school for this protest?"

"We're preparing for up to a hundred."

"One hundred students. Less than five percent of our student body."

"What do you mean by that?"

"Take a good look at that five percent. You and I know who they'll be: the same ones who are willing to take up any cause, just to get their names in the paper. The ones who can't come to terms with themselves, to say nothing of coming to terms with the rest of humanity. The ones who give the whole school a bad name because they get their kicks out of using marijuana and other drugs. The five percent who are so fierce about 'protecting their rights' that they walk all over the rights of everyone *else*."

"Leonard, the last thing I need right now is a sermon."

"But, Mr. Guthrey, this type of student isn't representative of the younger generation. Certainly, teenagers are making themselves heard, and many of their protests are justified. But in this case? Aren't school athletics still a privilege, not something a student is automatically entitled to?"

"You're right, of course. Still—" Guthrey slumped forward in his chair. "Rioting. Narcotics. Right here in our school. What's the world coming to, Leonard?"

"It would help if the parents of our fair village would wake up to the fact that these things aren't just problems you read about in the paper. They're here in Aldershot—and in a lot of other smug little suburban communities across the country."

"Unfortunately," Guthrey grumbled, "that five percent are the ones who'll make the headlines tomorrow if there's any property damage, or if anyone gets hurt here today. That's why I wanted to see you, Leonard."

"You want *me* to stop them?" asked the teacher in genuine surprise.

"Not exactly." Guthrey allowed himself a sickly smile. "But the kids respect you. I'd feel easier if I knew you were in the building, keeping an eye on the doors. Just in case they *do* try to break in."

"Do I get some help? Or will I be all alone, like Horatius at the bridge?"

"All the doors will be locked, of course. And Inspector Adams has assigned two police officers—Drescher and Sturdevant—to keep an eye on the outside of the building. But they can't watch all the doors simultaneously. Each of them will have a key, in case he needs to get inside in a hurry."

"Sounds as if you've touched all the bases," said Mr. Strang. "Our own little maximum-security schoolhouse. Well, why not?" Stiffly, the slender teacher rose to leave.

"I'll be doing some patrolling myself," said Guthrey. "Be careful, Leonard."

"When it comes to protecting life and limb—especially my own—I'm the soul of caution," replied Mr. Strang. "One shout of warning is the most you can expect from me. After that, I'll be off and running, looking for a place to hide. I'm no hero, Mr. Guthrey, just a teacher."

At three-thirty that afternoon, Mr. Strang trudged through the deserted halls of Aldershot High. Idly kicking a piece of paper lying on the floor, he rounded a corner and headed toward the gym and shop areas to check the exit door near Mr. Haxton's woodworking shop.

As he passed the entrance to the boys' locker room, he heard a sound. It might have been water gurgling down a drain somewhere, but still—

He listened carefully, but the sound didn't repeat.

He walked into the locker room, wrinkling his nose at the combined smell of leather, sneakers, and sweat. The room was deserted. With a shrug, he stepped back into the hall.

Wait, there was the sound again. He glanced down the hallway. The door to Mr. Haxton's shop was open. Funny. But maybe Mr. Haxton had been particularly anxious to get out of the building early today. Mr. Strang went into the shop and glanced around.

As usual, the huge space was almost spotless. The tools were in their proper places in racks on the walls, while the benches and machines had been brushed and wiped until they nearly gleamed. All sawdust, wood chips, and other rubbish had been carefully deposited in two metal drums standing against one of the walls. Mr. Strang turned to leave ...

... and saw what was behind the door through which he had entered the room. Cold sweat popped out on his face.

On the floor lay a man in a police uniform. One side of the officer's face was bloody, and a noise was coming from deep in his throat, as if he were trying to say something but couldn't. Mr. Strang knelt over the man, wondering how badly he was hurt. The officer's eyes were closed, but his lips were moving. The teacher bent closer.

"Sawhorse," came a muffled sob. "Sawhorse—saw-horse—saw—"

And then silence.

It took perhaps ninety seconds for Mr. Strang to make his report of an injured policeman coherent enough over the intercom that the main-office secretary could understand it. Perhaps another minute and a half was spent locating Mr. Guthrey, who immediately called the police. Two minutes after that, the siren of an ambulance was heard approaching the school, followed by a stream of police cars. Within six minutes of the discovery of the unconscious officer, he had been placed in the ambulance with an intern attending him. The school was surrounded by police officers, and the students who had gathered on the front lawn for their demonstration were shouting their annoyance, because, as one of them put it, "Every time I go to scratch my head, there's fuzz breathing down my neck!"

Six minutes. To Mr. Strang, it seemed like an eternity.

"Sit down, Mr. Strang." Detective Paul Roberts took the chair from behind Mr. Haxton's desk and settled the trembling teacher into it. In his previous dealings with Mr. Strang, Roberts had always found the old man to be hale, chipper, and completely in command of every situation. Now, however, the pallor of his wrinkled features had the detective worried.

"Feel up to telling me what happened?" Roberts asked.

"There's not much to tell, Paul. I found him lying over there behind the door. He had blood on his face and—Paul, he's going to be all right, isn't he?"

"I think so," replied Roberts. "The intern said lacerations and possible concussion. But remember, Sturdevant's a tough old cop."

"How did it happen? I mean—"

"Somebody hit him with this." Roberts held up a large wooden mallet.

Glancing at the tool rack, Mr. Strang saw several similar implements.

"Now," the detective said briskly, "let's get your story."

Mr. Strang outlined the manner in which he had found the injured policeman.

"*Sawhorse*, huh?" mused Roberts, when the teacher had finished. "Well, there are three of them over by the lathe." He walked over and gave each of them a quick examination. "Just ordinary sawhorses," he said finally. "By the way, Mr. Strang, did you touch Sturdevant at all when you found him?"

"I don't know. I might have. Just to see how badly hurt—"

"No, I don't mean that. Did you loosen his clothing? To make him more comfortable, maybe?"

"I'm sure I didn't. Why?"

"Because his gun belt had been taken off. We found it under that second workbench."

"I didn't do that. But what—?"

"Everything that's usually on the belt is missing. Notebook, handcuffs—everything."

"Why would anyone want those things?"

"I don't know. And there's something else. His holster's empty."

"Then—"

"Yeah. We can't locate Sturdevant's .38 pistol."

Mr. Strang frowned. A policeman had been injured. Students were being held under guard. And now a gun was missing.

This wasn't education. It was war.

"Paul?" he said softly.

"Yeah?"

"I want to do something. I want to help."

Roberts looked at the teacher. He didn't normally like outsiders meddling in problems of law enforcement. But this was Mr. Strang. On other occasions, the gnome-like old science teacher's assistance had proven invaluable. And the current investigation hadn't gotten anywhere as yet.

"Okay, Mr. Strang," Roberts said, "you're in."

A plainclothesman younger than Roberts appeared in the doorway. "Sir?"

Roberts looked up. "Yeah, Buckler?"

Buckler held out his hand. Dangling from his index finger was a ring of keys. "We found these in the keyhole of the door that leads outside. They must be Sturdevant's—his name's on the tag."

Roberts took the key ring and fingered the black disk on which Joseph Sturdevant – Aldershot P.D. was printed in white letters. As Roberts was about to drop the keys into his jacket pocket, Mr. Strang spoke:

"Mr. Buckler, did you find those keys on the *outside* of the door?"

"Sure, where else? I mean, there's no keyhole on the inside, just the release bar."

"Is that what you expected, Mr. Strang?" Roberts asked.

"Yes. Now if you don't mind, I'd like to go outside for a minute."

"Aren't you feeling well?"

"As well as can be expected. But I want to look through the window in that door."

"Mind telling me why?"

"According to Mr. Guthrey, Paul, Officer Sturdevant was assigned to patrol the *outside* of the building. When he passed that door, he must have looked through the window and seen something *inside* that he thought needed investigation. So he used the key Mr. Guthrey had given him to unlock the door and come in."

"Makes sense. Only why couldn't Sturdevant have seen something through one of the classroom windows? Instead of the window in the door, I mean."

"The classroom windows are too high off the ground. That keeps people outside from peering in while classes are in session."

"Buckler, keep an eye on things in here," Roberts ordered. "Come on, Mr. Strang."

The detective and the teacher walked out of the shop and through the school's exit door. They could hear the students in the front of the building shouting objections to being kept under surveillance.

Shading his eyes, Mr. Strang peered through the window set into the upper half of the door. "Hmm," he muttered. "About twenty feet of hallway and three lockers."

"I beg your pardon?" said Roberts.

"Three student lockers, directly across from Mr. Haxton's shop. That's all I can see from here."

Roberts took out Sturdevant's key ring and was trying to locate the correct key when Buckler came racing up the hall, punched the release bar, and swung the heavy door open. He stood in the hallway, waving a pistol in one hand.

"I found it!" he said almost joyfully.

"Put that thing down before you hurt somebody," Roberts said curtly. "You found *what*?"

"Sturdevant's pistol. This is it. I found it in one of those barrels of wood scraps, way down at the bottom."

Roberts toyed with the idea of chewing out the younger man for destroying possible fingerprints on the weapon. But what was the use: this was Roberts' case, and he'd be held responsible for Buckler's mistake. "Good going," he said gruffly, taking the pistol and examining it.

"Has it been fired?" asked Mr. Strang fearfully.

"Nope. Whoever hid it in that barrel apparently just wanted to get rid of it."

"But why?"

"Who knows? This thing gets crazier by the minute. Did you find any of Sturdevant's other things, Buckler?"

"Not yet. But I'm still looking."

"Well, if you get any bright ideas, let me hear 'em real quick. I can't keep those kids out front much longer. Their parents will be on my back as it is." He turned to the teacher. "How about it, Mr. Strang? Are you as confused about this as I am?"

"I'm afraid so. It would help, of course, if we knew what Officer Sturdevant saw that brought him into the building."

"Maybe," Roberts began, "one of the kids coming—"

"No, Paul. The students leave school from the rear of the building, not here. The only people who'd be in this hallway are the ones who have their lockers here."

"We'll check them out. But what should we be looking for? Besides, I'd rather know why someone would take off Sturdevant's gun belt just to get rid of his pistol. But I'll tell you one thing: a cop's been hurt, and I'll find out who did it if I have to take this school and everybody in it apart, piece by piece."

"Take it easy," said the teacher.

"It burns me up," snarled Roberts. "Sturdevant only has eighteen months to go before retirement. This assignment was supposed to be a piece of cake for him, patrol around the school for a few hours. But he ends up getting slugged. For my money, it was one of those kids out front who did it. Smart-aleck punks who think the law doesn't apply to them! If we search them, I'll bet we find they're *all* carrying grass."

"Paul, you're letting your emotions run away with you. Don't lower yourself to the level of..."

The teacher's voice trailed off. He looked long and hard at the entrance to the shop, and then at the lockers set into the opposite wall. "What did you just say?" he asked, almost in a whisper.

"I said I'm getting tired of these kids who—"

"No, not that. You said 'grass.' That's slang for marijuana, isn't it?"

"Yeah: grass, pot, Mary Jane. Even the pushers don't like to call narcotics by their right names. What's on your mind?"

"I think I know what made Sturdevant come into the building."

Roberts' first thought was that the shock of the day's events had finally caught up with Mr. Strang. Then he asked, "Why don't you tell me about it?"

So Mr. Strang told him.

When the teacher finished, Roberts found himself trying—and failing—to find a flaw in the odd theory he had just heard.

"That might be it, Mr. Strang," he said grudgingly. "But there's no proof."

"I think I can provide the proof, if you'll let me."

"We could both get in a lot of trouble."

"A policeman's in the hospital, Paul."

"Buckler!" shouted Roberts. "Stay here and keep an eye on things. I'm going up to the main office with Mr. Strang."

After locating Guthrey, who allowed them to examine a file in the main office and then use the telephone, Roberts and Mr. Strang headed toward the building's front door. When they came out into the cool air of late afternoon, a hundred voices were raised in raucous cries:

"Hey, Mr. Strang! You still teaching, or have you joined the police?"

"Man, ain't you cops ever gonna let us go home?"

"We know our rights, fuzz! Book us or let us go!"

Ignoring the shouts, Roberts led Mr. Strang to one of the policemen surrounding the schoolyard. "This is Andy Drescher," he said. "He was on duty with Sturdevant."

"I recognize Andy," said the teacher. "You were in my chemistry class about twelve years ago, weren't you?"

"That's right," replied Drescher. Then he turned to the detective. "Any news about Sturdevant?" he asked grimly.

"Not yet," Roberts answered. "How are things out here?"

"The parents don't like us keeping their kids from heading home."

"Too bad." Roberts reached into a pocket, pulled out a slip of paper, and handed it to Drescher. "See if any of these three kids are in this mob. If so, I want to see them inside—

in the principal's office. Tell the rest they can go home."

Ten minutes later, one of the policemen hauled a portable loudspeaker from the back of his patrol car. "Boys and girls," he began, his amplified voice echoing in the still air. "It's all over. You can leave now."

Slowly at first, then faster, the crowd began to break up and move away from Aldershot High School.

Later, in Marvin W. Guthrey's office, Roberts and Mr. Strang sat in straight-backed chairs against one wall, looking at the seventeen-year-old boy opposite them. Avoiding their gaze, the boy slouched against the wall, fixedly examining the fingernails of his right hand, his left hand in a pocket of his tan sports jacket. Guthrey sat behind his desk, nervously considering the well-dressed man who stood in front of him, shaking an admonishing finger in the principal's face.

"I want—no, I *demand*—to know the reason you're detaining my boy!" the man shouted, with a dramatic sweep of his hand.

Guthrey glanced at Roberts.

"Mr. Beldeck," Roberts began, "a policeman was assaulted in this building today. I'm the detective in charge of the case. This isn't a formal hearing. We just thought you might like to hear what we have to say. Of course, if you'd like to call your lawyer—"

"My lawyer *will* be brought into this," said Beldeck, "the moment you make a single charge against my son that can't be proved in court. In the meantime, I think I'm capable of safeguarding his rights. And the first thing I'm advising him to do is keep his mouth shut. Do you understand that, George?"

The boy nodded, scowling at Roberts, and continued his perusal of his fingernails.

Roberts' heart sank. He could see his chances for further promotion fast disappearing. Perhaps he should never have placed so much trust in Mr. Strang. He turned to the teacher almost desperately. If there *was* any real proof, now was the time to bring it out.

Mr. Strang got to his feet. "I'm a teacher here, Mr. Beldeck," he said almost shyly. "My name's Strang. I suppose I'm the reason that George is here, but this isn't a trial. Nobody has yet been accused of anything. I just thought you might like to hear some of my thoughts about the case. Fair enough?"

"I'll reserve judgment until I've heard what you have to say," replied Beldeck.

"Your privilege," said Mr. Strang. "May I begin?"

Beldeck shrugged.

Whipping off his glasses, Mr. Strang perched on the edge of Marvin Guthrey's desk. This was the same pose he had assumed in front of his Aldershot classes for more than a quarter of a century.

"Officer Sturdevant—the injured man—was assigned to patrol the outside of this building around dismissal time today," he began. "Most of the students went home after school, but about a hundred remained to attend a protest meeting. One of those who stayed was your son."

"So he was at the demonstration," said Beldeck. "This is the first time he's ever showed any interest in this protest stuff. Was it a crime for him to attend?"

"Of course not. But to get back to Sturdevant: I believe that, as he passed the outside door near the wood shop, he saw something through the window, something that made him unlock the door and enter the building. He was in a hurry, too, so much so that he left his key ring in the lock. Now, the only students who would be in that hallway at dismissal time are those who have lockers there. And only three lockers can be seen through the window of that door—one of them belonging to your George. In fact, he's the only one of the students assigned to those three lockers who didn't go straight home after school. Mr. Roberts confirmed this by phone."

"Is that all you have to offer?" asked Beldeck. "My son has a locker within sight of that door and he went to a meeting today?"

"No, there's more. But it's important to present the facts in their proper order. Now let's consider what Officer Sturdevant saw at one of those three lockers."

"Well," Mr. Guthrey chimed in, "what *did* he see? And how do you know, Leonard? I thought the officer was still unconscious?"

"He is—but he told us himself," said Mr. Strang.

"How?"

"When I found him, just before he lost consciousness, he said the word 'sawhorse.' He said it several times. The fact that he was struck down in the wood shop was misleading. He wasn't referring to the wooden sawhorses there, but that's the way I first understood him."

"So what *was* he trying to say?" snapped Beldeck.

Mr. Strang looked from Beldeck to his son and back again. "Saw ... horse," he said slowly. "Two words, not one."

"I don't get it."

"*Horse,* Mr. Beldeck, is a slang term for the drug heroin.

And that's what I believe Sturdevant saw: someone taking packets of heroin out of one of the three lockers. The packaging of illegal heroin, by the way, is usually quite distinctive. It's a white powder, and it's often put into clear plastic pouches. Pretty hard to mistake it for anything else. So, if I'm correct, Sturdevant saw someone who was either a user or a pusher—or perhaps both."

"Oh, come on!" Beldeck strode up to the teacher, scowling. "Of all the far-fetched—assuming somebody, my son or someone else, had this 'horse' in his locker, why would he be taking it out today? Or was this afternoon's protest meeting for addicts only?"

"I think Mr. Guthrey can answer that," said the teacher.

"Me?" exclaimed the principal. "I haven't any idea—"

"You were on the telephone when I came into your office this morning," said Mr. Strang. "Who were you talking to?"

Guthrey thought for a moment. "Why, Miss Ansell, our librarian. She wanted a locker inspection to locate overdue books."

"A locker inspection this afternoon." Mr. Strang smiled. "So whoever had the horse in his locker had to get it out of there before it was found."

Beldeck took a long look at the teacher. "Ingenious," he said. "Very ingenious, indeed. But pure supposition, of course. And even if it's true, there's no indication that George—"

"Mr. Beldeck," said Mr. Strang reprovingly, "I call on everyone present to bear witness that not once have I mentioned your son in connection with what happened to Officer Sturdevant."

"Then why did you bring him here? Why am *I* here?"

"I'll get to that in a moment. When you interrupted me, I was explaining why I believe Sturdevant came into the building. To continue, it's my idea that he went into Mr. Haxton's shop to make the actual arrest. Perhaps he wanted to be sure there wouldn't be any interruptions from his captive's friends."

"Mr. Strang," said Beldeck, glancing at his watch, "it's getting late. Can we leave this high-flown theorizing and stick to the facts? You haven't got a shred of evidence against my son—or anyone else, for that matter."

"I didn't do anything," growled the boy sullenly.

"Of course not," said his father. "But these gentlemen seem to think you did. The proof, Mr. Strang, if you please?"

"All right," said the teacher. "Let's begin with the fact that the person who clubbed Officer Sturdevant removed his gun belt and concealed all of the items on it. Most of them haven't been found yet. Probably he hid the drugs at the same time. The belt was a neat bit of misdirection. Unfortunately for him, we found the gun."

"So?"

"So it occurs to me that whoever removed the belt was trying to cover up the fact that there was something else—something besides the gun—that was missing."

"Like what?" asked Beldeck.

Mr. Strang ignored him and turned to Roberts. "Paul," he said, "pretend I'm Sturdevant's prisoner, standing in front of that tool rack. Would you illustrate what a policeman does in such a situation?"

"Sure." Roberts got up and pointed at the teacher with his index finger. "Pretend this is a gun. Okay, now, Mr. Strang, hands against the wall. Spread your legs."

Mr. Strang assumed the required position, his arms above his head, his back to Roberts.

"Put your left hand behind your head." Mr. Strang did so. "All right, now I snap a handcuff around your left wrist. Next, I—ow! Hey, that hurt!"

Roberts rubbed the side of his head, where Mr. Strang, whirling quickly, had connected with a fist. "We all get careless sometimes, Paul," said the teacher. "I think you're supposed to hook a foot around my ankle to trip me if necessary, aren't you? I imagine Sturdevant also forgot to do so."

Beldeck was watching the demonstration with interest. "You're pretty fast on your feet for an old man, Mr. Strang."

"You're way ahead of me, Mr. Beldeck, aren't you?"

"Well, *I'm* not," said Guthrey. "What's this all about, Leonard?"

"I think what happened to Detective Roberts just now is the same thing that happened to Sturdevant. He got the first handcuff on, but, before he could lock the second one, his captive turned and hit him. Unlike me, though, that unknown person had a wooden mallet in his hand."

"Wait a minute," Guthrey said. "That would leave this person—whoever it was—with a handcuff still on his left wrist."

"Exactly." Mr. Strang smiled. "The keys of which were still on the ring in the lock of the school door, a fact the attacker couldn't possibly know. That was the reason for the removal of Sturdevant's belt, to conceal the fact that the officer's handcuffs were missing."

The teacher walked over to George Beldeck, who was still lounging against the wall. "George," said Mr. Strang, "at your father's request, you haven't said much during this discussion. You're within your rights if you don't say anything now. But I'd still be interested in the real reason you stayed after school today instead of going straight home."

He looked at Mr. Beldeck, then back at the boy. "You were afraid your parents would see it, isn't that right, George? Because you couldn't get it off!"

Slowly the old teacher extended a hand. "You've kept your left hand—and wrist—concealed in the pocket of your sports jacket all this time, George," he said softly. "Come on, prove me wrong. Show everybody I'm nothing but an old crackpot."

George Beldeck looked at the hand outstretched toward him. "You—you've got no right!" he shouted. "You can't make me! Dad, tell him!"

Mr. Beldeck saw his son's shoulders start to tremble.

"Dad?" pleaded the youth.

"Do what he says, George," said Beldeck, his voice shaking.

The boy's left hand came out of his pocket. A handcuff was tightly clamped to his wrist. The other cuff, catching the fading light coming through the window, dangled loosely from its short chain.

MR. STRANG LIFTS A GLASS

"Mr. Butcher will see you now."

The secretary smiled and pointed to a door at the opposite end of the outer office. Mr. Strang and the two Aldershot High School juniors nodded their thanks and padded across the thick carpet. When they reached the door, which led to the sanctum sanctorum of the president of Butcher's Department Store—"Aldershot's Biggest and Best"—the students wriggled apprehensively, and Mr. Strang gave them a wink of reassurance. He wished he felt as certain of success as he tried to appear.

Henry Kerrigan, whose long dark hair and full-sleeved shirt gave him a curious resemblance to Romeo Montague, turned to the girl beside him and crossed his fingers for luck. The girl, Jean Dumont, wore a blue dress short enough to have gotten her arrested when Mr. Strang was a boy. Nevertheless, it had been his idea that she wear it. Perhaps, if all else failed, Wade Butcher would be influenced by the sight of a trim feminine figure.

Taking the stubby briar pipe from between his teeth, Mr. Strang used it to tap gently on the door.

"Come in," rumbled a voice from inside.

The door opened quietly, and, when they had entered, it closed again with a respectful hushing sound. The office, with its modern furniture, modernistic statuary, and civic-award plaques on the walls, was clearly designed to awe visitors and convince them that this was indeed the sanctum sanctorum of a Successful Executive.

In one corner, a big man wearing a cashmere sports jacket had his back to them and was fiddling with the dials on one of the two television sets sitting on a stainless-steel table. He switched the set off and turned. Wade Butcher had a face that was handsome despite a double chin and receding hairline. His appearance was only slightly marred by a nose that had once been broken.

"Leonard Strang!" He walked toward the slender science teacher with his right hand extended, and Mr. Strang allowed his own hand to be enveloped in Butcher's huge paw. The students were introduced, and Butcher gestured toward seats in front of his huge desk. He then moved behind the desk and settled himself into a padded chair.

"What can I do for you, Mr. Strang?" he asked, taking a thick cigar from a teakwood box and sparking fire from a gold lighter.

"We need money, Wade—the school, that is." Mr. Strang ran a hand nervously across his wrinkled brow. He didn't like doing this; it seemed undignified.

"Oh? My secretary usually handles things like that. But I'm glad you dropped in, for old times' sake. How much? Ten dollars? Twenty-five?"

Henry and Jean looked at each other, and Mr. Strang took a deep breath. "We need a thousand dollars," he answered slowly.

Butcher stared at the teacher in silence. Then he began to shake with laughter. "You're joking!"

"Wade, don't just turn us down flat. Let me explain." Mr. Strang spoke rapidly, giving Butcher no time to voice a refusal to listen. "We're trying to get a student-exchange program going. Next year, there's a possibility of Henry and Jean spending a semester in France. But we've got to raise the money to send them there. We've tried shows and sales at the school, and we've asked for contributions from the community. We've made quite a bit, but we're still twelve hundred dollars short. If you'd give us a thousand, I'm sure we could raise that last two hundred. Think of it as an opportunity to—"

"This isn't an *opportunity*." Butcher shook his head ponderously from side to side. "It's a touch—and a hefty one."

"But the good will it would create for the store—"

"I'm more interested in profits."

"Yes, but I'm sure that, for something as worthwhile as this, the store can afford to—"

"Dammit, Strang, it's not the store. It's me. *I'm* the one who's turning you down."

Both men stopped abruptly. There was a silence in the office that could almost be touched. "Did you think I'd forgotten, Mr. Strang?" asked Butcher softly. "Not me. Not even after all these years. I knew that one day you'd have to come to me. I guess the time is now."

"What does he mean, Mr. Strang?" asked Jean, puzzled. The old science teacher looked at Wade Butcher, who turned to stare out the window behind him.

"I don't want to drag you into something personal between Mr. Butcher and me," Mr. Strang began, "especially since it happened so long ago. But he brought it up, so perhaps you'd better know.

"It was back around the end of the Depression—in 1937, I believe. Wade—Mr. Butcher—was a student in my general-science class at Aldershot High. Most of the families in town had little or no money, and many students came to school without bringing a lunch or the funds to buy one in the cafeteria. But Wade always had cash in his pocket. His father owned a dry-goods store and had managed to keep his head above water. Wade began to lend lunch money to his classmates. At first, I thought it was a fine thing for him to do."

"It sure was," said Jean. "But why—?"

"Later on, I found out that he was charging interest on those loans, six percent per week. Some of the students eventually owed him tremendous sums."

"There was nothing illegal about it," interrupted Butcher aggressively. "Everybody I loaned money to knew the kind of deal I was making. None of them complained—at least, not until it was time to pay me back."

"But if they were broke to begin with," asked Jean, "how did they ever—?"

"Mr. Strang gave them the money!" Butcher whirled in his chair. "*Gave* it to 'em! They paid me back, all right, and not just with cash. As soon as they were all out of debt, they ganged up on me one day after school. That's how I got *this*." He fingered his broken nose.

"When it happened, Wade, I told you how sorry I was. But that doesn't alter the fact that you were taking advantage of the other kids, just because you had cash and they didn't."

"Like I said, they went into the deal with their eyes wide-open. I never welched on any of *my* deals, did I?"

Mr. Strang had to admit this was true. Wade had always had a compulsion to follow any agreement to the letter. He could be as exacting on himself as he was on others. One time, he'd completed three weeks of homework by remaining up all night, simply because he'd promised it to Mr. Strang in the morning. His personal motto could have been: "Absolute justice—without mercy."

Although a thousand dollars was a pittance compared to the wealth of Butcher's Department Store, Mr. Strang knew there was no hope. He was being punished, according to Butcher's stern code, for a supposed injustice committed more than thirty years in the past.

He got up to leave.

"Mr. Butcher," said Henry, still in his chair. "You stink. Even if your nose *was* Mr. Strang's fault—and I think you had it coming—why take it out on us? Personally, I think you're just cheap, and the excuse about your nose is a cop-out. You'll spend money on toys like those two TV sets, but you won't give anything to our exchange program."

"Toys?" Butcher grinned, got up, and walked to one of the sets. "Not quite." He turned the set on, and a view of the store's perfume department appeared on the screen. "The store used to lose a couple of hundred dollars every day because of shoplifting and employee pilfering, until I had this closed-circuit system installed." He flipped the channel-selector knob to show the lingerie counter, housewares, men's clothing. There was no part of the store that was hidden from Butcher's view.

"The other set is for the second floor." Butcher clicked the switch off. "We catch thirty or forty people a day with this rig. The sets in the Security office are manned at all times when the store's open, and we make no secret of the fact that shoppers are under constant observation. Shoplifting has been cut to almost nothing."

"What happens when you see somebody taking something?" asked Jean. "Do you arrest them?"

"No. One of my men follows them outside. It's not technically shoplifting until the merchandise leaves the store. Then the shopper is brought in to our Chief of Security, Max Whittier."

"*Then* do you arrest them?"

"We just make them pay for the merchandise. Occasionally, we release the details to the newspapers—which we find warns off others who might be tempted."

"How much does a setup like this cost, Mr. Butcher?" asked Henry.

"About seven thousand dollars. And it's been worth every penny."

Anger or frustration might have accounted for Henry's next remark. But afterward, Mr. Strang was willing to swear that the boy knew exactly what he was doing—that, when it came to a thousand dollars, a high-school student could be just as ruthless as the president of a large store.

"Gee, Mr. Butcher," Henry said slowly. "I don't see how those dumb TV sets could stop *anybody* with a brain in his head. Why, I bet Mr. Strang could outwit them easy."

"I've heard Mr. Strang has occasionally acted as something of an amateur detective, but I doubt that he—"

Butcher cut himself off and smiled oddly. "Perhaps you've got something there," he said. "How about it, Mr. Strang?"

"How about what?"

"Like to try your hand at being a thief?"

"What's that supposed to mean?"

"I'll make a deal with you. If you can snitch something from my store—something I pick out, mind—and get it outside without being caught, I'll give you the thousand dollars you need for your project."

Mr. Strang began a vehement refusal. The idea was not only undignified but possibly illegal, even though Butcher himself would be in on it.

But then he glanced at Henry and Jean. Their eyes had the pleading look of puppies waiting to be fed.

"Well, ah"—the old teacher stared daggers at his students—"what happens if I get caught?"

"Oh, you won't go to jail, Mr. Strang. But the newspapers will have a field day. It'll be pretty embarrassing for you, especially since you'll probably have to answer to the School Board for your actions." Again Butcher rubbed his broken nose.

"I see. So this will be your revenge, is that it?"

"That's right. Unless you succeed, of course." He gestured toward Henry and Jean. "They seem to have a lot of faith in you."

Mr. Strang considered the challenge for a long minute. "What am I supposed to steal?" he asked. "I'm too old to lift a rowboat or a bedroom set."

"I've been thinking about that," said Butcher, "and I believe I've got the very thing." He pointed to the door. "Shall we?"

Five minutes later, Mr. Strang and Wade Butcher were in the gift department on the first floor of the store, leaving the two students behind in Butcher's office.

The store owner pointed to an object on one of the shelves. "That," he said. "That's what you've got to steal."

Mr. Strang scowled angrily. "*Arthropoda!*" he growled.

"Why, what's the matter? Don't you think you're clever enough to get out of here with a single glass?"

The object did have the shape of a glass—a shot glass, to be exact. It was the size of the thing that confounded the teacher. More than a foot high and just as wide, the glass seemed to have developed its own kind of pituitary trouble and grown to gigantic dimensions. It was the ugliest thing Mr. Strang had ever laid eyes on, and he couldn't understand how anyone had the nerve to charge seven dollars for it.

"It's supposed to be used as a punchbowl," Butcher explained. "So that's the deal. You get that glass out of the store, and the thousand dollars is yours—the school's, that is. Care to come back to my office and discuss it further?"

"I'll come with you," Mr. Strang replied, "if only to wring the necks of those two kids."

Seated behind the desk once more, Butcher turned to

Henry and Jean. "Mr. Strang's decided to accept my challenge," he said. "I tell you frankly, I don't think he's got a chance in a million of succeeding—and don't expect me to be sympathetic when he fails. You'll get nothing, but I'll get plenty of laughs, that I promise."

"Just to get the ground rules straight," said Mr. Strang, "what about help? Can I have any assistance?"

Butcher considered the question. "I don't see why not," he said at last, "as long as you don't use a professional shoplifter. Aside from that, use anyone or anything you like. Use black magic, for all I care. But when you—or your helper—is nabbed, you've got to agree to any publicity I want to arrange about your failure."

"That's *if* I fail," said the teacher. "But to get all things in proper form, just tell me once more, what are the exact terms of the agreement?" He took a small notebook from his jacket pocket.

Butcher pulled a desk pad toward him, snatched up a pen, and began to write.

"You select any day the store is open," he began, spacing his words to give each of them time to write down the terms. "On that day, you've got to get the glass out of the store without being caught." He folded the paper and put it in his pocket. "Simple enough?"

"Simple enough," Mr. Strang repeated.

But the following afternoon, as he sat perched on his classroom's demonstration table in front of Henry Kerrigan and Jean Dumont, it didn't seem all that simple.

"There must be *some* way, Mr. Strang," said Jean, slouching at her desk and resting her head on one hand. "I read somewhere about a person who shoplifted a piano. And there was a woman who almost got out of a store in New York with a TV set between her legs."

"I'll bet her skirt was longer than yours," said Mr. Strang with a puckish grin. "And as for the piano, that was arranged by altering a sales slip. The store itself delivered it."

"Then why couldn't we—?"

"Wade Butcher is no fool," Mr. Strang reminded them. "He picked what he wanted me to steal very carefully. That big shot glass wouldn't be delivered. It's not expensive enough, and the box it comes in probably has carrying handles. On the other hand, it's too bulky to hide under clothing, and of course it's rigid, so it can't be folded up. Besides, Mr. Butcher will have one of his men watching that part of the store on his closed-circuit TV, just waiting for me to try something."

"Couldn't one of us take it?" asked Henry, indicating himself and Jean.

"No. Definitely not."

"But he said you could have help."

"I know. But I'm not getting either of you in trouble because of an idiotic bet between Mr. Butcher and me. I'm the one he wants. I can see the headline now: 'Teacher Nabbed As Shoplifter.' *Mollusca!*"

Mr. Strang spent the weekend in a futile attempt to develop a foolproof technique for getting the shot glass out of Butcher's store. By Monday noon, he was about ready to admit defeat. Only the thought of Wade Butcher's smile of triumph—plus the loss of the all-important thousand dollars—prevented him.

"For a full-time teacher and occasional detective, Leonard," he mumbled to himself, as he stood by the lab sink polishing test tubes for use in his afternoon chemistry classes, "you certainly make an inept thief."

He considered again the conditions under which he had agreed to operate: "On that day, you've got to get the glass out of the store without being caught." It was so simple. Too simple. There didn't seem to be a single loophole.

He put the tubes in their racks and headed to the cafeteria and lunch.

Halfway through his meal in the teachers' dining room, he noticed the garbage cans into which leftover food and used paper napkins were dropped. He idly ran his fork through the gelatinous mass that the chef, with more audacity than culinary art, had labeled chow mein. He jammed the fork into the top of the pile of rice and vegetables, and it stood on its own like a miniature flagpole. Then he bolted out of his chair.

"Eureka!" he cried. "I've got it!"

Leaving his colleagues to ponder this Archimedian comment, he hurried to the telephone booth on the first floor. After a call to the Aldershot Village building, he dialed Wade Butcher's number.

It took almost two minutes to convince Butcher's secretary that he had to speak to the president personally and that he was unwilling to leave a message. Finally, Butcher came on the line.

"Wade, this is Mr. Strang."

"Want to call it off?" asked Butcher gleefully.

"No. Keep a sharp lookout for me on Thursday. I'll be in after school to filch your oversized shot glass."

And deliberately chuckling like *The Shadow* he remembered from old radio days, Mr. Strang hung up the receiver.

Butcher's Department Store was open until nine on Thursday and Friday evenings. So when Mr. Strang arrived shortly after five, he knew he would be a marked man for nearly four hours.

A moment after he entered the store, the telephone in Wade Butcher's office rang. "Yeah?" Butcher barked.

"Security," said the voice at the other end of the line. "That Strang character is here. The camera picked him up as soon as he came in."

"Okay. Keep him in sight, and be sure to get the whole thing on tape. I might want to run parts of it on a news program sometime."

"Right, Mr. Butcher. And I've got one of my men on the floor, watching that big glass full-time, just like you ordered."

"Good, Max. Don't let Strang or the glass out of your sight."

Mr. Strang seemed to be in no hurry to get anywhere near the glass. He took the escalator to the second floor and spent almost an hour thumbing through science volumes in the book department. Occasionally, he glanced around to smile at the TV camera mounted in the ceiling.

At five-thirty, Henry Kerrigan and Jean Dumont came into the store. Henry wore thick boots, a leather jacket with several zippered pockets, dark glasses, and a beret. Jean had on a bright-red maxicoat. They would have stood out at a masquerade party, to say nothing of a crowd of late-afternoon shoppers. It was Butcher himself who spotted them on the TV in his office after they had been in the store for more than twenty minutes. He picked up the phone and stabbed a button angrily.

"Max," he growled, "get a couple of your guys down on the floor to keep their eyes on those two kids in hardware. Leather jacket and long coat, that's them. You stay at the set and keep watching Mr. Strang."

Five minutes later, Henry and Jean caught sight of the two men from Security. "The big one should get his suit pressed," said Jean, laughing. "Let's split up and see what they do."

She left Henry in rapt contemplation of door hinges and made her way to women's wear. There she picked up the frilliest slip she could find and requested a fitting room to try it on. The man following her was stopped at the door to the fitting room by an outraged saleslady.

The shot glass remained on its shelf.

Mr. Strang headed for the lunch counter, where he ordered a fried-egg sandwich and a cup of coffee. Half an hour later, Henry sat on the next stool and ordered a hamburger. While he waited, he waved cheerfully at the camera above his head.

"Those damn fools are treating this like a game," Butcher said to himself, watching Mr. Strang and Henry play tic-tac-toe on a paper napkin. "When are they going after the glass?"

He switched the channel selector. All was well in the gift department.

At seven o'clock, Mr. Strang and Henry headed for the toy department, where they spent half an hour playing chess. By this time, Butcher had joined Max Whittier in the Security office. They both peered at the TV screen. "I just heard from Gould," said Max. "The girl finally came out of the dressing room. Look, there she is now."

On the screen, Jean moved into view, gathered up the chessmen, and packed them neatly in their box. Then she, Henry, and Mr. Strang turned toward the TV camera and bowed.

"Hell," said Max. "They must think they're on the *Ed Sullivan Show*."

It wasn't until eight o'clock that things began to pick up. The three potential shoplifters finally headed for the gift department. Butcher saw Mr. Strang stop to shake hands with the Security man assigned to watch the big shot glass. Then the teacher went to the shelf and, with elaborate care, took the thing in his hands.

"Max, he's got it!" said Butcher. "Get down on the main floor, right now!"

"You want me to pick him up?" asked Max.

"No, there's nothing we can do until he gets it outside. Just keep an eye on him—on all three of 'em."

Max hurried out of the office, and Butcher turned back to the screen. He was just in time to see Mr. Strang hand the glass to Jean. She moved her arm quickly, and her maxicoat billowed out. Suddenly the glass was no longer visible. She headed for the front of the building, as Henry walked quickly to the rear and Mr. Strang ambled off toward the escalator.

"Max!" screamed Butcher uselessly. "Get her—I mean him. Damn it, they're getting away."

But Max and the man guarding the glass were on their toes. One took Jean's arm as she walked through the store's front door, and the other nabbed Henry at the rear. They were both brought within range of a TV camera. After a quick search, Max telephoned Butcher.

"They're clean, Mr. Butcher," he said. "Neither one's got the glass."

In the confusion, Mr. Strang had disappeared. Desperately Butcher flipped through the channels on both sets. Home appliances ... power tools ... stationery ... books.

The teacher was finally found lurking—if so harmless and inconspicuous a man could be said to lurk—on the second floor, in sporting goods. He had the glass tucked under his arm like a transparent football.

He wiggled his fingers slyly at the camera, and Butcher switched channels as he scuttled into men's wear. From there, Mr. Strang went to the escalator and rode down, holding the glass triumphantly above his head until Max, still on the first floor with Jean and Henry, saw him.

The chase that followed would have done credit to the Keystone Kops. Mr. Strang did some fancy broken-field running through the aisles on the main floor, closely followed by Max and the other Security officer, neither of whom knew what he would do with the teacher if he caught him. In the curtains and draperies department, they lost him for a few moments, until Mr. Strang stuck his head through a fake window hung with elaborate drapes and shouted at them. At the lunch counter, the teacher sat down, and, when they sat beside him, he ordered each of them a cup of coffee and then moved on as they were getting ready to relax for a few moments and drink it.

At eight forty-five, a quarter of an hour before closing time, Max began to see a pattern in Mr. Strang's movements. After trying three ballpoint pens in stationery, the teacher insisted that his followers do the same. At the electric-razor counter, he treated himself to a free shave. In the clock section, he started four alarm clocks buzzing before a salesman stopped him.

As the minutes passed, Mr. Strang—with the huge glass tucked under his arm— was getting nearer and nearer to the store's big front doors.

Butcher watched him move onto the marble floor just inside the entrance doors. Shoppers leaving the building stared curiously at the man with the oversized glass.

And then a loud female voice boomed over the store's public-address system: "Ten minutes to closing time! Attention, shoppers: you have ten minutes to complete your business. The store closes at nine o'clock."

Butcher wondered if it was the announcement that startled Mr. Strang, or perhaps the smooth glass just *squirted* out of his grasp, his fingers now slippery with perspiration. For whatever reason, the teacher made a convulsive gesture, tripped, and the glass shot out of his hands like something alive. It arced through the air and struck hard against the unyielding floor—and shattered into dozens of jagged pieces.

On the TV screen, Butcher saw Mr. Strang fall to his knees, a pained expression on his face.

"All I need right now is to have him collapse in the store," Butcher moaned.

On the main floor, Max Whittier grabbed Mr. Strang under one arm and led him to the president's office. Meanwhile, the other Security guard signaled to a cleaning man, who began to sweep up the shards of glass.

"You seem to be feeling better, Mr. Strang." Wade Butcher lounged back in his chair, a satisfied smile on his lips. "I hope your ankle isn't too painful."

"No, I just turned it slightly. I'll be fine."

"You failed, you know. The store's officially closed, and you didn't make it out with the glass. Some of the TV tape we recorded will make interesting viewing."

Mr. Strang didn't answer. "May I go home now?" he asked at last. "It's been a hard day."

Butcher shrugged. "Max, find Mr. Strang's car in the parking lot and bring it around to the main entrance. I'll escort him out personally."

It was almost midnight when Wade Butcher arrived home. He was later than usual, because he and Max Whittier had stayed in his office to watch those parts of the tape that showed Mr. Strang dashing around the store. Butcher was still chuckling when he stepped into his living room.

He opened a desk drawer and took out a sheet of paper. He had a letter to write—a long, sarcastic letter to the gnome-like little teacher he'd sent scuttling from one end of his store to the other in a futile attempt to—

Butcher crumpled the paper and got another sheet. Somehow, the spiteful words weren't coming as easily as he'd expected. He started the letter four times, and each time got no further than "My dear Mr. Strang."

Hell, he'd be better off writing it in the morning, when his mind was fresh. At least the scrawny old buzzard wouldn't get the thousand dollars he'd been after.

"Wade?"

Butcher looked up from his fourth sheet of paper. His wife, Helen, was standing at the foot of the stairs, rubbing her eyes sleepily.

"Yes, dear? Why aren't you asleep?"

"I just wanted to tell you to be sure and put out the trash before you come up. The yard man forgot to do it today, and the truck comes early tomorrow."

"I'll take care of it. You go up and—"

Butcher's eyes suddenly widened. He reached into the pocket of his jacket, pulled out a slip of paper, and read the words on it: "On that day, you've got to get the glass out of the store without being caught."

He reached for the telephone next to his chair and dialed. The phone rang several times before someone answered. Butcher asked his question.

"They did?" he said. "About an hour ago?"

He slammed the receiver back into the cradle, crammed his hand into his jacket pocket, and yanked out his checkbook. "Damn!" he said, as he began to write.

At school on Monday, Mr. Strang received an envelope with the return address of Butcher's Department Store. There were two things inside. One was a note:

> Dear Mr. Strang,
> I concede. You outwitted me every step of the way, and, as you know, I never welch on a deal. I hope the enclosed will help with your project.
> This evening I saw a respectable dignified teacher make a fool of himself in front of hundreds of people, just to give a break to a couple of kids. Maybe—just maybe—I've been wrong about you.
> Anyway, I've been nursing a grudge for almost thirty-five years, and that's too long. Tell Jean and Henry to come and see me when they're getting their travel wardrobes together. I'll give them the best deal in town.
>
> Congratulations,
> Wade Butcher

The other item in the envelope was a signed check.

"I lived up to the exact wording of the agreement, of course," said Mr. Strang, when he met Henry and Jean during the lunch period. "He said I had to get the glass out of the store without being caught. And I did—every scrap of it.

All those antics we performed before I broke the glass were just misdirection to keep everyone's attention on me and away from the cleaning crew."

"But how did you know the crew would take the pieces of glass outside?" Jean asked.

"That was easy. When I phoned the village building just before accepting Mr. Butcher's challenge, the Sanitation Department assured me that the trash pickup for the whole of Aldershot is on Friday mornings. So I was sure that any rubbish that was collected in the department store on Thursday evening would be taken out of the store immediately and left at the curb for the morning pickup. I thought I'd have to explain to Wade how I won, but he figured it out for himself."

"I'm surprised he sent the check, though," Jean went on. "Someone else might have waited to see if you'd planned it that way or if you just realized you'd been lucky."

"Not Wade Butcher. He can be a hard man to deal with, but he's honest, scrupulously honest."

"Wait a minute." Henry Kerrigan had been examining the check, but now his eyes were on the teacher. "Mr. Strang?"

"Yes, Henry?"

"This check—it's wrong. You asked Mr. Butcher for a thousand dollars, but the check's only made out for nine hundred and ninety-two dollars"—he paused—"and sixty-five cents."

"Oh, that. That's another example of Mr. Butcher's attention to detail. He's given us a thousand dollars, all right—minus the cost of the glass, which was seven dollars plus tax."

MR. STRANG FINDS AN ANGLE

It was after five-thirty one afternoon in late fall, and Aldershot High School was nearly deserted. As he walked down the long hall that ran the full length of the building's second story, Murray Crofton—"Mr. Crofton" to his American History students—heard the click of brooms against chairs, reminding him that the night-crew custodians were busy cleaning up for the next day's onslaught of students.

Crofton was glad he'd stayed in school to mark that last batch of tests. Now he could take the groovy new typing teacher to the movies without wondering how'd he explain to the kids why their papers weren't ready. Besides, Mr. Guthrey, the principal, had stopped by on his way out and was clearly pleased by the sight of one of his faculty members working late.

Crofton felt that his first year of teaching was getting off to a good start. He passed the open door of a broom closet and reached the rear hall, which ran at right angles to the one he was in.

A rustling sound came from somewhere. Started, the young teacher turned to his left. At this spot, the rear hall went beyond the center corridor, forming a small, windowless area, an unlighted cul-de-sac about twelve feet square, lined with the metal doors of student lockers.

Something moved in a shadowy corner. A twinge of apprehension made the teacher's hands tremble. "Come out of there!" he snapped.

There was the crash of a locker door slamming shut.

"Why don't you just go home, Mr. Crofton," came a voice from the darkness, "and forget you seen anything?"

"Who—?" Crofton peered into the gloom. "Is that you, Sontag? Your locker's not up here. It's on the ground floor. And who's that with you?"

He approached the corner, where he could dimly see the outlines of two figures.

There was a sudden swift movement. Crofton gasped as an elbow smashed into his stomach. At almost the same time, a fist collided with stunning force just below his right eye. He struck out blindly, hearing a yelp and then a curse as the edge of his hand hit something. Then an arm raked his legs from under him, and he fell heavily to the floor, face downward. He tried to roll over, but a foot crunched into his ribs, and he fought to keep from blacking out.

Even as he shook his head to clear it, he saw—as if

through a dense fog—something above him sweep upward and then down. He put up an arm to protect his face. A heavy blow fell on the arm, and pain streaked up his shoulder as the bone snapped near the elbow.

Through slitted eyes, Crofton saw the upward motion repeated. Whatever it was that had hit him descended again, this time to the side of his head. A million lights spun before his eyes, and, for a fraction of a second, his brain seemed to explode.

There was the sound of feet running toward the place where he was lying and a shouting of voices.

But Murray Crofton heard none of that: he was unconscious....

The following morning, Leonard Strang—Aldershot's venerable science teacher—was late getting to school. His ancient purple car, like his own frail body, was reluctant to perform at its best on these nippy fall mornings. When he did arrive and had signed in, he was immediately buttonholed by Art Mickel of the math department.

"Leonard, I hope you haven't got any plans for after school today," said Mickel.

"Nothing I can't change, Art. Why? Not another curriculum committee meeting, I hope."

"Young Crofton, the history teacher, got beaten up yesterday after school, right here in the building. Terrible thing, just terrible. As head of the Teachers Association, I've asked Mr. Guthrey to hold a faculty meeting about it this afternoon, and he's agreed."

Mr. Strang nodded solemnly. "I'll be there. But what about Crofton? Was he badly hurt?"

"He's in critical condition in Beardsley Hospital. I'm going to call over there later today and see if I can get any more information."

"But shouldn't his parents be—?"

"His father's dead. His mother lives in Minnesota with a married sister, and she's not well enough to travel. He doesn't have any family in this part of the country. Under the circumstances, I think the Association has a duty to act on his behalf."

"Of course. Do we know who did it?"

Mickel nodded. "Four of the custodians heard the scuffling and nabbed the boys just after they knocked Crofton down. It was in that little dead end at the back of the second floor."

"Boys?" Mr. Strang looked at Mickel in amazement. "You mean it was some of our students who did it?" He felt as if a lump of lead had suddenly formed in his stomach. In all his years at Aldershot, he'd never heard of anything so foreign to the business of teaching school. Of course, there were bound to be fights with a student population of over two thousand. But they usually ended with nothing worse than a bloody nose or a black eye—and they almost never involved a teacher. Besides, this wasn't just a fight ... it was apparently a deliberate attempt to maim or even *kill* another human being.

The bell for first period rang, and students erupted out of their homerooms.

"See you this afternoon, Leonard," said Mickel, walking off.

At three-thirty that afternoon, almost all of the Aldershot teachers were present in the auditorium. Principal Marvin W. Guthrey waited patiently at a lectern on the stage while Cal Owens, the audio/visual director, got the hums and squeaks out of the microphone. Then he took a piece of paper from a manila file folder and began.

"I'm sure you've already heard," he said, his voice echoing from the loudspeakers, "that Mr. Crofton was injured yesterday. I have here a statement from the Board of Education concerning the incident."

The paper crackled as he placed it on the lectern and began to read: "At approximately six o'clock yesterday afternoon at the high school, Mr. Murray Crofton, one of our teachers, saw two students in the second-floor rear hallway. The students, whose names are being withheld pending further investigation, had no business being in the school at that hour. There was a scuffle between Mr. Crofton and the students, during which Mr. Crofton received several injuries. He is expected to be absent from his teaching duties for an indefinite period of time. The two students have been suspended for five days on the charge of loitering in the building. The Board intends to conduct a further investigation."

Guthrey folded the paper and put it in his pocket. "That is the end of the statement," he said. "It's signed by Frederick Landerhoff, the president of the Board of Education. Now if there are no questions—"

There were whispered conversations among the teachers that sounded like the humming of angry bees. Art Mickel shot up from his chair. "Mr. Guthrey!" he shouted, not waiting to be recognized. "Did I hear you say that Bradley Sontag and Luke Burroughs were given only five days' suspension?"

"I'd appreciate it if you wouldn't refer to the boys by name," replied Guthrey. "And, to answer your question, yes, I did say five days."

"Let's not beat around the bush," snapped Mickel. "We all know who it was. And now I'd like you to hear something. I phoned Beardsley Hospital today and talked with the doctor in charge of Murray Crofton's case. It took a little convincing, but I got him to tell me the extent of the 'several injuries' the Board mentioned in their statement. Mr. Crofton has three cracked ribs, Mr. Guthrey. He has a broken arm and a concussion, plus multiple bruises and abrasions. And a fractured skull, Mr. Guthrey—a *fractured skull*. As of noon today, the doctor wasn't sure whether or not he's going to live—and, if he does, whether or not his teaching ability will be impaired. The doctor also told me that, in his opinion, Murray was beaten with some kind of blunt instrument. And you're telling us that the punishment for all of this will be a *five-day* suspension? If the situation wasn't so tragic, I'd be laughing at you, Mr. Guthrey. *Loitering*?" Mickel snorted his contempt and sat down.

"You were pretty rough on him," whispered Mr. Strang, who was sitting next to Mickel.

"Rough, hell!" snarled Mickel. "The next time something like this happens, it might be you or me on the receiving end. If those two boys get away with just a slap on the wrist, I'm going to quit and find myself a nice *safe* job, like bomb disposal or test pilot." He looked at the steps leading up to the stage. "Who's that character in the Madison Avenue suit?"

"I don't know," said Mr. Strang. "But we're about to find out."

A tall, well-groomed man with a small mustache walked to the lectern and spoke to Guthrey. The principal nodded, and the stranger took the microphone.

"You're all concerned about what happened here yesterday," he said, "and I don't blame you. But while your concern is for the teacher, mine is for the boys involved. I'm Boyd Bankhead, and I'm a lawyer. I represent a group called FREE, the Fund for the Relief of the Educationally Exploited. Our purpose is to protect the rights of students whose parents can't afford to pay legal fees. The two boys—and you're right, they were Bradley Sontag and Luke Burroughs—fall into that category. I'm here to see that their rights aren't violated."

"Who's protecting Mr. Crofton's rights?" shouted a teacher.

"Frankly," Bankhead said, "I'd hoped for a less vehement

reception. Remember, please, I said I'm here to protect the boys' rights—not to get them off if they're proven guilty. But their guilt *must* be proved. Now, as you heard, Mr. Guthrey has suspended the boys. They were in the building when they shouldn't have been, there's no question about that. But as to any other alleged offenses, it will be up to Mr. Crofton to prefer charges—"

"How can he prefer charges when he's unconscious?" Mickel snapped. "He may never *regain* consciousness!"

"A legitimate point. But the Board's statement does promise further investigation. Conceivably, the Board could itself bring additional charges on the teacher's behalf."

"Excuse me." Slowly and stiffly, Mr. Strang rose from his seat. "I have a question. In any such investigation as the Board mentioned in its statement, you'll be representing Sontag and Burroughs. They'll be allowed to testify, along with any other witnesses you might care to call, and then the Board will make up its mind as to whether or not the boys did anything wrong beyond trespassing. Is that correct?"

"Essentially, yes," replied Bankhead.

"Then tell me," the teacher went on, "who'll be representing Mr. Crofton?"

"I beg your pardon, Mr.—?"

"Strang. Leonard Strang. And since hearings of the type you mention are usually conducted on the adversarial system—your side against our side, as it were—I'm wondering who's going to present Mr. Crofton's case?"

Bankhead took a close look at the old teacher, who was calmly toying with a button on his wrinkled tweed jacket. The old boy wasn't quite the bumbler he might appear to be, thought the lawyer. He whispered with Guthrey again and then spoke into the microphone.

"Mr. Strang," he said, "you've raised a valid point. Mr. Crofton probably won't be available for quite some time, and—since he's not in any position to hire legal aid—I've suggested to Mr. Guthrey that your Teachers Association make arrangements for someone to represent him at the Board's hearing."

Mr. Strang felt a tug at his sleeve and glanced down to see Mickel smiling up at him. "What about it, Leonard? Want to take the job?"

"Me? Shouldn't we get a lawyer?"

"This won't be a trial. It's just a hearing to see if the Board can find out whether the boys really did beat up Mr. Crofton. Of course, any facts brought out could be used later in formal legal proceedings. Besides, the Association's treasury is pretty low right now. We can't afford the sort of lawyer a thing like this would take. How about it?"

After a moment's thought, Mr. Strang nodded.

Mickel got up. "Mr. Guthrey," he said, "the Aldershot Teachers Association hereby appoints Leonard Strang to act for Mr. Crofton at the Board's hearing. He's a tenured teacher with longer service than anyone else in the building. Any objection, Mr. Bankhead?"

The lawyer shook his head, and Guthrey adjourned the meeting, asking Mr. Strang and Mr. Bankhead to meet with him in his office.

Ten minutes later, Marvin W. Guthrey was sitting in the leather swivel chair behind his desk, with Bankhead and Mr. Strang in padded chairs opposite him.

"Mr. Strang," Bankhead began without preamble, "I'd just as soon lay my cards on the table, because I don't think you've got a prayer of proving anything against Bradley and Luke except that they were in the building when they shouldn't have been."

"I see." Mr. Strang stoked up his massive briar pipe, emitting a cloud of pungent smoke. "Then Mr. Crofton's injuries are purely imaginary, is that what you're saying?"

"No, there's no denying there was a scuffle."

"Perhaps 'mugging' would be a more accurate word?"

Bankhead was about to shout "Objection!" but caught himself just in time. "Who's to say the scuffle or fight wasn't Mr. Crofton's own fault?" he asked in a reasonable manner. "Perhaps he grabbed one of the boys, the boy pulled away, and Mr. Crofton slipped and hit his head on one of the lockers or on the floor."

"And I suppose he smashed up his ribs and broke his arm at the same time," replied the teacher. "Dangerous things, those lockers. They'll leap right out and take a sock at you when you least expect it. No, Mr. Bankhead, that's too unlikely."

"But you'll agree it *could* have happened that way." Bankhead made it a statement instead of a question. "Remember, Mr. Strang, an accused person is considered innocent until proven guilty."

"*Ophiuroidea!*" shouted Mr. Strang, his voice ringing off the office walls. "Come off it, Mr. Bankhead! I'd buy the smashed ribs *or* the broken arm *or* the fractured skull as an accident, but not all three. Crofton was hit with a club or some other object, and we both know it."

"My responsibility is to the boys," said Bankhead. "It's not up to me to find the weapon. That's your job, and I wish you luck with it. Because you see, Mr. Strang, there was no weapon. That's the heart of my case: there *was* no weapon!"

The muscles of Mr. Strang's face suddenly went limp, and the pipe dropped from between his teeth, scattering ashes onto his lap. "No weapon?" he murmured, looking at Guthrey.

The principal nodded. "Four of our custodial staff reached Mr. Crofton not more than a few seconds after he fell. Bradley and Luke were still bent over him. The custodians grabbed them, of course, and then phoned me. I called the police and came right to the school."

"And none of you found anything that might have been used to inflict those injuries on Murray Crofton?"

"Not a thing. All of us—the police, the custodians, and I—searched the boys and that entire rear hall. There wasn't much to search, really. We even looked in the main hallway. Nothing."

"What about the lockers?"

Guthrey shook his head. "I opened all of them with my master key. Nothing but books and papers—nothing that could account for Mr. Crofton's injuries. One locker looked suspiciously as if the boys had been rifling it when Crofton caught them, but—"

"You can't *prove* the boys were in any of the lockers, though, can you, Mr. Guthrey?" asked Bankhead.

Guthrey shook his head.

"What were the boys carrying?" asked Mr. Strang.

"Nothing dangerous. Luke was empty-handed. Bradley had a paper bag filled with gym clothes and a pair of sweat socks. He told us he was taking them home to be washed."

"And their shoes?" Mr. Strang knew he was grasping at straws.

"Sneakers on both of them, and they were tight-laced."

"So there you are," said Bankhead. "Regardless of appearances, it would have been impossible for either Bradley or Luke to have inflicted those injuries on Mr. Crofton. Don't get me wrong—I feel sorry for the young man. But unless you can find a weapon, I think you'll have to agree that—"

"No, Mr. Bankhead, I don't have to agree to anything. If something struck Mr. Crofton, I'll find it."

"I wish you luck, Mr. Strang." With a sardonic smile, Bankhead rose and turned to Guthrey. "If you'll excuse me, I'm very busy. The hearing, as I understand it, will be next Monday in the boardroom at district headquarters. See you then."

Bankhead left the office, and Mr. Strang knocked the

dottle from his pipe and began to rise.

"Don't hurry off, Leonard," said Guthrey. "I want to talk to you."

Mr. Strang sank back into his chair.

"Leonard," began Guthrey haltingly, "the teachers will listen to you. I want you to explain my position in this distressing matter. I know there's going to be a lot of talk about the five-day suspension, but that's all I have the power to do. Any further measures can only be taken with the approval of the district superintendent. I called Superintendent Weyland three times today, practically begging him to let me expel those two boys permanently. But he won't budge until the Board has had its hearing."

"In other words," said the teacher, "you did everything you could."

"Yes, and now my hands are tied. Unless you can find whatever it was they used to hit Mr. Crofton, Bradley Sontag and Luke Burroughs will be back in school next week, and they'll be laughing up their sleeves at all of us. Find the weapon, Leonard, or life around here won't be worth living."

After school the following day, Mr. Strang spoke with Jesse Yates, one of the custodians who had belatedly come to the rescue of Murray Crofton. In answer to the teacher's first question, Jesse shook his head.

"Honest, Mr. Strang," he said, "us guys and the cops checked out those halls with a fine-tooth comb, looking for a club or *anything* those kids might have used to clobber Mr. Crofton. It didn't take long—I mean, where's to look? The floors are terrazzo, and the walls are tile halfway up and then cement. There ain't really any place to hide something like a club."

"Okay, Jesse," said the teacher. "I just wondered if you'd noticed anything."

"Nope. Neither did any of the other guys. I asked 'em. There wasn't anything out of the ordinary. Unless—"

"Unless what?"

"Well, you might think this is kinda weird, Mr. Strang, but, when I was running down the hall once I heard the fighting, suddenly it got awful quiet. I guess that's when Mr. Crofton went down for the count. It was right after that I thought I heard something."

"What did you hear?"

"That's the funny part. You know, my kid's got a pair of roller skates. And right out in front of our house is a piece of sidewalk that makes a hollow sound when the skates go over it."

"What's that got to do with—?"

"That's the kind of sound I heard. It wasn't as loud, but it sounded like my kid skatin' over that part of the sidewalk."

That evening, at the house where he rented a room from Mrs. Mackey, Mr. Strang lay on his bed, staring at the ceiling and thinking of roller skates. But how do you hide a roller skate? A little spot of light high up on one wall caught his eye. He looked out the window, but the night was completely dark. Then where was—?

He turned out the lamp next to his bed, and the spot of light disappeared. When the lamp was turned on again, the spot returned. Odd. The teacher glanced across the room at the bureau. Of course: above the bureau hung a large mirror. The spot of light on the wall was nothing more than a reflection of his own lamp. A line from the physics textbook flashed across his mind: "Incident light striking a flat reflective surface at any angle will be reflected at an equivalent angle."

The angle of incidence is equal to the angle of reflection. That scientific principle works for light, for sound waves, for—

As he thought these words, a vision of the corner hall where Mr. Crofton was attacked popped into the teacher's mind.

With a whoop, he bounced off the bed, skittered downstairs, and grabbed the telephone, startling Mrs. Mackey, who was watching an old Joan Crawford movie on TV. After consulting the phone book, he dialed the number of the Aldershot Bowling and Billiard Academy....

The hearing on Bradley Sontag and Luke Burroughs was called to order in the school district's boardroom at eight o'clock on Monday evening. It was a closed session, with attendance limited to those having an immediate connection with the case.

At one side of the room, behind tables set in the shape of a crescent, sat the Aldershot Board of Education: seven men and women elected by the community to determine the educational policies of the district. With them was Superintendent of Schools Lawrence Weyland and Alvin Beaney, the district's legal advisor.

In folding chairs facing the Board were the participants in the hearing. On the left were Bradley Sontag and Luke Burroughs, accompanied by their parents, in huddled conversation with Boyd Bankhead, the lawyer from FREE. Opposite them were Mr. Strang, Marvin W. Guthrey, Jesse Yates, and a fourth man, whom the science teacher introduced as Patrick Haliday, proprietor of the Aldershot Bowling and Billiard Academy. A secretary occupied a table in one corner of the room to keep a record of the proceedings.

Board President Frederick Landerhoff rapped his gavel for order, and Superintendent Weyland rose. A short, rotund man, he peered owlishly over his glasses and began to speak.

"This hearing," he said, "is being held in regard to events that took place in the high school last Tuesday. Certain facts can be agreed on. Murray Crofton, a teacher, discovered the two students, Bradley Sontag and Luke Burroughs, in the rear hallway on the second floor, just before six o'clock. In the course of subsequent events, Mr. Crofton received severe injuries. Are we in agreement so far, gentlemen?" He looked from Bankhead to Mr. Strang, both of whom nodded.

The superintendent went on in a voice as dry as an autumn leaf. "Mr. Bankhead, representing the boys, maintains that the injuries were accidental—that Mr. Crofton, in attempting to remove the boys from the building, slipped and hit his head against a locker door or the floor, and in a similar way received injuries to other parts of his body. Mr. Strang, on behalf of Mr. Crofton, alleges that he was deliberately and repeatedly struck by the boys. May I say for the record that each Board member has the doctor's report, listing Mr. Crofton's injuries.

"If the Board of Education finds at the conclusion of this hearing that the injuries were indeed accidental, the boys will be reinstated in school without delay. If, on the other hand, the Board rules that the injuries were deliberately inflicted, it has the power to expel the boys. In addition, the Board has the authority and the duty to turn any evidence of illegal action over to the police or the district attorney for possible criminal action. Naturally, any ruling of this Board may be appealed through the courts or to the Commissioner of Education. Any questions?"

There were none.

"This is a boardroom, not a courtroom," Weyland continued. "Therefore, I suggest a certain amount of informality. We're interested in facts, not legal niceties. Mr. Bankhead, I believe you asked to begin."

Bankhead got to his feet and honored the Board members with a charming smile. "Thank you, Dr. Weyland," he purred in a mellifluous tone. "Ladies and gentlemen, my speaking first is, as your superintendent indicated, somewhat irregular. Usually, it's up to the prosecution to prove that a crime has been committed before the defense begins its case. But in this instance, the entire position of my— shall we say 'opponent'?—rests on a single supposition that I will deal with in a moment."

Bankhead reached into his briefcase and removed a sheet of paper. "I refer you," he said, "to the doctor's report that Dr. Weyland mentioned earlier. It states that, in his opinion, Mr. Crofton was beaten with a club or blackjack of some kind. But that, to use his own word, is only an *opinion.*" He looked across the room at Jesse Yates.

"Mr. Yates, how long would you say it was between the time Mr. Crofton slumped to the floor and the time you reached the area where he and the boys were?"

"I dunno, maybe ten seconds?"

"Ten seconds. And did you find any sign of a club or blackjack or other blunt instrument?"

"Nope."

"Did any of your assistants find such a weapon?"

"No, but—"

"Just answer my questions, please. Did Mr. Guthrey or the policemen he called in locate anything?"

Jesse Yates shook his head.

"And now, Mr. Yates, would you tell us what the boys— specifically Bradley Sontag—had with them?"

"A bag. A paper bag."

"What was in the bag?"

"Gym shorts and a T-shirt. And a pair of sweat socks."

"That's *all* they had?"

"Uh-huh."

"And you searched the hall thoroughly?"

"We looked, yeah. But we didn't find nothing."

"Thank you, that's all." Bankhead turned to the Board. "There's my argument in a nutshell, ladies and gentlemen. While it may sound odd that a fall could produce the injuries Mr. Crofton suffered, that's what *must* have happened—unless you conclude that these two youngsters roughed up Mr. Crofton by slugging him with a T-shirt."

With a smile, Bankhead sat down.

For a moment, there was silence in the room. Weyland turned to Mr. Strang. "If I may be allowed an observation," said the superintendent, "Mr. Bankhead has presented a rather convincing argument in favor of the boys' innocence. I believe the ball's in your court, Mr. Strang."

His joints creaking almost audibly, Mr. Strang got to his feet. Whipping off his black-rimmed glasses, he slid them into a pocket of his jacket. "Dr. Weyland, ladies and gentlemen," he began, "an Aldershot High School teacher has been beaten unmercifully. He may *die* of the injuries inflicted upon him. For that, I ask that the perpetrators of this outrage should be punished. I don't ask this in a spirit of vindictiveness. I ask for punishment only so that the next individual who takes it into his head to resort to violence will be forewarned that he may not do so with impunity. I ask it so that the faculty in the Aldershot school system may perform their function as teachers without fear for their safety or their very lives.

"You will note that I did *not* say Mr. Crofton was 'accidentally' injured, or that he 'slipped and fell.' I said that he was *beaten*. And to make that fact perfectly clear, I intend to produce the weapon that Mr. Bankhead has claimed was nonexistent."

There was a murmuring among the members of the Board. Mr. Strang reached into his own briefcase and removed a white cotton sock, which he threw onto the table in front of Weyland.

"A gym sock," he said, "like the ones Bradley Sontag was carrying in his paper bag. I have the mate to it here." In his left hand, he held up a similar sock. "The sock in front of you is harmless, isn't it? Go ahead, pass it around. Feel how soft it is. It couldn't hurt a mouse, to say nothing of a human being. But what about this one?"

He raised the sock he was holding over his head and brought it down on the table. It struck with a tremendous *crash*, leaving a dent in the wood.

Fred Landerhoff looked at Weyland and then at Mr. Strang. "What have you got in that sock?" he demanded.

Mr. Strang turned the sock upside down, and a ball about two inches in diameter rolled out of it.

"A pool ball," he said. "It would make quite a dent if it hit you in the head, wouldn't it, Mr. Landerhoff?"

"Just a second," interrupted Bankhead. "Where would either of these boys get a pool ball?"

"I'm glad you asked," replied the teacher. "Mr. Haliday, would you answer that?"

"Sure." The owner of the Aldershot Bowling and Billiard Academy leaned forward in his seat. "A week ago tonight, young Sontag there was in my place shooting a few games. When he left, one of the balls from his table was missing. I had to get out a replacement for the next customer. We lose quite a few balls that way. I know the kids are making blackjacks by putting 'em in socks, but I dunno what to do about it."

"No one found a pool ball in the hall where Mr. Crofton

was injured," protested Bankhead.

"I'll get to that," said Mr. Strang. "But first, I'm going to take this ball out into the hallway. Jesse, I want you to listen carefully. Tell me if you hear anything familiar."

Mr. Strang walked out of the boardroom, leaving the door open behind him. Everyone listened intently, and then a soft whirring could be heard.

"Roller skates!" breathed the custodian.

"No, Jesse," said Mr. Strang, reappearing in the doorway. "That's the sound you heard the day Mr. Crofton was beaten. It's the sound of a pool ball rolling across the terrazzo floor of the hallway."

The teacher came back into the room, this time carrying a large board on which was mounted what looked like an architectural drawing. He set it up on a chair, so it faced the members of the Board.

"I have here," he said, "a scale drawing of the section of the second-floor hall where Mr. Crofton was found. It's as near perfect as the best student in our mechanical-drawing class could make it. You'll notice it shows both the main hall and the rear hall that branches off it. Mr. Crofton and the boys were in this section." He indicated the cul-de-sac with a pencil.

"If a ball such as the one I've shown you were rolled anywhere in the rear hall, it would have been found," Mr. Strang continued. "But suppose it were rolled in the direction of the main hall?"

"Why, rolling past that corner," said Weyland, "it would hit the far wall of the main hall and bounce off."

"Correct. Now tell us, Mr. Haliday, what do they mean by a 'bank shot' in the game of pocket billiards?"

"That's a shot that bounces off a cushion—the side of the table—before it goes into a pocket."

"And is there any rule about how those shots should be played—assuming there's no English on the ball?"

"Sure: whatever angle the ball goes into the cushion at, it'll come off at the same angle. With a little practice, you can make the shot every time. Well, *almost* every time."

"The scientific principle is that the angle of incidence is equal to the angle of reflection," explained the teacher.

"No kiddin'? I didn't know I was that much of a scientist."

"Now," continued Mr. Strang, "I believe we've ascertained that a pool ball rolled out of the rear hall into the main hallway would rebound from the wall at a predictable angle. Then, depending on the position from which it started, the ball would roll across the hall and strike the far wall somewhere between here"—he placed an X on the diagram—"and here." Another X.

"But why wasn't it found?" asked Landerhoff.

"I think Jesse Yates can answer that. Jesse?"

"Well, I—hey, wait a minute! There's a *door* between them two X's, the door to the broom closet."

"And wouldn't the door to the broom closet be *open* while your team was working after school?"

"Sure, we gotta get rags and water and—you mean the ball's still in there someplace?"

"That's right, Jesse." Mr. Strang turned to Landerhoff. "I believe that whoever clubbed Mr. Crofton rolled the ball away from him to get rid of it. It rolled out into the main hall, bounced off the far wall, and luckily—or unluckily, as the case may be—wound up in the broom closet."

"But isn't it odd," said Bankhead, "that none of the custodial staff found it there?"

"Mister," said Jesse Yates, "you oughta see one of them closets. They're jammed to the ceiling with all kinds of cleaning supplies. We might *never* find a thing as small as a pool ball unless we was 'specially looking for it."

"Then, if Mr. Strang is right, it should still be there," said Weyland.

"Of course, it's been an entire week since Mr. Crofton was injured," objected Bankhead, "during which time anyone could have planted a ball in that closet."

"Funny thing about pool balls," mused Mr. Strang. "They're hard and shiny—just right for taking fingerprints. If there are any on the ball, we'll not only be able to eliminate the possibility of the evidence having been planted, we'll also be able to tell which of the two boys clubbed Mr. Crofton."

"What are we waiting for?" said Landerhoff. "Let's send someone over to the high school to take a look in that broom closet."

Twenty minutes later, Jesse Yates found the pool ball wedged between two boxes of paper towels.

A few days after the Board meeting, Art Mickel met Mr. Strang in the high school's faculty room. "Congratulations again, Leonard, on a fine job. And I have great news: you'll be happy to know that Murray Crofton's condition is improving every day."

"You can hold the congratulations, Art," replied the teacher. "I'm sick to death of this whole rotten mess. Although that *is* wonderful news about Murray."

"Whichever of those boys actually slugged him," Mickel

said, "I suppose he'll be treated as a juvenile offender."

Mr. Strang shook his head sadly. "The prints on the pool ball were Luke Burroughs'," he said, "and Luke turned sixteen two months ago, so he's no longer considered a juvenile. Right now, he's in the county jail, awaiting trial as an adult."

MR. STRANG HUNTS A BEAR

"Leonard, I'm relieving you of all of your classes for the rest of the day." Marvin W. Guthrey, principal of Aldershot High School, watched as a scowl of annoyance twisted the already seamed face of the teacher seated on the opposite side of his desk.

Why was it, Guthrey wondered, that whenever they talked, Mr. Strang could fill him with a sense of uneasiness without saying a word? Certainly the thin old teacher didn't cut a very prepossessing figure. In his wrinkled suit and with his sparse crop of gray hair looking as if it hadn't been combed in weeks, he wasn't exactly Guthrey's idea of what a high-school teacher ought to look like. And now he wouldn't have to teach today. Couldn't the man show at least a *little* gratitude?

Mr. Strang was not grateful. His chemistry students desperately needed further review for their upcoming final examination, and the substitute teacher who had been hurriedly summoned to replace him turned out to have had all her preparation in English and couldn't tell an Erlenmeyer flask from a benzene ring. In addition, having taught at Aldershot for more than a third of a century, Mr. Strang knew that no teacher is ever called from his classroom unless the principal has some ulterior—and usually unpleasant—motive.

He silently began polishing his black-rimmed glasses on an acid-stained necktie.

"I got a telephone call about an hour ago," Guthrey went on. "The caller requested an appointment to see you."

"I see," replied Mr. Strang, though he didn't. Parent interviews were always held during a teacher's free period or after school, never during class time.

"The caller," said Guthrey, with almost religious awe, "was Letitia Ingraham Balt."

Letitia Balt, whom a New York newspaper had once referred to as "the globe-hopping grandma of the jet set," had moved into a huge mansion at the edge of the village of Aldershot some ten years ago, just after the death of her husband Mortimer. In his day, Mortimer Balt had possessed an uncanny knack for buying up barren pieces of land that, once he had acquired title, seemed only to need their surface scratched to pour forth limitless barrels of crude oil. Therefore, when Letitia came to the village, she was given almost as grand a welcome by the local bank as by Aldershot's social set.

For years, Letitia had only one interest in life: herself. She delighted in arranging "intimate little parties" at her home, at which a hundred or more guests were asked to meet her latest acquisition—a U.S. senator, a prize-winning novelist, a movie star. On completion of one of these affairs, she would jet off to some exotic locale to be feted by heads of state, artistic and cultural leaders, and the Beautiful People, each jaunt lovingly chronicled in the society pages of the nation's leading newspapers.

But the giddy whirl came to an abrupt halt when Letitia Balt received word that her only daughter and son-in-law had perished in the flaming wreckage of an airplane crash.

The couple left a child: Bobby, a nine-year-old boy turned into an invalid by severe rheumatic fever. Letitia sent for him. From the moment he arrived and was wheeled into her presence, she abandoned the life of the jet set and devoted herself wholly to Bobby's welfare. Some said her selflessness couldn't last and were surprised when it did. And, equally surprising, she seemed more happy when attending to her grandson's needs than ever before in her life.

And then the boy died....

"It was about six months ago, wasn't it?" asked Guthrey. "Weren't you giving the lad some private tutoring?"

Mr. Strang nodded. "He was pretty good in science, and Mrs. Balt called me one day and asked if I'd help him find the answers to some questions he had. We seemed to hit it off, and I arranged to show him some of the experiments he was too weak to perform himself. But I haven't seen Mrs. Balt since Bobby's death. I wonder what she wants?"

"So do I," said Guthrey. "I hope it doesn't mean trouble for the school. Her word carries a lot of weight in this town." He jabbed at the intercom on his desk. "Joanne," he said into the speaker, "send in Mrs. Balt."

He glanced across at Mr. Strang. "Please, Leonard," he pleaded, "be on your best behavior. Regardless of what she says, show a little respect—for my sake. If you don't, and with the connections she's got, I might be the first high-school principal to be fired by the President of the United States."

The door behind Mr. Strang opened, and Letitia Ingraham Balt entered the office. Slender and scarcely an inch over five feet tall, she bore herself with an air that was proud but not vain. Well into her sixties, she was still a classically beautiful woman.

As she approached the desk, Mr. Strang stood and turned to her. "Lettie," he said softly. "How good to see you again."

Guthrey wondered if he should ask Mr. Strang to use a more formal term of address. But as he pondered the problem, Mr. Strang took Mrs. Balt's hand gently in his own and brought it to his lips. As he kissed it, Letitia made a slight curtsy. The gesture, so old-fashioned and yet so thoroughly charming, brought to the principal's mind visions of another age, an age of Strauss waltzes and elegant horse-drawn carriages. He began to feel distinctly out of place in his own office.

"I suppose you'd like to talk to Mr. Strang alone," said Guthrey, hoping to be contradicted.

"If you don't mind," answered Letitia.

With a shrug and a final stern look at Mr. Strang, Guthrey left the office.

"Mr. Guthrey seemed upset about something," said Letitia with a slight frown.

"I imagine it was because I called you Lettie," replied Mr. Strang. "He's quite impressed with your position in the community, and he probably thought I was being too familiar."

"Good heavens, Leonard," replied Letitia with a trilling laugh, "after all you did for Bobby? Why, my grandson used to say that he never enjoyed anything as much as your visits with him. After the happiness you brought to that boy, you could call me Bawdy Mab if you wanted to. I hope we're good enough friends not to be too formal when it comes to names."

"Of course we are, Lettie." Mr. Strang offered her a chair and pulled up another for himself. "Now, what can I do for you?"

"It's about Bobby."

"Bobby? But he's..." The teacher's voice trailed off lamely.

"Yes, Leonard, he's dead. His heart was never too strong. But I want you to find something out for me."

"Find something out?"

"Yes. I want you to find out whether or not I killed my grandson."

The sudden silence in the principal's office was almost palpable. Mr. Strang stared at the woman seated opposite him, and she returned the stare without flinching.

"Lettie," breathed Mr. Strang, "it's not possible that—I mean, you couldn't—it's nonsense! You're not a murderer. Besides, the papers said it was his heart."

"No, it wasn't murder. But I think I killed him just the same. That's why I've come to you."

"But wouldn't a doctor—?"

"Oh, Leonard, I've talked to doctors from all over the world. I've even had the police in, and private investigators."

Mr. Strang didn't like the shrill, almost hysterical tone of Letitia's voice. He patted her hand soothingly. "But, Lettie," he said, "I'm only a teacher. What could I—?"

"One of the men I talked with about Bobby's death was an Aldershot police detective, Paul Roberts."

Mr. Strang smiled. "I know Paul quite well. A good man."

"He came to the same conclusion as everyone else, that I didn't kill my grandson. But he did say that, if there was anything new to be learned, you'd be the one to find it."

"That doesn't sound like Paul Roberts talking."

"Well"—Letitia's eyes twinkled through her tears—"his actual words were, 'That scrawny old goat's got a built-in crystal ball,' but it comes to the same thing."

Mr. Strang rose from his chair. "If there's anything I can do, of course I'll help you. But don't expect miracles. Now tell me about it."

"Leonard, I'd be very grateful if you'd see me home. Once we're there, I can explain. It'll be much easier than trying to tell you about it here."

"But Mr. Guthrey—"

"It's all arranged with Mr. Guthrey. And don't tell me you're too busy or give me any other excuse, because I've made up my mind. I'm not one of your students, Leonard Strang, who you can order about whenever you feel like it."

The teacher was grateful for the smile that appeared on Letitia's lips as she rose and took his arm.

Her huge foreign automobile was chauffeured by a young giant of a man who was introduced to Mr. Strang as Carl Drew. "I employed Carl just a few weeks before Bobby's death," she explained. "He was awfully good to the boy. You should see the small animals he carved, just to please a sick child. Now he's my driver, butler, and general handyman."

The Balt estate was just as Mr. Strang remembered it: immense. The main house was a Victorian architectural monstrosity. Its walls and roof sprouted bay windows, cupolas, and turrets in wild profusion. The grounds, however, sadly needed the services of a gardener.

"I've cut back on my staff since—it happened. I lost interest," said Letitia. "Now there's only Carl and Janet."

Mr. Strang remembered Janet Ramsey and greeted her warmly as she opened the front door for them. A pretty nurse in her early thirties, she had originally come to the

Balt estate seven years ago to care for Letitia during a bout of pneumonia. She had stayed on, and, when Bobby had arrived, her nurse's training had been invaluable.

"It's good to see you again, Mr. Strang," she smiled. "Mrs. Balt usually has tea about now. Can I get you something?"

"Coffee would be fine," said Mr. Strang, and Janet strode toward the kitchen, her starched skirt rustling.

Looking up the wide curving stairway, Mr. Strang considered the elevator chair that had been installed on the wall.

"I had that put in for Bobby," said Letitia, "along with a speaker system from his room to the kitchen. Janet had enough to do without climbing stairs all the time—and of course, unless Carl was around, it was impossible to get the boy from one floor to another without it."

Mr. Strang accompanied Letitia into the huge living room and sank into an armchair. "Let's get down to cases," he said, stoking up his briar pipe. "What's this nonsense about your having killed Bobby?"

"It started right here in this room," replied Letitia, "when I told him a ghost story."

"A ghost story?"

"Yes. I suppose it was foolish, considering his condition, but Bobby had a fondness for ghost stories. He read them every chance he got, and, when I saw how much he enjoyed them, I began telling him some. Not after dusk, with flickering fires in darkened rooms. I used to tell him a different story every day, while we ate lunch. Right here in this room, in broad daylight."

"I see. And how did they affect him?"

"He'd smile and clap his hands while I was talking. When I told him one he especially liked, he'd say, 'That's great, Grandma.' That's how he reacted to the story of the burning bear."

"The burning bear."

"That was the story I told him on the day he—he—"

"May I hear it?"

"It's not much of a story, really. It's about an Indian hunter who was out in the woods one winter, searching for something to feed his starving family. He came upon a cave where a bear was hibernating. He wanted to kill the bear, but first he asked for the blessing of the *manito*, an Indian spirit.

"He heard the strange voice of the *manito* come to him on the wind." Letitia cupped her hands about her mouth and began speaking in an eerie tone. "The *manito* refused permission to kill the bear. But the Indian didn't listen. Piling sticks in the cave, he set fire to them. When the fire died down, the bear had been burned to death.

"That night, while the Indian and his family feasted on the bear, there suddenly came a roaring from the forest around them." Again Letitia cupped her hands, this time making the sound of a large animal in pain. "Into the light leaped a huge bear. But instead of fur, its entire body was covered with green fire. The Indian fled, chased by the bear. Neither was ever seen or heard from again. But the little bits of foxfire you sometimes see glowing in the forest are supposed to be what was left of the Indian after the bear was finished with him."

She shrugged and spread her arms. "End of story," she said.

Mr. Strang puffed his pipe in silence for several moments. "I'm sorry, Lettie," he remarked finally, "but I can't find anything particularly unnerving about the fiery bear, especially if Bobby heard the story in broad daylight. What happened when you finished telling it?"

"Nothing. Bobby read until almost three o'clock, and then he went upstairs for his nap."

"Alone?"

There was a rattling of cups as Janet Ramsey entered the room, a tray balanced expertly on one palm. "Of course not, Mr. Strang," she said, pouring tea and coffee. "Bobby couldn't go anywhere except in a wheelchair. I put him on the elevator and walked up beside him." She turned to Letitia. "I'm sorry to interrupt, Mrs. Balt, but I couldn't help overhearing you."

"That's all right, my dear. We've gone over this story so many times—so very many times—there's nothing private about it anymore. Perhaps it would be best if *you* were to continue, Janet, since you put him to bed."

"There's really not much to tell. When we reached the top of the stairs, I settled Bobby back in his wheelchair. I remember that Carl was working on some pipes in the upstairs bathroom, and I had to tell him to be quiet. I helped Bobby into bed, pulled the covers over him, and closed the door. That's about all."

"Except that, that afternoon, Bobby overslept," added Letitia.

"Overslept?" Mr. Strang's eyebrows shot upward.

"Yes," said the nurse. "Usually Bobby woke up by himself between six and half past. But that day, when I'd finished preparing dinner, I saw that it was after seven and he was still asleep."

"What did you do?"

"At first, I didn't think much about it. You see, Mr. Strang, Bobby also sometimes suffered from what I call 'the shakes'—jerky, uncontrolled movements of the arms and head. The technical name is chorea. It's often a result of severe rheumatic fever."

The teacher nodded. "I've heard of it," he said. "We used to call it St. Vitus' dance."

"When he had these spells, he was exhausted most of the time. That day, I felt he needed whatever sleep he could get. But by seven-thirty I began to be worried. Carl was still upstairs, so I called up to him and asked him to wake Bobby."

"We were standing right over there," Letitia said, pointing, "at the foot of the stairs. We heard Carl knocking on Bobby's door, and then he came to the landing and called down that the door was locked and Bobby wasn't answering. Of course we rushed up to see what was the matter. That is, Janet rushed up. I followed a few seconds later."

"Why 'a few seconds later,' Lettie? You seem spry enough."

"I had to get the room key from the pantry where we keep it. And in my hurry I knocked a pot of strawberry jam all over a beautiful sketch Janet was making of the view from the kitchen window."

"I see. And after you got the key, you went up and joined the others outside Bobby's door?"

Letitia nodded. "When I got there, Janet was shouting, and Carl was in a positive panic trying to break down the door. Janet took the key—my hands were shaking too much for me to use it myself—unlocked the door, and opened it. Oh, Janet, you seemed to take *forever* to open that door."

"I didn't think we ought to burst in on him like a tribe of wild savages."

"And that's when he cried out, Leonard." Letitia buried her face in her hands and sobbed.

Mr. Strang placed a gentle hand on her shoulder. "He cried out," he said softly. "What did he say, Lettie?"

Letitia lifted her head to look at the ceiling, as if begging some higher power for courage. Her face was twisted with the anguished memory of that moment in her grandson's room.

"'The bear'," she whispered, the words seeming to force themselves past her lips. "That's what he screamed: 'The bear! It's coming after me!' Over and over again. Leonard, it was the most awful moment of my life."

"I switched the light on right away," said Janet, "and went to the boy. His heart was pounding as if it would leap out of his body. Then it stopped. He was dead before the doctor could get here."

"There it is, Leonard." Letitia wiped her eyes with a handkerchief and made a valiant attempt to pull herself together. "If I hadn't told Bobby that story, he'd be alive today."

Mr. Strang turned to the nurse. "I suppose the doctor certified the cause of death?"

Janet nodded. "Bobby was frightened, and, when his heart began to beat faster, his damaged valves couldn't handle the increased load. It's not uncommon in these cases."

Mr. Strang motioned for Janet to leave him alone with Letitia. She nodded understandingly and tiptoed out.

"Lettie?"

"Yes, Leonard?"

"You can't keep blaming yourself. It was an accident, that's all."

"But I'm so afraid I killed him!"

"It's not a case of anyone 'killing' him. You did what you thought would please the boy."

"He was all I had after my daughter died! I was going to see to it that, when I pass on, he would inherit everything."

Something occurred to Mr. Strang. "You were *going* to see to it? Did you in fact ever change your will?"

"No, I never got around to it."

"So, as things stand now, who will inherit?"

"Aside from a few small bequests, my entire estate will go to charity. My daughter's husband was quite wealthy, so she wouldn't have needed my money."

So much for hidden motives, thought Mr. Strang. He looked at the ashen face of the seated woman. He wished he had some words of comfort, but whatever he might say would be useless. In her own mind, Letitia had convicted herself of murder.

And yet....

"*Brachiopoda!*" he muttered angrily. There had to be *something* he could do.

"Lettie," he said, "I'd like to see Bobby's room."

"Of course. It's just as it was when he—on that day. I've kept it locked since then, as—as a memorial, I suppose. I clean it myself, and the only other people who've been inside it were the police and the investigators I employed."

They climbed the stairs and walked along the hallway until they reached a door at the far end. "It's not very big," said Letitia, turning the key in the lock. "But it's bright and cheerful, and Bobby loved it."

As the door swung inward, Mr. Strang noted that its lock was of the spring type. *That explains the locked door*, he thought. The catch snapped into place as soon as the door was closed, and no key was necessary to lock it.

Two windows threw the late-afternoon sun across the small bed. Underneath the windows was a bench that ran the length of the room. On it were a telephone, some pieces of scientific apparatus, and several wooden carvings. He picked one of them up.

"A bear," he said to Letitia. "Pretty good job of carving. Did Bobby do this?"

"No, that was Carl. He carved several things for Bobby, but this little bear was the boy's favorite."

"There's nothing frightening about *this* bear, at least." Mr. Strang examined the room and found nothing of importance. The autographed pictures of world-famous men and women that decorated the white walls were interesting but not helpful. A boy's clothing, showing none of the wear and tear of active play, hung from two rows of hooks fastened to the inside of the door through which they had entered.

There was a soft tapping on the door. Mr. Strang released the spring lock and opened it. Janet Ramsey looked past him to Letitia.

"Excuse me, Mrs. Balt," she said, "but it's nearly seven and dinner is ready. Should I—?" She nodded at Mr. Strang.

"Of course, Janet, set another place. Please say you'll stay, Leonard. Perhaps—"

"Certainly I'll stay," replied the teacher.

The meal was an elaborate affair at which Mr. Strang regaled Carl and the two women with wildly exaggerated accounts of his adventures as a teacher at Aldershot High. When it was over, Janet commandeered Carl to help with the dishes, while Mr. Strang and Letitia stood on the front porch, admiring the sunset.

"I suppose you'll have to be leaving soon," Letitia finally said.

The old teacher nodded. "I'm sorry I couldn't be of more help, Lettie."

"Oh, Leonard, I wish the sun would never set. I don't want to be here alone when it's dark and know that—Leonard, what's the matter?"

Mr. Strang had pulled the black-rimmed glasses from his face, and he was staring fixedly at the red half-disk of the sun on the horizon. "That's it," he said in a hoarse whisper. "That's *got* to be it."

"What are you talking about?"

Instead of answering, Mr. Strang took Letitia by the arm and hurriedly steered her back into the house.

"The key," he said, extending his hand.

"What key?"

"The one to Bobby's room. I'm going back up there."

"I'll come with you."

"No, Lettie, you stay here. Wait until the sun has set before you come up. And when you do, make sure Janet and Carl"—he jerked a thumb in the direction of the kitchen—"have something to keep them busy. Get them out of the house, if possible."

Letitia handed him the key, and he ran up the stairs, pausing when he reached the top to get his breath. He turned to look down at Letitia Balt and placed a finger to his lips. Then he scuttled to the door of the dead boy's room, unlocked it, and darted inside.

Twenty minutes later, seated in the darkness, Mr. Strang looked out the window and saw a light in the garage. Carl and Janet had walked across the lawn and entered the building. Seconds later, a small sports car raced off into the darkness.

He heard footsteps in the hall. There was a gentle tapping on the door. "Leonard, are you in there?" asked Letitia's voice quietly. "I sent Carl and Janet out to a movie. They'll be gone for the rest of the evening."

He switched on the lights, opened the door, and motioned for her to come inside. As she entered, he pushed the door shut behind her.

"I took the liberty of using the telephone," he whispered. "I hope you don't mind."

"Not at all. Whom did you call?"

Without replying, Mr. Strang gestured toward the bed. "I want you to lie down, Lettie," he said.

"Whatever for? Really, Leonard, I feel perfectly all right. I don't need to rest."

Mr. Strang whipped off his glasses and tucked them into a jacket pocket. "I think I've got the answer," he said. "I know how Bobby was killed, and you had nothing—almost nothing—to do with it."

Letitia stared at the old teacher, shaking her head in disbelief. "You mean I really *wasn't* responsible for—?"

"No, you weren't. But it won't do any good just to *tell* you about it. I've got to *show* you, so you won't have any doubts later. Lie down, please."

Slowly, still looking incredulously at Mr. Strang, Letitia made her way to the bed, lowering herself onto its soft mattress.

"Now close your eyes," Mr. Strang commanded. "Keep them closed while I talk to you."

"All right, Leonard." There was a soft click, and even through closed eyelids Letitia could sense that the lights had been turned off.

"The room is completely dark now," said Mr. Strang in a soothing voice. "Just the way it was on that day six months ago, when Bobby was awakened from his nap."

"That's right, it was dark outside. But what's that got to do with it?"

"That's the one thing I hadn't considered. It's now June, final-exam month. When we came up here just before dinner, there was still a good two hours of sunlight left. But Bobby died six months ago, in the middle of winter. The shorter days—as well as the fact that we weren't on Daylight Saving Time then—meant that, on the day he died, Bobby would have awakened in darkness. Isn't that the way it was, Lettie?"

She could hear a rustling of cloth somewhere nearby. "Yes, it was dark. But I don't see—"

Mr. Strang spoke slowly and softly, calming her jangled nerves. "Now, Lettie, I want you to use your imagination, but be sure to keep your eyes closed. For a little while, you're not the wealthy lady who owns this house. You're Bobby, an eleven-year-old boy with a rheumatic heart. On top of that, you're having an attack of chorea—what Janet calls 'the shakes.' You're exhausted, but, because of the twitching of your body, you find it impossible to sleep."

Despite herself, Letitia felt her arms jerk involuntarily.

"Perhaps you've been given something to calm you down. Phenobarbital, maybe. You're not fully conscious. Instead, you're experiencing a sort of 'twilight sleep.' You're too tired to move, but you have some awareness of the things going on around you."

"Nobody in his right mind would give phenobarbital to a person with a rheumatic heart," protested Letitia. "Even I know that."

"But Bobby wouldn't," the teacher droned on. "He wouldn't even know he'd taken it, if it were put in his milk or something. And you're Bobby now. Remember that: you're Bobby."

There was a sudden sound in the darkness. At first, Letitia couldn't make it out. Her eyes still closed, she strained to listen.

Mr. Strang was chanting the words of the *manito* in her ghost story.

The bear, the fiery bear. Oh, *why* had she told Bobby that story? It wasn't possible, of course, that the bear could actually exist....

And then the growling sound came to her ears. That had to be Leonard, too. But it was so *real*. She imagined some forest bear prowling about the room. She had to think the way Bobby would have thought. Leonard had told her to.

The growling stopped. Several minutes passed, and in spite of the odd circumstances Letitia felt her mind becoming foggy with sleep. This would never do. Still, Leonard was there to protect her from the bear—the bear—

She had almost dozed off when, from somewhere in the room, she heard pounding. "Bobby," said a muffled voice, "wake up!" Involuntarily, she opened her eyes and sat up. Startled, she shook her head to clear her mind. She looked about to locate the teacher in the inky blackness of the room.

And then she screamed.

The thing was poised beyond the bed like some diabolical nightmare. It had the shape of a bear, but such a bear as might appear from the deepest pit of hell. The outstretched forepaws, the huge torso, the slavering jaws loomed before her—all in a green fire that glowed in the dark.

And then the awful thing moved, moved—

"Leonard!" she shrieked.

The lights snapped on and, as abruptly as it had appeared, the bear vanished. Mr. Strang peered around the edge of the open door. He walked over to Leticia, his feet shuffling through a pile of boy's clothing.

"Now you know what really killed your grandson," said the teacher. "Imagine the condition you would be in now if your heart were as weak as his."

"But the bear," Letitia moaned.

"Luminous paint. The bear was drawn on the inside of the door. It wasn't noticed when the lights were on because, in the light, the color of the paint exactly matches the color of the door. I imagine the clothing hanging on the hooks helped to conceal it, too." He indicated the clothes on the floor.

"That's why none of your investigators ever found anything," Mr. Strang went on. "Either they searched this room in the daytime, or they opened the door at night and switched the lights on at the same time. I made the identical mistake, until I remembered how dark it would be in here at seven-thirty in the middle of a winter evening."

"But who—?"

"Janet," said Mr. Strang. "It had to have been her."

"She wouldn't do a thing like that! She *loved* Bobby!"

"Let me explain how it must have happened. Janet overheard your ghost story that day. She realized she could get rid of Bobby and make you believe *you* were responsible for his death. She came up here and drew the picture of the bear on the door—if she didn't already have a supply of luminous paint, she had plenty of time that afternoon to go into town and get some. And you've already told me she's a talented artist."

"What about the phenobarbital?"

"That's something I can't prove, but it seems plausible. As a nurse, she'd have access to it—or some other sedative. She'd know how much to give him just to make him drowsy, and while she was up here she took the clothing down from the back of the door—remember, Bobby couldn't see the bear in the daylight—and made sure the spring lock was set.

"After that, she went back down to the kitchen. I imagine she piped the chants and growls of your burning-bear story up to Bobby's room via the speaker system you mentioned. The kitchen is too far from the living room for *you* to have heard the sounds.

"Later on, Bobby didn't wake up at his usual time because of the drug he'd been given. The alarm was raised, and you all gathered outside his room, knocking and shouting—which was guaranteed to confuse and frighten a groggy boy. He opened his eyes, and—well, you know the rest."

"But we all went into the room together," said Letitia. "Why didn't Carl and I see—?"

"Because Janet was the first one in. You mentioned that she opened the door slowly—she had to be sure Bobby had seen the bear. Bobby screamed—"

"—and Janet immediately turned on the lights!"

"Exactly. And hung the clothes back on their hooks while your attention was on Bobby. Since then, Janet hasn't had a chance to paint over the bear, because you've had the room locked and the key in your possession."

"It's—it's ghastly," said Letitia slowly. "But I can't deny that there *is* a bear painted on the back of the door. What now, Leonard? The police?"

He nodded. "They should be here by the time she gets back. Right now, *except* for the bear on the door, the case against her isn't strong. What we know and what can be proven in court are two different things. But I think Paul Roberts and his men will come up with more evidence, once they're pointed in the right direction."

"Whatever you say, Leonard. Only—"

"Only what?"

"*Why?* After all these years, why would Janet *do* such a thing?"

"Oh, Lettie, Lettie, you must be the most generous person in the world. That's why."

"I don't understand."

"While I was waiting up here, I called your lawyer about your will, the one you hadn't yet changed in favor of your grandson."

"What about it?"

"Lawyer Simms is an old friend of mine. We went to school together. Still, he was a little reluctant to discuss your personal affairs—but I finally talked him into it."

"I don't see—"

"You told me that everything was going to charity 'aside from a few small bequests.' Isn't that the way you put it?"

"Yes, but—"

"Really, Lettie, we working people don't consider 'fifty thousand dollars to Miss Janet Ramsey for her faithful service' to be a *small* bequest."

MR. STRANG CHECKS A RECORD

There ought to be a law forbidding rain on Saturdays, thought Mr. Strang.

As the diminutive science teacher pulled his battered purple coupe out of Napoleon Drive and onto Wellington Avenue, rain beat against his windshield in sheets that made the flicking wipers almost useless. Even at ten in the morning, visibility was so bad that he turned on his headlights. Wiping moisture from the inside of the glass, he peered up the street.

Suddenly a figure in a black slicker loomed in front of him. A policeman. At the man's gesture, Mr. Strang pulled to the curb, switched off the ignition, and rolled down his driver's-side window. Drops of rain dribbled off the roof of the car and into his lit pipe.

"Yes, Officer?" he said, as the policeman approached. "Was I doing something wrong?"

"No, sir. But we've had an emergency in the white house over there. The street's pretty well blocked. You'll have to turn around."

Up ahead, Mr. Strang could see the revolving red lights of two Aldershot police cars and what appeared to be an ambulance. He nodded to the officer and pressed the starter.

Nothing. With an obstinacy that seemed almost human, the ancient automobile had selected another in its long list of inopportune times to break down.

"*Endoprocta!*" growled Mr. Strang.

"Probably the ignition got wet," said the policeman. "I'll call for a tow truck when I get the chance. Don't know how long that'll be, though."

"What is it, Gibbs?" came a voice out of the rain. Then a man appeared behind the policeman, water gushing from the brim of his felt hat. "Oh, hello, Mr. Strang. Having car trouble?"

"Paul Roberts." Mr. Strang peered up at the bulky and exceedingly damp form of his friend. "What's the trouble over there?"

"Well, I—" Roberts looked longingly at the dry interior of the teacher's car. "Do you mind if I come in out of the rain?"

Without waiting for an answer, Roberts walked around the car and climbed in on the passenger side. "What a day," he sighed, shaking water from his limp hat. "Until the doctor and the lab boys get through inside the house, there's nothing for me to do but wait. I might as well be dry while I'm doing it."

"If you're going to get my car wet," said Mr. Strang with a grin, "you'll have to pay for the privilege. What's going on?"

"The Bulland house," replied Roberts. "Somebody seems to have broken in. Mr. Bulland and his son were attacked. The boy got beat up pretty bad, and his father—"

Roberts paused. "I don't know why I'm telling you about it, Mr. Strang," he mused. "It's supposed to be confidential information."

"How confidential can it be, with all those people standing around the house? I promise I won't breathe a word, Paul. Come on, let's hear it."

Roberts shook his head. "Maybe this is just oddball enough to interest you," he said. "Like I told you, somebody broke in. The Bullands' car is at the shop, and whoever it was probably figured the place was empty. So he decided to walk in and grab a few things."

"Bulland? There's a Joey Bulland at Aldershot High School. Is that the boy you mean?"

Roberts flipped open his notebook and glanced at his scrawled notes. "Yeah," he said, "kid's a freshman. Anyway, once the burglar was inside, he must have run into Bulland and his son in the basement. Joey had his face pretty well bashed—two black eyes, multiple bruises, and some teeth loosened. But Bulland himself? Mr. Strang, I feel like an idiot putting it in my report. It sounds like something out of an old-time horror movie."

"Oh?" The teacher's grizzled eyebrows shot upward. "What happened?"

"Two small punctures." The detective indicated a spot about three inches below his left ear. "Right here, on his neck."

Mr. Strang considered Roberts curiously for several moments. Having worked with the stolid detective unofficially on other occasions, he knew that Roberts was not blessed with a vivid imagination. The punctures were undoubtedly real. Still...

"You suspect a vampire?" The teacher's mouth curved into a sly grin. "The walking dead? Bela Lugosi flitting about in a Dracula suit?"

"Cut it out," Roberts interrupted. "I didn't say anything about vampires. Look, I've talked too much already. I'll have Gibbs give you a hand with your car, and you can be on your way. The lab boys'll be about finished, so I've got to get back in there."

"Paul?" The wizened old teacher knocked the dottle from his pipe. "Let me come with you."

"Mr. Strang, nobody's allowed in the Bulland house except authorized persons."

"And who authorizes them?"

"Well, I do, but—"

"Then let's go." Mr. Strang opened the door and stepped out into the drenching rain. "As an avid viewer of monster films, I'll be your guest vampirologist."

With a resigned shrug, Roberts led the way to the rear door of the Bulland house. The area in front of the back steps had been transformed by the rain into a soupy mess, and as he walked through it Mr. Strang could feel mud squelching over the tops of his shoes.

"The intruder had to come in this way," said Roberts. "The front door was locked from the inside."

The rear door led into the kitchen, where dozens of muddy tracks on the linoleum had produced a surrealistic design that might have been called *A Housewife's Nightmare.*

"You guys hold everybody out of the rest of the house," Roberts told the two uniformed men in the kitchen. "So far, we've kept those white rugs in the living room and the dining room from getting all muddy. Let's keep it that way."

A flashbulb popped in a narrow doorway that opened onto a descending wooden stairway.

"That's the entrance to the basement, Mr. Strang. The intern from the ambulance is down there now, patching up Joey and his father and trying to calm down Mrs. Bulland. You finished, Stacey?"

The cameraman nodded and began buttoning his raincoat. Mr. Strang followed Roberts down the basement stairs. At the bottom, a group of men was gathered around a small figure lying on the cement floor, covered with blankets. Off to one side, a young man in a white uniform was attending to a heavily muscled seated man who was gingerly rubbing his neck. Beside him stood a slender middle-aged woman, her eyes red from weeping.

"That's Joey in the blankets," said Roberts. "The medic's already given him something for the pain, so he'll probably be pretty groggy. I guess his old man needed looking after, too."

Joey Bulland had indeed received a severe beating. One eye was swollen almost shut, and the other wasn't in much better condition. There were greenish-yellow bruises on one side of his face, and his nose was bleeding.

"Mr. Strang," mumbled the boy. "I know you. I seen you in school lots of times. What are you doing here?"

"In school?" Alexander Bulland's voice was deep and harsh. "What's school got to do with this, Roberts?"

"Take it easy, Mr. Bulland."

The intern thumped a hypodermic needle into Bulland's arm. "Tetanus shot," he explained, "for those punctures in your neck."

Mr. Strang bent forward and examined the two small wounds. They were almost two inches apart, and each had an angry red area circling it.

"They're fairly deep," said the intern. "It's lucky they missed the carotid artery and the jugular vein. He'll have a stiff neck for a few days, but that's all."

"Have you figured out what caused 'em, Doc?" asked Roberts.

"That's your job," was the answer. "I just fix 'em up. I don't explain 'em."

"Lemme alone," said Bulland, roughly pushing the intern away. "You've done enough. I've got a right to see my own doctor, haven't I?"

"Yes, but—"

"Then get hold of Dr. Kermit. I want *him* to check us out, not some kid who's still wet behind the ears."

"Easy, Mr. Bulland," said Roberts. "I'll call Dr. Kermit for you. But Joey will have to be taken to the hospital."

Mrs. Bulland looked up, startled. She turned her pale face toward her husband, bringing one hand slowly to her lips. "Oh, Alex," she breathed. "The hospital. What are we going to do? How can we—"

"Joey'll be all right," Bulland cut in, his loud voice drowning out his wife's whisper. "You go with him to see everything's taken care of. And keep a close watch on him, hear? I don't want nobody interruptin' him while he's slee-pin'."

As the intern left to get a stretcher, Roberts took out his notebook. "Feel up to telling us what happened?"

"Not much to tell. Whoever it was must have got down here awful quiet. We never heard him. He was on us before we knew what was happenin'. It—I don't remember much about it."

"And you, Mrs. Bulland? Did you see anything?"

The woman's wide eyes darted in confusion from her husband to Roberts and back. To Mr. Strang, she seemed on the edge of a nervous collapse. "I—no, I was upstairs. I didn't see anything. I couldn't possibly tell you—" She burst into tears and buried her head in her hands.

"Dammit, leave her alone," barked Bulland. "Can't you see she's had enough for one day?"

"Yes, sir," said Roberts. "Can *you* give us any kind of a description, sir? Anything at all?"

"I didn't see him real good. He hit me on the back of the head. I got a lump there. Then he must have come after Joey. Afterwards, when I come to, I told Joey to go upstairs and call the police. I guess whoever it was must be long gone by now."

"Yeah." Roberts sighed and closed his notebook. "Well, maybe Joey will be able to tell us something later. I'll check with him at the hospital tomorrow."

"Like hell you will," said Bulland grimly. "First you bug my wife, and now it's my kid. Leave him alone, you hear?"

"I'll have to talk with him, sir. It's my job."

"But he's *my* boy. So I want to be there when you ask your questions."

"That's fine, Mr. Bulland." Roberts looked over at the two men who were standing beside what appeared to be an undersized automobile body. Near it, in a crate made of narrow wooden slats, were a variety of hand tools.

"Prints?" asked Roberts.

"We're trying," said one of the men, "but everybody in the world must have been down here at one time or another. It'll take weeks to check them all out."

"Joey's friends like to come down and help him work on his car," said Bulland. "He's going to put a motor in it when he's done with the body work. He can hardly wait to get his hands on the family car, but this'll have to do till he's old enough. Anyway, he was nailin' the body stringers on when—when—say, how much longer are you gonna take, Mr. Roberts?"

"We're almost finished," replied the detective. As he spoke, the intern and an assistant came down the stairs with a stretcher. "You and your wife can ride along in the ambulance, if you like. I'll leave a man on duty here and meet you at the hospital. Maybe you'll remember something on the way."

"I doubt it," said Bulland. "It all happened pretty sudden."

Mr. Strang and Roberts went up the stairs, through the kitchen, and out the back door. The rain had slackened.

"You'd better go home," said Roberts to the teacher, "and get on some dry clothes. At least you got to see what police work is usually like: this was just another breaking-and-entering. With the attack on Mr. Bulland and Joey, we can probably add felonious assault, if we ever find the guy—which I doubt. I wish I could explain those marks on Bulland's neck, though. Aside from that, it's a fairly routine case."

Mr. Strang rammed tobacco into his pipe and peered over his glasses. "To me," he said softly, "those two marks are the only routine things about the whole business. It's the other things that are weird."

"The other things? What do you mean?"

The teacher shook his head. "Not now, Paul. I've got some checking to do first." He touched a match to his pipe and blew a cloud of acrid smoke into the damp air. "I might suggest, though, that you give serious consideration to the condition of the living-room rug."

"The rug? Why? The burglar never touched the rug. It's in perfect shape."

"Precisely," snapped Mr. Strang.

And before the detective could reply, he walked stiffly to his car and got in. By some miracle, the engine caught, and he drove off in a cloud of blue haze.

The following Monday morning found Mr. Strang in the Aldershot High School guidance office. Virginia Cannoughby, the youngest of the counselors, was at her desk, and Mr. Strang walked in without knocking.

"Good morning!" she said cheerfully, looking up from her work and honoring the teacher with a devastating smile. "What can I do for you, Mr. Strang? Is one of your students giving you a hard time?"

"No, Ginnie, it's not one of *my* students I'm concerned with today. It's a boy named Joey Bulland."

"I recognize the name. Ninth grader, a little guy, seems scared of his own shadow. Didn't I hear that, on Satur-day—"

Mr. Strang nodded. "That was Joey," he said.

"I don't know him very well, but his records are in the files. What are you looking for? Grades? Achievement tests? Conduct?"

"Attendance. Do you have a record of his attendance?"

"Well, for this year, the main office would—"

"Not just this year. I want a record of his attendance from the time he entered the Aldershot school system. Plus the reasons for any absences, if possible."

"Mr. Strang," sighed Miss Cannoughby, "I'd have to check with his grade school for much of that information. It'd be sort of—well, complicated."

"Ginnie," said Mr. Strang softly, "indulge an old man who's weak and feeble and desperately in need of your help. Get me the attendance records."

Virginia Cannoughby's eyes twinkled. "You old fraud,"

she smiled. "You're about as weak and feeble as a strip of rawhide. All right, I'll see what I can do. Meet me for lunch."

"A pleasure," replied the teacher, with a courtly bow.

During sixth period, Mr. Strang and Virginia Cannoughby sat in a corner of the teachers' dining room. "Here are Joey's attendance records," said the counselor, passing them across the table.

Mr. Strang broke off his consideration of a gelatinous mass of rice and gravy to leaf through the documents. When he finished, he pushed his black-rimmed glasses onto his forehead and rubbed his chin.

"Curious," he said.

"What is?"

"The pattern of absences. Every year, Joey's had three or four absences of five to eight days, always for the same reason: sickness."

"What's so odd about that?"

"First, the absences are evenly spaced, always about ten weeks apart. Second, there are almost no absences of one or two days. They're usually five or more."

"All right, that *is* curious. But I don't see—"

"Isn't it strange that the boy would have three or four serious illnesses *every* year?"

"Yes, but his marks are fairly good. So he's been able to keep up with his work."

"It's not his work that worries me. Excuse me, Ginnie, I've got a call to make."

"To Joey's parents?"

"No, to a Dr. Kermit."

Dr. Leland Kermit was unable to see Mr. Strang until after eight o'clock that evening. Finally, however, his last patient left, and Kermit waved Mr. Strang into his office.

"Your call was unusual," said the doctor, leaning back in his swivel chair. "I'm not in the habit of talking about my patients with outsiders. There's a question of medical ethics, as I'm sure you know."

"The question of ethics may well come up in the course of this conversation," replied Mr. Strang, "and I hope you'll remain true to your Hippocratic oath. But we're both in the business of helping others: you do it by healing the body, while I try to educate the mind. So please don't dismiss me until you've heard what I have to say."

"Well spoken, Mr. Strang. But before we go any further, just who is it we're discussing?"

"Joey Bulland. You know him, correct?"

"Of course. What about him?"

"Every school year, Joey's been absent several times with fairly long illnesses. All we have on record is that he was sick. I'd like to know what was wrong with him."

Dr. Kermit smiled. "Don't worry about what happened to him on Saturday. He'll be right as rain in a week or so. I'd say there isn't a healthier boy in Aldershot. I guess that's the trouble—he's got too much energy."

"But his absence records show—"

"Not illness, Mr. Strang— accidents. Joey's small and clumsy, and things *happen* to him, that's all. He falls downstairs, or a chair he's standing on collapses under him— things like that. The trouble with your records is that, any time a student is laid up for a few days, the school says he's sick."

"That's true," said the teacher. "We don't differentiate between disease and injury. Can you tell me about his last accident? The one about three months ago?"

"He was climbing a tree and fell, cut his face up pretty badly. I treated him here at the office and kept him in bed for a week, until the cuts were healed."

"You'd think his parents would look after him a little more carefully."

Dr. Kermit shook his head. "You're a bachelor, aren't you, Mr. Strang? Still, as a *teacher* you ought to know that a teenage boy's got more energy than a stick of dynamite. Besides, you can't wrap kids in cotton all their lives. They've got to get out and let off steam, and, if the price of their doing it is a few cuts and bruises, at least the kid's learned enough to be careful the next time he climbs a tree. See what I mean?"

"But if Joey's absences are all because of accidents, it would seem to me that his mother and father could somehow—"

The doctor waved a hand impatiently. "Listen, Mr. Strang, I've known Alex and Carol Bulland since I started practicing in this town, and there aren't two more devoted parents anywhere. You ought to see the way some kids are brought into this office. Torn and sloppy clothes, dirty faces, uncombed hair. Not Joey. Whenever his parents bring him in, he's wearing clean clothes, with his shoes shined and his hair combed. He looks the way a boy *ought* to look, not like a little tramp. No, I've got nothing but admiration for the way Carol and Alex are bringing up their boy."

Mr. Strang nodded. "Maybe you're right," he said. "I've seen Joey trip over his own feet in school. Tell me, what happened to him the time before he fell out of the tree?"

"Mr. Bulland told me he tripped and hit his head on the edge of a table. There was a big cut in his scalp. I had to take stitches. But I never saw a kid with more guts—no yelling or crying or anything."

"I see. Dr. Kermit, I've taken enough of your time. I'll be leaving—but there is one thing I'd like you to do for me." The teacher took a small notebook from a jacket pocket and scribbled three words on one of its pages. He tore the page out and handed it to Kermit. "I'd like you to look this subject up in your medical journals. Tonight, if possible, or first thing in the morning. Perhaps you've already done some thinking about it. Get all the information you can. Then, if you would, I'd appreciate your calling me at school."

The following evening, there was a knock on the door of the Bulland house. When Alexander Bulland answered, he found Paul Roberts standing in the doorway.

"C'mon in," said Bulland. "Carol and I was just gettin' ready to watch some TV. Hey, good news! Joey's comin' home from the hospital tomorrow." He turned toward the living room and shouted, "Carol, it's Mr. Roberts, the detective. I think he's got some information on who slugged—"

Mr. Strang and Dr. Kermit came into the front hallway behind Roberts.

"I didn't see you two out there in the dark," said Bulland. "But come on in. The more, the merrier."

"Mr. Bulland," said Roberts, "I know this is unusual, the three of us coming to see you this way."

"Yeah, I was wondering about that." As they entered the living room, Carol Bulland switched off the TV and gestured them to seats on the couch.

"Mr. and Mrs. Bulland," Roberts began, "this is Leonard Strang from the high school. He's got an idea about what happened to Joey."

Bulland rubbed the bandage on his neck.

"It took most of the day," the detective continued, "for him to convince me that I even ought to trouble you with it. What I mean to say is, we're all here strictly unofficially, and if you'd rather we left, you can just say so."

"Well," said Bulland, "it *is* kind of late. Maybe in the morning we could—"

"No, sit down," interrupted Carol Bulland, her face pale. "I'd like to hear what these men have to say, Alex."

Bulland leaned close to Roberts and whispered, "Who's the little guy again?"

"Mr. Strang. He teaches at the high school."

"I didn't figure him for a cop. Think he'd like a beer? I

wouldn't tell anybody, if you get what I mean."

Roberts shook his head. "I'd just like you to hear what Mr. Strang has to say, if you don't mind."

"Sure, why not?" Bulland eased into his chair.

"Mr. Bulland," the teacher began, "perhaps in the confusion you don't remember, but I was here on Saturday morning with Detective Roberts."

"If Roberts wanted you here, that's fine with me."

"Thank you. In any case, I saw something on Saturday that I considered rather unusual. I'm sure Mr. Roberts overlooked it only because he was much more interested in those strange punctures in your neck."

"What was it you noticed, Mr. Strang?" asked Carol Bulland, leaning forward in her chair, her lips pressed tight.

"The white rugs," the teacher said, "in your living room and dining room."

"They're old. We've been planning to replace them when we have some extra money."

"If you'll recall," Mr. Strang went on, "the kitchen was a regular quagmire from all the mud that had been tracked in. And yet there wasn't a mark on those white rugs."

Bulland shrugged. "So?"

"Mr. Bulland, consider the type of man we're talking about: a sneak thief. He comes into a supposedly empty house to steal a few items and then tries to get back out as quickly as possible, without being noticed. He must have come in through the back door, muddying his feet in the process. But judging from the lack of mud on those white rugs, he never went into the living room or dining room or up the stairs to the second floor, all places where he would logically expect to find things worth stealing. Instead, he seems to have headed directly for the basement. That doesn't make sense."

Bulland pondered this point. "I guess so," he said finally. "Only maybe he didn't make tracks because he wore boots or somethin' over his shoes. Or what if, when he came in, he heard Joey and me talkin' in the basement?"

Mr. Strang shook his head. "I doubt that a man who feared discovery at any moment would stop to remove his boots and then put them on again when he left. And if he heard voices, wouldn't he be more likely to move *away* from them, rather than *toward* them?"

"What are you gettin' at, Mr. Strang?"

The teacher ignored the question and glanced at Carol Bulland, who was staring at him fearfully. "Another thing," he continued. "When you regained consciousness, Mr. Bulland, you had a bump on your head and two wounds in your neck. Joey, on the other hand, had just received a severe beating. He was obviously suffering acutely from pain and shock. And yet, according to what you told the police, you sent him upstairs to phone for help instead of going yourself. That was strange behavior on your part, wouldn't you say?"

"My throat—I couldn't talk."

"You could talk well enough to tell—that's your own word—you 'told' Joey to call the police," replied the teacher. "It won't do, Mr. Bulland, it really won't. You and I both know there wasn't any burglar in this house last Saturday."

"Listen, Teacher, I got a kid in the hospital with his face beaten up. I took a sock on the head and these cuts on my neck myself. Are you tryin' to tell me I imagined the whole thing?"

"No, Mr. Bulland." Mr. Strang shook his head calmly. "I'm not saying you imagined it. But once the idea of an intruder is eliminated, only one possible cause for Joey's injuries remains."

"Like what?"

"Like *you*, Mr. Bulland. *You* were the one who beat Joey up."

For a moment, Bulland stared at the teacher, his face void of any expression. Then he started to laugh.

"That's a good one!" he roared. "This shriveled twerp is accusin' me of sluggin' my own kid. What do you think of that, Mr. Roberts?"

"An accusation has been made against you, Mr. Bulland," said Roberts in a flat voice. "You have the right to remain silent, but, if you do speak, anything you say—"

"Hey, wait a minute. Wait just a minute." Bulland waved Roberts into silence. "You jokers are *serious*?"

"Yes, sir," said Roberts. "Would you like to call your—"

"I don't need to call nobody. I heard all about that rights stuff on TV. But don't you try to con me. You got no case. How do you explain these?" He tore the bandage from his throat, revealing the two puncture wounds.

"I'd like to show you something," said Mr. Strang, "Mrs. Bulland, I wonder if you'd mind going down into the basement and bringing up that slatted crate Joey was using for a tool chest. Not the tools, just the crate."

"Hold it," said Bulland. "You got no right to—"

"I'll get it, Mr. Strang," said Carol Bulland, her voice shaking.

When she returned with the crate, Paul Roberts tugged at the slats, one by one. Finally he came to one that pulled easily away from the crate. At each end of the strip of wood, two nails gleamed wickedly.

"There seems to be blood on the nails on this end," said Roberts. "The lab should be able to tell us if it is or not."

"It will be," said Mr. Strang. "Come, Mr. Bulland, there's only one possible explanation in the light of what we've just seen. Joey was in the basement. Whether he was working there or hiding from you really makes no difference. In any case, you found him there and started to beat him. Either the slat was already loose or he pulled it loose during the struggle. To protect himself, he struck at you with it, hitting you in the neck. Perhaps you stumbled into something, or maybe Joey also hit you on the head, which is how you got that lump. You were probably unconscious for at least a few seconds. And that's when Joey broke away, ran upstairs, and made the call to the police—to get protection from you, Mr. Bulland."

"I'm tellin' you, the burglar was—"

"According to our log," Roberts cut him off, "the caller didn't mention a burglar. He just said police were needed at this address. Then, right in the middle of a sentence, the line went dead."

"You followed Joey upstairs, didn't you, Mr. Bulland?" said the teacher. "*You* broke the phone connection. But when you realized the police were on their way, you made up a story about a burglar and threatened Joey to make him go along with it. Then you took the boy back down to the basement, replaced the slat in the crate, and waited for the police to arrive."

"You characters make me laugh," said Bulland, his voice belligerent. "Of all the wild yarns I ever heard, this takes the cake. Just tell me one thing: *why?* Why would I beat up my own kid?"

Mr. Strang turned to Kermit. "Doctor?"

"Alex," said Dr. Kermit, "I can't keep quiet any longer. You're not the only one who does this. There are thousands of cases, all over the country."

"Cases? Cases of *what?*"

"One name for it—the three words Mr. Strang wrote out for me yesterday—is 'battered child syndrome.' The victims are usually younger children, but not always. For some reason, a parent becomes unreasonably angry over real or imagined misbehavior by the child, who might be crying or refusing to obey—almost anything. The parent reacts violently and with a complete lack of concern for the child's safety. Children have been beaten, burned, scalded—and when the parents come to their senses and seek a doctor's help, they invariably call it 'an accident.' Doctors generally don't report suspected cases of battered child syndrome to the police, because they're so hard to prove. But I can't go on with this, Alex. I can't stand by and see this happening to Joey anymore."

"I—I don't believe this. What proof—?"

"The proof is there, Alex. I've suspected it for quite a while, and Mr. Strang was able to gather the facts I didn't have. The periodic long absences from school to allow bruises to heal. The 'emergency calls' after Joey was carefully prepared to see me and dressed in his best clothes. The refusal to allow an examination by another physician. Medical reports are full of such cases. If it hadn't been for Mr. Strang, I might never have had the nerve to stop you. But I know now I'm not mistaken about what's been happening to your son."

"Mistaken? I'll show you mistaken." Bulland jerked a thumb toward the front door. "Get out of here, all of you! This is my house, and I don't want you in it no more. If you say one word in public about this, I'll sue the three of you for every cent you've got in the world. The idea I'd beat up on my own boy and—"

"Alex, stop it!" screamed Carol Bulland. "They *know*! Somebody besides me finally knows what you've been doing to Joey all these years. Oh, God, at *last* somebody else knows!"

Her body convulsed, and she threw herself into Roberts' arms. "I—I tried to stop him," she said, burying her face in the detective's overcoat. "But if I tried to protect Joey, Alex beat him all the harder. I couldn't turn him in to the police—he's the father of my child. So I kept quiet, praying someone else would find out about it. And now you've come. Thank heaven, you've come!"

"Why does he do it, Mrs. Bulland?" asked the detective gently.

"It's always little things. Once Joey cried after he got in a fight with another boy. 'Tough guys don't cry,' Alex told him, and then he *hit* Joey with a cane. Another time, Joey spilled some things out of his tackle box. Or he used a tool and didn't put it back where it belonged. Always little things. And then Alex would hit him, beat him unmercifully. It was always so senseless."

"Senseless, huh?" Bulland stood with his fists clenched, like an animal at bay. "Lemme tell you somethin'. Last Saturday, you noticed that the car was gone, right? Well, that was a new car, brand-new, first new car I ever owned in my life. I saved for six years for that car. Six *years* of no beers at the tavern on payday and stayin' away from poker parties and wearin' Sunday clothes that was thin enough to see through. Finally, I got it, just last week, all bright and shiny, with the engine turning over like a cat purrin'. After the old clunker I had before, it was the most beautiful thing in the world.

"So I put it in the garage, and Joey had strict orders not to go in there. Strict orders, you got that? Except Saturday morning I heard a noise out there. I jumped out of bed and ran down. It was Joey. He was foolin' around in the car—somehow he got it started. It jerked forward, and the whole front end bashed into the back wall of the garage. I didn't have the car *four days*, and the kid wrecked it. When the repairman towed it off to the shop, he said it'd cost at least two hundred bucks to fix it. Two hundred dollars! Where was I gonna get that kind of dough after just buyin' a new car?"

Bulland's voice grew louder and more incoherent. "I *told* him to stay out of the garage! So I had to teach him a lesson. What else could I do? Answer me that! What *else* could I do?"

He was still shouting when Roberts picked up the phone and began to dial.

MR. STRANG FINDS A CAR

For nine blocks, the nondescript gray four-door sedan followed the yellow bus with ALDERSHOT CENTRAL SCHOOL DISTRICT painted on its side. When the bus turned into the long curving driveway behind Aldershot High School, the gray car continued to follow. Louis Markham, the bus driver, found nothing odd about this. Many parents dropped their kids at school on their way to work. On reaching the rear corner of the building, the car stopped. From this vantage point, there was a view of both the teachers' parking lot and the fenced athletic field, where almost two thousand students were milling about, waiting for the entrance bell.

The driver of the gray car kept his eyes riveted on the bus—Number 81—as it pulled up to a gate in the fence. He took little notice of the slight gray-haired teacher who stood near one of the building's doors, waving to the students as they climbed out of the bus, chattering like magpies, and walked to the gate.

Then the last student, a boy, got off. A tall, lanky, studious type, the boy wore thick glasses mounted on his beak of a nose. His sweatshirt, on which appeared a picture of the dog Snoopy dancing with joy, seemed to accentuate the boy's rounded shoulders and skinny arms. The boy stood for a moment, examining the thick bundle of books under his arm.

The driver of the gray car slammed it into gear. There was the roar of a racing engine, and two tracks of scorched rubber were laid on the smoking asphalt as the rear wheels fought for traction. Rocketing forward, the car bore down on the boy—who looked up wide-eyed at the noise, saw the deadly grillwork of the car's radiator headed directly at him, and froze in panic.

A massive hand reached out from the door of the bus and yanked at the neck of the sweatshirt. Stumbling backward, the boy collapsed into a sitting position on the bus's step as the gray car shot by, only inches from his knees. Before the boy could thank Louis Markham, the gray car skidded to a halt and shifted into reverse. The boy quickly scrambled onto the bus.

The gray car screeched to a stop next to the bus's door. For a fraction of a second, Markham and the car's driver regarded each other. Markham's face was a study in shocked surprise. It was difficult to see the expression of the other man, who wore a wide-brimmed hat and dark sunglasses and, despite the heat, had his jacket collar turned up. With a clash of gears, the gray car roared forward again, down the driveway and out into the street. Markham attempted to get its license number, but the plates were smeared with mud.

It was several minutes before Mr. Leonard Strang, at his position by the school's rear door, could calm his queasy stomach. It had all happened so fast. But for the quick thinking of Louis Markham, Richie Hatch would be lying dead on the pavement. On rubbery legs, Mr. Strang approached the bus and asked Richie and Markham to accompany him to the principal's office to report the incident.

Marvin W. Guthrey, principal of Aldershot High School, looked incredulously at the two men and the boy seated on the other side of his desk. "Be reasonable, Mr. Strang. You, too, Louis. Why would anybody want to run down a student, especially right here in the school parking lot? Maybe the accelerator jammed—that's happened to me."

Markham banged an angry hand on the arm of his chair. "We were out there, Mr. Guthrey, remember? I tell you, this guy *deliberately* tried to run Richie down."

"Not only that," added Mr. Strang, still trembling, "but when he failed the first time—thanks to Louis's quick thinking—he came back for a second shot. Fortunately, Richie was inside the bus by then."

"Whoever it was probably just returned to make sure Richie was all right," replied Guthrey.

"Then why didn't he stop?" growled the bus driver. "At least he could have given us an apology or something. No, sir, Mr. Guthrey. I got a good look at that character. He wasn't sorry for what he done—unless he was sorry he missed."

"I thought you said his face was almost completely covered?" asked the principal.

"Yeah, but—" With a helpless shrug, the bus driver turned to Mr. Strang. "You tell him, will you? He won't listen to me."

Mr. Strang pulled a pipe from his pocket and rammed tobacco into the bowl as he gathered his thoughts. "A few minutes ago," he said finally, "Richie was almost run down in the school parking lot. Let's take that as our starting point, Mr. Guthrey. You say it was just an accident, while we maintain it was deliberate. Right so far?"

The principal nodded.

"Well, consider the following two things." The teacher ticked them off on his fingers. "First, we were on the scene when it happened, and you were not. I ask you: who would make the more reliable witnesses?"

The principal tried to interrupt, but Mr. Strang went on implacably. "Second, even though it's quite warm this morning, the man wore a hat and dark sunglasses and had his collar turned up. Doesn't that suggest a disguise? And remember those muddy license plates, Mr. Guthrey. All the accoutrements of a deliberate hit-and-run attempt."

"And on the basis of what you tell me," asked the principal nervously, "I'm supposed to do—what?"

"Why, call the police, of course," replied the teacher. "Get somebody down here to look into this."

"But no one was actually hurt," said Guthrey. "So what am I supposed to tell them? I can't have police in the building every time somebody makes a little mistake."

"And what if it wasn't just a 'little mistake'?" asked the teacher, puffing out a thick cloud of acrid smoke.

"What do you mean?"

"Let's assume, in spite of what we've told you, that the chances are, say, a hundred to one *against* the incident's having been deliberate. Even then, would you want to take the chance, Mr. Guthrey?"

"What chance?"

"He means, if it was deliberate, the guy might try again!" shouted Markham. "For some reason, somebody wants Richie out of the way. Are you going to let them have another crack at him?"

Reluctantly, Guthrey picked up his phone.

In the small conference room, Richie Hatch, Mr. Strang, and Louis Markham sat in straight-backed chairs, flanked by Aldershot police detectives Paul Roberts and David Bell.

"It's crazy," Bell said. "Just *crazy!*"

"What is, Bell?" asked Roberts.

"Us being here. We're working four breaking-and-enterings, one possible kidnapping, and that sex molester who's supposed to be prowling the neighborhood. Plus there's that APB on the armored truck that was hijacked over in Wolverton, the plans for guarding the mayor during the parade tomorrow, and whatever else the lieutenant might throw at us. And now we're expected to waste time listening to this malarkey, just because somebody's car went out of control?"

"Nobody twisted your arm to get you out of uniform and into detectives," growled Roberts. But he couldn't help agreeing with Bell. The whole thing seemed such a trivial incident. If it had been anyone but Mr. Strang...

Roberts had built a considerable respect for the teacher since the day, several years ago, when Mr. Strang had kept him from making a fool of himself in connection with a stolen car. Since then, the wizened little science teacher had assisted Roberts unofficially on several cases, and the detective had a growing faith in Mr. Strang's abilities of observation and logical analysis. Even if there *wasn't* a real problem this time, Roberts guessed he owed the old boy at least a hearing.

"Richie," said Bell, "just tell me one thing: why the hell would somebody want to run you down?"

"I don't know, sir," answered the boy.

"You see, that's the hang-up—no motive. Think about it, Richie. What could a school kid possibly do that would make someone want to kill him? What do you do after school? What crowd do you hang around with? Do you have any enemies?"

"I don't hang around with anybody too much," replied the boy. "Usually, I go right home after school and do my homework. Then I mow the lawn or do whatever else my mother wants. We have supper at about seven—that's when my dad comes home—and after that I either watch TV or work on my insect collection."

"Richie's quite an entomologist," added Mr. Strang proudly. "His collection won second prize at the county Science Fair."

"Yeah, great," muttered Bell. "Maybe that car was driven by a mad tsetse fly."

"Lay off, Bell," snapped Roberts. He turned to Mr. Strang, tearing a sheet from the yellow-lined pad in front of him. "I guess that's it," he said. "Here's a preliminary report on what you've told us. I'd like the three of you to read it over. If you have no additions or corrections, I'll see what I can do about locating your gray sedan. But I can't guarantee any results. You haven't given us much to go on."

Mr. Strang scanned the report, then passed it to Richie, who flipped his thick glasses up onto his forehead and peered at the writing.

"You believe us, don't you, Paul?" asked the teacher.

"I believe a car came close to hitting Richie. But as for it being deliberate—well, I dunno, Mr. Strang. You make quite a thing of the guy not stopping. But maybe he was just embarrassed. After all, he almost killed somebody. He came back to make sure no one was hurt, and then, when he saw Richie was okay, he just got out of there before anyone could tell him what a numbskull he was."

"Oh, *ctenophora!*" snapped the teacher. "Somebody tried to kill Richie. I don't know the reason. But there's got to be an answer somewhere."

As the detectives were about to leave, Bell turned to Mr. Strang. "Maybe you just aren't asking the right questions," he drawled.

"Shouldn't the boy be given some kind of protection?" Mr. Strang asked Roberts, ignoring Bell's remark.

Roberts shook his head. "This is too far-fetched," he said. "The lieutenant wouldn't authorize it." Seeing Mr. Strang's hands quiver, the detective went on in a softer voice. "Tell you what, I'll pick Richie up after school and drive him home myself. He ought to be safe in his own house. That's the best I can do."

That afternoon, Richie Hatch left the front door of the school accompanied by both Paul Roberts and Mr. Strang. As they headed for the detective's car, none of them noticed the heavily muscled man in the green sports shirt lounging against the telephone booth down the block. On spotting Richie, the man entered the booth, dialed a number, and spoke into the mouthpiece, as Roberts' car passed within a dozen feet of the booth.

Ten minutes later, the detective pulled into Waverly Crescent. That road, nearly a quarter of a mile long, formed a huge semicircle. This densely wooded area on the outskirts of Aldershot had once been a favorite destination for Mr. Strang's biology classes' nature walks. Now, four houses were spaced along the length of the crescent, and the builder had said there would be more to come. Richie Hatch's house, a shingled split-level, was at the far side of the semicircle.

"Mom must be out," said Richie, as Roberts pulled into the driveway. "Her car's not here. Thanks for the lift, Mr. Roberts. I'll see you tomorrow, Mr. Strang."

From the rear seat, the teacher waved vaguely. "The right questions," he whispered, watching Richie pad across the lawn toward his house.

"What's that, Mr. Strang?"

"Nothing, Paul. I was just thinking about what your partner said this morning. Maybe we aren't asking the right questions." Suddenly, he rolled down the window and shouted, "Richie, stop!"

Startled, Roberts turned around in his seat. "Did he forget something?"

"No, I did." The teacher beckoned to the boy, who was just unlocking the front door.

Richie returned to the car. "What's the matter?" he asked.

"Council of war." Mr. Strang motioned the boy back into the car and tapped Roberts on the shoulder. "Detective Bell is smarter than I thought," he murmured, smiling. "The right questions—I should have thought of that myself."

"What are you getting at?" asked Roberts.

The gnomelike science teacher rubbed his hands together. "Let's assume for a moment that whoever was driving that car this morning *did* deliberately try to kill Richie. When we talked about it earlier, we questioned his motive. Why, we asked, would anybody want to do such a thing? But that's the wrong question. Try this one: why would anyone want to do it *on the high-school parking lot?*"

Roberts shook his head in confusion. "I don't get you."

"If someone wanted to kill Richie, wouldn't the high-school parking lot be the *last* place they'd choose, with teachers on duty and about two thousand potential witnesses nearby? It was only dumb luck that Richie was the last student to get off the bus, and that he was alone when the car tried to hit him."

"Not really," said the boy. "I'm the first one on in the morning, Mr. Strang. The bus has to come way out here just for me, and I always take the rear seat. The bus doesn't even come all the way to the far side of the crescent. I cut across the lots to where Waverly meets the main road and get picked up there."

"All right, all right," said the teacher impatiently. "But that doesn't change the fact that you live in a comparatively deserted area. If somebody wanted to kill you, the obvious place would be *here*, not a crowded schoolyard. Why, then, did the attempted crime take place where it did?"

"If there *was* a crime," said the detective. "What you've just said is a pretty good indication that there *wasn't.*"

"Wait, Paul. If the attempt *was* deliberate, why in such a public place?"

"I'll bite," said Roberts. "Why?"

"There's only one reason I can come up with that makes any sense," said the teacher. "Paul, something must have happened early this morning, before Richie got on the school bus. He either saw or heard something—something the driver of that gray car felt would be dangerous to him. Before Richie could be intercepted out here, he reached the school bus and was picked up. Our mysterious Mr. X felt that Richie had to be stopped at any cost before he could communicate whatever he'd seen or heard. So he followed the bus to school and made a desperate attempt to kill Richie."

Mr. Strang turned to the boy. "Come on, Richie, what

was it? What did you see this morning? What did you hear?”

There was a long pause, as Richie pushed his glasses up onto his forehead and gazed at the teacher. “I don’t know,” he said finally. “I don’t remember seeing or hearing anything.”

Both Mr. Strang’s face and spirits drooped. “Nothing?” he asked with a plaintive sigh.

Richie shook his head.

“Okay, that’s enough.” Roberts turned the key, and the car’s starter whirred. “Let me take you home, huh?”

“Just a minute.” Mr. Strang waved his hand impatiently. “Richie, maybe you don’t realize that what you saw or heard was important. Please, tell us everything that happened to you this morning, from the time you got up until you got on the bus—everything, no matter how trivial it might seem.”

Richie considered the question. “Well, first I got dressed. Brushed my teeth. Then I went down, and Mom gave me my breakfast. It was oatmeal.”

“Then what? After you left the house.”

“I cut through the woods in back on my way to the bus stop. Did you know there’s a bee tree out there, Mr. Strang? They were buzzing like crazy this morning.”

“Never mind Mother Nature,” groaned Roberts. “Get on with your story.”

“I walked through the Killians’ backyard and put out food for their spaniel. They’re away for the month, and they asked me to feed and water the dog. I saw a praying mantis on the windowsill of the garage. It was eating a beetle, and I got real close to it. Mr. Roberts, do you know that mantises kill all sorts of harmful—”

“Spare me the bugs, Richie, *please*. Just finish your story, so Mr. Strang and me can get out of here.”

“All right. Back in the woods, I found a place where some kids must have been digging. There was a deep hole near the stream that goes through there.”

“A hole,” mused the teacher. “Anything in it?”

“Nothing but a broken robin’s egg. I spotted three gray squirrels just before I came out of the woods, and I could have sworn I heard the chirping of a—”

Paul Roberts thought he would go mad.

A car rolled by them and pulled into the driveway. “Mom’s home,” said Richie. “Would you like to meet her?”

“Some other time,” said Roberts in a tired voice. “And, Richie, when you tell her what happened today, don’t make it too dramatic. A car went out of control, and you came close to being hit—that’s all. This other stuff? Well, sometimes Mr. Strang lets his imagination run away with him.”

The teacher folded his arms and stared ahead in stony silence.

In the woods behind the Hatch house, a large woman wearing a dark green coat that blended with the foliage ducked back behind the trunk of a huge willow tree and lowered a pair of high-power binoculars. Kneeling next to her was a stocky young man in blue jeans and a T-shirt, under which his muscles bulged.

The man looked up at his partner. "What do you think, Doris? What did you see?"

"The kid's with two men, like Larry said on the phone. The scrawny one with the gray hair wouldn't be hard to handle, but the big one's got cop written all over him. We'd better lay low, at least until Larry gets back."

"A cop," muttered the man. "Hell's bells, Doris, if that kid told the cops what he saw—"

"Take it easy. I don't think he realizes he saw anything important. Otherwise, this whole area would be swarming with police. Probably he just told the cop about Larry almost running him down this morning."

"Too damn bad he missed," the man grumbled. "That kid might remember any time now. Hey, look! The car's leavin'. Now's my chance to get over there an'—"

"Calm down," said Doris. "The kid's inside the house with his old lady. What happens if you try to break in there and one of 'em gets to a phone? The kid's forgotten all about it, I tell you. And we'll be out of here in another few hours."

"When? What time?"

"We can't start unloading till after ten. About midnight, I guess."

"And what about the kid? Shouldn't he still be wasted?"

"Maybe. Let's see what Larry says."

*

When Paul Roberts dropped him off at his boarding house, Mr. Strang was still furious. "Let my imagination run away with me, do I?" he grumbled. "I'll show him!"

But the teacher wasn't really prepared to show the detective anything. What could Richie have seen? A bee's nest, a praying mantis, a hole, a robin's egg, some squirrels? All that seemed innocent enough.

"*Platyhelminthes!*" He spat out the word—Phylum VI in the classification of animals—in a tone that would have brought a blush to the face of a muleskinner. Then, feeling somewhat better, he sat down with the newspaper to await his supper.

A short while later, a mouth-watering smell from the

kitchen brought the teacher to his feet. Pot roast. He tip-toed downstairs to the kitchen door. A large kettle was bubbling on the stove. He lifted the lid, and a cloud of steam rose upward.

Tiny droplets of water settled onto Mr. Strang's glasses, and, for a moment, he was blind. Replacing the lid, he removed the glasses to polish them on his tie. But then he stopped.

Holding the glasses in front of him, he glanced first at the lenses and then at the wall behind the stove. There was something else Bell had said this morning, something about—

And then he remembered.

Hoping against hope that he wasn't already too late, the teacher scuttled into the living room, picked up the telephone, and dialed Paul Roberts' number.

It was after nine o'clock, and darkness had fallen when Roberts, accompanied by Mr. Strang, again reached Waverly Crescent. The detective pulled his car to the curb, turned off the ignition, and killed the lights. "We'll walk from here," he whispered. "Good thing there aren't any street lights out here."

"There's a full moon, though," replied Mr. Strang. "We'll have to be careful."

"I hope you're right about this," said Roberts.

They passed two houses, keeping to the shadows on the opposite side of the street.

The Killian house was completely dark. "Figures," breathed Roberts. "Richie said they're away."

The two men crept closer, keeping trees between themselves and the house.

Finally, they reached the garage. "There's a border of rocks along here," Roberts told the teacher. "Be careful you don't trip. I'm going to use my flashlight. I'll try to keep it masked as much as possible, but—what's that?"

There was a rustling sound from the far side of the garage, followed by an odd moaning. The teacher snapped to attention, then relaxed. "The dog," he whispered. "He's behind the house, in a kennel."

Roberts brushed a film of dirt from the garage window with the sleeve of his jacket. Cupping one hand carefully around his flashlight, he held it against the windowpane.

Mr. Strang peered through the glass. The car inside would have been close enough to touch, had the window been open. "Gray four-door sedan," breathed the teacher. "I'll give you odds that's the car that almost ran Richie down this morning."

"Yeah, sure," replied the detective impatiently. "Only—holy Moses on a bicycle! Look!"

As he moved the light, Mr. Strang could see the huge thing that reared up on the other side of the two-car garage. It was constructed of thick plates of steel, held together with many rivets, the heads of which spotted the brown surface like warts on the back of some prehistoric monster.

"There's lettering on it," said Roberts. "B-I-L-L-I—Billikin!" He breathed the word in an awed voice. "The Billikin Armored Car Service. One of their trucks was hijacked near Wolverton two days ago—with over a hundred and fifty grand in silver bars inside."

The teacher nodded. "Detective Bell mentioned that this morning."

"You were right, Mr. Strang, there *is* something important in this garage. I've got to get word back to headquarters. If we're lucky, maybe the silver's still there."

"It is. But your luck's about run out."

At the sound of the voice behind them, Roberts and Strang whirled. The teacher could just make out the figure of a woman in the moonlight—a mountainous figure in a dark coat. And as Roberts pointed the flashlight in her direction, they both saw a pistol glittering in her hand.

"Point that light the other way," rumbled the woman. "At your own face. You're the two who were at the kid's house earlier, aren't you?"

There was the slamming of a door, and a second figure—a man—appeared beside the woman. "What have we got here, Doris? A couple of snoopers?"

"Yeah, Larry. I guess the kid finally remembered."

"Mr. Strang here was smart enough to figure it out," said Roberts. *Keep them talking,* he thought. *Get the woman's mind off the gun. Maybe there'll be a chance to grab it.* "You might as well tell 'em about it," he said gruffly. *Come on, Mr. Strang, stall for time.*

The teacher picked up the cue. "You saw Richie this morning, didn't you?" he asked.

"The kid? Sure," said the woman. "He had his nose less than a foot from the garage window. I looked out from the kitchen, and there he was."

"He was only looking at a praying mantis—an insect—on the windowsill."

"Maybe, but he couldn't help seeing the armored car."

"As a matter of fact," said the teacher, "it was *impossible* for him to see the armored car."

"So you say," rumbled the man. "How come?"

"Richie's near-sighted," Mr. Strang explained. He crouched as if terrified by the menace of the gun. "He needs glasses, but only for seeing at a distance. For close observation, he has to take the glasses off or move them up to his forehead. I saw him do that twice today, but I only realized the importance of it when I had to take off my own glasses. Anyway, if Richie was watching a mantis at close range, he wouldn't have been wearing his glasses." Mr. Strang crouched still lower, seeming to cower before the pistol.

"That's right," said the woman. "He had 'em on his forehead, like a flier's goggles."

Roberts had the light turned on himself, which left Mr. Strang in the dark. Bending forward from his crouched position, the teacher's hands made contact with one of the large rocks that formed a border beside the garage. Lifting it slightly, he estimated its weight at about fifteen pounds.

"The armored car's on the far side of the garage," the teacher continued. "It would have been nothing but a blur to him. Besides, the garage was dark and the glass is dirty. No, your secret was safe—until you tried to run the boy down, that is."

The woman turned to the man beside her. "See, you idiot!" she barked. "I *told* you it would be all right. But no, you had to go after him. You had to try a hit-and-run at the *school*. Of all the stupid—"

Mr. Strang took a deep breath and heaved the rock, his joints cracking at the unaccustomed effort. He could hardly have missed so large a target at such short range, and, sure enough, the rock struck the woman full in the stomach.

"Ow!"

"Doris, what—"

"Hold it, both of you!" barked Roberts, pulling his own pistol. "Mr. Strang, get the gun. And make sure you don't come between me and them."

Mr. Strang made sure.

Roberts had just finished handcuffing the two when he heard the rear door of the house slam and moved his light in that direction.

A man in the doorway shook his head groggily, rubbing his eyes with huge fists. "Doris," he mumbled, his voice heavy with sleep. "Turn that thing off. You were the one said no lights. An' keep the chatter down. How's a guy supposed to sleep when—"

He was not yet fully awake when Roberts jammed his pistol into his ribs and forced him to lean against the wall to be searched.

A few moments later, the three prisoners were marched up Waverly Crescent. When they reached Roberts' car, the detective put in a call on his two-way radio. It wasn't long before two patrol cars arrived to take the criminal trio away.

The old teacher gingerly handed Roberts the pistol he'd been holding. "Do you suppose the Killians were in on it?" he asked.

"We'll check them out," replied Roberts, "but I doubt it. It wouldn't be hard for those three to spot an empty house whose owners were away on vacation."

He got into the car and slammed the door. "C'mon," he said. "We've got to get back to Richie's house."

"Why, Paul?" asked the teacher. "You don't think he's still in danger?"

"No. But in a few minutes this street will be crawling with police, men from the DA's office, and reporters. And before I talk to them, I've got some high-powered apologizing to do for not believing Richie and you in the first place."

MR. STRANG EXAMINES A LEGEND

"The Reverend Abraham VanderBoj was born of a Dutch father and an English mother in London in 1713. It is thought that the strict upbringing he received accounted for the grim and forceful nature of his religious beliefs. Sailing to the colonies in 1738, he traveled throughout New England, preaching of hellfire and damnation. Indeed, his sermons equaled and even surpassed in vehemence those of his contemporary, Jonathan Edwards."

Mr. Strang yawned. He only half listened to the fat lady in the print dress and floppy hat, unctuously delivering her prepared lecture as she pranced among the picnic tables at which Aldershot High School's honors history class was seated. The students, God bless 'em, were pretending an interest that the old science teacher was sure they didn't feel.

"Isn't she awful, Leonard?" a voice whispered in his ear. He turned to look into the pert face of Nancy Woodhull, the social-studies teacher who had planned this Saturday trip for her class.

"I feel like a fool, dragging you fifty miles in that rattling old school bus just to listen to her drone on and on," continued Nancy. "I'll bet you had lots of better things planned for today."

"But none of them could have been done with such charming company," replied Mr. Strang gallantly. "Besides, she's bound to finish sometime. Then maybe we'll be allowed to see the house."

The fat woman delicately patted perspiration from her face with a lace handkerchief. "I am Miss Bunt," she lilted, "and I will be your guide. As we walk along the path and through the trees to the house, I hope a bit of magic will take place. Try to imagine you are living at a time two centuries ago and that you have come to pay a call on the Reverend VanderBoj. You will see his rooms, his belongings, just as they were when—"

"Excuse me." One of the students raised his hand, peering at the woman through thick glasses. "But are we gonna see the place where VanderBoj committed suicide?"

"Oh, my, you *have* been doing your homework, haven't you?" Miss Bunt clasped her hands across her ample bosom and smiled archly. "Of course you will. That was in the buttery, one of the last parts of the house we'll see. But, before that, you'll be able to examine the last page of his journal. Perhaps then you'll understand the state of mind that drove poor Reverend VanderBoj to suicide."

"They're no fools, anyway," Mr. Strang muttered. "Those kids'll sit still for anything to get a look at the place where an authentic historical corpse once hung."

"Doing himself in was one of the best things VanderBoj ever did, as far as the popularity of the house as a historical site is concerned," said Nancy. "If he hadn't hanged himself, people wouldn't walk across the street to look at this place. As it is, history students come from all over the country to see if they can add a little something to the legend of the VanderBoj suicide."

"Everybody up!" called Miss Bunt, clapping her hands brusquely. "Follow me, please. And I wonder if you two"— she indicated Nancy and Mr. Strang with a stabbing finger—"would mind bringing up the rear."

And with that she was off, like a mother duck followed by a troop of ungainly ducklings.

The path led down a slight incline and through a grove of maple trees. Just beyond, in the center of a freshly mowed lawn, stood the VanderBoj house.

The exterior of the two-story building was of rough-hewn planking, which had weathered to a uniform gray. The white door was flanked by two windows, each with several small panes, and three similar windows were on the second floor.

"You'll note that the windows contain glass," said Miss Bunt. "Quite a rarity in an eighteenth-century Colonial home. But the people of this community built the house to VanderBoj's specifications, and he insisted on the best."

She walked to the door and opened it with a massive key. "As you enter," she went on, "please note the room to your right. That was the reverend's study. It was here that he wrote some of his most famous sermons. Over the fireplace are two portraits, one of Abraham VanderBoj himself and the other of his young wife, Barbara."

It took quite some time for the students to file through the doorway and into the room. Finally Nancy and Mr. Strang reached it.

"Quite an old buzzard, wasn't he?" said Nancy, nodding toward the portrait on the right. "I'd hate to have to tell him about my sins."

Mr. Strang looked at the painting, his seamed face wrinkling distastefully. For his portrait, VanderBoj had stood in the doorway through which they had just entered the house. His flat tricornered hat, surmounting a lean body dressed in unrelieved black—except for the silver buckles on his shoes—almost touched the top of the opening. His face was like a chunk of gnarled hickory log to which a beak of a nose had somehow been attached. The mouth turned down in a disapproving frown, and his eyes could have been those of a vengeful and self-righteous patriarch of the Old Testament, glaring their disapproval of a sinning world.

"VanderBoj was fifty-seven when the portrait was painted," Miss Bunt explained. "Barbara's picture was done at the same time. It was the summer before he killed himself."

Barbara VanderBoj's picture was that of a girl in the full bloom of youth. The artist had captured her beauty, but there was a tenseness about the figure. Perhaps it was in the hands, gripping tightly at the arms of the chair in which she was seated. And the eyes—didn't they have a hint of fear in them?

Clomping along the bare wood floor of the hallway, the gnome-like teacher reached a rack holding canes and riding whips. Sneaking a guilty glance in the direction of the guide, he lifted out a walking stick. When he placed its tip on the floor, its knobbed grip extended a full six inches above his belt. Crudely carved into the wood was an inscription: *V.derB. facit.*

The group stopped before another doorway. "This is the living room or, as it was called then, the front parlor," explained Miss Bunt. "Notice the absence of any of the creature comforts. Heat was provided by the single fireplace, and it was reported that the Reverend VanderBoj took pride in seeing how few logs he could use to get through the winter. The bookcases, now empty, were reputed to hold a Bible and other religious texts. As was the case when VanderBoj occupied the house, there are no rugs or curtains."

She motioned to the group to follow. In a long hallway, she held up an imperious hand.

"On your right are the stairs leading to the second floor," she said. "Note the door beneath the stairs. This small room was made available to divinity students who sometimes came to receive training in religion and rhetoric from the reverend. In return, they were expected to care for his horses and do other odd jobs about the place."

The room was indeed small. A bed—a corn-husk mattress on a rope frame—and a tiny chest of drawers almost completely filled it. On the bed was what looked like a covered frying pan with a wooden handle almost four feet long.

"The warming pan on the bed was necessary on winter nights," said Miss Bunt. "This room has no fireplace. The pan was filled with hot ashes—probably from the living-room fire—and rubbed over the sheets to warm them."

Suddenly Miss Bunt's voice dropped to a conspiratorial hush: "Here is where we begin to speak about that last fateful night in the fall of 1771—the night that Reverend VanderBoj hanged himself. Here is his journal," she went on, indicating a glass case opposite the foot of the stairs, "written in his own hand. The exposed page was written that last night"—a dramatic pause—"just before he died."

As the students filed by the illuminated case, Mr. Strang could hear rumblings.

"It's too faded. I can hardly make it out."

"Man, that guy's spelling is worse than mine."

"How come all the *s*'s look like *f*s?"

When it came to his turn to view the journal, Mr. Strang had to agree with the students. The final entry, written in a spidery hand, might well have been impressive, but it was also illegible.

"Anyone not practiced in reading such script," said Miss Bunt with a simper, "is sure to have difficulty with it. Therefore, I will—ah—translate. As I do so, picture Abraham VanderBoj walking through this house, a portable desk in his hand, writing these last words in his journal."

Her voice dropped, trying to approximate a masculine register. "'It nears midnight, and the catarrh from which I have suffered these last several days continues to worsen. It invades my brain, enfeebling my soul and making my thoughts mean and destructive. The very air this night seems charged with evil. Without, a high wind shakes the house to its foundation, seeking entrance through any opening, be it ever so small. And what is this? My wife, in manner quite unlike her usual wont, has left her chamber door unbolted. The devil will mock me no longer. I will pursue him to his hell below and there do battle. O woe! O misery! Alas for me!'"

In the gloom of the old house, Mr. Strang had to admit that it was a striking performance. Beside him, he could feel Nancy Woodhull trembling. Miss Bunt's outstretched hands pointed up the stairs.

"As you go up," she said, "you will see the reverend's portable writing desk still lying in the hallway. Please step carefully around it. It is lying in the same spot where he dropped it on his way to the buttery to put an end to his life."

Mr. Strang felt the change that had come over Nancy Woodhull's students. No longer was Miss Bunt a silly old woman in an absurd print dress. Instead, she was their guide to a mysterious event that had occurred two hundred years ago, when a man recorded on paper the very moment his mind slipped beyond the bounds of reason.

They tiptoed respectfully around the small writing desk, not much more than a shallow box with a hinged lid. In a socket at one corner was a tiny glass inkwell.

"This first door to the left," said Miss Bunt, "is to Abraham's bedroom. Kept awake by his illness, he must have slipped outside into the hallway here, carrying the writing desk with him. From this point, he made his way along the hall to the next room on the left, that of his wife Barbara." She moved to the next doorway.

"He tried Barbara's door and found that it was open. Perhaps frightened by the wind, she had forgotten to lock it. And then, for some unknown reason, the reverend's mind snapped. He considered himself an avenging angel, fit to do battle with the devil. Flinging the writing desk from him, he plunged down the stairs. From there, he went into the buttery—the next stop on our tour."

Peering into the bedroom of the late Mrs. VanderBoj, Mr. Strang felt a little like a Peeping Tom. There was the bed, its homespun coverlet lumpy over the rude mattress. Beside the bed was a small table on which stood a bowl and pitcher. On the wall was a rude drawing of Moses carrying the Ten Commandments. To the teacher's left, an interconnecting door stood half-open on hand-forged hinges, revealing a similar bed and table in Abraham VanderBoj's room.

"Lead on, Miss Bunt," said the little teacher finally. "Where's that buttery you've been telling us about?"

In the large kitchen, the students were allowed to examine the cave-like fireplace with its hooks and spits, pots and kettles—where, Miss Bunt assured them, Barbara VanderBoj prepared all the meals, her husband being much too frugal to employ a servant. Finally the class was herded into the buttery.

"It's what we'd call a pantry nowadays," said Miss Bunt. "Note the trough over there lined with metal. Water from a spring was pumped into that trough, providing a crude method of keeping foods cool in the summer."

"Where'd VanderBoj hang himself?" asked one of the students without preamble.

"Ah, yes, I did promise to show you that, didn't I?" Miss Bunt gave a girlish titter. "Look up. You see the beams overhead? In the main part of the house, they're covered with a plaster made of shells, but here such decoration was thought to be a luxury and therefore unnecessary."

Mr. Strang reached up and slapped a hand along the side of the oak beam under which he was standing. There was a dull *thunk* of flesh against wood.

"Oh, they're strong enough," said Miss Bunt. "Whole

sides of beef used to hang from those beams."

"And which one," the teacher began, "did VanderBoj—?"

"The very one you have your hand on," said Miss Bunt with a smile. "Barbara found her husband hanging there when she got up the following morning. His neck was broken, and a stool was lying on its side near his dangling feet. Villagers were called to cut him down and prepare him for burial. And there is one interesting sidelight."

"What's that?" asked Nancy.

"Because of the suicide, it was impossible to find a clergyman willing to offer prayers for VanderBoj. Finally Barbara herself had to say the prayers over her dead husband. A few days later, she abandoned the house forever."

Opening the door at the rear of the buttery, Miss Bunt stepped out into the sunlight and gave a slight curtsy. "And that concludes our tour of the VanderBoj house," she said with a smile. "If you'll just follow the path to the top of the hill, you'll find our pavilion. Refreshments are available there, as well as souvenirs of your visit. Our offices are also located there—if you have any questions you'd care to ask, Mr. Kimbrough is the man to see. He's considered quite an authority, not only on the house itself but on the events surrounding Abraham VanderBoj's suicide."

Nancy Woodhull and Mr. Strang walked along the path behind the flock of students, many of whom were making choking noises and holding their necks in odd positions while others giggled.

"Charming place I brought you to," said Nancy, ironically. "I'm sorry, Leonard, but Mr. Guthrey insisted I needed a second chaperone." A long pause. "Leonard Strang, are you listening to me?"

"Huh?" Startled from his reverie, Mr. Strang blinked his eyes and grinned ruefully. "Sorry, Nancy," he said. "It's just that—oh, I guess history isn't really my field."

"It wasn't very interesting, was it? I mean, except for the suicide it would be just another old house."

"Interesting? Nancy, I was fascinated." They reached the pavilion and found an empty table. Mr. Strang held a chair for Nancy and took another for himself. After carefully polishing his black-rimmed glasses on his necktie, he stoked up his pipe and puffed away, staring at the ceiling. "I just seem to be drawing all the wrong conclusions," he mused.

"What are you talking about, Leonard?"

"We both heard the same things down there at the house—Miss Bunt's talk and that page from the journal. Well, to me it just doesn't add up to suicide."

"Excuse me."

Nancy and Mr. Strang looked up to see a rather portly man standing at their table. "Kimbrough's my name," he said with a smile. "Harold Kimbrough. Thought I'd see how your class liked the house, and I couldn't help overhearing your conversation. Now, I'll admit that the ladies who act as guides sometimes emphasize the local color a bit too much, but generally they've got their facts straight. What's troubling you, Mr.—uh—?"

"Strang," said the teacher, extending his hand. "Leonard Strang. And I wonder if you'd mind telling me how you came to the conclusion that Reverend VanderBoj committed suicide."

"Well, the hanging's pretty well authenticated—diaries of other people, medical reports, and all that. Besides, there's that last entry in old VanderBoj's journal. 'The devil will mock me no longer. I will pursue him to his hell below and there do battle.' It's perfectly obvious VanderBoj had lost his marbles. And to a man in his condition, what better way to seek out the devil than by committing suicide?"

"And you figured all that out from the journal?"

"Yes, but—"

"Have you got a copy? A legible one, I mean?"

Kimbrough walked to the souvenir stand and spoke to the girl behind the counter. He returned carrying a picture postcard and handed it to Mr. Strang. "On the left is a photo of the actual journal, and there's a transcription on the right."

There were a few moments of silence while Mr. Strang read the words. "Now let me get this straight," he said at last. "On the basis of this journal, you've concluded that, on the night of his death, Abraham VanderBoj was wandering through the upper hallway of his house, writing his final thoughts. He tried the hall door that led into his wife's room and found it unlocked. Then, for some unknown reason, he took leave of his senses, rushed into the buttery, and hanged himself. Is that about right?"

"Well, yes," replied Kimbrough. "But remember, the journal isn't all we have to go on. There are eyewitness accounts from people who saw the body even before it was cut down. And the position of the writing desk has also been authenticated. The local surgeon himself examined the body at that time and pronounced it a suicide."

"Oh, *hemichordata!*" exclaimed the little teacher. "Do you mean to tell me that for two hundred years historians have been taking the word of some part-time doctor who probably earned the better part of his living by cutting hair? Why, the whole thing is as plain as the nose on old Abraham's face."

"What's plain, Mr. Strang?" asked Nancy.

"Abraham VanderBoj didn't kill himself. He was murdered in cold blood."

The word "murdered" brought students flocking to the table where the slender teacher was seated. Across from him, Kimbrough smiled indulgently.

"Come now, Mr. Strang," chuckled Kimbrough. "I hardly think a murderer could have remained undiscovered for two centuries. After all, the death of VanderBoj has been the subject of some pretty intensive study. I did my master's thesis on it myself."

"Would you care to listen to my theory?" asked the teacher, his eyes twinkling. "Maybe I can give you a head start on your doctoral dissertation."

"The floor is yours," replied Kimbrough. "But I warn you: it'll be tough to convince me."

The teacher rose, stalked to the head of the table, and turned to face his audience. Whipping his black-rimmed glasses from his nose, he placed them in a jacket pocket.

"First," he began, "I ask you to consider the portrait of Reverend VanderBoj—the hard set of his mouth, the determination in those eyes. VanderBoj was clearly the captain of his fate. As soon as I saw that portrait, I knew that such a man might be hard or even cruel, but he would *never* have committed suicide. Self-destruction is the refuge of weaklings—and VanderBoj, whatever he was, was no weakling."

"Hardly proof, Mr. Strang," said Kimbrough. "You'll have to do better than that."

"All right, let's take another aspect of the portrait. In it, VanderBoj's head almost touches the top of the doorway. Therefore, he must have been an exceptionally tall man. My impression that he was taller than average was confirmed when I examined a cane with his initials on it. Only a very tall man could have used it comfortably."

Kimbrough nodded. "Score one for your side," he said. "VanderBoj was almost six and a half feet tall. But I still don't see what this has to do with murder."

"Consider for a moment that beam in the buttery," replied Mr. Strang. "I'm rather short myself, yet I was able to reach up and place the flat of my hand against the side of the beam. A person as tall as VanderBoj would have at most only a couple of inches of clearance between the beam and the top of his head."

"So?"

"Mr. Kimbrough, when a man is properly hanged, he falls a distance of at least a foot—perhaps more, depending on his weight. In any case, it's far enough so that the knotted rope, slamming against the victim's head as it jerks tight, breaks his neck. But now consider VanderBoj, dangling from the beam with his feet off the ground. His head must have been actually touching the beam. He couldn't have fallen any distance at all. He might have died of strangulation, of course. But under the circumstances, he couldn't possibly have broken his neck during the hanging."

"But his neck *was* broken," said Kimbrough. "All the accounts agree on that point. How do you suggest it happened, Mr. Strang?"

"I'll get to that. But first, another inconsistency in the legend. Previous to the hanging, VanderBoj was supposed to have been wandering though the house in the middle of the night. In one hand was his writing desk. In the other, presumably, a quill pen. So I ask you this, Mr. Kimbrough: how did he hold the candle?"

"Candle? What candle?"

"He had to see to write, didn't he? Therefore he needed a candle or a lantern or *something*. And it couldn't have remained in a fixed position, since VanderBoj was pacing along the hallway. So where was the candle? Did he hold it clenched between his teeth? No, Mr. Kimbrough, it just won't wash. There was no candle, because VanderBoj *wasn't* in the hallway when he wrote that final entry in his journal."

"But the journal says—"

"The journal is the one thing about this whole affair that makes sense. It is not, as you seem to think, the ravings of a madman."

"Mr. Strang?" A lanky boy dressed in blue jeans and a tie-dyed T-shirt raised his hand.

"Yes, Cal. What is it?"

"Well, sir, you've been telling us all the things that are *wrong* with the story we heard down at the house. But that's not good enough, is it? I mean, maybe the story's full of holes, but it's what we're stuck with. That is, unless you can tell us what *did* happen to Reverend VanderBoj."

"The boy has a point, Mr. Strang," said Kimbrough. "I'll admit you've given me some things to think about. But the original story will have to stand—with some minor alterations—unless you can prove this murder theory of yours. It's easy enough to be negative, to tear down the legend. But you have yet to prove a murder."

Mr. Strang took a deep breath and let it out slowly. "Very well," he said. "Let's consider the house, not as it stands today, but as it existed two centuries ago. The straightlaced master is the Reverend Abraham VanderBoj. He is tall, forbidding in appearance, and, I have no doubt, given to frequent sermonizing on the horrors that await those who commit the slightest sin, either in deed or in thought."

"As your students would say, 'Right on,'" said Kimbrough. "You've described the old boy just as if you'd met him personally."

"VanderBoj had only been married a short time," continued the teacher. "His wife is a pretty young thing only a year or so older than the girls in our class here. The union was probably arranged by Barbara's parents, overjoyed that such an eminent person should have been attracted to their daughter. But what would have been the reaction of the girl herself at being forced to marry such a man?"

"I'd have been scared to death of him," said a girl seated on the floor. "What a disgusting person to have as a husband."

"Disgust. That's the very word," said Mr. Strang. "Consider the plight of that poor creature, condemned to live her life as the wife of that man. Is it any wonder she bolted the door of her room at night?"

"What makes you—?" began Kimbrough.

"The journal says so," replied the teacher, referring to the postcard. "'My wife, in manner quite unlike her usual wont, has left her chamber door unbolted.' Therefore, she usually kept it locked. And now," he went on, "I ask you to think again about the impossibility of VanderBoj's breaking his neck by hanging himself from the rafter."

"Is that your idea?" said Kimbrough. "That VanderBoj's body was hung there *after* his neck was broken?"

"Exactly!"

"Really, Mr. Strang." Nancy Woodhull's voice was filled with skepticism. "I find it awfully hard to believe that a tiny thing like Barbara VanderBoj could have carried that big man anywhere, to say nothing of hauling him up to the rafter at the end of a rope."

"It would have been absolutely out of the question. And that's why we have to postulate the presence of a third person in the VanderBoj house that fateful evening."

"Impossible," objected Kimbrough. "VanderBoj had no servant."

"Do you really find it so surprising?" asked the teacher. "What about that little room under the stairs? VanderBoj was in the habit of giving lodging to divinity students. And a reasonably muscular young man would have no trouble moving VanderBoj's body and hanging it from the beam."

"I'll bet he had blue eyes," tittered one girl.

"And wavy blond hair," giggled another.

"I suspect," snorted Mr. Strang, "that he could have been as homely as a mud fence and Barbara would still have been attracted to him. Anything would have looked good to her after living with VanderBoj."

"Okay, okay," said Kimbrough. "VanderBoj couldn't have broken his neck by hanging from the beam. Therefore he had to have been moved there. And Barbara couldn't have moved him herself. So I guess the idea of the young divinity student is a reasonable speculation. Go ahead, Mr. Strang."

"Let's get to the night in question," said the teacher. "Because I think we're finally ready to put that last entry from VanderBoj's journal into its proper context. He mentions suffering from 'the catarrh'—most likely a head cold—and feeling miserable. So he did just what you or I would do under the same circumstances."

"He went down to the buttery and hanged himself?" suggested Kimbrough drily.

"No, he simply went to bed. The hours passed. VanderBoj tossed and turned, but his head cold prevented him from falling asleep. Instead, he lit the candle on the table beside his bed, planning to write in his journal. He sat up in bed, his writing desk across his knees."

"This is all pure conjecture on your part," said Kimbrough.

"True," Mr. Strang replied. "But it's certainly a lot more convincing than that business about carrying the desk through the outer hall with a candle between his teeth. Besides, see how it fits with what was written in the journal: VanderBoj first complains about his cold. Then he mentions the wind and the drafty old house. He looks up, clearly surprised. And what does he say next? 'My wife, in manner quite unlike her usual wont, has left her chamber door unbolted.'"

"But it would have been impossible for VanderBoj to see the door to his wife's room from his bed," protested Kimbrough. "I mean, unless he first opened the—the…"

His voice trailed off uncertainly. "That's got to be it," he finally murmured. "VanderBoj wasn't referring to his wife's *hallway* door at all."

"You're beginning to see it," smiled the teacher. "The door he spoke of was the *connecting* door between the two bedrooms, his wife's and his—the door that VanderBoj realized hadn't been bolted because a draft was slowly blowing it open."

"And what did VanderBoj see in his wife's bedroom?"

asked Nancy Woodhull, her eyes wide with excitement.

"It's what he *didn't* see that's important," answered Mr. Strang. "In spite of the fact that it was midnight, Barbara's room was empty. She hadn't come to bed! Not being a complete fool, VanderBoj must have realized that his wife, who he may already have suspected of being attracted to the visiting divinity student, was downstairs with the young man at that very moment. Thus the final entry in the journal: 'The devil will mock me no longer. I will pursue him to his hell below and there do battle.' The *devil*, of course, was the student, and the *hell below* was the room under the stairs. So you see, those words aren't the ravings of a lunatic, but simply VanderBoj's statement of what he planned to do.

"Scrawling the final phrases in the journal, he left his bedroom, angrily flinging the writing desk into the hallway. Once he'd reached the main floor downstairs, he undoubtedly threw open the door of the student's room and—well, I doubt the two just sat and talked. After all, the bed occupies most of the space in that tiny room."

"That's it," repeated Kimbrough dazedly. "That must be it. There'll be a lot of red faces at the next meeting of the historical society."

"But how did VanderBoj get his neck broken?" asked one of the students.

"I doubt we'll ever know all the details," said Mr. Strang. "I'd suspect, however, that either Barbara or the student clobbered him at the base of the skull with the warming pan. Afterward, of course, they carried his body to the buttery, strung it up on the beam, and tipped over a stool to give the appearance of suicide and divert suspicion from themselves. The student left—followed, shortly after the funeral, by Barbara. The townspeople who viewed the body were too much in awe of Reverend VanderBoj to question the suicide story. Thus the wording of the journal has been misinterpreted for two hundred years."

This last remark was followed by the honking of a horn from outside.

"That's our bus, Mr. Strang," said Nancy.

The teacher whipped out his black-rimmed glasses and settled them on the bridge of his nose. As he was about to follow the students from the pavilion, Kimbrough plucked at his sleeve.

"Mr. Strang, you've just made about a thousand dollars' worth of guidebooks and pamphlets completely worthless," he said. "Still, I appreciate what you've done for the VanderBoj house. Come back and see us again—on a Sunday, if possible."

"Why Sunday?"

"Because that's the only day we're closed. And once your story gets out, this place'll be mobbed any time we're open. There's nothing like a nice brutal murder to promote a healthy interest in history."

MR. STRANG INVENTS A STRANGE DEVICE

It was hot for the middle of May, thought Mr. Strang, as he stood in the sunlight just outside the main entrance to Aldershot High School. Through open windows he could hear the buzzing of voices coming from classrooms at the front of the building. *Be inconspicuous*—that's what his principal, Mr. Guthrey, had said. The old science teacher wondered just how inconspicuous he could be with sweat pouring from his balding brow and fogging his thick glasses.

"Heads up!" someone shouted.

Mr. Strang stepped to one side, as Warren Seabert—Aldershot's new young baseball coach—lurched through the door, carrying over one shoulder a lumpy duffel bag with the handles of several baseball bats protruding from the narrow opening at one end.

"Excuse me," Seabert panted. "We've got a game over in Farley Ridge this afternoon, and I want to put these in my car."

"What's the matter, did the team bus break down?" asked Mr. Strang.

"Nope, but I like to have a car at away games, in case of emergency." With a wave of his free hand, the coach was off toward the blue station wagon parked at the curb.

Moments later, he returned, his T-shirt stained with perspiration, and flopped down on the wide stone steps. With an audible cracking of his aging joints, Mr. Strang sat beside him. The little science teacher liked Warren. Not much taller than Mr. Strang himself, the new coach had a nose that had been broken at least once, a mop of bright red hair that topped his head like a battle flag on a castle turret, and a breezy informal manner that the older teacher found refreshing.

"The sun's really beating down, man," said Warren, wiping his forehead. "Let's go inside, where it's cooler."

"I can't," Mr. Strang replied. "I'm on duty."

"Duty? What duty? It's the junior/senior lunch period. All the action's out back, on the athletic field."

"You mean you haven't heard about Mr. Guthrey's theft patrol?"

"Theft patrol?" Warren's eyebrows shot up. "What theft patrol? You're putting me on."

"No, silly as it may sound, I'm not. Several articles have been stolen from the building, and—"

Mr. Strang paused as the front door opened and Mary Dakin, a senior who was in his third-period chemistry class, came outside, a large shopping bag clutched in one arm.

"Hello, Mary," said the teacher. "Going home for lunch?"

"Oh, hi, Mr. Strang. Yeah, I thought I would." She indicated the bag with a nod of her head. "This has to go home today, and I've got an appointment after school."

As she started down the steps, Mr. Strang rose quickly. "Mary?"

The girl turned. Her shoulders slumped, and a look of disgust passed across her face. "Mr. Strang, you're not in on this, too!"

"I'm afraid I am, Mary. May I have a look in the bag, please?"

"Oh, gee, it's just some stuff I did in sewing class." She looked at the young baseball coach, her cheeks reddening.

"I'm sure it is. But I'm supposed to check everything. You understand, don't you?"

"But you know I wouldn't—"

All at once she flung the bag savagely at the teacher. "All right, *here!*" she shouted. "Check the dumb thing. I've never been so embarrassed in my whole life!"

Reluctantly, Mr. Strang began pulling objects from the bag. An apron. A peasant blouse. And then behind him he heard Warren chuckle as Mr. Strang extracted two pairs of shocking-pink hotpants.

At the sound of the laughter, the girl burst into tears. Grabbing her clothing, she stuffed it back in the bag and ran down the steps. Mr. Strang stood beside Warren Seabert and wished the earth would open up and swallow him.

Marvin W. Guthrey's theft patrol had struck again.

"I don't care what the reason is, Mr. Strang. It's embarrassing for us kids, and it's just not fair!"

At the end of the day, Kenneth Byington—Aldershot High's Student Council president—had made it a point to see the science teacher in his classroom. "We're not blaming you, Mr. Strang. But is it right that every student who leaves school with a package has to be searched? I mean, what kind of place are you running here, anyway?"

"I tried to make that point to Mr. Guthrey when he first brought up this theft-patrol business, Kenny, but he couldn't see any other way around the problem."

"But it's not even legal." Kenneth paused and looked Mr. Strang straight in the eye. "Is it?"

"According to Mr. Guthrey, we're within our rights as long as we don't make any accusations and don't search anyone who insists on being left alone."

"Sure," answered Kenneth sarcastically. "And anybody who doesn't want to give the teacher a look at what he's carrying is automatically guilty, is that it?"

"Kenny, perhaps you don't realize the problem we—"

"Come on, Mr. Strang. Things are getting stolen from the school, and whoever's ripping the stuff off has got to get it out. That's the way you figure, isn't it? So instead of going after the guilty person, you make like *all* of us are crooks or something. Why, Mary Dakin was crying all afternoon. And just because somebody took a couple of colored pencils or something."

"It was more than a couple of colored pencils," came a voice from the classroom doorway.

Both Kenneth and Mr. Strang swiveled their heads toward the sound. "Oh," said Kenneth softly. "Hello, Mr. Guthrey."

"Good day, Kenneth," said the principal with a nod. "I heard you planned on seeing Mr. Strang this afternoon. And, since the idea of the theft patrol was mine, I thought it best for me to answer any questions personally. I'd like to begin by saying that Mr. Strang was against the idea of searching students from the start. He's doing it only because of my orders."

"But *why?*" asked Kenneth hesitantly. "What's the big deal about a few things that have disappeared?"

"Early last month," Guthrey began briskly, "someone broke into four cartons of books that had been left outside the door of our library and took seventeen volumes. Most of them were bestsellers, but one was a book of colored prints of old maps, worth over twenty-five dollars. A few days after that, the same person—at least, we assume it was the same person—cleaned out a locked supply closet in the Physical Education office. Two weeks later, down in the back hall, twelve boxes containing a total of a gross of typewriter ribbons disappeared. And just today—I only got word of this an hour ago—two boxes of canned fruit in the cafeteria were opened, and every last can was taken. Our losses on all these items are close to four hundred dollars."

Guthrey walked across the room and crammed himself into one of the chair-desks. "So you see, Kenneth," he concluded, "this isn't just penny-ante theft. And, with another month of school to go, there's no telling what'll disappear next." He gave a rueful laugh. "I swear, I expect to hear at any moment that the whole chemistry lab is missing."

"And the only way you can figure out to catch your thief is to search everybody with a package, is that it?"

"Well, Ken, it's the taxpayers who'll get stuck with the bill," replied Guthrey. "I might add that the PTA is firmly behind my theft-patrol idea. But if you can come up with something better, I'll be glad to hear it."

Kenneth shook his head slowly. "I'm no detective," he said. "It just doesn't seem right that *everybody's* got to get it in the neck because of one person."

"Well," said Guthrey in his most reasonable tone, "what would you do in my place?"

"I dunno. You've *got* to stop it, I guess. But look, Mr. Guthrey, why just the kids? I'm sorry if I'm out of line, but, like I said to Mr. Strang, it's just not fair."

"I don't understand what you're trying to say, Kenneth."

"I do," interrupted Mr. Strang. "Two thousand students come into this building every school day. And we tell them they've got to be searched if they bring anything home, as if this were some kind of penal institution, rather than a school. But what about the others who come in and go out of the building? The custodians, the salesmen, the delivery-men? We don't insist that *they* be searched before leaving."

"But the students are—"

"Oh, sure," said Mr. Strang with magnificent irony. "They're just kids. Who cares about *their* rights or feelings?"

"Mr. Strang!" said Guthrey indignantly. "Are you suggesting that visitors to our building—including parents—*all* be searched?"

"Fair's fair," replied the teacher blithely. "Remember, your theft patrol's been around for three weeks, now, and hasn't found a thing. Oh, yes, and one more point."

"Yes?"

"Don't forget the teachers—and the administration." He pointed a finger directly at the principal. "Including *you,* Mr. Guthrey."

"But you don't—I mean, I can't—" Guthrey got up angrily. "And just who'll do the searching?" he asked.

"Yes, that's a problem, isn't it? The whole thing—including your theft patrol—is kind of ridiculous. So I'd like to make you a proposition, Mr. Guthrey."

"What proposition?"

"You call off your theft patrol—as of tomorrow morning—and I'll guarantee to find your thief within two weeks."

"You? But we've even had the police in. What can you—?"

Mr. Strang jerked a thumb at his own narrow chest. "I'm not the police," he said.

"I don't know, Leonard. I admit there've been a few situations around here that you've managed to clear up, but in this case—well, I just don't know. How would you go about it?"

"Professional secret," said Mr. Strang with a straight face.

"Two weeks, eh?" Guthrey considered the teacher, who was wiping his glasses on an acid-stained necktie. "I suppose it would get me off the hook with the students. All right, Leonard. But remember: if you haven't produced the thief within two weeks, I will hold you personally responsible for anything else that's stolen." Guthrey stalked out of the room, leaving the teacher to ponder his parting shot.

"Hey, Mr. Strang," said Kenneth admiringly, "that was great! You're really something else. I didn't know you had a plan. Tell me, how are you going to find out who did it?"

"Kenny," replied the teacher, shaking his head sadly, "I haven't the faintest idea."

At odd moments during the rest of the week, Mr. Strang mulled over the problem he had set for himself. Keeping watch for whoever was doing the stealing was out of the question—there were just too many halls and storerooms, doorways and closets. For a while, he considered dusting all packages with either methylene blue or gentian violet. Either of those chemicals would stain the hands of the thief with brilliant color, and any attempt to wash the hands would merely spread the stain. Unfortunately, neither chemical was selective: it would also stain the hands of those legitimately entitled to touch school supplies.

By Friday afternoon, the teacher only had two facts to go on. First, the thefts had occurred at irregular intervals, beginning the first week of April. And second, all the stolen articles were things that could easily be converted into cash, once they'd been removed from the building. There was no way they could be traced back to the school.

How had the supplies been taken from the building? That was the key to the whole thing. Books, typewriter ribbons, canned fruit—how could anyone possibly spirit such things away without being spotted?

"I just wish I could design a package that would hoist a red flag and yell, 'Stop, thief!' when it was being stolen," mused the teacher.

That afternoon, as he went to the office to hang up his keys before going home, Mr. Strang glanced idly at the teachers' bulletin board on the wall beside the key rack. Summer job openings, announcements of college courses, spring sports schedules, new fire-drill instructions, an announcement that the wife of one of the foreign-language teachers had given birth to a baby boy—the bits of paper, neatly typed or printed, were an ever-changing journal of the affairs of Aldershot High School.

Then something caught Mr. Strang's eye. Whipping his glasses from his jacket pocket, he perched them on his nose and peered closely at one of the announcements. He read it twice and then scribbled something quickly in a small notebook.

"*Asteroides*," he mumbled. In the parking lot, he angrily kicked the front tire of his battered purple car before getting in.

Even though the knowledge was proving painful, he now knew who had been doing the stealing and how the supplies had been taken from the building. But proving it would be something else again....

That evening in his small room at Mrs. Mackey's boarding house, Mr. Strang made several rough sketches of a device that looked on paper as if it might have come from a science-fiction story. He didn't know if it would work, or even if it would be possible to construct it. But he intended to find out.

The following morning, he drove to the Aldershot Surplus Warehouse at the end of the business district and spent most of an hour wandering among shelves filled with battle jackets, helmets, tools, obsolete swords and knives, and other items that the military in its wisdom had decided it no longer needed. Finally he found what he was looking for. The cost was more than he'd expected to pay, but, if his scheme worked, it was possible he'd be reimbursed by the school district.

His second stop was at a low brick building with a sign on top that read *Tommy's Machine and Tool Shop*. Thomas Mulvahey, the owner and entire labor force of the establishment, looked up from a milling machine as Mr. Strang entered.

"Hi, Mr. Strang!" he called, wiping his oily hands on a rag. "What brings you to these parts?"

"I want something made, Tommy," said the teacher. He showed the machinist the sketch he had drawn and explained the purpose of the device. "Can you do it?"

"Shouldn't be too hard. I've got an old timing mechanism in the back room that I could use. When do you need it?"

"As soon as possible. Monday morning, if that won't be too much trouble. And, Tommy?"

"Yeah?"

"About payment," said the teacher. "I can't afford more

than—"

"Forget it," replied the machinist. "This job's on the house."

"I didn't mean—"

"Mr. Strang, two years ago my Joey was having trouble with physics. You tutored him at my place for a solid three months and wouldn't take anything more'n a cup of coffee and some cookies for your trouble. I couldn't afford a private tutor, but you came anyway. I've always wondered how I could do something to pay you back, and here's my chance."

"In that case, I accept," said the teacher. "I hope it won't be too difficult to make what I have in mind."

"Piece of cake," smiled Tommy. "I'll drop it off at your place tomorrow afternoon."

On Monday morning, Mr. Strang arrived at school more than an hour early. From the back seat of his car, he took a cardboard box about nine inches square and eighteen inches high. He left it in the custodians' office with explicit instructions to set it outside his classroom door at approximately ten-fifteen on Wednesday morning.

At ten-twelve on Wednesday, the box was delivered. The classroom was empty, since Mr. Strang had charge of a study hall at the far end of the building.

At two o'clock that same day, Mr. Strang asked his principal for permission to call a meeting of the entire faculty as soon as the students were dismissed. An announcement of the faculty meeting was read over the school's public-address system.

At two-twenty, Art Mickel—president of the Aldershot Teachers' Association—was at Mr. Strang's door, his jaw thrust forward belligerently. "Leonard," he barked, when Mr. Strang answered his knock, "as soon as I heard the announcement, I went to see Mr. Guthrey. I told him he's got no business holding a meeting on such short notice. He said you were the one who wanted it."

"That's right," Mr. Strang answered.

"But you can't! I mean, *Tuesday's* supposed to be meeting day. And, besides, Mr. Guthrey says nobody—but *nobody*—is supposed to miss this meeting of yours."

"Also correct," replied the teacher.

"C'mon, be reasonable. The tennis team has a match today, the baseball team has a game, and the Debate Club's supposed to have practice right after school. Besides, some of us have college courses we have to get to. This is bad planning on your part, Leonard, admit it."

"Art, you've known me for a good many years. This is important, or I wouldn't have asked Mr. Guthrey to call the meeting. Please take my word for it that *everyone* on the faculty has to be there."

Mickel looked at Mr. Strang questioningly. "I could file a grievance, you know."

"File away, but I'd advise you not to."

Mickel was silent for a long moment. "Ah, you know I wouldn't do a thing like that," he said at last. "But this had better be good, Leonard—your meeting, I mean. Otherwise, there'll be hell to pay among the teachers."

"Let 'em holler, Art. Just get everybody to the meeting."

By three-thirty, the auditorium held more than a hundred grumbling teachers. The microphone squawked twice as the amplifier was adjusted, and then Marvin W. Guthrey stood up to speak.

"I know that having a meeting at this time is inconvenient," he began, and there were murmurs of agreement. "I'm as mystified about it as you are. As you know, there have been thefts of materials and supplies from the building, and Mr. Strang has taken it upon himself to investigate. I understand that he's called this meeting to issue something in the nature of a progress report."

"How long are we going to be here?" someone shouted.

"I'll let Mr. Strang answer that one," said Guthrey, and the science teacher rose and walked to the microphone.

"I understand your annoyance," Mr. Strang began. "So first let me say that this shouldn't take more than half an hour—perhaps less."

There was a patter of light applause.

"You're all aware," the teacher went on, "of the thefts that have been taking place. For a time, we were searching the students, trying to find some trace of the stolen goods. But then the Student Council president made a point I hadn't considered."

"What point?" called out Steve Weissman of the math department.

"He said that, since we were already searching the students, why not search everybody?"

"The kid's a wise guy," a voice shouted.

"No, he's not. You see, we all *assumed* a student must be doing the stealing. But there was no evidence of that, except our own preconceived notion. It was only when I started considering the fact that *anyone*—student or staff member—might be guilty that things began to make sense."

"Are you trying to tell us," said Art Mickel, with fire in

his eyes, "that a *teacher* could be guilty?"

"Why not, Art? Four hundred dollars is a lot of money."

"*Did* a teacher do it, Leonard?" Mickel persisted. "And can you prove it?"

"To the first question," Mr. Strang replied, "I think so, yes. And to the second, I hope so."

"Okay, I'll bite: how did this unknown teacher get the stuff out of the building?"

"That puzzled me for a long time, Art," said Mr. Strang. "But then I got to thinking about something. The typewriter ribbons, for example, were stolen outright—that is, just as they came from the factory. But the books, on the other hand, were taken out of their cartons, as were the cans of fruit. Why?"

A hundred and twenty-three teachers leaned forward in their seats.

"There seemed to be only one explanation," Mr. Strang went on. "The typewriter ribbons were in small boxes, but the boxes of books and the cartons of canned goods were quite large. Our thief obviously had some receptacle to carry out his stolen goods, and that receptacle must have been able to hold everything that was stolen. Bulky items, however, were being broken down into smaller units. This suggested that, while the container was large, its opening was rather small."

A murmur of assent passed through the group.

"That still doesn't prove it was a teacher, though, does it, Leonard?" asked Mickel.

"No, of course not. But then I thought about the supplies taken from the locked Physical Education closet. That theft would require the use of a key. And keys are in the hands of us teachers, not our students."

"Hey, wait a minute!"

Heads turned as James Whitiker, the head of the Phys Ed department, rose from his seat. Whitiker had a thick shock of iron-white hair, below which his scowling face seemed carved of granite.

"Yes, Jim?"

"I don't like the way this is going," said Whitiker, "not one little bit. In the first place, it's not impossible for a kid to have gotten hold of a key to that closet. And, if not, then you're accusing a member of my department of doing the stealing, because we're the only ones with keys to that closet."

Mr. Strang stared at the floor. "I don't know that it's my place to accuse anybody, Jim," he said slowly. "I just want to present the facts. Then you can make up your own minds."

"Don't play word games with me, Leonard," snapped Whitiker. "Who do you think did it?"

"Jim," said Mr. Strang, in a voice so soft his listeners had to strain to hear, "were you aware of the fact that every one of the thefts took place on days when the baseball team was playing an away game? I saw the schedule on the office bulletin board. The similarity between game dates and the days the stealing happened couldn't be missed."

"Yeah, sure. And how did our mysterious thief get the stuff out of the building? Did he hide it in a baseball?"

"No, it's my belief that he hid it in that big duffel bag—the one Warren Seabert packs. Nobody thinks twice about seeing him in the building with that bag on the days when there's a game. And the narrow opening at the end would explain why the cartons of books and cans had to be opened."

"But wouldn't Warren notice the extra weight? Explain *that*, Mr. Detective."

"He might notice—but he wouldn't *care*, if he himself were the thief," said Mr. Strang, wiping perspiration from his brow. "And once the stolen stuff was in his car, he could drop it at his home before going on to the game."

"Hey, man, let's hold it right there." Warren Seabert had popped up from his chair. "Let me get this straight. Are you saying *I* took all that stuff, Mr. Strang? Because, if you are, I'm coming up there and knock your—"

"Just a moment, please," said the teacher. "Warren, in science we start with a hypothesis—a theory. But no theory—including one that says you were the thief—can be accepted without proof. So I decided on a little experiment."

"What kind of experiment?" demanded Jim Whitiker.

"I made our thief an offer he couldn't refuse."

This catch phrase from *The Godfather* brought a few laughs. Others, however, were not amused. It is seldom that one teacher baldly accuses another of being a criminal.

"Today," Mr. Strang went on, "there is an away baseball game. So this morning I had a box left outside my classroom door. On the box were stenciled the words 'Fire Extinguishers.' The box was of a size that might have held four of the little red extinguishers we have in all the science labs—the kind that could easily be resold for home use. Not only was the box taped neatly shut, as if it had just come from the factory, but it was small enough to fit into Warren's duffel bag without being opened. I made sure of that."

"So?"

"So sometime this morning, while I was out of my classroom, the box was stolen."

"Oh, sure." Warren jabbed a finger at Mr. Strang. "I get it. Now all you have to do is search my station wagon and look inside the duffel bag, eh? Well, no dice, Mr. Strang. My car is locked, and it's going to stay that way."

"A search won't be necessary, Warren."

"Huh?"

"Last week, I considered the possibility of creating a package that could signal for help if it was stolen. And I think I found a way to do it. You see, the box outside my room this morning did *not* contain fire extinguishers."

"Yeah? What, then?"

"On Saturday," said Mr. Strang, "I arranged to have made for me a rather strange device. It's basically a valve. The valve is operated by a spring-wound timing mechanism. Without going into all the details, let me just say that the valve can be set to open at any prearranged time. It's quite ingenious, really."

"I still don't see how that proves that I—"

"The valve, Warren, is inside the fire-extinguisher box, and it's connected on one side to a small tank of compressed air. The other side of the valve is attached to a war-surplus inflatable life raft. When deflated, the raft fit into the box, but *inflated* it would measure about four by six feet."

By this time, Mr. Strang had his colleagues' undivided attention.

"The valve was set to open," he went on, glancing at his watch, "about five minutes ago."

Guthrey jumped to his feet. "Are you telling us, Mr. Strang, that if someone here stole that box, he has a fully inflated life raft in his car right now?"

The teacher nodded. "I think we can assume so—as long as Tom Mulvahey constructed the valve correctly. Suppose we go outside and take a look."

Almost as one being, the teachers rushed from the auditorium and headed for the front of the building, where Warren Seabert had parked his station wagon. A woman with a shopping bag under one arm was standing beside the vehicle, looking incredulously through its window.

"I was just passing by," she said, wide-eyed, "when I saw that big yellow thing kind of *growing* out of a little brown box."

The rubberized raft lay upside down, completely filling the wagon's cargo area. It had jammed the canvas duffel bag against the rear window, and the onlookers saw that one of the bag's seams had burst open.

Mr. Strang saw Jim Whitiker looking from the raft-filled station wagon to a grim, red-faced Warren Seabert. "*Why,*

Warren?" the department head said. "I was ready to back you to the hilt, but I can't ignore that damn life raft. Why did you do it?"

"For the bread, man. The money. Did you ever try to make ends meet on a beginning teacher's salary?"

Whitiker looked about at the assembled Aldershot High School faculty. "Yes," he said, without emotion. "I guess we all have. It gets tight sometimes, sure, but none of us ever thought that *stealing* was the answer."

Mr. Strang felt someone pluck at his sleeve. It was the woman with the shopping bag who had first seen the raft in the station wagon.

"What an odd thing that is," she breathed. "Do you suppose it's some kind of safety device?"

"No," said the teacher. "I think it's some new kind of burglar alarm."

MR. STRANG FOLLOWS THROUGH

The brutal murder of Shirley Capehart in her own apartment early on a Monday morning shook the village of Aldershot. Within hours, dozens of police cars were cruising the streets, their steely-eyed occupants stopping often to question anyone who appeared even remotely suspicious. Young matrons, alone during the day, breathed easily only after their husbands had come home and their houses were locked up tight. The village's clergymen prepared sermons in which Aldershot was depicted as a modern-day Sodom or Gomorrah.

The town gossips, of course, had a field day. And out of the mass of misinformation that was passed along over back fences and through overworked phone lines, a few facts emerged:

- Miss Capehart, a girl in her early twenties, had been a substitute teacher in the Aldershot school system.
- She had been murdered in her apartment in the Aldershot Arms sometime between seven o'clock in the morning, when she had been called to take a substituting job, and eight, when her body was found.
- The murder had been committed with a long knife or some other sharp, pointed weapon. She had been stabbed multiple times in the abdomen, and there were other cuts on her head and neck.
- The girl's own pen had been used, presumably by the murderer, to print on the painted apartment wall a quotation that was quickly identified as coming from the Second Book of Kings: "Go, see now this cursed woman, and bury her."

Although there was some talk of this being a dying message that the girl herself had left, Aldershot's most astute gatherers of information were unable to confirm or deny that rumor.

At three-thirty on the day following the murder, Leonard Strang entered the main office of the James K. Errington Elementary School, one of the six primary schools in the village, which annually sent its graduating eighth graders on to Mr. Strang and his fellow faculty members at Aldershot High School for the continuation of their educations. He approached the secretary's desk and tipped his battered felt hat to Miss Dockett.

"Good afternoon," he said, nodding in the direction of the principal's office's closed door. "My name is Strang. I have an appointment with Mr. Hafgardt to take a look at your eighth-grade science achievement tests, just to get an idea of what kind of kids we'll be getting next year at the high school."

"He's in a conference," replied the secretary. "Something terrible came up. Would you care to wait, Mr. Strang?"

The teacher nodded. As he turned toward the row of chairs along one wall, he felt Miss Dockett pluck at the sleeve of his jacket.

"Mr. Strang," she whispered, "wasn't that awful about Miss Capehart? I mean, who could have *done* such a thing?"

"A madman, from what I've heard."

"Did you know she was scheduled to sub here yesterday?"

Before Mr. Strang could reply, a familiar voice boomed out from behind the principal's door.

"Mr. Hafgardt, I don't give a *damn* about your reputation. There's been a murder, and I intend to get to the bottom of it!"

The office door banged back, and Tom Hafgardt stood in the doorway. A slender man in his early thirties, his face was white with rage. "Out!" he barked. "I'm certainly willing to cooperate with the police, but nobody comes into my office and accuses me of murder!"

A tall, heavyset man wearing a tan overcoat and carrying a briefcase appeared behind Hafgardt. "I didn't accuse you of anything," he said. "But we have reason to believe you know more than you're telling us. By your own admission, you phoned her at seven yesterday morning to ask her to substitute. Less than an hour later..."

The man's voice trailed off as he noticed the gnome-like little science teacher. "Mr. Strang," he said. "What are *you* doing here?"

"As a teacher, Paul," said Mr. Strang with a grin, "I often find myself in school buildings. What are *you* doing here?"

"You *know* this imbecile, Leonard?" said Hafgardt. "Detective Roberts is here to grill me about the murder of Shirley Capehart. And of all the heavy-handed, dim-witted—"

"Oh, Paul's not as bad as all that. As a mutual friend, perhaps I can help?"

From Hafgardt: "Yes, you can tell this idiot to get out of—"

From Roberts: "Either this guy talks to me or I pull him in for—"

Mr. Strang's eyes flashed behind his black-rimmed glasses. He flung out an arm and pointed. "Get back in there, both of you," he snapped, biting off each word.

The principal and the detective both felt like schoolboys who had been caught in some mischief. With hangdog expressions, they returned to the inner office. Mr. Strang followed them in and closed the door behind him.

"Sit down," the teacher commanded, "and let's get to the bottom of this. You first, Tom."

Hafgardt flicked an angry glance at Roberts. "Yes, I called Shirley yesterday to offer her a sub job. One of my third-grade teachers had called in sick. Her lesson plans were in perfect order, so I knew Shirley wouldn't have any trouble, even on such short notice."

"A nice, easy day's pay for cute l'il Miss Capehart, eh?" said Roberts, with more than a tinge of sarcasm in his voice.

"As a matter of fact," continued Hafgardt, gritting his teeth and looking fixedly at Mr. Strang, "I also wanted Shirley to take a job for today, subbing for Mrs. Bledsoe, our vocal music teacher. Mrs. Bledsoe doesn't make lesson plans, and trying to get a class of first and second graders to sing on key is anything *but* easy. In any case, when Shirley didn't show up by eight yesterday morning, I called her apartment again. This time, the phone was picked up by this"—he jerked a thumb in Roberts' direction—"this—"

"A call was put in to the police a little before eight," Roberts said grudgingly. "It was placed by Eileen Jenns, who has the apartment next door to the Capehart girl's. She'd heard scuffling sounds, but she didn't think much about it at first—figured Miss Capehart was moving some furniture around or something. When she left her own apartment, she noticed that Miss Capehart's door was open. She looked inside and saw the body. The officer said she was almost hysterical on the phone. The station called me, and I got right over there. I'd no sooner entered the apartment when the phone rang. It was Hafgardt."

"I see. Tell me, Paul, what makes you think Tom Hafgardt knows any more about this case than he's already told you?"

The detective closed his mouth with an audible click and clutched his briefcase to his chest. "That's official police business," he said.

"I see," responded the teacher. He turned to Hafgardt. "Throw the fuzz out of your office, Tom, that's my advice. And don't say another word to him. There's no reason for you to cooperate."

"Hey, wait a minute!" cried the detective. "We've been

friends for more than five years, Mr. Strang. You've even given me a hand on some of my cases. What's the big idea?"

"Paul," the teacher replied, "it's true that you're my friend. But Tom is both a friend *and* a colleague, and you're taking too hard a line with him. You want him to be completely honest with you, but you refuse to do the same with him."

"I don't know what you're talking about," muttered Roberts.

"Oh, come on, Paul, you're not here just because Tom phoned Miss Capehart. You've *got* something on him, and, from the way you're hugging that briefcase, I'd say it's in there."

"Anything in my case is official police documentation, Mr. Strang. I don't have to—"

"You don't have to do *anything*, Paul," said the teacher. "On the other hand, Mr. Hafgardt doesn't have to give you his willing cooperation. But I was hoping we could handle this like reasonable men."

Roberts took a handkerchief from his pocket and mopped perspiration from his face. "The lieutenant will kill me for this, but—well, okay." He opened his case and drew out a glossy color photograph. "This is a shot of a page from a loose-leaf notebook that was on the desk in Shirley Capehart's living room. I had it enlarged, and I think it'll answer your question."

The photo was exceptionally clear—even the horizontal blue lines on the paper were visible. On the page, two concentric red circles surrounded some penciled letters. Other blobs of red appeared elsewhere on the page.

"Those circles were drawn by Shirley Capehart in her own blood. We know that, because there's a clear fingerprint at the base of the outer circle, and it matches her right index finger. The way we figure it, she staggered to the desk after she'd been stabbed and circled the printing on the page. It's pretty clear she wanted to draw our attention to it."

Mr. Strang took the photograph and examined the scrawled capital letters inside the pair of circles:

T. OMHAF
EIL

The teacher nodded thoughtfully. "Paul's got a point," he said to the principal. "Those letters on the first line do seem to be spelling out your name."

"But I—"

"On the other hand, Paul, there's that period, and the gap between the T and the other letters on the line. How do you explain that?"

"I wish I could. To be perfectly honest, Mr. Hafgardt isn't the only person this photo has made us suspicious of."

"Yes," nodded Mr. Strang. "The bottom line—EIL—might be a reference to Miss Capehart's neighbor. Her name is Eileen Jenns?"

"Right. And then there's someone else."

"Who's that?"

"An old man who lives on the top floor of the Aldershot Arms, Anthony Olmhoff. He has a piano in his apartment, and on several occasions he invited Shirley Capehart up to his place to play it."

Mr. Strang stroked his chin. "I see," he said thoughtfully.

"Well, I don't," said Hafgardt. "How do you figure this Olmhoff character might be the killer?"

"The diminutive for 'Anthony' is 'Tony,'" Mr. Strang explained, "and OMHAF could be a misspelling of his last name."

"Not only that," added Roberts, "but Olmhoff was under the care of a psychiatrist a few years back. Acute depression." He glanced at Hafgardt. "Have you ever been to one?"

"Certainly not!"

"Okay, take it easy. Consulting a shrink isn't a crime." Roberts flopped into a swivel chair and leaned back, breathing a long sigh. "So there you have it," he said. "A clue left by a dying woman that might indicate any one of three people. And no other evidence—not an iota."

"And you're sure that the murder was the work of a maniac?" asked Mr. Strang.

"No doubt about it. The living room of that apartment is a bloody mess, but nothing's missing. We even found forty-two dollars in a desk drawer. And another thing, the medical examiner said some of the stab wounds were made *after* death. Finally, there's that writing on the wall."

"Paul, doesn't it seem odd to you that an otherwise normal person would suddenly go *so* berserk? I mean, wouldn't there be some history of previous mental illness?"

"We thought of that." Roberts turned to the principal. "I don't mind telling you, Hafgardt, that in the past twenty-four hours we've gone over your life with a fine-tooth comb. If it'll make you feel any better, you seem to be about as normal as they come. But the same goes for Eileen Jenns. And Olmhoff, too—except for that business with the psychiatrist."

"Paul?"

"Yeah, Mr. Strang?"

"This problem intrigues me—to say nothing of the fact that I'll sleep better at night once the killer is caught. Is there any chance of my getting in to see the Capehart girl's apartment?"

Roberts shook his head. "No way. You're a pretty sharp old geezer, Mr. Strang—no offense!—but nobody but the police goes in there until the case is solved."

"Then I guess I'll have to use another way."

"Other way? What other way? Hey, Mr. Strang, come back here! You can't—"

But the diminutive teacher had already left the office and was on his way out of the building.

At four-thirty the following afternoon, Mr. Strang presented himself at the door of the Aldershot Arms and buzzed for admittance. The door was opened by the building's caretaker, a little cricket of a man with a wrinkled face and watery blue eyes, who introduced himself as Timothy MacDonald.

"An' ye'd be Muster Strang, I'll wager," said MacDonald in a thick Scottish burr. "Miss Jenns said to be expecting you. Doon the hall there, then turn right. Number nine."

As he passed the door of Shirley Capehart's apartment, Mr. Strang noted the seal over the keyhole and the notice stating that entrance was forbidden without police permission. Less than four days previously, Miss Capehart had been killed within a few feet of where he stood.

He rang the bell of the next unit. An eye appeared at the peephole, and then came the sound of bolts being thrown back. He bowed stiffly as Eileen Jenns opened the door. She was a tall girl, whose voluptuous body was surmounted by a rather homely face.

"I'm very grateful you were willing to see me," said the teacher, laying his hat on a chair. "You understand, I hope, that I'm in no way connected with the police."

"It's a good thing you called first," Eileen replied. "After what happened, I don't open my door to *anyone* unless I'm expecting them. And I took the precaution of calling the high school and asking your principal to describe you."

"Very wise," the teacher nodded. "Tell me, do all these apartments have the same layout? Rooms, closets, and so on?"

"Like they were stamped out with a cookie cutter," Eileen said. She took the teacher through the living room into a small kitchenette. "The bath's through there, and there's the bedroom."

Mr. Strang walked by a cheap dressing table and peered through the bedroom window at the cans of rubbish in the alley behind the building. "Charming view," he said wryly. "And you're sure Shirley Capehart's apartment is just like this one?"

"Her furniture's more expensive, and her walls are painted instead of wallpapered. Aside from that, you can't tell one from the other."

"Just one more thing, Miss Jenns," said the teacher, stoking up a pipe and applying a match. "Did you hear anything at about the time Miss Capehart was—er—"

"Just some bumping around. I didn't think anything of it at the time."

"Doesn't it seem odd to you that she didn't scream?"

"Not really. I asked the police about that. They said the shock of being stabbed might have made screaming impossible." She shivered. "I don't like all this talk about killing. And the idea that I'm suspected makes my flesh crawl. I— I'm afraid."

For supper that evening, Mrs. Mackey—Mr. Strang's landlady—treated the teacher to a Lucullan feast of pot roast, boiled potatoes, and tossed salad. She might just as well have served rubber boots and hay: Mr. Strang's mind was not on food.

Later, in his room, the old teacher sat in his chair and puffed on his pipe. The puzzle of Shirley Capehart's death circled his mind like a mechanical rabbit at a dog track. He considered the quotation written on the wall. The "cursed woman" was Jezebel—but Shirley Capehart was no Jezebel ... except, perhaps, in the deranged mind of her killer. But was that person Tom Hafgardt, Eileen Jenns, or Anthony Olmhoff?

Idly, he switched on the radio. A full symphony orchestra was playing an incongruous arrangement of "Row, Row, Row Your Boat." He took a scratch pad from his desk and scrawled letters on it:

T. OMHAF
EIL

As the music on the radio changed to "Three Blind Mice," Mr. Strang stroked a horizontal line at the bottom of the **F**. Now the upper row of letters read **T. OMHAE**. Interesting, but of no help whatsoever.

"And now for an old favorite, known to us all," said the

radio announcer. As the music began, Mr. Strang drew two more lines on the pad.

All at once, the hand holding the pencil began to tremble. The music boomed against the old teacher's ears, and he stared at the paper before him, his eyes wide.

"*Gnathostomata!*" he shouted, scuttling across the room to the telephone beside his bed. After consulting the directory, he dialed the home of the village's sanitation commissioner and asked a single question.

After hearing the answer, he hung up the receiver and made a hurried call to Detective Paul Roberts.

Eileen Jenns sat reading in her small apartment. According to her watch, it was eight o'clock, but it was already dark outside. The dressing gown she was wearing rustled softly. She really shouldn't have bought it—it was much too impractical for a single girl. Still, it was a pleasure to wear, especially after taking off the severe starched uniform she wore at her job.

There was a soft knock at the door.

"Who is it?" she called.

There was a muffled reply in a familiar voice. She turned the bolt and opened the door.

Suddenly, she felt herself spun viciously about. She opened her mouth wide, but, before she could scream, a hand clapped tightly over it. "Jezebel," a voice grated in her ear. "Whore of Judah! You paint your face and look out at a window. Temptress! Even as Jehu had Jezebel slain, so will I slay you!"

Something flashed in the air. A knife. Eileen steeled herself against the pain to come.

And then the hand was jerked violently from her mouth. There were scuffling sounds behind her. She whirled.

There were Detective Roberts and that funny little teacher, Mr. Strang. They each held an arm of the man struggling between them.

It was the caretaker of the Aldershot Arms, Timothy MacDonald.

Both hands of the clock at the station house were pointing straight up when Paul Roberts finally came through the doors at the rear of the building to confront a still-trembling Mr. Strang.

"MacDonald hasn't stopped ranting and raving since we brought him in," said the detective. "I don't know if they'll ever get him calmed down, even with tranquilizers. By the way, I had his rooms searched. Seems he kept a diary. You

ought to see it. Sigmund Freud would have had trouble figuring him out. We'll be able to make a murder case against
him, although I expect he'll plead insanity and beat the
rap."

He paused, considering the white-faced teacher. "Hey,
you don't look so good. Sure you don't want me to drive you
home?"

"I'll be all right, Paul. I'm just too old for these last-min-
ute rescues."

"I know what you mean. So what was it that tipped you
off, Mr. Strang? I mean, I wouldn't have figured MacDonald
for the killer in a million years."

"Those letters in her notebook, Paul. That was the first
thing. You see, they were written in pencil."

"So?"

"Does it seem logical to you that Shirley Capehart, after
being stabbed, would write a cryptic message in pencil—
and then put the pencil *down* and circle the message with
her own blood?"

"Well, no, I guess not, but—"

"Therefore, inference one: the letters, at least when Miss
Capehart originally wrote them, had nothing to do with her
murder. It was only *after* she was stabbed that they became
relevant to the case."

"I see that. But then what was that writing in the notebook?"

"She was a substitute teacher, and she'd just been
called about two assignments—third grade on Monday and
primary vocal music on Tuesday. Lesson plans had been
prepared for the third-grade class, but there were none for
vocal music. Now, if she had a few minutes to spare, what
would she have done with that time?"

"Are you saying she was writing down what she was going to teach in the music classes?"

Mr. Strang nodded, but the puzzled expression didn't
leave the detective's face.

"I still don't get it," he said.

"It was that second line that threw me, Paul: E-I-L. But
it must have happened this way." From his pocket, Mr.
Strang drew a small notebook. Turning to a blank page, he
rapidly printed the letters E and I. Next he made a vertical
line and then a short horizontal one to form an L.

"This is where she was interrupted—either by a knock
at the door or by the murderer's actual entrance into her
apartment. She never finished printing that third letter on
the second row."

The teacher quickly added two more short horizontal

lines, turning the L into another E. "And now I'll complete the second line of writing," he said, continuing to print.

Roberts took the notebook and read the letters from the page. "E, I, E, I, O," he said. "But what—Holy Saint Jude Thaddeus!"

"Sounds familiar, doesn't it? The note, if Shirley hadn't been interrupted," he said, jotting additional letters above the ones he'd already printed, "would have looked something like this."

Roberts peered intently at the modified page and saw:

T. OMHAF
EIEIO

"And," Mr. Strang concluded, "I can only think of one piece of music for primary students that would fit."

"O, M, H, A, F," Roberts read aloud. "'Old MacDonald Had A Farm.' And *that's* how you knew it was the caretaker."

"Exactly."

"But what about that first T? How does *that* fit in?"

"It probably stands for Tuesday, the day she was scheduled to teach the music class."

"One more thing. What led you to believe Eileen Jenns might be in danger tonight?"

"The bedroom windows of both girls' apartments look out on a back alley where the building's rubbish cans are kept. Rubbish is collected on Mondays and Thursdays in that part of town, according to the commissioner of sanitation. What would be more natural than for MacDonald to be out there, making sure everything was ready for pickup? I imagine that, if the girls were a little careless about pulling down their shades, he might have seen enough to arouse him."

"That all hangs together, all right. Only how come Shirley Capehart was killed in the morning and MacDonald came after Eileen Jenns at night?"

"Ah, well, that just shows that—in one regard, at least—Timothy MacDonald is absolutely normal."

"What do you mean?"

"For the Monday collection, he had the choice of getting the cans ready the night before or doing it early in the morning. And like the rest of us, Paul, Timothy MacDonald doesn't like to work on Sunday."

MR. STRANG DISCOVERS A BUG

It was only the end of the third period, but already Mr. Strang knew he was going to have a bad day. An exploding test tube in chemistry class had spattered his shirt, tie, and jacket with a bright red dye that he knew no amount of cleaning would remove. He had unwittingly touched the business end of a fully charged Leyden jar, thus receiving a jolt of electricity that not only numbed his hand but caused his few remaining hairs to stand out from his head in a halo effect that embarrassed him and brought gales of laughter from his students. And the gouramies in the fish tank were all suffering from acute indigestion as the result of a feeding of shavings from the pencil sharpener, administered by someone who preferred to remain anonymous.

But now a free period was coming up, and the old science teacher wanted nothing more than to lie on the couch in the faculty room of Aldershot High School and sip hot coffee. So, when the intercom buzzed as he was about to leave the classroom, it was only with difficulty that he restrained himself from wrenching it from the wall by the roots and dashing it to the floor.

"Guthrey here. Leonard, I wonder if you'd mind dropping by my office this period."

Marvin W. Guthrey, Aldershot's principal, had a habit of summoning teachers to his office without mentioning the purpose of the call. The result was to instill in his faculty a degree of nervousness and insecurity, emotions that Mr. Strang was experiencing as he knocked on the principal's door.

"Come in," called Guthrey. He sat at his huge glass-topped desk, flanked by three telephones on one side and stacks of papers on the other. A balding man in his early fifties, wearing a wrinkled tweed suit, was in the chair reserved for visitors.

"Leonard," said Guthrey, rising, "this is Mr. Wesley Bilik, the head of Bilik Motors, here in town. He's also the president of the Aldershot Chamber of Commerce, and—"

"—and besides that," interrupted the teacher, "he plays a mean game of poker every Thursday evening, but he has a tendency to draw to inside straights." Mr. Strang removed his black-rimmed glasses and winked broadly at Bilik. "Hello, Wes," he smiled.

"Good morning, Leonard." Bilik turned to Guthrey. "Mr. Strang and I already know each other," he said needlessly.

"So I see." Guthrey sat down again. "Then perhaps we can handle this problem in a somewhat less formal manner."

"Problem?" Mr. Strang looked from Guthrey to Bilik and back again. "What problem, Wes?"

"Do you remember coming to see me a couple of weeks ago?" Bilik asked. "We talked about the work-study program here at the high school."

"Of course I remember," said the teacher. "Some of the kids were having trouble in school, and we thought the answer might be to have them attend classes in the morning and work at jobs during the afternoons."

"Yes," said Bilik dryly. "And you asked me to use my connections to see if local businessmen would provide work. If you'll recall, I wasn't too crazy about the idea. I mean, the kind of students who can't make it in school fulltime just didn't seem to be the ones I'd like working for *me*."

"But you did offer to give it a try, Wes. You promised to hire Vince Quale at your place, and, if he worked out, you said you'd recommend the program to the Chamber of Commerce."

"I hired Vince ten days ago," said Bilik. "That's why I'm here."

"I don't understand," said the teacher, his brow wrinkling.

"I had to fire Vince yesterday, Leonard."

"Oh." Mr. Strang nervously polished his glasses on his necktie. "Look, Wes, maybe Vince isn't the brightest kid in the world. It'll take him time to learn what you want him to do. But he'll try, I'm sure of it."

"He's good with cars. That isn't the problem."

"Well, if he's damaged something, I'm sure we could work out a way to pay you for—"

"Dammit, Leonard, *stop*!" Bilik stared at the teacher, his eyes flashing angrily. "What kind of a person do you think I am? I wouldn't fire anyone just because of an accident. But this was deliberate."

"What was deliberate, Wes?"

"He spied on me. Gave out information that was supposed to be confidential. I don't know how much he got paid, but—"

"Wait a minute." Mr. Strang shook his head vehemently. "Vince Quale has his problems with the books, but he's never done a dishonest thing in his life. I'd stake my reputation on that."

"Leonard," said Guthrey in a calm voice, "I think you already have. And the school's reputation, as well. Now, Mr.

Bilik has been kind enough to assure me that he won't go to the newspapers with this, but—"

"—but Vince Quale won't be able to get a job in Aldershot as long as he lives, is that it? Besides which, the entire work-study program will go down the drain, just to save the school a little embarrassment." Mr. Strang's words crackled with disdain. "What is Vince supposed to have done, Wes? Given away national-defense secrets? Did he sneak around with his miniature camera photographing documents?"

"No, Leonard, of course not."

"What did he say when you accused him of this spying business?"

"He denied it, of course. But the whole thing is so clear that—"

"It's not clear to me!" Mr. Strang slipped his glasses on and peered owlishly at Bilik. "Suppose, before we hang the boy, you tell me what happened."

"It was the day before yesterday," Bilik began patiently. "J.J. Calish, my service manager, was with me in my office. We were preparing the bid."

"What bid?"

"Every two years, the Aldershot Police Department solicits bids for new police cars. There are always just two bidders: Bilik Motors, and Halbert Automotive over on the other side of town. Sometimes we get the bid, and sometimes Halbert does. But this year there was more than just police cars involved."

"What's that supposed to mean?" asked Mr. Strang.

"The village Sanitation Department let it be known that they're in the market for new trucks, several of them. And they're going to look pretty closely at the police-car bids to help them decide who they'll get the trucks from. The cars and trucks together could mean a tidy profit for the company that gets the contracts."

"I see," nodded the teacher. "Okay, you and Calish were preparing the bid. What then?"

"We went into the office just before eleven," replied Bilik. "J.J. made a couple of phone calls to the service department and the salesroom to tell them we weren't to be disturbed. Then we sat down at the table to get our figures together."

"So far, Vince hasn't entered the picture at all. Where does he come into it?"

"Around twelve-thirty, J.J. went to the door and shouted at one of the mechanics to send the kid—that's what we call Vince—to the deli for rolls and coffee. Vince was out to lunch, but the mechanic said he'd tell him as soon as he got back."

Bilik leaned forward in his chair and eyed Mr. Strang closely. "Now the time here gets pretty important," he said. "At about one-thirty, we had our figure ready: twenty-two thousand, five hundred dollars. I wrote it down on the work sheet in front of me. It was only a few minutes after that when Vince entered the office with the coffee and rolls. He put 'em down on the table right next to the sheet the bid was written on. He couldn't help but see it."

"So?" shrugged the teacher. "You ordered lunch and he brought it. No crime in that."

"No? We'll see. It took J.J. and me another couple of hours to prepare the bid forms and do the rest of the clerical work. It was after three-thirty when we drove to the village hall to submit the bid. We were just under the wire, because all bids had to be in by four o'clock. The clerk said that Halbert Automotive's man had been there before us— at about three o'clock."

Bilik paused and mopped his brow with a handkerchief. "The bids were opened yesterday," he went on. "Halbert Automotive got the contract for the cars."

"So this year you lost," said Mr. Strang. "I still don't see—"

"Dammit, Leonard, Halbert put in a bid of twenty-two thousand, four hundred and fifty dollars." Bilik gripped the arms of the chair. "On a bid of over twenty thousand dollars, Halbert was just fifty bucks below us."

"Hmm." Mr. Strang scratched an ear with one gnarled finger. "No chance of Halbert's bid being a coincidence, I suppose?"

Bilik shook his head vehemently. "Both Halbert and us," he said, "have always rounded our bids to the nearest hundred dollars. It would be a miracle if, just this once, Halbert decided to go to the nearest fifty. And I don't believe in miracles, Leonard."

The teacher bit his lower lip. "So you contend that Vince saw the bid when he brought in the coffee at about one forty-five. And sometime between then and the time you went to the village hall, he passed the word to Halbert Automotive."

"*Contend* nothing. I *know* that's what happened."

"What makes you so sure?" asked the teacher grimly.

"Because there's no other way it *could* have happened. Only Calish and I knew what our final bid would be. And we were together right up to the time we went to the village hall."

Mr. Strang considered this point. "I don't suppose," he

began hesitantly, "that there's any possibility of a hidden microphone or—"

"Hold on." Bilik waved his hand impatiently. "When I heard about Halbert's bid, I was fit to be tied. But I didn't want to accuse Vince without proof. So I got some experts to examine my office that same afternoon. It cost me a bundle, and they didn't find a thing. No microphones, no wires, no sign that anything had been tampered with."

"What about the possibility of some type of miniature radio gadget? A thing that wouldn't need external wires?"

Bilik turned his thumb downward. "The outer walls and the ceiling of my office are of sheet steel. Radio waves wouldn't broadcast through that, according to the men I hired. They told me flat out that there was no possibility of the office being bugged."

"It sounds open-and-shut to me," said Guthrey, "if we don't get carried away with Mr. Strang's superspy gimmicks. Vince walked in, saw the bid, and told Halbert Automotive."

"And picked up a couple of hundred bucks for doing it, I imagine," added Bilik bitterly.

"But Vincent Quale just isn't the type of boy who'd do a thing like that," said Mr. Strang. "He was very grateful to you for giving him the job. He wouldn't have betrayed you that way."

"You can't explain away the facts," said Bilik.

"Oh, *ciliata!*" snapped the teacher. "Scientists have been 'explaining away' the so-called 'facts' for centuries. Galileo was imprisoned for insisting that the earth goes around the sun when everyone *knew* the opposite was true. And Einstein's theories—"

"Look, I don't want to fight with you, Leonard," interrupted Bilik. "I'll tell you what. Drop by my office when you get a chance. See for yourself that Vince Quale was the only one who could have gotten that bid to Halbert. Then you'll understand why I can't support the work-study program with the Chamber of Commerce."

"I forbid it," said Guthrey. "Leonard, you've embarrassed the school too much already. If this gets to the papers—"

"Done, Wes," said Mr. Strang, ignoring the principal's outburst. "I'll be there after school today. But there's one condition."

"What's that?"

"If I find something that leads to the reasonable conclusion that Vince Quale is innocent, you'll have to rehire him with an apology—*and* endorse the work-study program to the other businessmen."

"Now I see why you play such a mean game of poker,"

grinned Bilik. "Okay, it's a deal." He stood and shook the teacher's hand. "I'll see you later," he added.

It was nearly four o'clock when Mr. Strang pulled his ancient purple car to the curb outside Bilik Motors. The shiny machines in the showroom windows seemed to look down their noses at the dented intruder, as if the teacher's automobile were some kind of disreputable relative they would prefer to disown.

Entering the building, the teacher walked past the salesmen and found Bilik's office.

"C'mon in, Leonard," called Bilik, looking up from his desk.

Once inside, Mr. Strang looked around. The office, illuminated by fluorescent lights, had no windows. One theory shot down.

"Just a minute," said Bilik, drawing the telephone on the desk nearer. "I'll get J.J. Calish in here." He raked at the dial four times with a pudgy finger, and the teacher could hear a buzzing somewhere in the rear of the building.

"Hello, Service Department? That you, Mike? Tell J.J. to come to my office, will you? No, put one of the other men on that job. I want to see J.J. now."

Less than a minute later, the office door was opened by a large man in a gray shirt, with a face that seemed to have been hewn out of a log with a dull ax. There was a smear of grease on one cheekbone. "This is J.J. Calish, my service manager," said Bilik by way of introduction. "J.J, Mr. Strang."

"Yeah," muttered Calish, taking the teacher's hand in his own meaty paw. "Excuse me if I don't do cartwheels at the idea of you being here."

"It's quite understandable," replied Mr. Strang. "After all, I'm here to try and prove Vince Quale didn't reveal your bid, even if he saw it. And if Quale's innocent, it stands to reason that either by chance or on purpose you or Mr. Bilik must have let the cat out of the bag."

"We know where we stand," said Calish. "But the kid did it, no question."

"Perhaps. Was the office in this same condition two days ago, when you were preparing the bid?"

"That's right," said Bilik. "My desk over there. We prepared the bid at this table here. Not a thing has been touched. Hell, I haven't even allowed the ashtrays to be emptied."

Mr. Strang nodded. "And where were you sitting, Wes?"

"Right here." Bilik indicated a chair. "J.J. was there,

across from me."

"I see. Now I assume you were both equipped with pencils and paper. That sort of thing."

"Of course," said Bilik. "But if you're thinking of a note, Leonard—"

"I'm not thinking of anything just yet. I'm simply trying to get a picture of what was going on."

"I didn't do any writing at all," said Calish petulantly. "I just looked up costs for the special equipment on the cars and fed the figures to Mr. Bilik."

"He also smoked almost a full pack of cigarettes and whittled up a length of radiator hose into half-inch slices with a jackknife," smiled Bilik. "One of the hunks started smoldering in the ashtray. Stank to high heaven." He poked among the cigarette butts in the ashtray and pulled out a small black object. It was a hollow cylinder of black rubber nearly an inch in diameter and about half an inch high. He handed it to Mr. Strang.

"Looks like a washer, doesn't it?" said the teacher absently, and dropped it back into the ashtray. "Now, as I understand it, at twelve-thirty you went to the door over there, Mr. Calish, and yelled for one of the mechanics to get Vince."

"I called Harold," said Calish. "He'll remember. He said Vince had gone to lunch. I told him to send the kid out for coffee and rolls when he got back."

"And then what happened?"

"I went back to the table, and Mr. Bilik and I went on working on the bid. We got our final figure at about one-thirty."

"And then Vince came in with the coffee and rolls," added Bilik.

"You're sure he didn't show up until after you'd written down your bid figure?"

"Positive. But what—"

"Did Vince knock before he entered?"

"Yeah, he knocked," said Calish impatiently. "I told him to come in. If that makes me guilty along with him, then I guess I'm guilty."

"Take it easy, J.J.," said Bilik. "Nobody's blaming you for what happened." He turned to the teacher. "J.J.'s been a bundle of nerves for a couple of weeks now. Lots of extra repair work coming in. It gets to you, after a while."

"I'm sure it does," replied Mr. Strang. He walked back to the table. "Vince came over here where you were sitting, is that right?"

"He was standing right beside me," said Bilik. "And there

was the work sheet with the bid written on it. He couldn't help but see it."

"He left the coffee and rolls and took off," added Calish. "He probably realized what he'd seen right away and phoned Halbert as soon as he got out of here."

"Perhaps." Mr. Strang went back to the desk and picked up the receiver of the telephone. "One of your mechanics might have noticed something about Vince when he left here," he said. "Maybe that Harold you spoke about. Can I get your Service Department on this thing, Wes?"

"Just dial 2143," said Bilik. "That's Harold's station. Tell him I said to get in here."

Mr. Strang started to dial. Then he shook his head and pressed down the button in the cradle, cutting off the connection. "It might be better to get Vince himself down here first. Can I call outside?"

"Sure. Just dial 9 first. That bypasses the internal circuits. When you hear the tone, dial whatever number you want."

"I see." The teacher slowly replaced the receiver. "On second thought, I don't believe Vince's presence will be necessary."

"Well, at last," breathed Bilik, "you're beginning to see the light. You're finally willing to admit that Vince Quale was the only one who could have gotten that bid out of here, right?"

"Wrong," said the teacher quietly.

"What?" Bilik slapped his hand against the table impatiently. "Look, Calish and I were never out of each other's sight. And the kid was the only other person to see the bid. How else could the information have gotten out of here?"

"As I suggested this morning, Wes, your office was bugged."

"Like hell it was. The men I hired to look over this place are experts at finding any of that complicated spy equipment."

"There was nothing complicated about it," said the teacher. "It was beautiful and simple, as all truly great swindles are, to quote O. Henry."

"Just say the word, Mr. Bilik," growled Calish, "and I'll toss this little squirt out onto the sidewalk where he belongs."

Bilik held up a restraining hand. "Not yet, J.J.," he said. "I made a deal with Mr. Strang that, if he could prove the bid got out some other way, I'd go along with a program at the high school. Now I'm going to hear him out, even if I still think he's crazy." He walked to the desk and flopped down into the swivel chair. "Okay, Leonard," he said. "Who tipped off the bid?"

"J.J. Calish. Who else?"

"But he couldn't have! I was with him the whole time!" With a great effort, Bilik lowered his voice. "How, Leonard? Tell me *how*."

"Mr. Bilik, are you gonna listen to this sawed-off—"

"Easy, J.J. Let him make a fool of himself, and then you can throw him out. Leonard, the floor is yours," he concluded, the skepticism clear in his voice.

"Very well." Mr. Strang whipped off his black-rimmed glasses and placed them carefully in a jacket pocket. "I first became suspicious when you told me that Calish shouted out the door for a mechanic to get Vince to bring rolls and coffee."

"What's so suspicious about that?" Bilik shot back. "We were hungry."

"I'm sure you were. But there's a telephone on the desk that connects with the Service Department. Wouldn't it have been easier just to dial the extension, rather than getting up and going to the door and yelling?"

Bilik considered this. "Well," he said finally, "I guess so. But it's really not that important, is it?" He spun about to face Calish. "Why didn't you use the phone, J.J.?"

"I dunno. I guess that—"

"I'll tell you why," said the gnomelike little teacher. "He didn't use it because it was already being used—to pick up every word you two said in this office. That's your bug, Wes: the telephone right next to your hand."

Bilik considered the instrument as if it were some loathsome insect. "But it's been examined," he said. "There were no special attachments, and no taps on the line."

"I didn't say anything about special attachments or taps, just the phone itself. An ordinary telephone—a bit old-fashioned, but still in good working condition."

"But—but then *how*?" Bilik demanded. "Neither of us even picked it up after we came in here."

"*Echinodermata!*" snapped the teacher. "Stick to one story. You told me Calish used the phone just after you two entered the office."

"Yeah, that's true," replied Bilik thoughtfully. "He called the Service Department and the salesroom, so we wouldn't be disturbed by the phone's ringing. But we hadn't even started to prepare the bid then."

"Ah, but you don't *know* that he placed calls to the salesroom and the Service Department, do you, Wes? I mean, you weren't listening in on the line or anything."

"I saw him dial, and I assumed—"

"I don't care what you assumed. All you *know* for sure is that Calish dialed four digits and said something into the phone. Then he dialed four more numbers. That's a total of eight times he spun the dial."

"I don't have to listen to any more of this!" roared Calish. "Mr. Bilik, if you want me, I'll be—"

"You'll be right here until I tell you to go," snapped Bilik. "Otherwise, I'll fix it so you can't get a job repairing cars this side of the North Pole. Go on, Leonard. You were saying that Calish dialed eight numbers."

"Correct. Now, let's suppose the first one was a nine." Mr. Strang picked up the telephone receiver, jabbed an index finger into the 9 hole, and spun the dial around to the stop. "Now," he went on, "we dial three other numbers." He did so. "I speak into the mouthpiece, just as Calish did. But listen, Wes." He held the receiver to Bilik's ear.

"Nothing but a buzzing," said Bilik in surprise.

"That's because the call isn't yet complete." Mr. Strang dialed four more numbers. "What do you hear now?" he asked.

There was the sound of a ringing bell at the other end of the line, and then a woman's voice: "At the tone, the time will be four fifty-one and twenty seconds." A beep. "At the tone, the time will be four fifty-one and twenty-five seconds."

"So Calish dialed an outside call," said Bilik. "But, Leonard, how did he keep the line open? I mean, I'd have noticed if the receiver were off the hook all that time."

Mr. Strang put the receiver on the desk blotter and went to the table. He fished around in the overflowing ashtray and finally found the short piece of radiator tube.

"This was the gimmick," he said, holding it up with a flourish. "Calish cut a few extra ones while he was in here, just to throw you off the scent in case you found the one he'd brought in with him."

"What are you talking about, Leonard? How could that thing—"

Mr. Strang fitted the circle of tube over the button in the center of the receiver cradle. "You'll note that the tubing now prevents the button from being depressed and breaking the circuit," he said. "Now watch."

He replaced the receiver. Once it was in place, the black tubing was almost invisible. "Listen," said the teacher.

An eerie voice, high-pitched and somewhat metallic, came from the telephone: "At the tone, the time will be four fifty-three exactly."

"Essentially what I'm saying, Wes," concluded Mr. Strang, "is that, from the time Calish put through that call until after you'd finished the figures on the bid—which you must have said aloud at some point—there was an open line from this office to whatever place Calish had phoned. Every word you said in here was transmitted directly to Halbert Automotive. They had their papers all prepared except to insert the actual amount of the bid, so once they found out your figure they were able to beat you to the village hall. And as soon as Calish was sure Halbert had the information they wanted, it wouldn't have been hard for him to remove the tube and break the connection without your noticing it."

"But why?" Bilik turned to his white-faced service manager, who was shaking his head as if to deny the whole thing. "Why did you do it, J.J.?"

"I didn't do nothing," said Calish brazenly. "Yeah, it probably *could* have been done the way this nut of a teacher said. But he can't prove I did any of them things he's talking about. It was the kid, I tell you."

"Wes, you said Calish has been nervous for the last couple of weeks," said Mr. Strang. "I suggest that he's rather deeply in debt, and his creditors are pressing him. A couple of hundred dollars from Halbert for this information would have come in handy."

"That shouldn't be hard to check," said Bilik. "But J.J.'s got a point, Leonard. You've shown me that he *could* have done it this way. But that doesn't prove he *did* do it. Right now, I don't know who the guilty party is—Vince or J.J."

"Who takes over as service manager when Calish isn't around?" asked Mr. Strang. "The one who'd cover the telephone in the service area?"

"Manny Bates, a good mechanic."

"Get him in here."

Bilik dialed the phone and asked for Bates. In a few moments, there was a knock at the door, and Bates—a small fat man—entered.

"Mr. Bates," said the teacher, "think back to the day before yesterday, when J.J. Calish was in Mr. Bilik's office."

"Yeah?"

"Did Calish call you at any time to tell you he and Mr. Bilik were not to be disturbed?"

The mechanic scratched his head and thought about it. "Gee, I dunno," he said finally. "Maybe yes and maybe no. I forget."

Mr. Strang's face fell, and a smile played about J.J. Calish's lips.

"You see," said the service manager. "You can't prove a thing. It's just your word against—"

"Just one thing, Mr. Bilik," interrupted Bates in a squeaky voice.

"What's that, Manny?"

"Well, I *do* remember that, while you were making out the bid, I tried to call your office several times. Maybe I shouldn't have, but old Mrs. Winter was out there raising the dickens about some repairs we'd done. Nothing would make her happy except talking to you personally. Between eleven and one, I must have dialed your office number at least half a dozen times."

"And?"

"Well, your phone was always tied up. I mean, while you and Calish were in here, that receiver must have been off the hook the whole time."

Bilik looked from Mr. Strang to Calish, who seemed to sink lower in his chair. Finally, Bilik spoke to the teacher in a voice that was soft, almost sad.

"Tell Vince Quale how sorry I am about all this," he said. "No, I'll tell him myself. And I'll tell him he can come back to work here any time he wants to."

MR. STRANG UNDER ARREST

Mr. Strang wriggled about on the hard wooden chair, trying to find a comfortable position. He counted some of the acoustic tiles that made up the walls and ceiling of the small room and then calculated in his head the total number used. With a loud sigh, he began drumming his fingers on the hard surface of the table at which he sat. If only the room had a window, he could at least watch the rain, which he could hear guttering through the downspouts outside the building. But there was no window.

"*Coelenterata*," he growled in annoyance.

It was a Saturday morning, following a week of unrelenting rain in Aldershot. Mr. Strang's high-school students, unable to work off their high spirits outside, had generated a full head of steam and conducted themselves in a manner that might have been suitable to the hordes of Attila the Hun, but which was downright disgraceful in teenagers preparing for midterm examinations. The advent of the weekend found the old teacher exhausted in mind and body, with his aging joints aching from the damp weather. He had looked forward to sleeping late this morning.

But here it was, only a little after nine, and he found himself in an interrogation room at the Third Precinct police station.

The detective who had called on him at Mrs. Mackey's rooming house—a granite block of a man named Walter Fosse—had been unfailingly polite. He'd been sorry to disturb Mr. Strang, but he was conducting an investigation, and he wondered if the teacher would mind coming down to the station house to make a statement concerning his whereabouts between eight and ten the previous evening. Oh, yes, there was one other thing: would he mind driving his own car to the station? He could leave it in the police garage, out of the rain.

His mind still foggy with sleep, Mr. Strang had taken his car to the station, where he'd dictated and then signed a statement to the effect that, until a little before nine the night before, he'd been in the Aldershot Public Library. Then he'd driven home and spent the rest of the evening lying in bed and reading one of the books he'd checked out. Fosse had taken the statement when he'd left the interrogation room, his parting words being that he'd "be back in a few minutes."

The whole procedure had been so foreign to Mr. Strang that not once had he thought to ask what the police were investigating.

"Back in a few minutes, indeed," the teacher muttered waspishly. "It must be at least an hour he's left me here alone." He glanced at his watch. Ten minutes had gone by since Fosse's departure.

He rubbed his hands against his wrinkled jacket to dry the sweat that had suddenly begun to pour from his palms. It wasn't that he was afraid, exactly, but the situation was peculiar, to say the least. In the classroom, he was fully in charge, but a police station was unfamiliar territory. Fosse had his statement, so why couldn't Mr. Strang leave? He was being treated almost as if he were a criminal. Again he dried his hands on his jacket.

The interrogation-room door swung open, and Fosse entered, jerking his thumb toward the hallway outside. "C'mon," he said.

The detective led the little old science teacher along a dirty hallway that had been painted a *mal de mer* green around the turn of the century and into another, larger room that held a long table with three men seated along one side. The ferret-faced one with the gray Vandyke beard was John Kitrich, the manager of Aldershot Home Furnishings, and the redhead with the squinty eyes was Dan MacIver, who worked in the office of the village Sanitation Department. The third—a lanky blond youth with several days' growth of stubble on his chin—was unknown to the teacher.

On the opposite side of the table was a huge man with curly black hair and a full bristling beard that swept in ebony waves about his head and face, giving him the appearance of a satanic Santa Claus. And then, looking around the man's massive body, Mr. Strang caught sight of Detective Paul Roberts.

"Paul!" Mr. Strang felt distinctly relieved. Here at last was a friend, someone who could explain what was going on. "I've never been so glad to see anyone in my life."

"Sit down, Mr. Strang," said Roberts with a smile, motioning to a chair next to Kitrich. "Now that we're all here, I'd like to remind everybody that this is Detective Fosse's case."

"Case? What case?" Kitrich was on his feet, waving a finger at Roberts. "I was called down here to make a statement about where I was yesterday evening. Now that I've made it, I want to go home."

There were murmurs of agreement from MacIver and the other man.

Fosse strode to the head of the table and rapped his knuckles against its surface. The room immediately fell ominously quiet, and the detective quickly made the necessary introductions. The blond young man was Willard Quinn, a bakery-truck driver and sometime college student. The bearded colossus next to Roberts was Victor Wilson, who'd been on duty checking out books at the library the previous evening.

"I'd like to start," said Fosse, peering out from between twin thickets of eyebrows, "by apologizing to three of you four men. You're here needlessly. The trouble is, I don't know which three."

He leaned forward, resting his weight on his slabs of hands. "Right now," he continued, "there's a man named Clifford Berlinger lying in the hospital with a broken jaw, possible skull fracture, three cracked ribs, multiple bruises and contusions—you name it."

"Cliff?" said Mr. Strang involuntarily. "But I saw him just last night at the—"

Fosse nodded. "At the library. I thought you'd know him, Mr. Strang."

"Of course I know him. He's taught American history at the high school for almost as many years as I've been there."

"Do you happen to know what he was doing at the library last night?"

The teacher thought for a moment. "Cliff spends a lot of his spare time writing articles for obscure little history magazines. The one he's researching now is—let me see— 'Southern Colonial Coastal Shipping, 1670 to 1720.' I remember kidding him that he'd probably have a readership of about six."

"So that's why we're here," said MacIver. "We were all at the library last evening."

As Fosse nodded, Quinn shifted in his chair and ran a hand across his unshaved chin. "Man, this is really somethin' else," he said, shaking his head. "Sure, I was in the library. There were at least fifteen people there, so why pick on us four? Maybe we're the only ones who look like we get our kicks out of beating up old men?"

"Berlinger wasn't beaten up." Fosse was visibly restraining himself from launching an attack on Quinn. "It was a hit-and-run, right in the library driveway. Berlinger must have been standing there when the car struck him. He was thrown against the side of the building."

There was a low buzz of voices as the four men absorbed this information. "Mr. Fosse." Dan MacIver's voice had a trace of a Scotsman's burr. "I don't go along with the young man's probable opinion of the police, but his question is a good one. Would you mind telling us why, of all the people in the library, you selected the four of us as suspects?"

"Nothing's been said about suspects, Mr. MacIver. We've just asked for statements from you, that's all."

"D'ye take me for a loony, sir? You didn't draw our names out of a hat. Come now, why *us*?"

Mr. Strang shot to his feet. "Paul," he said, his eyes blazing at the detective seated across from him, "I don't like the way this thing is being handled!"

Fosse started to interrupt, but Roberts waved him to silence. "What do you mean, Mr. Strang?" he asked.

The teacher removed his glasses and placed them in a jacket pocket. "I feel as if I were doing a science experiment with only half the necessary chemicals. First, out of all the people in the library, you choose the four of us to come down and make statements, without a word about what they were for. All right, we've made them. Now you bring us all here together. Why? We're being spoon-fed information a little at a time, Paul, and I don't like it. Either tell us what information you have—all of it—or I, for one am going home."

As he stood looking down at the two detectives, they both began to feel a little like schoolboys who'd just received a scolding.

Fosse's face became fiery red. "I don't have to—"

"Come on, Walt," said Roberts. "He's got a point, admit it. Open up. What's the harm?"

"And while you're at it," added the teacher, "you might tell us what *he's* doing here." He pointed a gaunt finger at Victor Wilson. "He's obviously not a suspect. Wrong side of the table."

Fosse's eyes locked with those of Roberts, and it was Fosse who glanced down first. "Okay," he said finally. "We'd like to wrap this case up quick. We—that is, I—thought we'd get you in here and pick your brains to see if we could come up with something that would throw a little light on what really happened last night. If you have any objections to our handling things this way, you're free to walk out. Officially, we wouldn't question the motives of anyone who did. Unofficially"—he shrugged bulky shoulders—"we'd be forced to draw some unpleasant conclusions."

"I, for one, wish to contact my lawyer before saying another word," said Kitrich.

"That's your privilege," said Roberts. "But remember, Mr. Kitrich, nobody's accused you of anything." A puckish smile came across his face. "Yet," he added.

"As for me," said MacIver, "I'm not guilty of anything, and I'd like to say so out loud. But if you don't mind, Mr. Strang here has a brain that seems a bit more organized than mine. I'll let him do the talking for me."

"Right on, man," said Quinn. He turned to Mr. Strang, holding a clenched fist high. "Go to it, teach. Put the screws to the screws!"

"Okay," said Fosse quickly. "What do you want to know, Mr. Strang?"

"Everything. A friend of mine has been badly injured. That's shock enough for one day. But on top of that, I find myself one of four men suspected of the crime, and I don't mind telling you the situation has me scared stiff. So could you stop being so mysterious and tell us in detail just exactly what we're suspected *of*?"

"Let's take it from the top," said Fosse. He turned toward Victor Wilson. "You want to start?"

Wilson got ponderously to his feet. "I'm new to the village, moved into my sister's house over on Elm Court last Thursday. Maybe one of you know her: Mrs. Zoller?"

MacIver nodded. "The widow lady, spends every Saturday afternoon washing her new sedan. I see her—I live in the same neighborhood."

"At any rate," Wilson went on, "yesterday was my first day on the job as librarian. I closed the place promptly at nine and went out to my car and started the engine. As I drove down the driveway, I thought I spotted something white next to the building. I came very near not stopping. What I mean is, it was only a few minutes' drive to home, and I was tired and wet and all. Oh, dear, I'm making a mess of this, aren't I?" He looked in confusion at Fosse.

"Quite all right," rumbled the detective. "Just tell the story in your own way, Mr. Wilson."

"Well, since the library was in my care, I thought I'd better investigate. That's when I found Mr. Berlinger, lying on the ground next to the driveway. It was his cloth raincoat I'd seen. I tried to get back into the library to call someone, but I'd already set the spring locks and I don't as yet have a key to them. Heavens, the trouble I had finding a telephone at that hour of the night. I finally located an all-night drugstore and called from there. I—I guess that's all, Mr. Fosse."

"Wilson's call came in at nine-thirty," said Fosse. "I called for an ambulance and a patrol car. Then Roberts and me drove to the library. Mr. Wilson had waited for us, but we didn't keep him long, on account of his old sports car has a rip in the canvas top and water was pouring in on him. We checked Berlinger while the attendants were putting him in the ambulance, but if there was any evidence on his clothes it had been washed away by the rain. With the patrol car's spotlight, though, we got a good look at where he'd been lying."

Fosse fished into a pocket and brought out a small envelope, which he proceeded to open. "We found something near the body," he said. "Personally, I don't think it means a thing, but you might think different." He shook out the contents—two small bits of ridged glass.

"These came from an automobile's sealed-beam headlight," he said. "So we figured all we had to do was see which of the people in the library that evening had a car with a busted headlight."

"And?" asked Mr. Strang.

Fosse let out a deep sigh. "We've been working on this thing since ten o'clock last night," he said. "We checked the people who were in the library six ways from Sunday. The cards from the books that were taken out helped there. Finally we got a complete list. Then we went and looked at their cars. Fortunately, most people leave them outside— we only had to wake up a couple of 'em to get into their garages."

Fosse pounded his fist against the table. "Not one of the cars we saw had a busted headlight," he said. "Furthermore, none of 'em had a light replaced recently. So it's my guess the glass had been lying there quite a while and has nothing to do with this case. But we do figure the car that hit Berlinger hit him hard enough to wind up with a dent."

"So that's it." Mr. Strang felt relief flooding through him. "My old car has dents in its fenders."

"Its right front fender, to be exact," said Fosse.

"My jalopy gets creased by a taxi, and right away I'm a criminal," sneered Quinn.

"I told my boy to be careful when he used the car last week," MacIver chimed in. "Wait until he hears the trouble he got me—"

"All right," Fosse interrupted, "now you know. The mechanics and lab technicians down in the garage have been examining your cars while we've been talking with you. I doubt they found anything, or I'd have heard about it by now. So the only thing left to say is that, if one of you is guilty, you'll be doing yourself a favor by telling us now. We might be able to do something about lessening the charge. Maybe you'll get off with only a stiff fine. But if we have to dig up the evidence, we'll see that the guilty party gets the book thrown at him."

The four men looked warily at one another. Mr. Strang could feel sweat coursing down his back.

A uniformed officer escorted the four men to the door of the precinct house. As they left the building and stepped into the rain, Kitrich turned to MacIver. "He had no reason to bring us down here," said Kitrich, his beard quivering in outrage.

"Look, I agree that a dented fender doesn't make one of us guilty," said MacIver. "But they've got to start somewhere."

"But we have our rights as citizens!"

"Hey, man," giggled Quinn, as they headed for the police garage. "Do you suppose them fuzz will ever find out who did it?"

"I assume the police have their own way of answering that question," replied the teacher coldly.

The following Wednesday, Mr. Strang found out what the answer was.

The students and teachers at Aldershot High were buzzing with rumors about Mr. Berlinger's accident and the fact that Mr. Strang was under suspicion of hit-and-run. At the end of the day, after having been asked for the sixth time by Principal Marvin W. Guthrey if he had anything he'd like to get off his chest, Mr. Strang left the building.

Detective Fosse was standing by the teacher's car, waiting for him.

"Good afternoon," said Mr. Strang with a polite nod. "Something I can do for you?"

"Mr. Strang, I'm placing you under arrest on the charge of leaving the scene of an accident. You have the right to remain silent, but if you do choose to—"

As Fosse proceeded with the litany of an arrested man's rights, Mr. Strang shook his head in disbelief. His stomach churned, and for a moment he thought he might be sick. There was an unreal element about it, as if he were observing the arrest of a complete stranger. It was an awful dream, and in a moment he'd wake up. Fosse's final words did awaken him.

"Look, Mr. Strang, I don't want to have to use the handcuffs. It would have a bad effect on the kids. So just get in the car quietly, huh?" On limp legs, Mr. Strang allowed himself to be led to Fosse's car.

Fifteen minutes later, Mr. Strang was in the same interrogation room he had occupied the previous Saturday. He was seated at the table while Fosse and Paul Roberts spoke heatedly in one corner.

"Dammit!" snapped Roberts. "I told you to take it easy on him. He's an old man. Did you have to come on so strong?"

"I tell you, I didn't—"

"It's all right, Paul," said Mr. Strang weakly. "If I could just have a glass of water."

Fosse went for the water as Roberts sat down beside the teacher. "Take it easy, Leonard," said the detective kindly. "Do you want to tell me about it?"

"Paul, I swear there's nothing to tell. Believe me, I don't even know why I'm here."

"Fosse got to speak to Berlinger in the hospital this morning. Oh, hell, I know you're innocent, but—"

He was interrupted by Fosse returning with a glass of water in one hand and a portable tape recorder in the other.

"I guess Roberts told you where I was this morning," said Fosse. "Berlinger's jaw is wired up, so it's hard for him to talk, but I'm sure you'll be interested in what he had to say."

"I've known Mr. Strang a long time," snapped Roberts, "and I won't have him badgered, Fosse. Just play the tape."

Fosse pressed a button, and the recorder's reels began to turn.

"—only a very short visit," came a deep voice from the machine.

And then Fosse's voice: "Fine, Doctor, that's all I'll need."

The reels spun on in silence. Then Fosse was heard again: "Mr. Berlinger? Are you awake?"

Two soft groans might have been an affirmative reply.

"Do you know who it was, Mr. Berlinger? The man who hit you with his car at the library?"

"Yes." It was little more than a whisper.

"Who, Mr. Berlinger? Who was it?"

The reels made two revolutions. Then the weak voice whispered through wired jaws: "Teach…"

A shiver ran up Mr. Strang's spine as the voice trailed off into nothingness.

Fosse reached over and flipped the switch. "Okay," he said, "Paul tells me you're very sharp, Mr. Strang. We got four suspects: a store manager, a man who works in the Sanitation Department, a truck driver"—he paused for effect—"and a teacher. Now, you heard the tape. Who do you think Berlinger was accusing?"

Mr. Strang shook his head and stared at the table.

"Mr. Strang." Fosse spoke in a low, confidential voice. "Like Paul says, you're an old man. We can work something out. I'm sure no judge is going to give a person like you more than a few months. Why don't you just tell us how it happened?"

A few months in prison. And what then? Leave Aldershot—the only home he'd known for most of his life? How could he be expected to command honor and respect from his students after this? He'd be washed up as a teacher, wherever he went. It all seemed so unfair. Mr. Strang knew that he was innocent.

But then why that accusing word on the tape?

"What now, Paul?" Mr. Strang asked in a cracked voice.

"We'll let you phone a lawyer. If you hurry, maybe he can arrange bail before the court closes."

As they left the room, Fosse started to grip Mr. Strang's arm, but Roberts brushed the other detective's hand away. They went out into the hallway, where a plumber was trying to unplug the drain to one of the building's ancient drinking fountains.

Mr. Strang looked at the can of caustic soda in the plumber's hand. The word POISON was printed in big red letters along the side of the can, and something stirred in the teacher's mind.

Trancelike, he walked over and took the can from the plumber's hand.

"Hey," muttered Fosse to Roberts. "You don't think he'd try to swallow—"

But the teacher made no attempt to open the can. Instead, he was peering closely at its label.

"Paul," said Mr. Strang, "may I ask Mr. Fosse a question?"

Roberts looked at Fosse. They both shrugged. "Why not?"

"Tell me, Mr. Fosse, when you visited Cliff—Mr. Berlinger—in his hospital room, did he act at all strange?"

"He didn't act *any* way. In the first place, the doctors had given him something for the pain, so he was groggy. And second, he couldn't hardly move anything but his eyes. And he wasn't even looking at me, just staring through the door of the room."

"*Through* the door? It was open, then?"

"Sure. There's a big poster outside the room, on the opposite wall. It says *Speed Kills*."

"Is that all it says?"

"Yep. Underneath the words, there's this big skull and crossbones, and a hypodermic needle at the bottom."

Mr. Strang could almost hear the wheels whirring in his brain as he tried to remember something he'd heard in a high-school class nearly fifty years ago. And then the wheels stopped.

Jackpot!

"Geez, look at him, Paul," whispered Fosse. "This is really beginning to hit him. He's crying."

Mr. Strang whipped out a red bandanna handkerchief and blew his nose loudly. Waves of relief washed over him, and he longed to set his trembling body into a chair. But this was no time for weakness.

He drew his glasses from his jacket pocket and peered through them at the detectives as he might have regarded a class of students. "Here's what I want you to do," he said imperiously.

"What *you* want?" Fosse's face was starched with surprise. "Hey, you're in custody, mister!"

There was a grin plastered across Roberts' face. If Mr. Strang was acting like a teacher again, the truth was coming. "Shut up and listen, Walt," he said. "You might learn something."

"Mr. Fosse." The science teacher stood poised on a pinnacle of icy dignity. "If you want the person who really ran down Cliff Berlinger, I'll tell you what to do. Listen closely, because I'm not about to repeat myself."

For a moment, Fosse was back at St. William's, preparing to have his knuckles rapped by Sister Anne's ruler. He listened without interruption.

When the teacher finished, Fosse shook his head. "I dunno, Mr. Strang," he said. "It sounds like a mighty long shot to me."

"What have you got to lose by taking a look?" asked Roberts. "And just to make it interesting, I'll bet you a steak dinner Mr. Strang's right and you find it."

In less than forty-five minutes, Detective Fosse returned to the precinct house with a new prisoner in tow. "It's like you have second sight, Mr. Strang," he said in awed tones. "It was all there, the car and everything. He'd put in a new headlight, but I found the old one in the trash. It's down at the lab now, and if the piece of glass we found on the library driveway fits the rest, we've got our man. It's spooky how you knew all about it."

"Hello, Mr. Wilson," said the teacher. "I can't tell you how good it is to see you here."

The librarian mumbled something into his black beard and stared at the floor.

"Go on, Mr. Strang," said Fosse. "Lay out the case against him."

"You haven't got a thing on me," growled Wilson. "Both Roberts and Fosse saw my car at the library that night, and there wasn't a dent or a broken headlight on it."

"Of course there wasn't," replied the teacher. "Because the car they saw was not the car you were in when you hit Cliff Berlinger."

"You're crazy!"

"Come now, Mr. Wilson, the time for dissembling is past. Your car—the one you were in when Mr. Fosse saw you—has a leaky canvas top. It was raining on Saturday, so you must have borrowed your sister's sedan to go to work. But after the borrowed car hit Cliff Berlinger—and before you phoned the police—you drove back to your sister's house and stashed her damaged car in the garage. The trip couldn't have taken more than ten minutes.

"You then drove back to the library in your own car, stopping off at a drug store long enough to phone the police and still return before anyone else got to the library. That's why your call was made at nine-thirty, even though the library closed at nine. And the police never examined your garage for the car they were looking for, because at no time were you under suspicion. On the contrary, *you* were the public-spirited citizen who reported the crime."

Paul Roberts' grin threatened to touch his earlobes. It was good to see the old Mr. Strang back, instead of the pitiful creature the teacher had become during the time he was under arrest.

"I deny the whole thing," Wilson snapped.

"Then how," chided the teacher, "do you explain the broken headlight on your sister's car?"

"Anybody can break a headlight."

"You'll be singing a different tune when the lab matches the bits of glass I found with the headlight in your rubbish can," said Fosse. "And even if they don't, Berlinger's getting better every day. He'll identify you, all right." Fosse turned to the teacher. "Just one thing I don't get, Mr. Strang. How did you know it was Wilson?"

"Cliff Berlinger told me."

"But all he said was 'Teach.'"

Mr. Strang leaned down and picked up a book from the floor. "While you were at Wilson's sister's house, Paul and I got this from the library," he said.

"What is it?"

"One thing at a time. It's pretty obvious from the recording that all Cliff could manage to mumble was a word of one syllable. But he knows me well, and my name's easy to say. So why didn't he simply say Strang?"

"The doc had given him some kind of drug or something."

"Yes, he was certainly in a dazed condition. But he's a

historian, remember? And he had been researching a paper on shipping off the Atlantic and Gulf coasts in the early seventeen hundreds until a few minutes before the car struck him. Add that to his staring at the skull and crossbones on the poster. Don't those clues suggest something to you?"

"Poison, maybe, like on the can the plumber had?" Fosse scratched his head, still puzzled. "Or"—his eyes widened—"or pirates?"

"Go to the head of the class, Mr. Fosse: pirates. The time about which Cliff planned to write was the era of some of the famous buccaneers who plied the southern coastal waters."

"Excuse me, Mr. Strang, but—well, so what?"

"Now think of Cliff lying there outside the library. The driver of the car that struck him gets out. And Cliff sees a man bending over him, a man he'd never seen before that evening, a man whose name he didn't know. Our Mr. Wilson, who'd just moved to Aldershot the day before.

"In the hospital, Cliff could have used an identifying word like 'beard' but that might have implicated innocent people. Remember, Mr. Kitrich has a small beard, and even young Quinn was in need of a shave."

The teacher opened the book in front of him to a marked page. "Cliff wanted to describe a particular man," he went on, "a man who, in the words of an eighteenth-century writer, had a 'large Quantity of Hair which, like a frightful Meteor, covered his whole Face.' Wouldn't you say that was a fairly accurate description of Mr. Wilson?"

Fosse regarded the librarian's bushy black beard and nodded. "But who was that guy writing about?"

"A man who was undoubtedly a central figure in Cliff's article." The little teacher took a breath and lifted a triumphant finger high above his head. "Blackbeard the Pirate!"

"Hold it a minute," said Fosse, shaking his head impatiently. "Berlinger never said anything about Blackbeard."

Without a word, Mr. Strang passed the book to Fosse, pointing to one particular passage.

"Blackbeard the Pirate," Fosse read slowly, "the name given to Edward Teach, born in Bristol, England, died Ocracoke Island, North Carolina, in 1718."

"Once I'd connected Cliff's word 'Teach' with Blackbeard," said Mr. Strang, "the rest was easy. Since there was no damage to the car you saw, there had to be another car. It was a fairly safe bet the other car belonged to Wilson's sister, and he was keeping it out of sight until the case calmed down. It was sure to be at her house—Wilson wouldn't take the risk of hiding it anywhere else."

At that moment, the telephone on the wall behind them rang. Roberts picked it up. After a short conversation, he hung up and turned toward Wilson.

"Yo-ho-ho and a bottle of rum," he said. "C'mon, Blackbeard, Detective Fosse and I are going to book you into a nice jail cell."

"But—"

"That was the lab. The two pieces of glass by Berlinger's body fit the cracked lens of the headlight Fosse found in your sister's rubbish can."

MR. STRANG AND THE CAT LADY

It was a Wednesday in late fall. Fifth period was almost over, and Mr. Strang stood at the window of his classroom. The crumbs of the sandwich that had been his lunch lay unnoticed on his jacket lapels and rumpled necktie. He was speculating on how many more days it would be before the maple trees in front of Aldershot High School would be completely bare of leaves when he felt a tugging at the far reaches of his consciousness. Something odd had happened. Or rather, something had *not* happened, and that was what was odd. But it was several minutes before he realized what it was:

Miss Pinderek had not passed the school on her daily walk to the grocery store.

Until seventeen years earlier, Agnes Pinderek had been a history teacher at Aldershot High. Then, at the age of seventy-two, she had retired—with a minimum of fuss and fanfare—to her little cottage just around the corner. Few of the present staff even knew of Miss Pinderek's existence. But Mr. Strang knew, remembering the advice and encouragement she had showered on him long ago, when he was a young teacher just out of normal school.

He ran gnarled fingers through his sparse crop of gray hair, realizing that, by now, Agnes Pinderek must be almost ninety.

And yet despite her age, Agnes Pinderek walked by the school every day at twelve-fifteen on her way to the grocery store three blocks away. And every day at one o'clock she returned, head erect and spine ramrod straight, clutching a small paper bag as if daring anyone to try to take it from her. Rain, snow, sleet, and hail did not deter her. Through them all, she marched at her appointed times. In retirement, she was the same as she had been in the classroom: proud, punctual, self-sufficient.

But on this day, Miss Pinderek had not appeared.

Mr. Strang decided to pay her a visit as soon as school was over. He knew that this would not please her. While she sometimes returned to Aldershot to see old friends, she was adamant about refusing to allow visitors into her home. "I'm an old lady, Leonard," she had told Mr. Strang on one occasion, when he'd requested the privilege of making a call. "I've worked hard for my privacy, and now I intend to have it. I love chatting with you in your classroom, but my home is not open to visitors."

And that had been that.

Still, Miss Pinderek might be ill, perhaps too ill to summon help. And he might not need to enter her house. If he shouted through the door and received an answer, that would be enough to reassure him.

For the rest of the day, Mr. Strang's classes came and went: chemistry, general science, biology. And through them all, the old teacher couldn't get Miss Pinderek out of his mind. Finally, the school day ended. He placed a sign canceling the meeting of the Science Club on his door, took his key ring to the main office, and left the building as the last of the buses were pulling out of the driveway.

Miss Pinderek's tiny front yard was overrun with ivy that not only choked out the weeds but climbed the clapboard sides of the house, partially obscuring the fact that the structure was badly in need of paint.

Mr. Strang pressed the doorbell. He heard no chime or buzz inside the house. He rapped loudly on the door, his knuckles avoiding the panes of glass, three of which were cracked. The fourth was missing entirely, the opening blocked by a piece of cardboard.

No answer. He knocked again. Then he rattled the doorknob. The door creaked open a scant twelve inches and struck against something.

The teacher pushed his way through the opening. He found himself standing between two towering piles of boxes, one of which had kept the door from opening fully. Beyond the boxes, piles of ancient magazines and newspapers filled the entryway, leaving only a narrow passage through which he walked.

"Agnes? Agnes Pinderek?" he called. The piles of debris muffled the sound of his voice. There was no answer, except for the faint rustling of mice scampering for safety. When he reached the living room, it was there that he found the body.

Even as he absorbed the shock of finding the woman dead, Mr. Strang's brain was considering what must have happened. She had died painfully, horribly. The threadbare rug was pulled and twisted where she had thrashed about on the floor, and an old brass lamp had been toppled, breaking its white glass bowl. Several of the piles of books about the room had been dragged down, and a copy of Charles Dickens' *Bleak House* was lying beneath the body. The old lady's long fingernails had pierced the palms of her hands, silent testimony to the agonies she had suffered.

Someone had to be notified. Mr. Strang looked around for a telephone and found none. He walked toward the rear of the house, shivering uncontrollably. What kind of illness or injury could have caused such suffering?

He found a box of rat poison on a shelf in the kitchen. It was almost empty. In the sink were two white china cups and a teaspoon, all washed clean.

Pale and queasy, Mr. Strang left the house and hurried to the telephone booth on the corner in front of the school. From there, he called the Aldershot Police Department and asked to speak to Detective Paul Roberts.

As if by magic, a crowd collected in front of Miss Pinderek's house on the arrival of the police. A pair of uniformed patrolmen, beefy and poker-faced, was stationed at the front door, and others kept the onlookers behind hastily erected barricades. Official-looking men carrying briefcases, cameras, and bags of investigative equipment moved back and forth between the house and the line of cars parked at the curb. Miss Pinderek's body, covered with a sheet, was brought out on a stretcher to be taken to the morgue for examination.

Paul Roberts came out of the house and beckoned to Mr. Strang, who followed the bulky detective through the crowd to one of the parked cars. As Mr. Strang got in on the passenger's side, he couldn't help thinking how much Agnes Pinderek would have disapproved of all this fuss being made over her. Proudly independent for nearly ninety years, she was receiving in death the sort of attention she had spurned while alive.

Roberts sprawled onto the seat beside him and braced a clipboard against the steering wheel.

"Do you have any idea who did it?" asked the teacher.

"I dunno. She didn't seem to have any enemies, according to the neighbors. She lived a pretty lonely existence, as far as we can make out."

Mr. Strang removed his black-rimmed glasses and rubbed at his eyes. "Paul," he said, "are you sure it's murder? After all, Agnes—Miss Pinderek—was an old lady. Couldn't she have died of natural causes?"

Roberts shook his head. "The police surgeon says it was poison. Arsenic, with all the classic symptoms. She apparently died sometime yesterday afternoon."

"Was it the rat poison I found in her kitchen?"

Roberts shifted the holstered pistol at his hip to a more comfortable position. "That's how we figure it," he said. "A couple of spoonfuls of that stuff would have killed a horse. We tried to lift prints from the box, but the cardboard was so wrinkled and greasy we couldn't get anything worthwhile. The cups and spoon in the sink were clean, too."

"*Two* cups," said Mr. Strang. "So there was probably a visitor. But Agnes never allowed visitors in her house. Not even her closest friends."

"Yeah," Roberts mused. "Well, she had one yesterday."

"Any idea who it could have been?"

"We've got a pretty good—"

Suddenly Roberts clamped his mouth shut and looked at the teacher, shaking his head. "Always want to play detective, don't you?" He grinned. "Suppose I ask the questions and you answer them."

"All right, Paul, fire away."

"Okay, since Miss Pinderek didn't allow visitors, how come *you* were there?"

The teacher told Roberts about the old woman's daily trips to the grocery store.

"But today she didn't go?"

Mr. Strang nodded. "For the first time I know of in years. I came over thinking something might be wrong. But I never suspected—"

"Yeah." Roberts slapped the clipboard onto the seat beside him. He turned the key in the ignition, and the starter whirred. "Let's take a ride. It's not much of a lead, but I'd better follow it up."

"Follow what up, Paul?"

"The grocery store. That would be the supermarket on Ripley, the only one within walking distance. I'd like to know what Miss Pinderek usually bought there."

In the parking lot, Mr. Strang waited in the car. Roberts was gone less than fifteen minutes. When he returned, he shrugged dejectedly. "Cat food," he rumbled, frowning into the rearview mirror. "Damn!"

"What's the matter?"

"The clerks remember her, all right," Roberts replied. "One or two of the older ones used to have her as a teacher. Every day, she comes into the store about twelve-thirty. She picks up a few vegetables, maybe, or a loaf of day-old bread on sale. But there's one thing she buys every day: a can of Tabby-Yum cat food, tuna flavor."

"Well, that's innocent enough," said the teacher. "I doubt anyone would murder Miss Pinderek just because she kept a cat."

"Right, but tell me this: what *happened* to the cat?"

"I beg your pardon?"

"About thirty men have gone through Miss Pinderek's home with a fine-tooth comb this afternoon, and there's no sign of any cat."

"Perhaps it ran away."

Roberts shook his head. "No way, Mr. Strang. I know cats—we've got two of 'em at home. They tend to hang around wherever they're used to getting chow."

"Maybe it's at a neighbor's house."

Roberts rubbed his chin thoughtfully. "Could be. But you'd think we'd have found a food dish or a litter box— *something* to show a cat lives there."

"Paul, are you saying the murderer *took* the cat?"

"That would explain why it's missing. If the killer was after the cat, and if Miss Pinderek caught him—"

"Then what?" Mr. Strang shook his head. "I doubt she'd have offered him a cup of tea."

"That's true. But how's this: Miss Pinderek's visitor is let in. She offers him something—tea, probably. The visitor spikes Miss Pinderek's cup with the rat poison. She drinks it and dies. Then the killer takes away the cat and all its equipment. How does that grab you?"

"Frankly, Paul," said Mr. Strang, "it leaves me with a good many unanswered questions. Why, for example, did Agnes allow this one person in, when she'd been keeping all visitors *out* for years? And why did the killer choose a slow-acting poison like arsenic? And why was the cat taken away at all?"

"This is a weird one, all right," said Roberts, with a shake of the head. "The whole thing's crazy. No motive. A stolen cat. If we're dealing with a maniac, he's going to be devilishly hard to locate."

"But you do have another lead, don't you?" Mr. Strang regarded the detective with an owlish stare.

"Like I said, that's police business," said Roberts, starting the car. "You stick to teaching school. C'mon, I'll take you home."

It was two days later, on Friday evening, when Roberts called on Mr. Strang at the teacher's room in Mrs. Mackey's boarding house. Mr. Strang offered a chair, which was accepted, and a brandy, which was refused.

"I gotta have your help on the Pinderek case," said the detective reluctantly.

"Why, I wouldn't *think* of meddling in police business," said Mr. Strang, a smile playing across his lips. "I'm just a schoolteacher, remember?"

"Okay, so I shot my mouth off," said Roberts, "and I apologize. Seems like everybody in Aldershot knew of Miss Pinderek, and they're demanding action on her murder. The chief's been catching all kinds of flak, and he's given me twenty-four hours to come up with an answer."

"How can I help?" Mr. Strang asked.

"Do you know a kid named Gary Eklund?"

Mr. Strang stared intently at Roberts. "What's Gary got to do with it?"

"I just want to talk with him, that's all. If I drop by his house by myself, though, the whole family's going to get excited—a detective questioning their son and all that. But I understand Gary's in one of your classes."

Mr. Strang nodded.

"Well, that's the answer, then," said Roberts. "You come with me. You're his teacher. He'll be more open with you."

Mr. Strang shook his head. "Gary lives with his mother, Paul. His father's been dead less than a year. I'm not about to use my position as Gary's teacher to make him say things he wouldn't otherwise discuss with a detective. You'll have to do your own dirty work."

Roberts got up and jammed his hat onto his head. "I thought it would be easier this way, that's all. I guess I'll just have to pull the kid in for questioning."

He was almost to the door when Mr. Strang stopped him. "Wait, Paul. You must have some evidence against Gary. Tell me what it is. If what you've got is legitimate—if you're not just on a fishing expedition—I'll help you. I'm afraid of how Gary's mother would react to his being arrested."

Roberts came back into the room and sat down again. "Evidence," he said. "Yeah, we've got evidence. Apparently Gary Eklund was the visitor Miss Pinderek had on the day she died."

He took a notebook from his coat pocket, opened it, and removed a small piece of paper. "This," he said, "is a receipt for the school edition of the *Morning Record.* According to what we've found out, Eklund handles the deliveries to Aldershot High. Is that right?"

"Yes, I take the *Record* myself. Seven cents a day, thirty-five cents a week—a special school rate. Gary earns a few dollars distributing the papers to the classrooms."

"But he's not supposed to deliver anywhere except the school," said Roberts. "Correct?"

"Yes, but—"

"Then how come this receipt was found in Miss Pinderek's house? It was under the rug next to the body. It's dated the day of the murder—last Tuesday—and it's got Miss Pinderek's name on it. It's made out for thirty-five cents, and the words *Cancel Subscription* are written across the front of it ... and Gary Eklund's signature is at the bottom."

"Then Gary was in the house the day Agnes was murdered?"

"That's right. And there's another thing: have you noticed Gary's left hand, the last couple of days?"

"His hand? No, I—"

"According to his friends, Mr. Strang, there are scratches across the back of it. Scratches that look like they were made by a cat's claws."

The teacher sat down limply. "But Gary's only a boy."

"I know that. That's why I want you to be the one to ask him about the receipt and the scratches. Hell, I dunno, maybe it was an accident. I'm not out to frame the kid. I just want to know what really happened in Miss Pinderek's house last Tuesday."

"When do you want to see him, Paul?"

"Right away."

"I'll get my coat."

It was nearly eight when Roberts and Mr. Strang arrived at the Eklund house, a small shingled bungalow at the far end of town. Mr. Strang rapped at the door, while Roberts hung back in the shadows.

The door was opened by a frail, gray-haired woman in a faded housedress. "Why, Mr. Strang," she smiled, swinging the door wide. "What a pleasure to see you! Won't you come in?"

Mr. Strang entered the house, followed by Roberts. "We'd like to talk with Gary for a few minutes, Mrs. Eklund, if you don't mind. This is Paul Roberts, a detective with the Aldershot—"

There was a sudden scurrying at the rear of the house and the sound of a door opening and closing. Immediately, Roberts raced out the front door into the darkness.

For a moment, there was only the slap of footsteps circling the house. Then a scuffling sound, followed by a shrill yell. Finally Roberts' loud voice echoed through the evening stillness: "Get up, Gary, and come inside. I don't want to hurt you."

Roberts came back through the front door, almost carrying a youth wearing blue jeans, a flannel shirt, and once-white sneakers.

"Gary! Mr. Strang!" gasped Mrs. Eklund, her eyes wide, the palms of her hands pressed to her face. "What's happening? I don't understand."

"Sit down, Mrs. Eklund, said the teacher softly. "There really isn't any easy way to say this. You see, Detective Roberts believes Gary might know something about Agnes Pinderek's death last Tuesday."

"But—but that's impossible! Gary doesn't—"

"Tell me, Gary," said Roberts, staring down at the boy. "Did you visit Miss Pinderek at any time last Tuesday?"

"I don't have to talk to you." Gary turned uncertainly to the teacher. "Do I, Mr. Strang?"

After a glance at Roberts, Mr. Strang shook his head. He knelt beside the boy's chair. "Gary," he said softly, "I'm on your side. I don't think you did anything wrong."

Slowly, Gary raised his eyes to his mother's worried face. "But I did," he whimpered. "I did do something wrong."

There was a gasp from Mrs. Eklund.

"What was it, Gary?" the teacher asked. "What did you do that was wrong?"

"It was on Tuesday. I sneaked out of school during study hall. See, Miss Pinderek asked me to come to her house. And old Mrs. Lewis never takes attendance in study hall, so I thought nobody would know."

"Why did Miss Pinderek want to see you?"

Gary's mother gripped Roberts' sleeve, and her thin body was trembling.

"She takes the paper, Mr. Strang. I know I'm only supposed to deliver to people at school. But one day last year I saw her in the hall, and she said she'd like to take the paper if it was possible. She seemed real nice, and it was no trouble at all to go over there before homeroom, so I did it. I guess when they find out about this at the *Record*, they'll take my job away."

"So you've been delivering the paper to Miss Pinderek every day, is that it? That's the 'something wrong' you did? And she asked you to stop by on Tuesday so she could pay you?"

"Yes, sir. She owed me for last week. And that's when she said she wanted to cancel the subscription. I made out a receipt, so I'd have a carbon copy for the circulation manager."

"Did you go into the house, Gary?"

The boy nodded. "That was the only time she ever let me inside. It was kind of spooky in there, but she made me a cup of tea. I don't like tea, but she was nice, so I drank it. I didn't want to hurt her feelings."

"Did you see a box of rat poison?" asked the teacher.

Gary stared at him blankly. "I don't know anything about rat poison, Mr. Strang. After we had our tea, she paid me, and I left."

"Is that all?"

"That's all, honest! The next day, I was leaving school when I saw all the police cars by her house. When I got home, I heard on the radio that she'd been—been—"

Roberts tapped Mr. Strang on the shoulder. "That's all fine and dandy," he said. "But what about the scratches on the back of his hand?"

Gary considered his left hand as if seeing the scratches for the first time. "What's he talking about?" he asked Mr. Strang.

"The cat," Roberts said. "What did you do with the cat?"

"What cat?"

"Gary," said the teacher, rising stiffly to his feet. "Detective Roberts wants to know how you got the scratches on your hand. Was it Miss Pinderek's cat that did it?"

"It wasn't *any* cat," said Gary. "It was a girl. We were at the Malt Shop after school on Wednesday. In a booth. I was kind of—you know—playing around a little. She got mad, and she dug her fingernails into my hand. I pulled away, and that's how I got scratched."

"Holy Moses on a bicycle!" Paul Roberts shook his head in disgust. "Where did you dream up *that* fairy tale? If a girl did it, what's her name?"

Tight-lipped, Gary stared at the floor, shaking his head.

"There's no getting a straight answer out of this kid," said Roberts. "And we haven't gotten a single bit of information about the cat. Or the rat poison. Or—"

The teacher sank into a chair, staring at the opposite wall. "Rat poison," he murmured. "*Rat* poison. That's got to be it."

"What's got to be what?" asked the detective.

The teacher rose and faced the little group before him. From a jacket pocket, he took his glasses and began polishing them on his necktie. "Paul," he said, "it's pretty obvious that you think Gary is lying."

"Sure he's lying. How do you explain his taking off as soon as he found out I'm a detective? And what about that business with the girl? He won't give us her name. Why? Because there *wasn't* any girl. I'll grant I haven't figured out his motive yet. But of all the crazy yarns—"

"Paul, I want you to do something for me. It won't be easy, but try your best."

"Anything to get to the bottom of this, Mr. Strang. What is it?"

"I want you to assume for a short while that Gary is telling the absolute truth, and that he has left out nothing of importance."

Roberts stared at the teacher in amazement. "Oh, come on!" he barked, his tone outraged.

"If Gary's telling the truth," Mr. Strang went on calmly, "then he paid Agnes Pinderek a visit but left her alive and well. A day later, however, he finds out that she's been murdered. As perhaps the only visitor Miss Pinderek has had in years, he realizes he'll be the Number One suspect. And then this evening a police detective comes to his home. Would that explain his sudden flight out the back door? Gary tried to escape, not because he was guilty, but because he was afraid *you* thought he was."

"Well, yeah, maybe. But what about the girl scratching him? That's a load of—"

Mr. Strang held up a warning finger. "We're assuming Gary's telling the truth, remember? Now, Paul, when you were a boy, did you ever get fresh with a girl?"

The answer came grudgingly. "Yeah, a couple of times. One of 'em took a good sock at me."

"And would you have been willing to discuss those times with adults, if they'd asked you?"

"Not on your life! I mean—"

"So much for Gary's silence concerning the girl's identity," the teacher said. "Yes, he's afraid. He's afraid he'll lose his paper route because he was doing an old lady a favor by making deliveries to her outside of school. He's afraid he'll be disciplined for cutting school instead of going to study hall. He's afraid you suspect him of a murder he didn't commit. But I'm convinced he's telling the truth. He went to see Miss Pinderek on Tuesday afternoon. He collected what he was owed, gave her a receipt, and left. That's all."

"And what about the cat?" Roberts asked.

"Ah, yes, the elusive cat. I'm glad you brought that up, Paul, because that's what convinced me Gary was *not* lying."

"Where is it, then?" the detective demanded.

"The cat—which you thought must have made the scratches on Gary's hand, and which the killer supposedly did away with—can't be found for the simple reason that *it never existed in the first place!* The fleeing feline is a figment of the imagination, Paul. A phantom."

"But there *had* to be a cat!" exclaimed Roberts.

"Why, Paul? Why? There was no sign of one. No bedding, no food dish—nothing. And, once we eliminate the nonexistent cat from our thinking, Agnes Pinderek's death is much easier to explain."

"Hang on, Mr. Strang." Roberts held up a hand like a student during a class discussion, then furiously jerked it down again. "We know Miss Pinderek bought a can of Tabby-Yum every day. So how can you say she never owned a cat?"

"Because of the rat poison. Why would a woman who kept a cat—a cat big and healthy enough to consume a can of cat food every day—need rat poison? And yet the box was old and stained and nearly empty. Now, not even the most determined poisoner would need an entire box of rat poison. Clearly the poison was there because Miss Pinderek was plagued with rodents. But whoever heard of rat poison being necessary in a home where there's a healthy cat? Therefore, Miss Pinderek did *not* own a cat!"

There was a long silence. From deep in Roberts' throat came a noise like a clogged drain. "Why, I—I—" he stammered.

But Mr. Strang pressed on relentlessly. "Furthermore, when I first entered the house, I distinctly heard mice scurrying. Surely mice wouldn't run about so freely if there was a cat in the house."

"No cat," said Roberts slowly. "Okay, so Gary seems to have been telling the truth. But if Miss Pinderek was all right when he left her house, then what *did* happen? As far as we know, she had no other visitors. Who could have killed her?"

"The only person possible: Agnes Pinderek herself."

"Suicide?" Roberts whispered the word. "But *why*?"

"Paul, I knew Miss Pinderek for several years before her retirement. She was a fiercely independent woman. She told me many times of her dread of one day being forced to accept charity."

Mr. Strang removed a handkerchief from his pocket and blew his nose loudly. "Seventeen years ago, Agnes Pinderek retired. She'd made a few investments and felt that, with the income from them plus what she got from her retirement fund, she'd be able to get along.

"Now, whether the investments went bad or rising prices were more than her fixed income could take, I don't know. But look at her house. It's rundown in a way she'd never have allowed if she had the money for its upkeep. I also imagine you'll find that it's mortgaged to the hilt. She took to saving anything and everything that might one day be turned into cash. She bought stale bread, and she even got the daily newspaper at the school rate to save a few cents a week.

"Paul, the woman was a pauper. But she still wanted to maintain her independence. Therefore, she allowed herself no visitors who might see how badly off she was and take pity on her. Pity was the one emotion she couldn't tolerate.

"And then one day she realized she could go on no longer. It had become impossible for her to support herself.

But accept charity? Never, not Agnes Pinderek. There was, however, another way. A solution that a proud woman of ninety might have found quite acceptable—and certainly, from her point of view, much more honorable than the indignity she would have suffered from accepting public assistance.

"But first her affairs had to be put in order. That involved paying off her debts—including what she owed Gary. She invited him inside. We can only speculate on why she did this, after having kept visitors out for so many years. But he was the last human being she'd ever see, and she even remembered to tell him to cancel the newspaper. At her death, she would leave no loose ends behind.

"After Gary left the house, Agnes made a second cup of tea in the same cup she'd used before and mixed in the arsenic—which is tasteless and easily swallowed. Then she washed the cups and spoon, not to conceal evidence, but simply from force of habit. The cramps and stomach pains didn't come until later."

Mr. Strang rubbed one hand across his eyes, which were glistening wetly.

"You've drawn a helluva lot of conclusions from a box of rat poison and a missing cat," said Roberts. "How can you be so sure that—?"

A tear ran down Mr. Strang's cheek.

"It really *had* to happen like that, didn't it?" murmured Roberts. "I'll run a check on Miss Pinderek's finances, to make sure, but—well, how else could it have been?" With one hand, he rubbed at the back of his neck. "But I still don't understand about the cat food."

"Tabby-Yum costs about a third as much as a can of tuna," said Mr. Strang. "For the past few years, it was the only thing keeping Miss Pinderek alive."

MR. STRANG PICKS UP THE PIECES

It was Mr. Strang's free period. The little old science teacher was at the demonstration table in his classroom, preparing a chemistry experiment and wishing he could grow another pair of arms. If he held the Erlenmeyer flask in place on the ring stand with his left hand, he could insert the rubber stopper with his right. But that meant more than a yard of glass tubing would be projecting horizontally with no support whatsoever.

Flexing his gnarled fingers, he glared at the laboratory equipment. Then he tucked the tubing into his armpit, gripped the flask awkwardly, and—giving a perfect imitation of a man wrestling with a transparent octopus—brought it toward the dangling stopper.

At that moment, there was a knock on the classroom door.

"Oh, *Mastigophora!*" muttered the teacher, laying the apparatus down with a clatter. He walked stiffly to the door and opened it.

The muscular young giant who entered the room wore a conservative gray suit and gripped a briefcase in one hand. He extended the other hand and smiled. "Good morning, sir."

"How are you?" said the teacher, a bit less testily. "And *who* are you? I'm rather busy at the—"

"They told me in the office that I could come right up. I thought you'd remember me."

"Now that you mention it, you do look familiar. But I've had several thousand students over the years."

"Do you recall a time about ten years ago, when someone in your biology class dyed all the hamsters and guinea pigs bright green?"

"Of course I do. I could never prove it, but I always suspected a lad named"—Mr. Strang's memory leaped back, and a grin spread across his face—"Kempel, Brewster Kempel. Welcome back, Brewster."

Brewster Kempel, known during his time at Aldershot High School as "Bruiser," gripped Mr. Strang's arm with a huge paw that in earlier days had hurled footballs and paper wads with equally devastating accuracy. The diminutive teacher had often itched to tan young Kempel's britches. But the lad's infectious grin and outgoing personality made it impossible not to like him.

"Did you ever get the green dye off those animals?"

"I did—at the cost of a good deal of elbow grease. Can I assume that that was a confession?"

"Yes, sir. But I'll remind you that the statute of limitations has run out."

"Ah. I take it, then, that you followed through on your plan to become a lawyer?"

"That's right. Passed my bar exam just a couple of months ago. Matter of fact, the law is why I'm here."

"Oh?" Leonard Strang's eyebrows shot up in the direction of his receding hairline. "Have I done something illegal?"

"Not as far as I know," grinned Kempel. "But I could use a statement from you."

"What kind of statement?"

"Well, I'm with the county's public-defender office. Our job is to assist people who can't afford a lawyer. Right now, I'm on a case that—well, it looks pretty open-and-shut, Mr. Strang. Of course, my client insists he's innocent. I thought that, if I could get one or two people to testify to his good character, that might help him when his trial comes up."

"I'd be glad to help," said the teacher, "if I can. Who's your client?"

"Clifford Whitley."

"I see." Mr. Strang pursed his lips and stared at the floor. "So that's why he's been out of school the last couple of days. I've got to be honest, Bruiser: I don't know how effective I'd be as a character witness for him."

"Tell me, Mr. Strang," said Kempel in a flat voice, "are you shying away from this because Cliff's black?"

The teacher reacted as if he'd been slapped. His eyes flashed, and, when he spoke, his voice was little more than a whisper.

"I think you'd better leave, Brewster," he said. "If you don't know me better than that, I doubt we have anything more to say to each other."

Kempel shifted his weight from one foot to the other, like a boy caught cheating on an exam. "I'm sorry, Mr. Strang. I don't know of anybody who didn't get a square deal in your classes. But this is my first real case, and I want to do as well as I can by Cliff. I just—well, I spoke out of turn, I guess. But why *won't* you go to bat for him? He's a good student, isn't he?"

The teacher nodded. "His tests and homework are quite satisfactory. But he's also extremely militant. That's understandable, up to a point. But he can become violent in reaction to anything he considers an insult. The slightest remark can set him off, and, when that happens, there's no reasoning with him. If he's hurt someone during one of his tantrums, he's got to take what's coming to him. What's right is right, regardless of skin color."

Kempel stared curiously at Mr. Strang. "Who said anything about Cliff hurting anyone?"

"If he needs a lawyer, I assumed—"

A smile crossed the young man's face. "Clifford Whitley's charged with burglary, a smash-and-grab out of a store window. Nobody hurt, nobody even threatened. And Cliff didn't put up any resistance when he was arrested." Kempel jammed his hands into his pockets and rocked back on his heels. "It's improper to jump to conclusions. You taught me that, Mr. Strang."

"A hit, Bruiser, a direct hit. I stand properly rebuked." Mr. Strang sat down at his desk. "Under the circumstances, I'll do everything I can to help. I find it hard to believe that Clifford could be guilty. He might break a few heads over a chance remark, but I don't think he'd ever steal. He has too much pride for that."

"Mr. Strang, you don't even know the facts of the case."

"And you, Bruiser, don't know Clifford Whitley—not the way I do. Before we get to my statement, I want to hear what *did* happen."

"But there isn't—"

"Of course there's time. My next period doesn't start for fifteen minutes. Sit down, please."

Mr. Strang pointed imperiously at a chair, and Kempel slumped into it with a sigh. He took a yellow legal pad from his briefcase and thumbed through its pages.

"It happened Tuesday evening, about seven o'clock. Bainbridge's Jewelry Store, down in the Village. Do you know where it is?"

"Of course," said the teacher. "It's in Peacham Lane, the area they advertise as 'a little bit of Olde London Town.' Pseudo-nineteenth-century architecture, narrow cobblestone streets, and so forth."

"That's the place. The way Louis Bainbridge tells it, he and his clerk, Jerome Osborn, spent about an hour working on inventory after closing the store. Finally, Bainbridge told Osborn to go home. Maybe five minutes after he left, Bainbridge was in the back room when he heard a loud crash in front of the store—and, at the same time, his burglar alarm began bonging. He came out to see what was going on—"

"—and what *was* going on?" asked the teacher.

"The display window in the front of the store had been smashed, and Clifford Whitley was running down Peacham Lane toward Main Street."

"A couple of questions, if you don't mind," said Mr. Strang. "First, I've always understood that jewelry stores have some kind of special glass in their display windows. Devilishly hard to break. What about that?"

"The place was originally a boutique," said Kempel. "The guy who was supposed to move in broke his lease, and Bainbridge took over. He was always 'going to' put in one of those special windows, but he never got around to it. He settled for installing that metal tape around the original windows and wiring it into an alarm system. He thought that would be safe enough for a while."

"I see." Mr. Strang took out his briar pipe and blew into the stem. "Another thing. At seven o'clock, it must have been quite dark in Peacham Lane, even considering the lighted shop windows. How can Bainbridge be so sure Clifford Whitley was the boy he saw running away?"

"Easy," grinned Kempel. "It seems one of the local cops, a man named Joe Bell, drives his patrol car up Peacham Lane every evening at about seven for a look around. He heard the burglar alarm and spotted Cliff right away. Bell didn't have any trouble catching him—Cliff practically ran right into the front end of the patrol car. Before he had time to turn and go the other way, Bell was all over him. Cliff insisted he was just out for a walk and got scared when the window broke, but—" The lawyer shrugged.

Mr. Strang sucked absently at his empty pipe. "I assume there was something missing from Bainbridge's window? Otherwise, the most they'd have on Cliff would be malicious mischief."

"Right. A couple of detectives were sent over and had Bainbridge sort through the stuff in the window. There were all kinds of things on display, from men's watches to gold key chains to who-knows-what. Plus a lot of broken glass. Bainbridge and the detectives went through the whole shebang and discovered there were three engagement rings missing. Good stones in all of them, worth close to four thousand bucks altogether."

"And the rings, of course, were found in Clifford's possession?"

"No," said Kempel. "He was clean when they searched him, and he insists that he doesn't know a thing about the rings. But Detective Roberts figures he must have tossed them away when he saw the police car."

"Wait a minute," interrupted the teacher. "That wouldn't be *Paul* Roberts, would it?"

"Yes, that's him. He's in charge of the case. Do you know him?"

"Quite well. He should be able to help us cut through a lot of red tape, once we begin looking into this."

Kempel was puzzled. "Looking into what, Mr. Strang? All I want from you is to be a character witness for Cliff."

"Bruiser, from what you've told me so far, this case doesn't strike me as being 'open-and-shut.' A window was broken, and a scared boy ran away. There's nothing criminal there."

"But Cliff was the only person near the window when it was broken. It *had* to be him."

"Who says so? According to what you've told me, Bainbridge was in the back of his store when the window was broken."

"Two separate eyewitnesses, that's who says so," said Kempel.

"Oh." The pipe between Mr. Strang's teeth drooped. "And who are these witnesses?"

Kempel flipped through the pages of his legal pad. "The first is Milton Gage, who owns a haberdashery right across the street from Bainbridge's. Gage was working on a window display of his own. When he heard the glass break, he looked up from a jacket he was fitting onto a dummy. There, on the other side of the street, was the smashed window and Clifford Whitley running away."

"And the other witness?"

"Jerome Osborn, Bainbridge's clerk. He must have seen almost the exact same thing Gage did. He was standing right outside Gage's store, in front of Gage's window, reading his paper. Since he'd worked late, he'd phoned for a taxi, and he was waiting for it to pick him up."

"Let me get this straight," said the teacher. "Both men were on the street, directly opposite the jewelry store. Is that right?"

"That's it. In a perfect position to see what happened."

"Yes, but, if what you've told me is true, neither one of them actually saw Clifford break the window."

"Of course they did!" cried Kempel. "I just finished telling you that—"

"You told me," said Mr. Strang, in his most professorial manner, "that at the instant of the crash, Gage was dressing a dummy in his own window and Osborn was reading his paper. Neither man saw the alleged crime itself, just the aftermath: the broken window, and Cliff running away."

"Mr. Strang, be reasonable," said Kempel. "Yes, technically you're correct. But the fact is, *there was nobody else* in Peacham Lane at the time. How could the window have *been* broken, if Cliff didn't do it?"

"Have you considered the possibility of a projectile of some kind, fired or thrown from some vantage point?"

Before Kempel could reply, there was the sound of a bell in the hallway outside, followed by hundreds of shuffling feet. The period was over.

Mr. Strang got up and stuffed his pipe into his pocket. "My chemistry class wouldn't be the best place to continue our discussion, Bruiser," he said. "Tell Detective Roberts we'll be calling on him tomorrow afternoon—about four."

By four-ten the following afternoon, Detective Paul Roberts had a few thousand well-chosen words he felt like using on Brewster Kempel and Mr. Strang—but with a reluctant bow to the squad's public relations, he limited himself to just one:

"No."

"But, Paul," said the teacher, "we just want a few moments to discuss—"

"*No.*"

"If only," Kempel tried, "you'd—"

"*No!*" Roberts shook his head stubbornly. "Kempel, we had a deal. You advise young Whitley to plead guilty, and we'll go as easy on him as we can. Now you want me to help you get Whitley off? I'm not out to railroad anybody, but in this case the prosecution has all the marbles. You've got nothing at all on your side, so why make trouble?"

"I no longer think it's that clear-cut," said Kempel. "Mr. Strang and I talked on our way over here, and he was pretty convincing."

"Yeah, he usually is," grumbled Roberts. "Mr. Strang, we can put Clifford Whitley right next to that window at the exact moment it was broken. Two eyewitnesses right across the street *saw* him there. Now you've suggested the possibility of some kind of object being thrown at the glass from a distance. That's out of the question, and you know it. A bullet would have made a single small hole in the glass, and any object big enough to smash the whole window would have been lying around somewhere for us to find.

"We went over the display case behind the window with a fine-tooth comb while Bainbridge was checking to see what was missing. But there was nothing. And don't give me any jazz about some kind of sonic beam. We considered that possibility—for about fifteen seconds. Setting up a rig like that would have cost more than the whole caper was worth."

"Paul," said the teacher. "If the glass was broken from the inside—"

Roberts shook his head. "Except for a couple of shards on the sidewalk, all the glass fell *into* the display case. The window had to have been hit from outside. And Whitley was the only one who could have done it. The only one. Period."

"But there are still a few things that aren't explained," said Mr. Strang.

"Like what?"

"Like why did Cliff pick up the engagement rings, rather than a watch or a key chain or something more in keeping with a boy's interests?"

"I dunno. Maybe he just took the first things he laid his hands on. Anyway, the rings were a lot more valuable than any of the other stuff."

"Another thing," Kempel cut in. "Cliff's a sharp kid. Why try a stunt like this at the one time of day when a police car could be expected to come by?"

"He didn't know about the car," growled Roberts in annoyance. "Who do you know who checks patrol-car routes and schedules?"

"If I were contemplating a crime," said the teacher, "*I'd* take the trouble to find out about them."

"This wasn't planned ahead of time, Mr. Strang. Whitley saw a chance and took it, that's all."

"But what about those two men across the street, Gage and Osborn? They both heard the crash and looked up. How long would that take? A fraction of a second?"

"I guess so," said Roberts, his patience beginning to wear thin.

"Then how could Clifford possibly have had time to reach into the window after he'd broken it and grab *anything*?"

There was a long moment of silence. Then Roberts slouched lower in his chair and pointed a finger at Kempel. "That question," he said. "That's your case, is it?"

The lawyer nodded.

"Well, lemme tell you something, counselor: time is relative. Maybe Gage and Osborn looked up right away, and maybe they didn't. Maybe they were confused about where the sound came from and spent a couple seconds looking up and down the street. I don't know—but if that's the best you can come up with, take my advice and plead young Whitley guilty. It'll go easier on him if he pleads."

Fifteen minutes later, Brewster Kempel and Mr. Strang were driving back to the teacher's rooming house. "Detective Roberts is right," said the lawyer glumly. "Cliff doesn't have a chance."

"That's why we're going back to my place," said Mr. Strang. "You and I are going to spend the evening figuring out what really happened on Peacham Lane."

Mrs. Mackey, the teacher's landlady, seemed to sense the seriousness of the situation. Usually as garrulous as a stuck phonograph record, she served supper to the two men in Mr. Strang's room without a word.

By eight o'clock, the floor was littered with scraps of paper, each covered with a diagram of Peacham Lane. Arrows and dotted lines were slashed across them, indicating the possible movements of Clifford Whitley, Bainbridge, Osborn, and Gage at the time of the burglary.

By eight-thirty, both men had to admit they were getting nowhere. Devices as varied as boomerangs, gigantic yo-yos, and trained monkeys had all been considered and discarded. The broken window and the theft of the jewelry remained a mystery.

Unless, of course, Clifford Whitley was indeed guilty. Reluctantly, Mr. Strang admitted to himself that that seemed the only logical answer.

At nine o'clock, there was a soft knock at the door. "It's me, Mr. Strang," said Mrs. Mackey, her voice like a breeze from the Lakes of Killarney. "I thought ye might like some coffee."

Mr. Strang took the tray and thanked her. Closing the door with a hip, he offered a cup to Kempel. "There's cream and sugar, if you want it."

Kempel took a large spoonful of sugar from the bowl as Mr. Strang returned to his desk.

"Any new theories?" the teacher asked, sipping from his cup. "Because, if not, I suggest we close down Kempel and Strang, Private Investigators, forthwith. I guess I had Cliff wrong. Much as I hate to admit it, he has to be guilty."

"*Pfoo!*" cried a guttural voice behind him.

"I beg your pardon?"

"Ugh," gasped the lawyer. "This coffee!"

"Mine's all right," said Mr. Strang.

"That's because you take it black. Mine's full of—of *salt.*"

"It can't—" The teacher stopped himself, then nodded. "Actually, it *can.* Mrs. Mackey keeps canisters of salt and sugar next to each other on the bottom shelf in her kitchen. Sometimes she's not too careful which one she picks up. Just last week, she made a similar mistake and served a candied beef stew that had my taste buds begging for mercy. Wait here, and I'll go down and get you some—"

His voice broke off. For a moment, his mouth was just a small round opening between nose and chin. And then a grin spread across the old teacher's face.

"That's it!" he exclaimed.

"What's what?" asked the lawyer, heading for the bathroom to rinse the salt from his mouth.

"The way it was done. The broken window. Oh, what idiots we've been! It's not that the case is too complicated. On the contrary, it was too simple."

"What are you talking about, Mr. Strang?"

"About Clifford Whitley. I didn't *think* I could be that wrong about him. He didn't steal anything. He's taking a hobo's blame, or whatever you call it."

"A bum rap?" suggested Kempel.

"Yes, that's it."

"How do you figure?"

"No time now, Bruiser. Here's what I want you to do. Get in touch with Paul Roberts. Call him at home, if he's not in the squad room." He scribbled words on the back of one of his diagrams. "Give him this."

"And where'll you be?"

"Down on Peacham Lane. Where else?"

Peacham Lane was deserted when Mr. Strang got there. Three streetlamps, designed to look like old-fashioned gaslights, were all that illuminated its length. Fortunately, one was directly across the street from the boarded-up window of the Bainbridge Jewelry Store.

Mr. Strang shivered, only partly because of the cold. The atmosphere of the place was effective, he had to admit that. He half expected Bill Sykes, Abel Magwitch, or some other sinister Dickensian character to emerge from the shadows.

He found what he was looking for at the curb directly in front of Bainbridge's. His gloved hands fumbled for several minutes, but finally he was ready to leave. As he got stiffly to his feet, he heard the grinding rumble of a distinctly modern garbage truck headed in his direction.

When he arrived at Paul Roberts' house, the detective and Kempel were waiting for him. "Can you cut this short, Mr. Strang?" asked the detective. "The news is coming on the tube, and I don't want to miss it."

"As short as you like, Paul. I just want to show you a couple of things and ask if you can arrange a meeting of everyone involved in this case. Tomorrow after school, if that's possible."

"I guess I can manage it, if you've got something really important. What do you want to show me?"

"These." The teacher extended his hands toward the detective.

*

The little interrogation room was jammed almost to overflowing by the time Mr. Strang got there. In one corner, Brewster Kempel was murmuring something to Clifford Whitley and patting the scowling youngster's shoulder. Opposite them, Louis Bainbridge and Jerome Osborn were whispering, waving their arms in broad gestures. At the table in the center of the room, Milton Gage was explaining to Paul Roberts the inconvenience of having to close his store in the middle of the day.

As Mr. Strang entered, Roberts got to his feet. "Glad you got here. I wasn't sure how much longer I could hold 'em without somebody threatening to walk out. I hope you can make good on what you told me last night. I sent a couple of men out, but they haven't phoned in yet."

"Hey, Mr. Strang!" called Clifford. "You the dude what's gonna spring me? Man, I hope so. This cat what they got for my lawyer sure ain't been much good so far."

"If you keep talking like that," replied the teacher, "I might just let them keep you here. Your street vernacular is like something from a bad movie."

"I'm sorry, man—uh, Mr. Strang."

"Well, *I'm* sorry you called this ridiculous meeting," snapped Bainbridge. "I've got a store to run. And it's going to be twice as hard as usual to attract customers with my display window gone. Let's get on with it."

"Very well," said the teacher. He carefully removed his glasses and polished them on his necktie. That finished, he waved them about in his right hand, at the same time inserting his left into a jacket pocket.

"Problem," he began. "How does one break a window and remove some of the most expensive jewelry behind it in the twinkling of an eye, without anyone observing the actual theft?"

"But," Gage began, "we *did* see—"

"No, sir, you did not. The parties involved heard a crash and saw Clifford Whitley running off down the street. But the actual theft of the jewels was not observed."

"So what?" said Osborn. "Did the diamond rings jump out of that broken window by themselves? This young man *has* to be the one who stole them. There's no other way anybody else could have got at them."

"Oh, but that isn't quite true." Mr. Strang turned to Bainbridge. "Is it?"

"Well, I don't see how else—"

"Come now. All those watches and things didn't leap into place through the solid back wall of the display case.

How do you arrange the displays in your window, Mr. Bainbridge?"

"The back of the case opens up inside the store," was the reply. "That's how we get things in there."

"Exactly. And that's the way they were taken out, too."

"Hey, wait a minute." Bainbridge was on his feet, his face a fiery red. "I was inside the store, remember? I'd have seen anyone who—"

"Of course you would—assuming the jewelry was stolen at the time the window was broken. But that wasn't the case. The rings, in fact, had been taken earlier that day. Given the number of items in that window, a few missing pieces wouldn't be noticed, except on close examination."

"I don't like the way this conversation is going," said Bainbridge.

"Neither do I," Osborn chimed in. "Are you saying that Mr. Bainbridge stole his own stuff? For the insurance or something?"

"Certainly not," said the teacher.

"Then—"

"Mr. Bainbridge couldn't have been the thief, Mr. Osborn. Because you were."

Osborn rushed to the table where Paul Roberts was sitting and shouted at the detective. Roberts took it for almost a minute. Finally, he rose—towering over the smaller man—grabbed him by the arm, and half led, half carried him back to his chair.

"Let Mr. Strang have his say," he murmured. "Then, if he's wrong, we can all sit around and tell him he's got rocks in his head. Go on, Mr. Strang."

"Very well. Mr. Osborn here removed the rings during the course of the day—probably while you were out to lunch, Mr. Bainbridge. He simply put them in his pocket, I imagine. However, he knew that they'd eventually be missed. So he developed a plan to make the missing jewelry look like a burglary. All he had to do was break a window."

"Yeah, and that's where your half-baked theory falls apart," snapped Osborn, stabbing a finger in the teacher's direction. "When that window was broken, I was on the other side of the street, right outside the window where Milt here was working. I couldn't have been more than a couple of feet from him."

"That's true, Mr. Strang," said Gage. "Of course, I was busy dressing the dummy, but I'm sure I'd have seen Jerry run across the street and back. When the window shattered, I looked up almost immediately."

"Oh, Mr. Osborn didn't run across the street," Mr.

Strang replied calmly. "He remained right there in front of your store, Mr. Gage."

"Then how could I have broken the window?" Osborn demanded.

"It was easy: you threw something at it."

Osborn stalked over to the detective again. "I'm telling you, Roberts, this—this *schoolteacher* is the one who should be locked up. You were at the store. You and Mr. Bainbridge examined the window. How could I have—?"

"Mr. Gage," interrupted Mr. Strang, "just before you heard the glass break, Osborn was standing right outside your window. And he was doing what?"

"He was reading the newspaper."

"A newspaper that had to have been bought earlier in the day," said the teacher, "because all the stores on Peacham Lane were closed by the time he got out of work."

"Yeah, yeah," said Osborn. "I got the paper at lunchtime. I always do that. So what?"

"But you also purchased something else on your lunch break, didn't you? Something you had wrapped up in that newspaper when you left the store. And then you waited in front of Mr. Gage's haberdashery, knowing he would furnish you with a perfect alibi.

"At last you spotted Clifford Whitley coming toward you on the opposite side of the street. The perfect person to complete your plan. Who'd believe him, no matter how loudly he denied any knowledge of what had happened? As he passed the Bainbridge's window, you took the object from inside your newspaper and hurled it across Peacham Lane, so it crashed through the window of the jewelry store opposite you.

"Mr. Gage didn't see that quick movement of your arm, because he was involved in his work. And the road is so narrow you could hardly have missed. Clifford was startled by the noise and took off. And that's when Officer Bell picked him up."

"Wait a minute," said Bainbridge. "Jerry's been working for me for almost a year. I'm not going to believe he took those rings unless you can do better than this, Mr. Strang. I mean, what could he have thrown across the alley that *nobody could find afterward*?"

"I didn't figure it out until yesterday," replied the teacher. "It was when my landlady made a mistake and brought Bruiser—Mr. Kempel—and me salt for our coffee instead of sugar. Those two substances look so much alike that—well, it's almost impossible to tell them apart just by looking at them."

"What's that got to do with anything?"

Mr. Strang reached into a pocket and took out a piece of paper. "I made a few phone calls during my lunch period today. One of them paid off. I have here a sales slip from the Aldershot Hardware Store. The clerk is ready to swear that Mr. Osborn made the purchase recorded on it."

"What purchase?" Bainbridge demanded.

"One pane of extra-thick glass, twelve inches square."

"Glass? But—"

"Don't you see? Osborn kept the glass inside the newspaper. Then, at the proper moment—as Cliff passed the window—he scaled it across the narrow street in much the same manner that children fling those toys shaped like plastic discs. The glass struck the window and shattered it. At the same time, the piece that Osborn had purchased broke, either when it hit the window or when it fell to the street, leaving fragments of glass that nobody would notice, just more debris to pick up and toss in the trash. Who'd ever go to the trouble of reconstructing a whole window, just to see if there was any extra glass left over? Especially when there was a ready-made suspect right at hand."

"Y'know," said Bainbridge skeptically, "all this sounds fine, Mr. Strang. But it's just a theory. There's no *proof.*"

"There's proof, Mr. Bainbridge," said Roberts. "Last night, Mr. Strang went back to Peacham Lane, and he was lucky. You had a trash can full of broken glass at the curb, but the collection truck hadn't come by yet. He found two pieces of glass. Two special pieces."

"Why special?"

"Because one of 'em's only about two-thirds as thick as the other. It doesn't matter which is which. The fact is, there were *two kinds* of glass in that mess where your window was. But the window itself was one solid piece of glass, so the second kind had to come from somewhere else."

Before Bainbridge could put his next question, a uniformed officer came to the door of the interrogation room and motioned Roberts outside. As he left, Osborn turned to the teacher, a smirk on his face.

"Maybe you think you're going to hang this on me," he sneered. "But I bought that piece of glass to fix one of my fish tanks. Yes, I keep fish as a hobby, anybody in my apartment building will tell you that. So where's your fancy theory now, Mr. Schoolteacher?"

Before Mr. Strang could reply, Roberts was at the door again. He looked at Kempel with a smile. "You and Cliff can go any time you want," he said. "But I think, Mr. Osborn, that you and I had better have a little talk."

"Why?"

"Because on the strength of the difference between those two pieces of glass that Mr. Strang found, I got a judge to issue a warrant to search your apartment. My men have been there since shortly after you left. They found the stolen rings hidden in the gravel at the bottom of one of your fish tanks."

MR. STRANG BATTLES A DEADLINE

It was only eight-thirty in the morning, but already Marvin W. Guthrey, the principal of Aldershot High School, knew it was going to be one of those days. He leaned forward dolefully in his chair and considered the appointment calendar on his desk. Overdue teacher observations to complete, a meeting of the math curriculum committee, a complaint from the art department about the lack of supplies, irate parents to be placated...

Chung, chung, chung, chung, chung. The hands of the clock on the office wall clicked ahead in fits and starts. The clock now read four-eighteen. With a groan of annoyance, Guthrey pressed the intercom button.

Miss Baird, his secretary, came in from the outer office. "Yes, Mr. Guthrey?"

"Joan, you'll have to work the passing bells by hand again today. When's that repairman coming to fix the master clock?"

"He's here now. Almost finished, he says. Would you like to talk to him?"

"No, just tell him to do it *right*. Sheer idiocy, every clock in the building showing a different time."

"Yes, sir. By the way, there are three book salesmen here, and they all insist—"

"Tell them to come back next week—or next year." Guthrey's patience was stretched to the limit. "And get me some coffee like a good girl, huh?"

Joan Baird made a grim face. An ardent Women's Lib advocate, she was angry at being thought of as a "girl" whose job included fetching coffee on demand. Guthrey knew this, but today he didn't give a damn. When *he* suffered, everyone *else* had to suffer, too.

He picked up the top envelope from the morning's stack of mail. Slitting it open, he drew out a typewritten note and read it. Then, in disbelief, he read it a second time.

The minor problems of the day vanished from his mind like snow before a fiery blast. Laying the note on his desk as if it were a poisonous serpent, he punched the outside-line button on his phone. He could feel sweat starting along his spine, and a tic jerked at the corner of one eye.

"Get me the police," he barked. "Hurry!"

The desk sergeant identified himself in a bored voice. But by the time Guthrey finished speaking, he was no longer bored. The call was transferred, and in seconds Chief

Corey Heksher was on the line.

Their conversation lasted less than half a minute. Hanging up the phone, Guthrey got up and marched out to the outer office. Without a word, he gripped the handle of a small red box on the wall.

He pulled it, and there was a crunching of breaking glass, followed immediately by a loud clanging.

In his homeroom on the third floor, Mr. Strang had just finished making a diagonal slash across the date box of one of the attendance cards when the fire alarm bonged. He peered out through black-rimmed glasses at his twenty-eight seniors, who stared back at him expectantly.

"Well, let's get going," he said in a gruff voice. "Two lines down the stairs—and *walk*, don't run. My sciatica's acting up, and I don't want to be trampled."

By the time Mr. Strang's class reached the ground floor, the athletic field behind the school was nearly half-full of students. It was a constant source of wonder to the old teacher that more than two thousand students, all bent on "being independent" and "doing their own thing," could be gotten out of the building in an orderly fashion in less than three minutes. Along the ball field's third-base line, he formed his group into something resembling a straight line and motioned them to sit down.

The last of the students had just cleared the building when the sirens were heard, accompanied by a loud cheering from the teenagers. Something was up, the teacher thought. During practice drills, the connection to the Aldershot Fire Department was disabled. Probably a false alarm—the smoke detectors were particularly sensitive to squirt guns.

Fire trucks careened into the parking lot, firemen climbed down to the pavement—but, to Mr. Strang's astonishment, they made no attempt to enter the school or even unpack any equipment. Instead, they seemed to be waiting for something.

It wasn't long in coming. Another siren, shriller this time, and a police car pulled up alongside the trucks. Its rear door opened, and a man resplendent in a blue uniform with glittering gold braid got out.

The teacher recognized Chief of Police Heksher. His daughter Susan was in Mr. Strang's sophomore biology class. Heksher, the fire chief, and Mr. Guthrey had their heads together.

Half an hour passed. Finally, a fireman with a bullhorn walked over to the athletic field, his black rubber coat flapping against booted legs.

"We're sending everyone home," he announced, his voice electronically amplified. "The buses have been called, and they're parked over on the next block."

"Man, doesn't that frost you?" someone growled. "First time something *good* happens around this place, and we're sent home so we can't see it."

The fireman ignored the comment. "You're to leave the school grounds through the gates in the fence at the back of the field," he went on. "Do not go into the building. Leave the school grounds through the rear gates immediately."

A few students got up reluctantly and headed off. But, despite the fireman's warning, most of them remained where they were. If something was going to happen, they wanted to be in on the action.

Finally, the fireman made a beckoning motion, and the crew of one of the trucks began unloading lengths of hose and fastening them together.

"They're gonna spray us!"

"Damn, I ain't gonna get my threads soaked just to watch a bunch of dumb firemen. Let's go!"

Slowly, like the beginning of an avalanche, small groups and then the entire mass of students headed for the rear gates. Within fifteen minutes, the athletic field was empty, with the exception of a few faculty members. Five minutes later, most of the students were across the street from the high school's main entrance, but by that time Chief Heksher had police lines organized and the building isolated.

"You teachers can take off," said the fireman. "If you've got cars in the parking lot, leave 'em. You can pick 'em up tomorrow."

"Want to tell us what this is all about?" asked football coach Hank Foley.

"Look, fella, I'm just following—"

The fireman paused when a police officer trotted up to him. They held a whispered conversation, and then the fireman turned back to the teachers.

"Is one of you named Strang?" he asked.

Mr. Strang raised his hand.

"Guthrey wants to see you. Go with this officer. The rest of you, clear out, okay?"

Stiffly, Mr. Strang followed the uniformed man to a spot by one of the trucks, where Mr. Guthrey and Chief Heksher were whispering intently.

"This is the teacher I was telling you about," said Guthrey, as Mr. Strang approached.

"Hiya, Leonard," said Heksher.

"Good morning, Corey. What's all the excitement?"

Guthrey and Heksher exchanged glances. Finally, the police chief shrugged. "Might as well tell him, Marvin. He's got to know sooner or later."

"Know what?"

"There's a bomb inside the building."

"In the school?" Then, strangely, the teacher began to chuckle.

"It's not funny, Leonard."

"Oh, come on, Mr. Guthrey. This idiocy's been going on for five years. Somebody calls and says there's a bomb." He turned to Heksher. "At first, we used to take everybody outside, like today. A couple of periods wasted, every time. Finally, we started just ignoring the calls—and nothing's ever happened. After all, any kid with a dime in his pocket can pick up a phone on his lunch hour and—"

"Take a look at this," interrupted Heksher. "Guthrey got it in this morning's mail."

He handed the teacher a sheet of paper. The typing was single-spaced. Mr. Strang perched his black-rimmed glasses on his nose and read:

```
There is a bomb in Aldershot High School. Please
clear the building of all students and staff. The
minutes are clicking away, and at 2:30 it will be
too late. This is not an idle threat, and I have
no wish to take human lives. Act now!
```

"You think this threat is real, then?"

"Leonard," said Heksher, "remember reading a couple of months ago about that church over in East Whorton? The explosion in the steeple that blew off half the roof?"

"Yes, I think so. But—"

"The pastor got a note the morning of the day it happened. He didn't take it seriously. After the explosion, every police department in the county got a copy of it."

He passed the teacher a photostat:

```
I have planted a bomb in your church. Evacuate
everyone — congregation, clergy, and custodians.
As the seconds tick by, 4:15 draws nearer. Please
believe I mean what I say, but I don't wish phys-
ical harm to anyone. Act now!
```

"The letter 'g' in both notes has a little gap in its upper loop," said the chief. "I'm sure they're from the same—"

"Yes, I see," murmured the teacher. "That church was

almost a hundred years old. A pity what happened to it."

"I don't like to think what could have happened to the people inside," replied the chief. "There was a service in progress at four-fifteen. Luckily, the roof timbers didn't give way, and no one was hurt."

"I read of a similar case about a month or so ago," said Mr. Strang. "Iron Wells, the town hall. Do you think that was—?"

Heksher nodded and produced another photostat:

```
A bomb has been placed in the Iron Wells Town
Hall. Everybody must leave — politicians and pub-
lic alike. The hours glide on, and 5:00 will be
here sooner than you think. I am serious about
this; however, I don't want a death on my con-
science. Act now!
```

"That time, the police knew better, and the building was evacuated," said Heksher. "The bomb squad searched the place, couldn't find a thing. But at five o'clock on the nose, *boom!* The blast took off the whole front of the building. Brand-new, it couldn't have been up more than a year or so."

"Okay, I agree that whoever sent this note has to be taken seriously. But why me, Corey? You let all the other teachers go home. Why was I elected to be placed in danger? I don't know much about bombs, but when it comes to being a coward, I'm at the top of the list."

"Because," said Guthrey, "you've taught in this building for longer than anyone else. You've seen it grow from a small school to what it is now. Three separate additions, and you were here while every one of them was built."

"But what's that got to do with—?"

"Everything," said Heksher. "You must know places where a bomb could be concealed that none of us would dream of. You've got to help us find it before it goes off."

Mr. Strang was horrified. "You want me to go back *in* there?"

"Of course not." Heksher reached through the window of his car for the radio microphone. "All right, bring it in," he said.

A moment later, a flatbed truck painted a brilliant red turned into the school driveway. On the rear was mounted what appeared to be a large open container of heavy-gauge steel. The single word DANGER was lettered in black paint on its doors.

"That's Doretti and Simmons," said Heksher, "from the

county bomb squad. I had 'em keep out of sight until we cleared out the kids. We don't want to cause a panic."

The two men who got out of the truck were wearing body protectors, and each carried a metal helmet that was made to cover the entire head, with a single thin slit to see through. The effect was that of a pair of baseball umpires who had decided to take up welding.

"We'll stay right here," said Heksher, after the introductions had been made. "These gentlemen will go inside. I'll be in contact with them by walkie-talkie."

"Better you than me," said Mr. Strang to Doretti. "Going in there would take more nerve than I've got."

"All part of the job, sir."

"The custodial staff is still inside," said Guthrey. "After I called you, I instructed them to search all the lockers and classrooms."

Mr. Strang's eyebrows shot up. "Isn't that dangerous?"

"I don't think so," said Hecksher. "The other two bombs went off at the exact times stated in the notes. Besides, whoever hid the bomb would know that the lockers and classrooms would be the first places we'd look. We're fairly sure he chose a better spot. But we have to know for certain." He turned to Guthrey. "How much longer, Marvin?"

The principal glanced at his watch. "The whole process should take about two hours," he said. "They should be finished in another fifteen minutes or so."

"That'll bring us to about eleven o'clock," said Heksher. He pointed to Doretti and Simmons. "You two had better get busy. How about it, Mr. Strang? Where should they start?"

"One of them might try the boiler room," said the teacher thoughtfully. "It's in the center of the building, in a kind of half basement. The other?" He paused, considering. "The main office and guidance complex, I suppose."

As the two men headed for the building, the side doors were flung wide and a dozen men in gray work clothes burst out with expressions of relief on their faces.

One of them, a huge man with a gap-toothed grin, approached Guthrey. "They's nothin' in the lockers or rooms," he said in a rich drawl. "We hauled out books an' everything. Left it kind o' messy, but we'll clean up tomorra. If they *is* a tomorra."

"Tell your men to go on home," said Guthrey. "They can take the rest of the day off. Oh, and Sackett?"

"Yessir?"

"Tell them I said thanks."

At eleven-thirty, a gravelly voice came over the chief's

walkie-talkie. "This is Sergeant Simmons. You there, Chief?"

"Yeah, Jerry, what have you got?"

"Nothing. Boiler room's clean, unless the bomb's hid inside the plumbing—and the pipes don't look like they've been touched in years."

"How about Doretti?"

"He's done with guidance and the main office. Tell the principal our master keys opened all the file cabinets, but we had to jimmy his desk. Sorry about that. It was all clean."

"Okay, hang on." Heksher turned to the teacher. "Where now, Mr. Strang?"

"Why, I—I don't know. Tell me, how big is the bomb supposed to be? I mean, is it a lump of plastic explosive, or gunpowder poured into a pipe, or—?"

"Dynamite, probably. We found traces of waxed paper and fuller's earth at both the church and the town hall. Four sticks, maybe five."

"What about the detonator?"

"I'd guess electric. With a couple of batteries and a timing device—probably a cheap watch."

"I see. So the whole thing would be about the size of a shoebox?"

"Yeah, that sounds right."

Mr. Strang stared at the ground. "Tell one of your men to check the custodians' tool room, particularly the drums of sweeping compound. They'd hold a bomb easily."

Heksher relayed the instructions. "What about the other man?"

"Send him up to the bell tower. The bomber tried that once, and he might do it again. On the way up the stairs, have him check out the little door on the first landing. There's a tiny room in there where I used to sneak naps." The teacher glanced at Guthrey. "When—uh—I was much younger, of course."

"Of course." Guthrey shook his head in wonder. "I never even knew there *was* such a room," he said to Heksher.

While they waited for the next reports on the search, Mr. Strang sat on the running board of one of the fire engines and looked up at Chief Heksher. "Why?" he asked.

"Why what, Leonard?"

"Why would someone *do* a thing like this? Hide a bomb in a building full of kids, I mean."

"Hard to say. A way to get attention, maybe. My job's to locate the thing—and, of course, to catch the man who hid it, if possible. I'll leave it to the headshrinkers to figure out his motive."

"It's pretty clear the man—assuming it *is* a man—doesn't

want anyone hurt. He's certainly given enough advance warning of his intentions. If he mailed the note yesterday or the day before, he had to know it would be delivered this morning."

"Yeah. And my bet is he's in that crowd beyond the police line right now. He'd want to be on hand when the building blows."

"*When* it blows? You don't sound as if you have much confidence in those men inside."

"I've got plenty of confidence in them," said Heksher. "But there are so many possible hiding places and not enough time to check them all."

As if to underscore Heksher's worry, Sergeant Simmons reported minutes later that both the bell tower and the tool room had been searched without results.

Twelve-thirty.

Over the next hour, the machines in the industrial-arts shops were examined, the gym lockers were searched, and the soft-drink machine in the faculty lounge was dismantled.

Nothing.

"Only one hour to go," said Heksher glumly. "A little less, in fact. I want to pull those men out a few minutes early—can't have them inside when the balloon goes up."

Mr. Strang suggested searching the cafeteria kitchen and the area above the false roof of the gymnasium.

At one fifty-five, both Simmons and Doretti reported no results.

Mr. Strang could feel perspiration soaking his collar.

"What next?" asked Heksher, a desperate tone in his voice.

"Book rooms," snapped the teacher. "Have 'em look in the book-storage rooms. And lavatories. There's one that's sealed shut on the second floor—it's been out of commission since someone pulled the sink away from the wall."

Heksher barked orders into the walkie-talkie. "And if you don't find anything, get out!" he commanded. "Fifteen more minutes is all I can give you. We can't be sure the kook's watch isn't a little fast." He glanced at his own watch for reassurance as the teacher stared at him blankly. "Don't feel bad, Mr. Strang. You did the best you could."

"Something. Something." The teacher pounded the top of his balding head with the knuckles of his right hand. "*Something* in those notes. Let me see them again, please, Corey."

"It's a little late to—"

Mr. Strang snapped his fingers impatiently. "The notes!"

With a shrug, Heksher passed them over.

Two-fifteen.

Two-eighteen.

Hecksher was about to call the men again when Doretti reported in. "Nothing in the johns, Chief."

Immediately after that came a one-word comment from Simmons: "Nothing."

"All right, get to the nearest exit and—"

"No!"

At the shout, Heksher whirled, startled. Mr. Strang was waving the notes triumphantly, looking somewhat like an ecstatic owl.

"It's too late, Leonard," said the chief. "We've got to—"

"No, you haven't! There's one more place to look!"

A voice came from the walkie-talkie: "What's all the shouting?"

"Teacher here thinks he knows where the bomb is. I'll leave it up to you: wanna try?"

A pause.

Then: "Sure, we'll take a chance."

Heksher extended the walkie-talkie to Mr. Strang. "Tell 'em, Leonard," he said. "Tell 'em where the bomb is."

So the little teacher told them.

"Just like he said." Sal Doretti shook his head and looked at the teacher. "A simple rig—we tore out the detonator by hand. The sticks of dynamite are over there in the back of the truck, harmless as a newborn kitten."

"Okay, Mr. Strang," added Simmons, "give. How'd you know where to look?"

"I'll be interested in the answer to that one myself," said Heksher.

"Very well." Mr. Strang whipped off his glasses, jabbing with them to punctuate his remarks. "The three notes were quite similar—as you pointed out, Corey. Corresponding sentences in each gave basically the same information. Each note even has an alliterative phrase in its second sentence: 'congregation, clergy, and custodians,' 'politicians and public,' 'students and staff.' And then of course the identical final sentence: 'Act now!'

"These similarities," the teacher went on, "disguised a single essential *difference* between the notes. A difference I'm sure the writer was quite unaware of."

"Get to the *point*, Leonard," pleaded Guthrey. "What difference?"

"It's in the third sentence. The first note says, 'the seconds tick by.' In the case of the Iron Wells Town Hall: 'the hours glide on.' And today's note tells us that 'the minutes are clicking away.' The conclusion is obvious: whoever planted the bomb has more than a passing interest in *clocks*."

"It's hard to argue with the results," said Doretti skeptically. "When we pried loose the face of the master clock in the main office, there was the dynamite staring us in the face, just like you said, with the batteries and detonator rigged to the clock mechanism itself. But I still don't see how you figured it out from what it said in the notes."

"Come on, Leonard, admit it," Guthrey said. "You got lucky."

"Not at all," said Mr. Strang. "Consider a one-hundred-year-old church. Its clock would either be spring-driven or operated by weights—in any case, a pendulum. On such a clock, wouldn't the time 'tick by'?"

"Yeah," agreed Doretti. "And the new town hall in Iron Wells would have an electric clock in the lobby somewhere, right?"

"Right," nodded the teacher, "with the hours 'gliding on.' However, at Aldershot High School the classroom clocks are tied to what we call a master clock. Every sixty seconds, the minute hand jumps ahead. Accompanied, I might add, by a distinct *click*."

He paused, polished his glasses on his acid-stained necktie, then continued. "The first two explosions occurred inside a church steeple and in front of a public building. I asked myself what those two locations had in common."

"Clocks," admitted Guthrey grudgingly. And then he looked blankly at Chief Heksher. "The repairman," he said. "He was here this morning. Do you think *he*—?"

"We know he did," said Heksher. "At Mr. Strang's suggestion, I had my men out front look for a truck from a clock-repair service. One of 'em spotted it up at the end of the block—with a few leftover sticks of dynamite stashed in the back. Like I figured, the guy had stuck around to get his jollies when the explosion happened. He's in custody now, but it'll be up to the psychiatrists to say if he'll stand trial. It'll take a better man than I am to figure out what's going on inside his head."

As he turned to get into the police car, a bell mounted on the side of the school building rang loudly.

Guthrey glanced at his watch. "Dismissal bell. Right on time, too." The principal smiled sardonically. "Well, at least he managed to get our system working properly," he said.

MR. STRANG ACCEPTS A CHALLENGE

MONDAY: THE CHALLENGE

The twenty-nine students in Mr. Strang's classroom gravely considered the two sentences scrawled across the freshly washed blackboard:

> All A's are C's.
> All B's are C's.

"The apparent conclusion—that all A's are B's—does have a certain allure," he said, "a kind of appealing logic."

Mr. Strang blinked myopically, his wrinkled face resembling that of a good-natured troll. Then he whirled, and his chalk drew a large screeching X through both sentences.

"Of course," he snapped, "it's also dead wrong. Its error can easily be seen by substituting 'teenager' for A, 'ostrich' for B, and 'two-legged' for C in the original premises. Thus, 'All teenagers are two-legged' and 'All ostriches are two-legged,' and therefore 'All teenagers are ostriches.' I doubt you'd accept that conclusion."

"I dunno," guffawed a voice from the back of the room. "Melvin's a teenager, and he *looks* like an ostrich."

Laughter, in which Mr. Strang joined. The student's comment hadn't been spiteful, simply an attempt to inject some humor into a period of intense mental activity.

Mr. Strang's elective course in Logic and the Scientific Method was one of Aldershot High School's most popular classes. It was also one of the most difficult in which to enroll. Those students finally accepted—invariably seniors—had risen to the top of the academic ranks like cream in fresh milk. With these students, a teacher could pull out all the stops and be not so much an instructor as a participant in a free give-and-take of theories and ideas.

The politeness of the members of the class was tempered by their skepticism. They were willing to weigh and consider the most heretical hypotheses, mercilessly rejecting what they believed to be sham, hypocrisy, or incompetence. After each period, Mr. Strang felt exhausted yet exhilarated, somewhat like a runner who has broken the four-minute mile. In Teacher Heaven, *all* classes would be like this one.

"Let us consider, then, the Fallacy of the Undistributed Middle." He drew a large circle on the blackboard, with two smaller circles like staring eyes inside it. "If the large circle represents Category C, and the smaller ones are Categories A and B—"

He paused. In the far corner of the room, three students had their heads together and were whispering earnestly. "We seem to have a rump session over there," said the teacher. "Mr. Cornish, Miss Doyle, Mr. Lockley—what is it?"

There was a moment of embarrassed silence.

Then, "I yield to the gentleman in the maroon sweater," Mr. Strang said. "What's going on, Jerry?"

Jerome Lockley was big, black, and beautiful. As he slowly uncoiled from his seat, it seemed as if he wouldn't stop until his head hit the ceiling. Looking down from a height of over six and a half feet, he bestowed a sly grin on the old science teacher.

"Well, Mr. Strang," Jerry began, "you understand we all dig the way you teach this class. I mean, you keep us hopping, but it's kind of fun, like basketball drills. And you're a right guy, personally. If somebody gets in a little trouble, you try to help out instead of just dropping a dime on him. So I wouldn't want you to take anything I say the wrong way."

"Take *what* the wrong way?"

"Since we've been in this class, we've hypothesized, syllogized, and organized. We've deduced, induced, inferred, and referred. Right?"

"Right, Jerry. That's what the course is all about."

"Yeah, but, the first day, you told us all this logic stuff would help us out in the real world." He jerked a thumb at the window. "Out there, where it's all at. But so far, all we've seen are little X's that are all Y's, and stuff about ostriches, and diagrams like that one on the board."

"We still have nearly seven weeks left in the semester."

Jerry shook his head. "Not good enough, Mr. Strang." He pointed at the boy and girl with whom he had been conferring. "Richie and Alice and me, we'd like to know right *now* if what we've been learning is really gonna help us, or are we just spinning our wheels in here? How about it? Did you mean what you said on the first day, or were you just jiving us?"

"The last part of the semester will be devoted to practical applications. But until you've learned the basic theories—"

"Right on, Mr. Strang, we dig that. But *you* know all those theories, don't you? I mean, *you* could put 'em to use, if you had to?"

"I hope so, Jerry. Although I must admit that emotion tends to—"

"Okay, then, prove it. Prove to us that this logic of yours

really works."

Mr. Strang chuckled, but in his mind there was a twinge of foreboding. "I assume you have a particular test in mind?"

The others in the class looked up expectantly at the tall boy.

Jerry thrust his head forward, daring the old teacher. "We want you to figure out how Simon Winkler was wasted."

Mr. Strang reacted as if a bucket of cold water had been thrown over him. For long seconds he gazed at Jerry Lockley, speechless. "But that happened last summer," he said at last. "And even the police haven't been able to—I mean, there's no evidence, really, that he *was*, uh, 'wasted.' I assume you mean murdered?"

Jerry shrugged. "Come on, man. Them two ladies was standing right there, weren't they? *And* the priest. As for the fuzz, what do they know? They never took this class, did they?"

In a daze, Mr. Strang shook his head.

In the far corner, Richie Cornish tugged at Jerry's sweater. "Sit down," he whispered fiercely. "He's not gonna try it."

"Sure he will," argued Jerry. "Mr. Strang's my main man. And he'll figure it out, too."

"Half a dollar?"

"It's a bet!"

Jerry turned back to the teacher. "Now, you got this deduction thing down pat. And it's not like you've got no facts to go on: that case was on the front page of the papers for weeks, and we all know you got connections with the local cops."

"But I can't just barge in and reopen a police investigation that—"

Jerry cocked his head to one side. "You *can't*, Mr. Strang?" he asked cynically. "Or you *won't*?"

So there it was. The gauntlet had been flung down, the challenge hurled.

The old teacher took a deep breath and sat on his high stool, indecision written across his face.

The twenty-nine students waited for his answer.

"Very well, Jerry," Mr. Strang said at last. "I don't guarantee success, but I'll give it a try."

"Right on, man!" Jerry extended an arm rigidly, his fist clenched.

The bell rang, and the students streamed out of the classroom, the sound of their excitement buzzing in the old teacher's ears. He slumped over the demonstration table, cradling his head in his hands.

"*Vorticella!*" he said harshly. "Leonard Strang, you are a

fool!"

TUESDAY: THE CASE

Detective Paul Roberts stood at the front of the classroom, looking about warily. The kids had been decent enough, so far, but who could tell what they might be plotting? Who in hell *ever* knew what was going on inside kids' heads these days?

The only reason he was here was that he hadn't been alert enough to think of a plausible excuse when Mr. Strang had called him yesterday evening to invite him to come to the classroom and discuss the Winkler case. Oh, sure, he did owe the old teacher a favor—many of them, in fact. But standing here in front of this group of sharp-eyed youngsters ... Roberts envied Mr. Strang his classroom cool.

The old boy had done his homework, right enough. There was Father Raymond Penn over in the corner, the case's only unbiased witness. The young cleric's unkempt hair and bushy beard made him look more like a hippie than a priest, in spite of the black suit and the turned-around collar. Roberts was glad he'd stopped by the precinct's records section to pick up the still-open file on the Winkler case. It wouldn't do to annoy Mr. Strang by showing up unprepared.

He cleared his throat. "Last July twenty-first," he began, "in the Bay Ridge section of Aldershot, Simon Winkler died. The cause of death was a blow to the head—a powerful blow, since not only was the skull shattered but two of the cervical vertebrae were crushed.

"Simon's aunts, Agnes and Lucille Winkler, were within a few feet of him when he died, and they both had every reason to want him dead. And yet it's impossible for either of them to have struck him down. We investigated the idea that the whole thing might have been some kind of freak accident, but that was equally impossible. You see, not only can't we figure out how the fatal blow was landed, but whatever object struck Simon Winkler seems to have disappeared."

The students leaned forward, like bloodhounds on the scent.

"I don't have to worry about withholding information," the detective went on, "because there's nothing to withhold. By the time we're through here today, you'll know as much about the case as I do, and I was the man in charge of it. But the police were really stumped by this one. I guess the newspapers were, too: all over the state, they headlined it 'the weird Winkler death.'"

"That's all right," Jerry Lockley drawled. "Mr. Strang'll figure out what happened, with logic and all that jazz."

Roberts made a wry grin. "Just a word of warning," he said. "Although Lucille Winkler died last month of a stroke at the age of eighty, her older sister Agnes—an invalid in a wheelchair—is still alive in a nursing home. So no rash accusations, okay? The laws concerning slander and defamation of character apply here in your classroom just as much as anywhere else."

"Paul," said Mr. Strang ingenuously, "we merely intend to examine the evidence and see where it leads."

"Oh, sure, Mr. Strang," the detective said, facing the teacher. "Just like you always do."

A loud guffaw came from the back of the classroom, and Roberts returned his attention to the students. "I'll start things off by saying that, when Simon Winkler called on his aunts that day, he was in the process of trying to take their house away from them by some kind of sharp legal ploy. The two old women hated his guts. They made no bones during the investigation about how much they despised their nephew. So Simon's visit was hardly a social call."

He motioned to the priest. "Now I'd like to introduce the man who was actually present in the house at the time of Simon's death. Want to step up here, Father Penn, please?"

Raymond Penn came to the front of the classroom, where he used a finger to hook the white collar tab out of his shirt and undo the top button. To most of the boys, the young priest seemed like a "right guy," and many of the girls found him adorable. He jammed his hands into his pants pockets and looked out at the class as if bewildered by the human condition.

"By the time Lucille Winkler got in touch with me," he began, "Simon had already phoned her more than once. She'd put him off with one excuse after another, but when it became clear that she'd eventually *have* to see him about who really owned the house, she set a date and asked me to be there. She wanted a witness, you see.

"When I arrived at the Winkler house that afternoon, the weather was about as wet as it could be. Rain had been pouring down for the last three days and nights, and the weatherman had predicted more of the same. I banged the knocker on the front door and heard Lucille fumbling with the lock, but, by the time the door opened, my hat was just a mass of soaked cloth.

"Lucille took my hat and raincoat to dry them off at the stove in the kitchen. Since she also had to tend to Agnes in her wheelchair, she left me alone in the living room for quite some time."

He shrugged. "Matter of fact, I read three chapters in a book on fishing that was on the coffee table. I was just thinking about whether I'd spend my next vacation catching bass in Canada or blue marlin off the coast of Mexico when she came back, wheeling Agnes in front of her. She'd been gone about half an hour, I'd say."

Roberts looked significantly at Mr. Strang. Puckishly, the teacher wiggled his fingers.

"We chatted for a while," Penn went on, "mostly about the weather. Lucille prattled about spending most of the previous week, which had been dry, dragging the lawn sprinklers around that big backyard of theirs, but now they had so much rain it was like living under a faucet.

"Finally, Agnes looked out the window. 'I think Simon has arrived, Lucille,' she said. 'We must have some tea.'

"Outside, Simon Winkler was getting out of a cab. From what I could see, he was about fifty or fifty-five years old."

"Fifty-four," Roberts put in.

The priest nodded. "But then I glanced back at Lucille, and she was giving her sister the oddest look. She said 'I'll put the water on' and went out to the kitchen, but she was only gone for a minute or so."

Penn took a deep breath, and his eyes went wide. "Now we come to the part the newspapers called weird. Me, I say it's downright eerie. Just as Lucille came back, there was a loud knocking at the front door, and Simon Winkler was shouting for someone to hurry and open up. 'I'm soaked to the skin!' he yelled. I felt sorry for him, because I'd been through the same thing just an hour before. Lucille was fumbling with the bolt again—she had arthritis in both hands—and I was wishing there was a window in the door so I could at least signal him that we were opening up as fast as we could. And then"—the priest's voice grew low and sonorous—"then there was the sound of a dull *thump* from outside. It was followed by another sound, like something heavy sliding down the length of the door."

The students looked at him in rapt silence. This was what they had been waiting for.

"Seconds later, Lucille got the door open at last. The rain poured in on us, because there was something propping open the outer storm door."

Penn pulled out a handkerchief and mopped his brow. "The thing holding open the storm door," he continued, "was the body of Simon Winkler. He was lying on the front stoop with blood gushing from his head. There were some gardening implements on the stoop—a bushel basket and some other things—and the blood had stained them all red, even in the rain. I was numb, didn't know what to think or do. Finally, I felt for a pulse. There wasn't one. Winkler was dead."

A pencil falling to the floor sounded like a cannon shot.

"Well," said Penn, "I tried to get the women back into the house. But they just stared at the body. I told Lucille to go inside and call the police. Agnes and I remained in the door-way. The rain was coming in, but it seemed obscene just to leave the body there without anyone—I mean—"

He swallowed loudly, mopped his face with the handker-chief, and sagged into a chair.

"What hit him?" asked Richie Cornish.

Roberts got to his feet. "That's what *we'd* like to know, young fella," he said. "It was at this point that the police entered the case. The first patrol car to arrive found Father Penn and Agnes Winkler looking down at the body in the doorway. The officers draped a sheet over the body, though it was immediately soaked with rain and blood."

Roberts drew out a report form from the file folder he was holding and consulted it. "I arrived on the scene at four thirty-five. We ran a grease-pencil outline of the body on the stoop and then had it taken to the morgue. By that time, the door was closed again, but I looked around a bit before I knocked. On one side of the stoop was a bushel basket with a handful of weeds in it and a metal sprinkling can lying on its side. On the other side of the stoop was a shiny new pair of grass shears and a little trowel. And that was all."

The detective's expression was grim, and he stared almost belligerently at the class. "Each of those objects weighed a pound or two at most. Sure, some of 'em could give a man a headache or even knock him out, if they hit him with enough force. And the shears would have made a perfect stabbing weapon, except Winkler wasn't stabbed. His skull was crushed like an eggshell. And, dammit—excuse me, Father—there just wasn't anything around that was heavy enough to have done it. We checked the stoop and walk for loose cement and to see if a part of the wrought-iron railing might have been pulled away. Nothing."

He spread his hands. "There you have it. Oh, sure, we went inside and questioned Lucille, Agnes, and Father Penn—and got the same story you heard just now. I had the house searched, and it was neat as a pin, everything in its place. There was absolutely no indication that anyone else besides the two women might have been living there or hiding there.

"And now," he said, "let's take a look at the scene." The detective nodded at two boys in the back of the room. One of them lowered the window shades, and the other pressed the switch of a slide projector. A shaft of light lanced across the room, and on the screen at the front appeared a picture of an ugly house surrounded by what seemed to be acres of badly kept lawns and gardens.

"The Winkler house," Roberts said. "It's off by itself on a private lane. Hipped roof, with three gables evenly spaced out along its upper section, well back from the eaves. Front door in the center, with a window on either side of it. More windows on the second floor. No fancy woodwork. Just a completely functional house."

"Looks like a big old barn," commented a student.

"It should," Roberts replied. "When Andrew Winkler—Agnes and Lucille's grandfather—had it built, he used the plans of a barn. Andrew was as rich as Midas, but he was too cheap to hire an architect. In fact, the records show that he pulled some kind of financial gimmick, so he didn't have to pay the builder more than *half* of what the job was worth."

Somewhere a student chuckled.

"When Andrew died," Roberts continued, "his son Jacob got the house, and *he* added those three gables. According to the stories, Jake was something of a character: he showed his patriotism by flying a huge American flag he hung from that big pole sticking out from the center gable there, and at the same time increased the family fortune by robbing the government blind back in Roosevelt's day."

"Franklin D.?" said a boy brightly.

"No, Teddy. Anyway, Jacob Winkler had three children: first Agnes and Lucille, and then, much later, a boy who grew up to become Simon's father. When Jacob died, he left the house and grounds to the two women." He paused. "Are you getting all this straight?"

"Yeah, we're right with you," said Jerry Lockley. "But enough history. Let's get back to the good stuff."

"Just a bit more background. It seems that, about a year ago, Simon Winkler discovered a flaw in his aunts' title to the house and property. By that time, the women had gone through nearly all of their inheritance. They lost a bundle in the stock-market crash of 1929, and the house was about all they had left. But Simon saw an opportunity to get it for himself, leaving Lucille and Agnes with nothing. A heartless attitude, of course, but in my business we see this sort of thing all the time.

"Anyway, he wrote to the aunts, outlining his position,

and indicated that, within a short time, he'd be prepared to take them to court over the ownership of the place, unless they could reach some kind of settlement with him."

"And that's what the meeting last July was all about?" asked Alice Doyle.

"That was it. So you see, the women make perfect suspects, as far as motive is concerned. But means and opportunity? No way."

The detective shook his head. "And there you have it: the death of Simon Winkler. Was it a perfect crime? Was it an accident? We just don't know. Frankly, the case seems immune to any logical approach. But I'd be very happy if Mr. Strang could shed any light on it. I don't like cases that remain in our 'Open' file." He chuckled. "And neither does my lieutenant."

Silence. Twenty-nine pairs of eyes looked expectantly at Mr. Strang, who was staring off into space.

"Any questions?" asked Roberts finally.

Jerry Lockley's hand shot up, and Roberts nodded in his direction.

"I been thinking, you know," said Jerry. "Couldn't those ladies have tossed something out the window of that center gable—something heavy? *Whammo*, down it comes on ol' Simon's head. What about that, Mr. Roberts?"

The detective shook his head. "First of all, both women were old and weak. They could hardly have *lifted* a heavy object, much less toss it out a window. And even if one of them could have managed it, the gable is set back from the roof's edge. The distance down from the gable to the eaves is about eight feet. So the object would have either had to punch a hole through the shingles, or roll over the edge and smash the gutter, or else it would have stayed on the roof. Our investigation showed shingles and gutter intact, and nothing on the roof that didn't belong there. Plus, remember, both Agnes and Lucille were at the front door with Father Penn at the moment of death. And finally, any object heavy enough to smash Winkler's skull couldn't have come to rest very far from the body. But we found nothing."

Jerry sank into his seat.

"What if somebody hit Winkler and then ran away?" someone called.

"Uh-uh. A person—especially one carrying off a heavy object—would have left tracks in the soft earth, unless he went straight down the front walk. And that walk's long enough that even an Olympic runner couldn't have gotten away before the door was opened. He would have been seen."

Silence.

"Anything more?" Roberts asked.

"Just one thing, Paul," said Mr. Strang softly.

"Yes?"

"Is there a laundry room on the ground floor of the house?"

Roberts screwed up his face, puzzled. "Yeah," he said, "in the back, right next to the kitchen. A little room with a washer at least fifteen years old. Why?"

"Does the laundry room have an outside window?"

Roberts consulted his folder. "A little one, yeah. But—"

"Thank you, Paul," said the teacher. "Thank you very much."

"Hey," said Jerry Lockley, "you got a handle on this case, Mr. Strang?"

The teacher nodded.

"Well, give!"

Before Mr. Strang could reply, the bell rang.

Over the excited humming of the students as they shoved their way toward the door, Jerry Lockley's voice rang out loudly:

"Well, all *right!*"

WEDNESDAY: THE CONCLUSION

"Glad to see you back, Paul," Mr. Strang began. "I'm just sorry Father Penn couldn't make it." He turned to address the class. "The murder of Simon Winkler—"

"Wait a minute!" the detective called out. "I told you yesterday, without proof you can't accuse—"

"To be sure, but Winkler *was* murdered. By his aunts, of course. The problem is *how* they did it. And I hope to explain that today." He pressed his fingers together thoughtfully. "Agnes and Lucille Winkler were represented to us yesterday as a pair of sweet, frightened, rather doddering octogenarians. And yet their grandfather did a builder out of his rightful payment, their father swindled the government, and their nephew was preparing to take the roof from over their heads through legal chicanery. From one generation to the next, the Winkler family has not only been devious, but completely without scruples. If only from the standpoint of heredity, could we expect any less from the ladies?

"I say no. Their method of murder was not only heartless, as all murders are, it was also devilishly clever, as might be expected from the descendants of Andrew and Jacob Winkler."

"Hardly proof, Mr. Strang," said Roberts. "What about the weapon?"

"Ah, yes, the weapon. I was struck, Paul, by your description of the gardening tools at the front door. Would two women who kept their house 'as neat as a pin'—your words, Paul—have left those objects lying about? I doubt it. Furthermore, you mentioned a *shiny* new pair of grass shears. Shiny, after three days and nights of wet weather? Not a speck of rust on them? Come now.

"No, the tools were put there, probably just before Father Penn's arrival, for one purpose: to camouflage the murder weapon.

"Now what are the requirements for such a weapon? Primarily, it must be heavy—massive, in fact. Therefore, we eliminate the basket, the trowel, and the shears. All too light."

He bent down behind the demonstration table and brought up an object that *bonged* as it hit the table's hard surface.

"A sprinkling can," he said simply. "Borrowed from my landlady—and similar, I daresay, to the one you found, Paul. Weight, perhaps a pound or two. But—"

He moved the can underneath the curved faucet at one end of the table and turned the water on full. In a few seconds, the can was brimming. Mr. Strang hooked a spring scale to the handle and lifted.

"Fourteen pounds," he announced. "A massive club, indeed, a weapon fit for a Samson. That's what struck down Simon Winkler. Heavy and deadly when full"—he emptied the water into the sink and tossed the can into the air—"but light and harmless when empty."

"But—" Roberts began.

"But how was the blow delivered? Jerry Lockley's theory yesterday was close to the mark."

Roberts shook his head. "Mr. Strang, neither of those ladies could toss something that heavy eight feet from the second floor onto—"

"No, Paul. It was eight feet from the gable to the eaves, but that's on a diagonal"—the teacher's finger traced a diagonal line in the air—"down a sloping roof. The actual *horizontal* distance couldn't have been much more than four feet, maybe less."

"Even so, a full can of water thrown *four* feet? By two old women who weren't even upstairs, anyway? What are you trying to give me?"

"You're forgetting something. On that center gable, there was a means to suspend the can beyond the edge of the roof. Think, Paul. All of you, think back to Jacob Winkler. Remember what—"

"The flagpole," cried Jerry Lockley. "Yeah, a can attached to the rope on that flagpole and pulleyed out to clear the roof."

"And since the pole was for a *large* flag, it would be fairly sturdy," nodded the teacher.

Then Jerry shook his head. "No way, Mr. Strang."

"Why not?"

"Look, the can is hanging there, right? Maybe getting full of water from the rain. But you want us to believe it just *happened* to break loose at exactly the right time? I ain't buying that."

"Of course not. You see, when the can was hauled out to the end of the flagpole, it was empty. And the rain was simply a cover for what really happened."

"Huh?"

"What did Lucille Winkler tell Father Penn she'd been doing the week before the rain?"

"Moving lawn sprinklers. So what?"

"So *hoses*," said the teacher. "Think of the lengths of hose required to water that huge yard. Put together, they'd be quite long."

Jerry's finger moved upward and then horizontally, making an inverted L in the air. Then a broad grin split his face. "That's why you asked about the laundry room, ain't it?"

"You mean—?" began Roberts.

Mr. Strang nodded. "Imagine a length of hose attached to a faucet in the laundry room—a faucet that must have been threaded, to accommodate the washing machine, and to which a garden hose could therefore have been attached. Imagine that hose snaked out the laundry window, up the rear of the house, through the upper hallway to the middle gable, and out along the flagpole, with its open end directly over a sprinkling can hanging there."

"I see what you mean," said the detective. "But you still haven't answered the boy's question: how could the can be made to break loose at exactly the right time?"

"As I said earlier, the gardening tools were out of place, considering the weather," Mr. Strang answered. "But there's another incongruous element here, Paul. Do you recall what Father Penn was reading while waiting in the living room for Lucille?"

"A book on fishing. So?"

"In a house inhabited by two aged spinsters? Highly un-likely reading material, wouldn't you say? No, that book was in the house for a specific purpose."

"What purpose?"

"Research. On fishing line."

"Huh?"

"Fishing line," Mr. Strang repeated. "It's the one type of string or cord that's made to extremely close breaking tolerances. That's so that those who catch fish on lighter lines will receive more credit for their skill than those who use heavier tackle. And there's a type of line that will break at a strain of twelve pounds, within an ounce or so. I verified that yesterday after school, with a call to Morey's Sport Shop."

Mr. Strang preened, brushing at the wrinkled lapels of his jacket as if he were wearing regal finery. "In summary, class—and Paul— here's how the murder must have been committed:

"The Winkler women invited Simon to call on a day when heavy rain was a certainty. That morning, Lucille lowered a long length of hose from an upstairs window to the window in the laundry room, and attached one end of the hose to the tap *in* the laundry room. The other end was led to the front center gable, where both hose and sprinkling can were tied to the flagpole rope by the same piece of twelve-pound-test fishing line. This apparatus was hauled out to a point directly above the front stoop. The sheer wall of the house, which left neither Father Penn nor Simon Winkler protected from the pelting rain, also had nothing to divert the can when it fell. I'm sure Lucille must have tested the rig several times over the previous weeks, to get the trajectory exactly right. Just as I'm sure she tested the amount of time it took the can to fill to the point where the line would break.

"On the appointed day, the sisters invite Father Penn—an incorruptible, unimpeachable witness—to visit. Finally, the three of them see Simon arriving. At that point, Agnes suggests tea. Why? As an excuse for her sister to leave the room, of course. Then the sisters had their private little joke."

"What joke?" asked Roberts.

"You'll recall that, as Simon was getting out of his taxi, Father Penn noticed a strange look that passed between the ladies. And then what did Lucille say to Agnes?"

"Why"—Roberts' eyes widened—"she said, 'I'll put the water on.'"

There was a collective gasp from the audience.

"I see you catch my meaning," said the teacher. "On her way to the kitchen, Lucille goes into the laundry room and turns on the tap to a degree determined by earlier practice. As Simon arrives at the door, the can above his head is filling."

"Wouldn't he have seen it hanging there?" asked Roberts.

"Unlikely. In a rainstorm, the tendency is to lower the head into the collar of the coat." Mr. Strang demonstrated. "Inside the front door, Lucille fumbles with the bolt. After all, the timing may not be absolutely perfect. She must wait for the can to drop.

"At length it does, smashing into Simon's skull with almost the force of a cannonball. The can drops to one side, spilling its contents onto the already soaked earth, and lands innocently among the strategically placed garden tools. The hose above snaps back to the roof, and its stream of water sluices across the shingles and into the gutters, joining the torrent rushing down the leaders."

"But weren't those two taking a big chance?" asked Roberts. "I mean, what if Simon had moved just a little bit to one side or the other?"

"Not *too* big a chance," came the reply. "You see, Simon had to open the storm door to get at the knocker. When he heard Lucille fumbling with the lock, it would be instinctive for him to hold the storm door open, so he could get inside in a hurry. At that point, his position would be as predictable as the phases of the moon."

"But wouldn't we have seen that hose draped through the house when we came to investigate?"

"Probably—if it had been left in place. But Lucille went back into the house to call the police. I suspect it was then she turned off the water in the laundry room and disconnected the hose. Then she slipped upstairs, dragged the rest of the hosing through the house, and pushed it out the rear window. Once it fell to the ground out back, it became just an ordinary length of rubber tubing."

The old teacher made a stiff but elegant bow to his class. "Alpha and omega," he said, grinning. "Do any of you have any questions?"

Jerry Lockley whispered, "Pay up, Richie," and that statement was followed by a clinking of coins.

For several moments, Detective Roberts considered Mr. Strang's solution. "It hangs together, I'll say that for it," he finally announced. "Weird, like the papers said, but that *had* to be how it was done. Only—"

"Only what, Paul?"

"How are we going to prove it?"

"Is that really necessary?" Mr. Strang caressed the briar

pipe in his pocket. "With Lucille already dead, and Agnes in a nursing home with little time left—"

"Oh, I wouldn't take any official action. I'd just like to be sure, for my own satisfaction."

"Perhaps you might begin by checking the local sporting and camping stores. Lucille must have purchased that fishing line *somewhere.*"

The detective patted the teacher on the back. "Mr. Strang, you're something else. I don't suppose you'd ever consider taking up police work on a full-time basis?"

"Sorry, Paul. My class and I have an appointment with the Fallacy of the Undistributed Middle." The teacher drew a large circle on the chalkboard, with two smaller circles inside it. "And we're three days late as it is."

MR. STRANG BUYS A BIG H

Marvin W. Guthrey, principal of Aldershot High School, was usually a model of unflustered leadership. But as he headed toward Mr. Strang's science room it was evident that he had lost a large portion of his administrative cool. The degree of his agitation could be ascertained by the fact that he was going up the down stairway.

Nervously, he rapped three times on the glass pane of the classroom's door. Mr. Strang left his students, who were grouped around the demonstration table, and opened the door.

"Leonard," whispered Guthrey. "Down in my office—the police. It's that Detective Roberts and—"

"Paul Roberts is a friend of mine," said the teacher, peering over the tops of his black-rimmed glasses. "I'm sure it's nothing serious."

"I don't know, Leonard. The man with him—a Mr. Warne—is with the government." Guthrey's eyes widened. "The *Federal* government. They're here on official business. They want to see you."

"But what about my class?"

"I'll stay with your class. Just go. I'd like those men out of the building before the dismissal bell rings. Loading the buses in this rain will be problem enough without any additional confusion."

Mr. Strang shrugged. "Whatever you say, Mr. Guthrey. But be sure and put the corpse back in the storage-room freezer before you lock up for the day."

Guthrey paled. "The corpse?"

"Caligula, our white rat. He died last night, and we were doing a dissection to see if we could find the cause. He'll be pretty ripe tomorrow if he isn't kept on ice."

Before Guthrey could reply, the little old science teacher was walking stiffly down the stairs toward the office.

Detective Paul Roberts and a young man, both wearing damp raincoats, were seated at the conference table in Guthrey's office when Mr. Strang entered. Roberts raised his voice over the raindrops pelting against the window.

"Mr. Strang, this is Hal Warne. He's with the FBI."

"Treasury, actually," said Warne leaning across the table to shake the teacher's hand. "Paul here tells me you're not only a good teacher, but you can keep your mouth shut when the situation calls for it."

"I'd like to think I'm reasonably discreet," said the teacher, sliding into a chair. "What's this all about?"

Warne shot a glance at Roberts, then looked back to Mr. Strang. "We—we're really not at liberty to say."

"Isn't that a bit irregular?" asked Mr. Strang. "You call me away from my class, but you won't tell me *why*? So what now? Do we just sit here and stare at each other until the students are dismissed for the day?"

"What Hal's trying to say, Mr. Strang," said Roberts, "is that we want you to do something for us. But we can't tell you the reason. If we do, you'll ask a lot of questions that we can't answer right now."

"Can't or won't?"

Warne looked at Roberts and shrugged.

"Do you want me to do something illegal, Paul?" Mr. Strang asked the detective.

"No, it—well, we just can't talk about it, that's all."

"You've certainly aroused my curiosity. What is it you want?"

"There's a boy here in town. We want you to tutor him in science. Twice a week ought to do it. He's very bright."

"Is he sick? Can't he come to school?"

Warne held up a hand. "No comment," he snapped. "You don't know him, Mr. Strang. He's never been to this school."

Mr. Strang grimaced. "Curiouser and curiouser. May I know his name?"

Roberts and Warne conferred in whispers, and then Warne spoke in a hushed tone. "It's Yanak. David Yanak."

"Yanak," Mr. Strang said thoughtfully. "I remember that name from back in the Sixties, don't I? There was a Yanak who was tried for—"

"We'd rather you wouldn't jump to conclusions, Mr. Strang," Roberts interrupted. "Suppose we forget that the government is asking. Will you do this for me, as a personal favor?"

"Well, Paul, if you put it that way, how can I refuse?"

"When can you start?" asked Warne.

"Right now, if you like. I'll talk with the boy and see what he already knows. How do I get to his house?"

"I'll take you," said Warne. "I'll have my car at the front entrance in ten minutes."

"I'll follow along later," said Roberts. "And, Hal, don't forget the Big H."

"I beg your pardon?" Mr. Strang blinked through his glasses. "The big *what*? Or shouldn't I ask about that, either?"

Roberts grinned. "David Yanak has a craving for junk

food, particularly the Big H, the pride of Harold's Heavenly Hamburgers. It's a glob of ground beef drenched in some kind of sauce and served on a synthetic-tasting bun."

"Plus French fries and milk," added Warne. "We'll pass by Harold's on our way, Mr. Strang. I'll pick the food up then."

But a quarter of an hour later, as Warne circled the block on which Harold's Heavenly Hamburgers had erected its plastic palace, the errand proved more difficult than the government man had expected. The rain had apparently given half the population of Aldershot a yen for a Big H, and there wasn't a parking spot to be found.

"A shame to disappoint the boy," said Mr. Strang. "Why don't you let me go in and get it? You can drive around the block until I come out."

Warne stopped the car. "Okay," he said. "I'll meet you right here."

Within ten minutes, Mr. Strang was back in the car with hamburger, fries, and a carton of milk on a cardboard tray the downpour had soaked.

Warne's car glided through Aldershot's wealthy East End, finally pulling into the curved drive of a Tudor-style mansion set well back from the street and nearly concealed by a towering wall of privet hedge.

"The front door's unlocked," said Warne, stopping the car. "There's a foyer inside. You can wait there, out of the rain. Ring the bell, and someone will open the inner door. I have to put the car away."

The teacher nodded and, gripping the sodden tray in both hands, trotted through the pouring rain, threw open the door, and ducked inside with a sigh of relief.

He found himself as promised in a small entranceway. In front of him, a massive locked door with a peephole barred admission to the house itself. On a side wall, a second door—probably to a coat closet—stood ajar. Opposite it was a table on which sat a deep wicker basket containing quite a lot of mail. Mr. Strang inspected his damp features in the mirror that hung above the table, pressed the bell button, and stood there listening to the drip of water from his raincoat onto the rubber mat on the floor.

There was a click, the door opened, and he was grasped gently by the shoulders. "Your coat, sir," said a voice in a clipped British accent. "I'd be glad to take it."

Mr. Strang allowed his coat to be stripped off—no easy job, since it was soaked through. Finally, he stood with his back to the closet door as the as-yet unseen man held the wet coat inches from the teacher's face.

"It's a bit damp, sir," the man went on, with magnificent understatement. The coat lowered to reveal a jowled face wearing no expression whatsoever. "I am Alston, sir. I manage the affairs of the house."

"I see. A kind of butler?"

"You might use that term, I suppose. And you must be Mr. Strang. Please come in. We're expecting you. I'll see that your coat is dried."

Mr. Strang followed Alston into a living room the size of a basketball court, richly furnished in Oriental style. The soggy cardboard tray was beginning to sag in the middle, and Mr. Strang clutched it tightly.

Before the butler could close the door, Warne darted inside and took off his raincoat. "We'll go right up and meet David," he said, gesturing toward the curving staircase.

At the top of the stairs, the two men walked along a hallway. Where it made a right angle, Mr. Strang noticed that a mirror had been cunningly placed so that it would be impossible for anyone to approach sight unseen.

In front of a door at the far end of the hall stood a mountain of a man whose receding brow and prominent jaw reminded Mr. Strang of the Easter Island monoliths.

"Who's dis?" the giant rumbled in a deep voice.

"Mr. Strang," said Warne. "David's teacher. You were told he was coming."

"Got to frisk him. Boss's orders."

"But you can't—"

Warne sighed his annoyance. "Mr. Danko is on guard here, Mr. Strang. He takes his job very seriously. Suppose you let him search you. That'll make him feel better."

Danko patted the teacher's pockets expertly, made a quick inspection of the cardboard tray, then reluctantly allowed Mr. Strang to enter the room, followed by Warne.

David Yanak was dressed in shorts and reclining under a sunlamp in the corner of his bedroom. On the boy's chest, a tiny white kitten was standing with one paw raised. Scooping up the animal and placing it gently on the floor, David got up and took off his shaded goggles.

Warne performed the introductions.

"Hi, Mr. Strang," the boy smiled. "Thanks for coming. I can use the help, and it'll be good to have somebody to talk with besides Cueball."

"Who?"

"Cueball, my kitten." David pointed to the kitten, who was toying with a tassel on the bedspread. "He's a *lot* more interesting company than Danko."

"I'll leave you two," said Warne. "Let me know when

you're ready to leave, Mr. Strang." He went out, closing the door behind him.

Mr. Strang sat down and took a notebook and pencil from a jacket pocket. "Suppose we get started," he said. "First, I'd like to know—"

"You brought it!" yelled David, noticing the tray of food the teacher had placed on the night table beside the bed. "Thanks!"

He fell on the hamburger like a starving man, emitting little sounds of pleasure between bites. When it was finished, he sucked at the grease on his fingers.

"Suppose you save the rest for later," said Mr. Strang. "Let's get going."

"Sure," said David. "Here, Cueball, how about a little milk?" He opened the carton and poured a generous portion into the kitten's dish. Cueball lapped at it with his tiny pink tongue.

"I've been doing some reading in chemistry already," David said. "Most of it I get, but the chapter on precipitates is—"

He paused, looking strangely at the kitten. Cueball took two tentative steps to one side of the dresser. Then the kitten's head and tail drooped, and it fell to the floor, a tiny mound of white fur.

David went to the kitten and picked it up. He raised the limp paws and examined the closed eyes. Finally he looked at the teacher with a puzzled expression. "It—it's dead, Mr. Strang."

"It can't be. A moment ago, it was frisking about like—"

The teacher picked up the milk dish and sniffed at it. Then he put it on a table with exaggerated care and wiped his hands with a handkerchief. "Prussic acid," he said, almost to himself. "The odor of bitter almonds is quite distinct. It's in the milk."

David's eyes widened with terror. "Danko!" he screamed. "Help! He tried to kill me!"

The door banged against the wall as Danko stormed into the room. He grabbed Mr. Strang, lifting the frail teacher clear of the floor. As the massive man's grip tightened, the air was squeezed from Mr. Strang's lungs. Red spots swam before his eyes, and he knew that, if the pressure increased, his ribs would crack like dry twigs.

"Danko, stop!" The unfamiliar voice was high, almost womanish. And yet there was a note of authority in it, the voice of a man who expects to be obeyed.

Reluctantly, Danko lowered Mr. Strang to the floor. Gasping for breath, the teacher's first impression of the man who now stood in the doorway was of an aureole of white hair atop a face seamed and wrinkled by the years, deep-set eyes almost obscured by bushy brows.

Then Mr. Strang saw the scar. It started high at the man's left cheekbone and drew an angry white line almost to the point of his chin.

"Yanak," said the teacher. "Jacob Yanak."

It had been years before—during the late Fifties and early Sixties—that the old man's face had appeared in the papers under sordid headlines that screamed of bribery, payoffs, kickbacks, and other assorted chicanery. The hair, of course, was darker then, the face not so lined. This one man had maintained absolute control over an organization that had succeeded in turning dozens of nationally known politicians, government officials, and businessmen into criminals—and as many criminals into supposedly legitimate businessmen.

The old man nodded his head in acknowledgment. "Nobody ever forgets the scar," he said, tracing it with a slender finger.

There was a pounding of feet in the hall outside, and Warne, Alston, and Roberts burst into the room. Roberts' tie was askew, and the butler had lost his look of cool efficiency. Even the razor creases of his trousers had disappeared, replaced below the knee with wrinkles and bagging.

"What is it?" gasped Warne. "What's going on?"

"Tell them, Davie," said Yanak.

"He—he tried to kill me," the boy said, pointing an accusing finger at Mr. Strang. In frantic phrases, he blurted the story of Cueball's death.

"It seems, Roberts," purred Yanak, his voice deadly calm, "that your Mr. Strang isn't as trustworthy as you made him out to be."

The teacher stood in the center of the room, eyes boring at him from all directions. "Surely you don't think," he began incredulously, "that I—"

Warne examined the dish of milk and emitted a long sigh. "What do you expect us to think? Paul, I'm not sure if this is your jurisdiction or mine, but my office would appreciate the first crack at questioning him."

"Just a minute, Mr. Warne!" Mr. Strang was every inch the teacher, now, lecturing a naughty boy. "I'll remind you: it was *you* who came to *me*, not the other way around. You insisted I come here, but your explanation of *why* was sketchy, to say the least. Nevertheless, I obliged you—for Paul Roberts' sake. Now, scarcely an hour later, without even an *attempt* at an investigation, you practically accuse me of attempted murder. Well, gentlemen, enough is enough. Before I leave this room, I demand to know what's going *on* around here."

Warne turned to Roberts. "Damn it, Paul, you said he was feisty, but this is ridiculous."

Mr. Strang glared at Warne indignantly. "I demand it, sir! Or shall I inform the press? What will happen to your precious secrecy then?"

"Why not do as he asks, Hal?" said Roberts. "Fair's fair. Besides, despite how things look, I don't think he did it."

"Hell, Paul, that's beyond my instructions."

"What instructions will you get if it turns out later that he's innocent?"

Warne looked for support to Yanak, who merely shrugged. "Okay, Mr. Strang," he said at last. "Danko, get some chairs. We'll talk in here, so none of the rest of the staff will hear what's happened."

When they were all seated, Warne faced the gnomelike little teacher and began. "As you probably read at the time, Jacob Yanak was convicted of several counts of bribery in 1963, and the judge threw the book at him. No one expected he would ever come out of prison alive. But some months ago, Mr. Yanak communicated with government officials and offered to give us information about some of the country's biggest narcotics operations—cases the FBI couldn't crack without his help."

"I see," said Mr. Strang. "And in return he'd be released from prison, is that it?"

"We promised him a little more than that. There would be no way to keep quiet the fact that our information was coming from Yanak, and we knew the Syndicate would be out for revenge. The usual procedure in cases like this is to give the informant a whole new identity—new Social Security number, new name, new driver's license, new place to live, the works. That's what we tried to do with the Yanaks. The first time we tried it, though, it didn't work."

"The first time?"

"That's right," said Jacob Yanak, who was seated on the bed. "Me and my family—my son, his wife, and David here—were living in Seattle and using the name Schneider. I don't know how, but they found us. The Coast Guard discovered my son's body floating in Puget Sound. He'd been dead three days with a bullet in his head. His wife—David's mother—still hasn't been found."

"And that meant we had to start all over," Warne continued. "We took this house and staffed it, just as a temporary thing until we could arrange the paperwork for Jake and

David's new identities, all in the strictest secrecy. But—well, Jake, you'd better tell what happened next."

"I got a letter. No signature. It said that, even though everybody else was satisfied I'd been hurt enough when my son died and his wife disappeared, he—the guy who wrote the letter—wanted more. He wanted Davie, too."

"But how could he find out—?"

"I don't know. But the letter was addressed to this house. It's an old trick: get a person scared enough, and he's bound to make a slip."

"We're doing all we can to protect Jake and David until we're ready to move them," said Warne. "We even brought in the local police, which is what Roberts is doing here."

"What about Danko?" asked the teacher. "He doesn't look like police."

"He was with me in the old days," said Yanak. "I trust him with my life—and Davie's."

"But David was missing out on his schooling," Roberts chimed in, "cooped up in this house and all. And, hell, Mr. Strang, I've known you for years. Your coming here seemed like a perfect solution."

"Look, Mr. Strang," said Warne, "I'm willing to be reasonable. We had you checked out before contacting you, so we know you're *not* the man we're looking for. But maybe he got to you, huh? I mean, there was that ten minutes or so between the time we talked to you and the time you got in my car. Did you get a phone call? Or make one? Maybe somebody sidled up to you in the hamburger joint. Just tell me, I'll give you every break I can."

"Cut it out, Hal," said Roberts. "Mr. Strang is as straight as can be. I mean, a man his age—and a *teacher*..."

Mr. Strang threw the detective a withering glance.

"Yeah?" queried Warne. "Then how do you explain the poisoned milk? When he had it in his hands the whole time?"

"Well," Roberts spluttered, "I, uh—"

"The man does have a point, Paul," said Mr. Strang. "All the evidence *does* seem to point straight at me. But, Mr. Warne, I'm going to ask your indulgence."

"What do you mean?"

"*I* know I had nothing to do with trying to poison David. Therefore, in spite of appearances, there has to be some other explanation. I'd like to attempt to find it—with your permission, of course."

"Where would you have to look?"

"Right here will be fine. All the principals are present."

Warne looked at Roberts in confusion. "Can he do that?"

"*You're* supposed to be the legal expert. I'm used to going by the book, but the book doesn't mention anything like this."

"That's not what I mean. I mean, is the schoolteacher here any good in the brains department? Or is he just trying to get himself off the hook?"

Roberts thought of all the cases where Mr. Strang's assistance had been invaluable. "Oh, he's good. He's *damn* good."

"And there's an added bonus, Mr. Warne," said the teacher.

"What's that?"

"If I'm successful, you'll have the man you really want." Mr. Strang directed another glance at Roberts. "Not just a broken-down old schoolteacher."

Warne drummed the top of the dresser with his fingers. "Okay, what's the harm? I'll give you half an hour, Mr. Strang."

"That should be ample. First, I'd like a closer look at that milk carton."

"We haven't checked it for fingerprints."

"Mine are all over it. A few more shouldn't hurt."

Warne handed him the carton, and Mr. Strang peered at it intently. "Is there a magnifying glass about?"

"I've got one I use for my stamp collection!" David Yanak rummaged through a bureau drawer. "Here it is."

The teacher accepted it and examined the carton, paying particular attention to its top. "Ah, yes," he said, "as I suspected. Take a look, Paul, right there where the tear ends. See that?"

"Hey, yeah: a little hole, like a pin's been jabbed through the seam of the cardboard."

"Not a pin. A hypodermic needle. So now we know how the poison got inside the carton."

"Great," said Warne sarcastically. "Somebody came up to you and said your milk needed a vaccination, huh?"

"No, it would have taken several seconds to locate the seam and a few more to press home the hypodermic's plunger—I'd have noticed. Tell me, Mr. Warne, when did David ask you to get him the hamburger?"

"Paul and I were just heading out to the school to see you. David came to the top of the stairs and shouted down to us that he wanted a hamburger, fries, and milk."

"I see. He was loud enough to be overheard, then. So you two came to the school, where you talked with Mr. Guthrey and then with me. We drove to Harold's and then here. Would an hour and a half be a reasonable estimate of the amount of time you were gone?”

“Yeah,” shrugged Warne, “I guess so.”

“And now to you, Mr. Yanak.” The teacher spun in his chair. “Did anyone leave this house during the time Warne and Detective Roberts were gone?”

“What do I know? I was upstairs with David. Ask Alston, the front door is his responsibility.”

“What about it, Alston?”

“I really couldn’t say, sir. You see, the grocery boy made a delivery, and it’s Cook’s day off. I spent part of that time period in the kitchen.”

“How long?”

“Perhaps twenty minutes? Otherwise, I was at the front door the entire time.”

“But there were twenty minutes when someone could have slipped in or out without your noticing?”

“Out, perhaps,” said Alston, “but not in. The door’s always locked.”

“What are you driving at, Mr. Strang?” asked Roberts.

“Paul, I suspect that a substitution was made. The carton of milk I purchased at Harold’s was not the same one from which David poured Cueball’s milk. There’d be no way of telling: the two cartons were identical.”

“You know something, Mr. Strang?” Warne took two long steps and stood looking down at the teacher. “You remind me of an animal with its foot in a trap, struggling to get free. What difference would it make if an *army* of people walked in or out the front door, or if one of them had *fifty* extra cartons of milk? The fact is, you had that tray of food in your hands from the time you bought it until David took it.”

“I know that, confound it. *Haemosporidia!* That’s the one hitch in every theory I’ve been able to imagine. Let me see: I came out of Harold’s and got in the car. The ride to this house, inside, up the stairs—”

The teacher made small movements with an index finger as if he were an orchestra conductor, guiding his own thought processes. Then the finger slowed to a stop, and the hand was still.

“Yes, by heaven, that’s it! It *had* to be that way.”

“Are you on to something?” asked Roberts.

“Oh, yes. Beautiful, beautiful! I feel like emulating Archimedes and running through the streets shouting, ‘Eureka!’ Of course, *I’d* wear clothes.”

“What is it?” asked Warne.

With a dramatic gesture, Mr. Strang swept his black-rimmed glasses from their perch on his nose and crammed them into a pocket. “From what we know, we can assume that it *was* possible for someone to leave this house, purchase a carton of milk, and add the poison without anyone else being the wiser. Correct, Mr. Warne?"

Warne waved a hand indulgently. "For the sake of argument, I'll agree that it *could* have been done. But so what? A second carton couldn't have been substituted for the one you brought while you were holding the tray in front of your own eyes every moment."

"Exactly. I was holding the tray the entire time. Except—"

The silence in the room was eerie. Then Jacob Yanak spoke.

"Except when, Mr. Strang?"

The teacher's index finger pointed upward triumphantly. "Except when Alston helped me off with my coat! I had to set the tray down to get my coat off."

Frowning, Roberts pantomimed the process of removing a coat. "Couldn't you have passed the tray from one hand to the other, Mr. Strang? Just long enough to pull your arms out of the sleeves?"

"Impossible. The tray was too soggy from the rain. It would have collapsed or broken."

Warne cocked a skeptical eyebrow. "So you're saying Alston tried to poison David? *He's* the guy we've been looking for?"

"I am saying exactly that, Mr. Warne."

"That's the craziest thing I ever heard in my life!"

"Is it? Hear me out, then do with me as you will. But I warn you: Alston must not be given another chance to get at David."

Yanak snapped his fingers and pointed at Alston, who seemed to shrink in his chair. Danko moved ponderously behind the perspiring butler.

"First," the teacher went on, "who's involved here? You two policemen? Not likely suspects. Danko? He's known and respected Jacob Yanak since before David was born. Yanak himself? Ridiculous.

"But Alston? You said yourself, Mr. Warne, that your men inspected this house and staffed it at the same time. That presumably would include Alston. In other words, he came on the scene at *precisely* the time an assassin could be expected to show up. But he had to find a way of killing without throwing suspicion on himself. To compound his problem, there was the formidable Danko, always at David's door. But then Alston heard something that greatly interested him."

"What did he hear?" asked Roberts.

"He heard David at the top of the stairs, shouting down to Warne and you that he wanted a Big H hamburger with French fries and milk. That was Alston's opportunity. Once you two set off for the school, he left the house, drove to Harold's, and bought the substitute carton of milk. In this huge house, he knew he'd never be missed."

"I—I never left the house," said the quivering Alston.

"But you did," replied the teacher. "Your clothing is immaculate, Mr. Alston, as a perfect butler's should be. But the crease in your trousers disappears below the knees—exactly what happens when a man wearing a raincoat goes out in a storm like the one we're having. His body is protected by the coat, but his lower trouser legs get pretty well drenched."

All heads turned to consider the lower half of Alston's trousers.

"Alston returned," the teacher continued, "and injected the poison into the milk. A bit later, I arrived with David's snack and stood in the entranceway. When he looked through the peephole, I suppose Alston was expecting Mr. Warne, but this was no problem.

"He gripped the shoulders of my coat to assist me in removing it—or so I thought. And I automatically put down the tray, the most natural thing in the world. So natural I'd forgotten all about it until a few moments ago. And where would be the most natural place to set the tray? On that handy little table across from the coat closet, of course. And on that table sits a rather deep wicker basket, used to hold mail. What better place to conceal the carton of poisoned milk than under the mail?

"Alston cut off my field of vision by waving my coat in my face with one hand, while with the other hand he quickly made the substitution. And then, all innocence, he allowed me to take the tray up to David—and, presto, the perfect crime! Except for the unexpected intervention of Cueball."

Warne sat silent for several seconds. "Interesting," he said finally. "Very interesting, Mr. Strang. But not conclusive. Sure, it *might* have happened that way. But I don't buy pinning this on Alston simply because of the way his pants are pressed. I need more proof than that."

"Proof? Yes, of course. So let's consider Mr. Alston's rather urgent disposal problem." Mr. Strang pointed to the container of milk on the table. "Here we have the poisoned milk. But what about the other carton? Its contents could be poured down the nearest sink as soon as Alston could retrieve it from the basket. Still, he could hardly throw the carton itself away. A second one found so soon after the poisoning would be damning evidence indeed. Burn it? But where? Waxed cardboard would take quite a long time to burn and has a distinctive odor. Even if he used a fireplace, he risked someone seeing him and asking what he was doing.

"No, if I were Mr. Alston, I'd simply fold the thing up and stash it in my pocket. No suspicion was likely to fall on him, and he could get rid of it later."

"Danko," snapped Yanak, "search him."

Danko patted Alston's clothing, then reached into the butler's left jacket pocket. When his hand emerged, the thing between his fingers was crushed and bent. But the vivid green letters on a yellow background were easily legible: *Harold's Heavenly Hamburgers.*

"You want me to take care of him, Mr. Yanak?" rumbled Danko.

"No, you big ape. We've gone respectable, remember? Let the law have him."

"Mr. Strang," said Warne, "I'd like to apologize for—"

"Nonsense," said Mr. Strang with a blithe wave of his hand. "All in all, I've had a grand time. As a mystery buff, I've always wanted to be in on a case where the butler really *did* do it."

MR. STRANG UNLOCKS A DOOR

It was Friday, the thirtieth of May, and the sunshine was bright outside the office window. There hadn't been a parental complaint in nearly a week, an incipient food fight in the cafeteria had been averted by the simple expedient of putting pizza back on the menu, and the school's baseball team had won its last four games in a row. For Marvin W. Guthrey, principal of Aldershot High School, life was good. With a contented sigh, he snuggled into the smooth leather of his high-backed swivel chair.

The office door flew open with a bang. In the opening stood the rumpled figure of Leonard Strang, Aldershot's veteran science teacher. He held some papers in one hand, and his other fist was tightly clenched. On the gnomelike teacher's face was an expression of total outrage.

Mr. Strang had been at Aldershot High for thirty-three years, sixteen more than Guthrey himself. In all that time, he'd been a stickler for politeness, for observing the amenities of civilized behavior. So Guthrey knew that Mr. Strang's barging unceremoniously into the principal's office spelled Trouble with a capital T.

"Leonard," said the principal solicitously. "What's wrong?"

"I am annoyed!" replied Mr. Strang. "More than that: I am provoked, irritated, and incensed! In all my years of teaching, I have never seen such a brazen attempt—"

He stopped abruptly and made a sweeping gesture with his hand. "In!" he ordered.

Two boys slunk silently into the office. Guthrey recognized both of them. Arthur Osgood was scarcely an inch taller than Mr. Strang himself. In his green jacket, peering about through bulbous eyes, the boy put the principal in mind of a myopic frog. By contrast, Ralph Milleridge was a colossus, his muscles rippling beneath a sweatshirt with ALDERSHOT ATHLETICS stenciled on it.

"Sit!" ordered Mr. Strang. The two boys sat, and the teacher looked across the desk at the astounded Mr. Guthrey.

"Today," began Mr. Strang, "I collected research papers from my advanced biology class. The papers were assigned last September and represent a full year's work. Much of the final mark for the year is based on—"

"Okay, okay," said Guthrey. "What's the problem?"

"I glanced through the papers at lunch," the teacher replied. "Take a look at this." He placed a stack of pages on Guthrey's desk.

"I see Arthur wrote about cloning," said the principal. "Let me see: 'To the average person, the word *clone* brings to mind images of huge monsters or zombie-like humanoids designed to do the bidding of their masters.'" Guthrey looked up. "Not bad, so far."

Mr. Strang began reading from the top sheets of the papers still in his hand. "'It should be understood, however, that at present cloning—the use of a single cell from a living organism to produce an exact genetic duplicate of the donor—is limited to—'"

Guthrey frowned and pointed to the paper on his desk. "That's exactly what this one says."

"Yes," replied the teacher. "It seems that one of these two papers is itself a clone. They're identical, from beginning to end. Fourteen pages of solid research by one of these boys—and of cheating by the other."

"But which is which?"

"That's what we're here to find out. I'll probably have to fail the cheater, and—as this is a class for seniors only—he may not be able to graduate. I thought the problem was serious enough to bring to your attention."

"Of course," said Guthrey. "But because it *is* so serious, we'll have to be absolutely sure who the guilty party is."

There was a long silence. Then Arthur Osgood spoke up. "I—I know how this looks, Mr. Strang," he said in a hoarse whisper. "But that paper's my own work, I swear that—"

"C'mon, man," interrupted Ralph Milleridge. "You tried a little scam, Artie, and it didn't work. Didn't you think Mr. Strang would notice your paper's just like the one I wrote?"

Teacher and principal looked at each other. The answer they were searching for wasn't going to be found easily—if indeed it was to be found at all.

"Both papers are typed," murmured Mr. Strang. "Footnotes, bibliography, all identical. They were done on different machines. The quality of your typing seems to be much better than Arthur's, Ralph."

"My father's got an office at home," said Ralph, "with a computer and everything. All the latest equipment, including one of those typewriters with a TV screen, so you can correct any mistakes and then the machine prints out a perfect copy. But just because Dad let me use his office doesn't mean—"

"It isn't neatness we're concerned with," said Mr. Strang, "it's honesty. Tell me, Ralph, when did you finish your paper?"

"About three weeks ago. It was the day of the game against Bentley. I remember because I pitched that day."

Guthrey consulted his calendar. "That would be May tenth, a Saturday."

"And you?" the teacher asked Arthur.

"Last weekend. Sunday afternoon."

"You see?" said Ralph. "My paper was finished two weeks ahead of Artie's. So he had to be the one who copied."

"Perhaps," said Mr. Strang. "I don't suppose either of you has any kind of proof—aside from your unsupported word—that you completed your paper when you say you did."

"No."

"Yes."

"Yes?" Mr. Strang peered at Ralph Milleridge over the tops of his black-rimmed glasses. "You can *prove* you finished your paper on May tenth, Ralph?"

"I sure can. I mailed myself a copy."

"You what?"

"I sealed a carbon copy of my paper in an envelope and mailed it to myself. Dad does that sometimes, when he writes something and doesn't want anybody to steal his idea. The postmark tells when you did the work. Here, I'll show you."

Ralph leafed through the notebook on his lap and came up with a nine-inch by twelve-inch brown manila envelope, which he handed to Mr. Strang.

"Looks like the flap is sealed with tape," said Guthrey.

"Sealed? It's practically bound and gagged." The teacher examined the shiny strips that crisscrossed one another over the envelope's flap. "And the tape's got glass fibers running through it. The adhesive's strong, and the tape itself can't be broken. You'd have to cut it. This flap hasn't been tampered with, that's for sure."

He turned the envelope over. In addition to Ralph Milleridge's name and address, the message *First Class Mail* was printed and underlined.

"The stamp cancellation seems to be in order," muttered Mr. Strang, peering closely at it. "Part of the postmark is smudged where it printed onto a strip of tape that was folded over the edge of the envelope. But it was mailed in Aldershot."

"The date, Leonard," said Guthrey impatiently. "What's the postmark date?"

"May thirteenth."

"See?" said Ralph. "The tenth was a Saturday. I mailed this late the following Monday, after school. So it got postmarked the next day, Tuesday, the thirteenth.”

Mr. Strang picked up a long pair of scissors from Guthrey's desk. With some difficulty, he worked the point under the layers of tape sealing the flap. Cutting through both tape and flap, he opened the end of the envelope.

Inside was a small stack of papers—a carbon copy of Ralph Milleridge's work. The teacher removed the first page, glanced at it, and shook his head sadly.

“Read it,” ordered Guthrey. “Read it out loud.”

“‘To the average person, the word *clone* brings to mind images of huge monsters or—’”

Guthrey turned to Arthur Osgood. “You've already admitted you didn't finish your paper until this past weekend, Arthur. That's about ten days after this was mailed. It's pretty evident that you must have copied Ralph's work. As a result, I'm forced to—”

“No! I didn't cheat!” And with a loud cry, Arthur ran out of the office.

Driving home through the peaceful streets of Aldershot late that afternoon, Mr. Strang growled angrily at himself, and the pipe between his clenched teeth emitted clouds of foul-smelling smoke. Arthur had cheated, that was evident. The sealed envelope containing Ralph Milleridge's carbon copy and dated May thirteenth was proof beyond all question.

Still, Mr. Strang had doubts. Why, for example, had Ralph mailed himself a copy of his paper in the first place? And why would he have the envelope with him in the principal's office? It was almost as if he had expected someone to copy his work. Or else—

The teacher swung the wheel sharply, drove two blocks out of his way, and stopped at the Aldershot post office. The postmaster, Dewey Langdon, was a former pupil of Mr. Strang's, and he greeted the teacher jovially.

“Hi, Professor! Read any good books lately?”

Mr. Strang smiled—a bit grimly, perhaps—and put the first of his questions.

“Dewey, are you acquainted with a boy named Ralph Milleridge?”

“Sure, he's in here from time to time. Darnedest thing, now that I think of it. He was in here a few weeks back, mailing a letter to *himself.*”

“Oh? What did it look like?”

“One of those big brown envelopes. The flap was taped down real good, as if there was something valuable inside. I weighed it in and gave Ralph fifty-four cents in stamps.

Four ounces, first-class mail. He stuck the stamps on the envelope and mailed it."

"Fifty-four cents? You remember that?"

"Sure do. One of the quarters he gave me was Canadian. I had to ask him for a U.S. quarter—that's why I remember the incident. Something else I can do for you, Mr. Strang? We've got a sale on fifteen-cent stamps today: two for thirty cents." Dewey's hoarse laugh rang out in the small post office.

So much for the theory that the tape had been added after the envelope was delivered, thought the teacher as he drove off.

Mrs. Mackey, the owner of the house where Mr. Strang rented a small second-floor room, was out when he got home. She'd left a note saying she was visiting her nephew and wouldn't be back until late. So, as the teacher sat at the kitchen table eating a bowl of canned soup and watching the sunset through the rear window, he was surprised to hear the front door open and then close.

"Who's there?" he called.

There was a rustling sound in the living room, and Mr. Strang went to investigate. At first, he saw nothing. But then he spotted a dim figure sitting in a gloomy corner. He snapped on the lights.

"Arthur Osgood," he said. "What are you doing here?"

Arthur—red-eyed, with tears streaming down his cheeks—spoke in a reedy voice. "Don't get mad, Mr. Strang. The doorbell didn't work, and the front door was unlocked, so—so I just came in."

Mr. Strang went to the door and shot the bolt. Then he returned to Arthur. "You don't just walk into people's houses unannounced and take a seat." He was about to go on when the distraught expression on Arthur's face silenced him.

"I had to see you, Mr. Strang. I wouldn't ever—I didn't—"

Mr. Strang sat down opposite the boy. "Arthur," he said, "I don't know what to tell you. All year long I've stressed the importance of that paper to your final grade. Why did you have to—?"

"But I *didn't*, Mr. Strang! I swear I didn't cheat! And now I'm not going to graduate, and—and—"

"Arthur, you'll graduate. You have enough credits even without my class. Maybe I came on a bit strong in Mr. Guthrey's office, but you'll graduate. Does that make you happy?"

"No, sir, it doesn't."

"Then what is it you want?"

"I—I don't want to leave school with you thinking I cheated on my work."

For a moment, the old teacher felt as if someone had jabbed him in the solar plexus. In the long silence that followed, tears welled up in his own eyes. He blinked them back and looked at the blurred figure of Arthur Osgood.

"Does my esteem really mean that much to you?" he asked softly.

The boy nodded.

"As I live and breathe," muttered the teacher. "In this day and age, to find a young person who values the good opinion of others—remarkable! Even in our era of 'being cool and doing your own thing,' there are still a few kids who put reputation above all else. Remarkable, indeed!"

"Huh?" said the boy.

"Nothing," replied Mr. Strang, with a shake of his head. "Nothing, Arthur. But for what it's worth, I believe you, despite the evidence. I don't think you copied Ralph's paper. Anyone who did something like that wouldn't come calling the way you've done this evening."

"Thanks, Mr. Strang. That means a lot to me." Arthur let out a long sigh. "But I guess everybody else will figure I cheated."

"I suppose they will."

But then Mr. Strang pounded the arm of his chair. "No, confound it! If *you* didn't cheat, then Ralph Milleridge did, and he came up with that envelope gimmick to prove his innocence. The question is: how did he manage it?"

For several moments, both teacher and student pondered the problem. Could the flap have been tampered with? No, Mr. Strang was sure that was impossible, especially in light of what Dewey Langdon had told him. Could a duplicate envelope have been used, or the postmark forged? In fiction, perhaps, but not by a high-school student in real life.

"All right, Arthur," said Mr. Strang finally. "Let's start at the beginning. Is there any way Ralph could have gotten a look at your work?"

Arthur thought about this. "I don't see how," he said. "I mean, we were both doing our papers on cloning, so we talked about the references we were using and stuff like that. But the only time I took my paper out of my house was—"

"Was when?"

"Last Monday. I was all finished, but I wanted to check what I'd written against one or two books in the school library. So I brought the paper to school, and—"

"And what?" Mr. Strang could barely contain his impatience.

"Ralph told me he was all done with *his* paper. But he wanted to have a look at a book on cloning I had at my house. So we walked home together."

"Did he ever see your paper? Even for just a minute?"

"I don't see how he could have. It was in my notebook the whole time. On the way home, we stopped off at Ralph's so he could pick up some notes. He went upstairs, and I waited in the kitchen. Mrs. Milleridge gave me a cupcake."

"Aha! And where was your notebook then?"

"On a chair in the living room, where we left our coats."

"Better and better," said Mr. Strang, rubbing his hands. "So while you were in the kitchen, Arthur could have taken your paper and written out—"

"We were only in the house for about five minutes, Mr. Strang, just long enough for Ralph to get his notes. He wouldn't have had time to *read* my paper, much less write out a copy."

The teacher's triumphant smile faded.

"Then we went to my house. I found the book, and Ralph asked if he could borrow it, and I let him. He took it home. But he forgot to take the rest of his stuff. I had to bring it to school the next day."

"Wait a minute," said Mr. Strang. "You mean Ralph left *his* notebook at *your* house overnight?"

"Sure, but—"

The teacher made a wry face. "Not good, Arthur."

"What do you mean?"

"You said Ralph couldn't have copied your paper. But you just told me you had access to his books—and presumably *his* paper—for at least twelve hours. You'd have had plenty of time to copy—"

"But I didn't, Mr. Strang. I *didn't*." Fresh tears sparkled in Arthur's eyes.

"All right, son, all right. But you can see how bad it looks for you. You had an opportunity to copy Ralph's paper. And then there's that confounded envelope. *Ciliata!* If I could figure out how *that* was managed, I'd—"

The sound of a doorknob rattling came from the kitchen. Mr. Strang lifted his head, wondering who'd be trying Mrs. Mackey's rear door. Then a key was inserted, and the lock snapped back.

"Who's there?" called the teacher.

"And who d'ye *think*'d be comin' calling at this hour o' the night?" Mrs. Mackey's rich Irish brogue carried with it hints of the green fields of Kilkenny and peat fires glowing in small cottages. "Seems only right I should be allowed entrance into me own house." She waddled into the living room, her ruddy smiling face belying her stern words.

"Why didn't you come in the front way?" Mr. Strang asked.

"Because *some* fool bolted the door on the inside, so even with my key it wouldn't open. You wouldn't have no idea how that door got bolted, now, would you?"

The teacher's face reddened. "Guilty as charged," he said. "After Arthur came in—"

"Ah, ye've got a guest. Yer pardon for disturbin' you. No harm done, 'twas no trouble coming in the rear way. I'll be off to bed now. Help yerselves to what's in the fridge."

With that, Mrs. Mackey ponderously climbed the stairs.

Mr. Strang looked after her, his face blank. Then he turned to Arthur. "Did you hear what she said?"

"Sure, she said she was going to bed."

"No, no, before that."

"She was bawling you out for bolting the door and making her come in through the kitchen. I don't see what that's got to do with—"

"But that's *it*, Arthur! It has to be!"

"What has to be what, Mr. Strang?"

The teacher rose stiffly from his chair and extended a hand. "Arthur Osgood," he said dramatically, "I hereby pronounce you innocent of any wrongdoing in regard to your research paper."

"But how could Ralph—?"

"Not now. When I explain what really happened with those two papers, I want Mr. Milleridge in the room. Just so I can see the look on that young rascal's face!"

On Monday, Mr. Guthrey called a meeting in his office after school. Those attending were Mr. Strang, Arthur Osgood, and Ralph Milleridge. When all were present, Mr. Guthrey dismissed his secretary and closed the office door.

"Mr. Strang says he's gotten to the bottom of this term-paper business," said the principal, from his exalted position at the head of the large conference table. "So I'll turn the—er—program over to him."

"What's going to happen to Artie?" asked Ralph. "You're not going to be too hard on him, are you?"

"Nothing's going to happen to Arthur," replied Mr. Strang, "for the simple reason that he's done nothing to deserve punishment."

"Done nothing?" cried Ralph. "He stole my paper, didn't

he?"

"Oh, Ralph, Ralph," sighed Mr. Strang, "this won't do. It really won't. Why not save us all a lot of trouble and own up to what you've done?"

"I haven't done anything, and I can prove it. The envelope—"

"Yes, the envelope," said the teacher. "Similar to this one, wasn't it?" He removed a brown manila envelope from his briefcase. "Sold at Pen and Ink Stationery here in Aldershot? Nine-by-twelve size?"

"Yes, that's the kind I used."

"Good. Then perhaps you'll indulge me while I perform a little demonstration."

Mr. Strang removed his black-rimmed glasses from his pocket and put them on with a flourish. Over the years, thousands of his students had seen him make this same gesture in the classroom just before an experiment was about to begin.

"This envelope is similar to the one Ralph mailed his paper in." Again Mr. Strang reached into his briefcase. "And here I have a sheet of blank paper. Will you place it in the envelope, Ralph? And seal the flap, please?"

The paper was inserted. Ralph Milleridge bent the metal fastener up and licked the flap of the envelope. Then he pressed down on the flap carefully and locked it into place with the fastener.

"Still not good enough," declared Mr. Strang, reaching for the briefcase once more. This time, it yielded a roll of plastic tape.

"Just like the stuff you used, Ralph. Go ahead, seal the envelope with it, the same way you did with the other one."

Mr. Guthrey furnished a small penknife, with which the tape was cut into short lengths. When Ralph finished flattening the strips into place, the flap was proof against anything short of a sharp pair of shears.

"Now, Mr. Guthrey, would you please draw a stamp right where the one was on the other envelope? That's it, just opposite the flap. Make your sketch as ornate as you like, something you'll recognize when you see it again. Put your initials on it. That's fine."

The teacher produced another sheet of paper. "Finally," he said, "I'd like each of you to make some identifying mark or marks on this page. Sign your names or put down anything else you like, just so you'll know this paper when next it appears."

When this was completed, Mr. Strang took the sealed envelope and the paper—which now had three signatures scrawled across it—and got to his feet. "I must ask your indulgence for about ten minutes," he announced. "At the end of that time, the demonstration will be completed." And before anyone could comment, he left the office.

He returned in less than ten minutes. The envelope, still tightly sealed, was in his hand. The signed paper was nowhere in sight.

"Here," he said dramatically, "is your envelope, Mr. Guthrey. Will you verify that it has the stamp you drew on it and initialed?"

"Why, yes," said the principal. "That's it, all right. But—"

"Now, will you open it, please? Your penknife should do the trick."

Guthrey hacked his way through the layers of tape and finally made an opening clear across the end of the envelope.

"Now remove what's inside," said Mr. Strang, leaning forward like a cat about to pounce on its prey.

"Leonard, it's got to be the blank paper we put—good lord!" Guthrey drew a sheet of paper from the envelope. On it were three signatures: Ralph Milleridge's, Arthur Osgood's, and Marvin W. Guthrey's.

"How," Guthrey sputtered. "How did you—?"

"First, will you agree that, within reason, I've duplicated what went on here last Friday?"

"Of course. But how did you unseal that flap?"

"That flap," said Mr. Strang with a chuckle. "That glued-down, clamped-down, taped-down flap. The one part of the envelope that, with all its adhesive trappings, attracted our attention. It's so obviously the only entrance to our miniature locked room that I'll admit I was as baffled as anyone— at least until my landlady said something that cleared up the mystery."

"What was it?" asked Guthrey. "What did she say?"

"She came in through the back door the other evening, after I'd bolted the front one. 'Twas no trouble coming in the rear way,' she told me."

"I don't understand, Leonard."

"When she said that, Mr. Guthrey, it suddenly occurred to me that the envelope has a kind of 'rear way,' too."

"It does?"

"It does. You see, it *doesn't* have just one flap. It has two."

"Two flaps?"

"Of course. The one that's so tightly sealed was the one we focused on. A bit like a magician waving one hand wildly to attract his audience's attention, while he palms a coin with the other."

"And?"

"*And*, at the other end of the envelope is another, smaller flap. Oh, it's glued shut, but otherwise unprotected. And with the application of a little steam, the glue loosens quite easily. The envelope's contents can then be removed through the 'back door'"—Mr. Strang looked sternly at Ralph Milleridge—"and anything else can be inserted. When the small flap's glued shut again, there's no evidence of any tampering. Especially if you go over the flap with a hot iron, as I just did down in the home economics room."

"Well, I'll be—"

"Wait a minute!" Ralph Milleridge rose to his feet. "Okay, Mr. Strang, it *could* have been done that way. But you haven't proved it *was*. I mean, how could I have gotten a look at Artie's paper in the first place?"

"Simple. He was at your house, wasn't he? With his books in the living room while he ate a cupcake in the kitchen?"

"Yeah, for maybe five minutes. But I didn't have time to copy—"

"Oh, stop it, Ralph! You talk about 'copying' as if you were one of the ancient scriveners, writing everything down in longhand. Yet you yourself mentioned your father's home office, with its ultramodern typewriter and even a computer."

"Right, but the typewriter and computer couldn't—"

"Surely, Ralph, such a setup would also include some kind of copy machine?"

The look on Ralph Milleridge's face told Mr. Strang that his shot had struck home. He pressed the advantage.

"In five minutes, you could have copied fifty to a hundred pages with such an apparatus. A mere fourteen would have been nothing. Afterward, your leaving your books at Arthur's overnight *could* have been an accident. Or, on the other hand, it might have been a deliberate attempt to throw suspicion on him by giving him ample time to copy *your* non-existent paper."

"You—you—" Arthur Osgood glared at Ralph, furious. He started to rise, but Guthrey urged him back into his chair.

"I've seen it before," Mr. Strang told Ralph. "A student lets the days turn into weeks and then months, with no work done on a major project. Suddenly, it's spring, and there are all sorts of interesting activities at hand. Yet the research paper looms large. With only a month or so to go, you had to come up with something. So you mailed yourself an envelope three weeks ago with blank sheets of paper in it, and then just sat back and waited for a chance to get at Arthur's paper. A little talk around school about the imaginary 'work' you were doing on your own paper would be enough to impress everyone with your studious ways."

Ralph Milleridge was shaken but still not ready to admit to Mr. Strang's charges. "You can't prove anything," he whispered.

"Unfortunately, Ralph, I can. There are two things you overlooked—understandable in a scheme as complicated as this one. First, there's the matter of the references you supposedly used. I checked 'em out in the school library. There are seven books listed in your bibliography. You checked out three of them last month, according to the book cards. Getting your story in order, were you?"

"No, I—"

"The other four were checked out just a week ago today—weeks after you'd supposedly completed your paper ... and *one day* after you had the opportunity to copy Arthur's work. The inference is clear: you'd seen Arthur's bibliography, and you wanted a look at those books in case anybody questioned you about your paper."

The effect on Ralph Milleridge was shattering. The boy seemed to shrink visibly. "I—I had to do something," he almost sobbed. "My folks would have killed me. What am I going to do, Mr. Strang? What am I going to do?"

Mr. Strang walked behind Ralph's chair and patted him gently on the shoulder. "Come and see me tomorrow," he said. "We'll talk about it. Maybe we can work something out."

Later, after the two boys had left the office, Guthrey gazed at Mr. Strang with an awed expression. "Leonard?"

"Yes, Mr. Guthrey?"

"You said there were *two* things Ralph overlooked. What was the second one?"

"I was saving that in case he still maintained his innocence." Mr. Strang shook his head sadly. "But, heaven help me, I broke him down. Is the second thing really important now?"

"I suppose not. Just curiosity on my part."

"The postage," said Mr. Strang. "Ralph mailed the envelope before he'd seen Arthur's paper, and he put in too many blank pages. First-class mail, fifty-four cents—one fifteen-cent stamp and three thirteens—four ounces. But the fourteen pages of the actual paper—plus the envelope— only weighed a bit over *two* ounces, so Ralph should only have had to pay for three—forty-one cents. I checked the weight of the paper this morning. Dewey Langdon weighed it for me.”

“That’s weak, Leonard. Mr. Langdon might have made a mistake.”

Mr. Strang shook his head. “Not Dewey. Even as a student, he was meticulous. Of all the kids I’ve taught over the years, he’s one of the few I could trust never to make an error like that. Especially where money was involved.”

The teacher jammed his felt hat onto his head. “I really can’t take much pleasure in what I’ve done today,” he said. “Ralph Milleridge’s scheme had to be exposed, of course. But to do it I had to break the boy in the same way a fine wild horse is broken to the saddle. I just hope Ralph’s got enough backbone in him to put the pieces back together again.”

The little teacher sighed. “I have a bitter taste in my mouth, Mr. Guthrey. Perhaps a good stiff brandy will remove it. And you’re buying.”

MR. STRANG GRASPS AT STRAWS

It was a raw evening, and a dreary rain pattered against the windows of Mr. Strang's rented room. The gnome-like teacher sat at a table, muttering in annoyance as he marked a batch of test papers written by ninth graders, most of whom seemed blithely ignorant of what had been going on in class during the previous three weeks.

Thomas Avila Edson was the frist man who invented the light blub.

For a moment, Mr. Strang pondered the good fortune that had made "Edson" the "frist" man to invent the mysterious and somewhat menacing "blub." How many others had invented similar blubs, he wondered, after Edson's triumph?

"*Ctenophora!*" the teacher grumbled, his blue pencil flicking across the page like the tongue of an adder, deducting two points here, giving partial credit there, and elsewhere sketching a gigantic question mark indicating his mystification.

Downstairs, Mrs. Mackey was watching television—a police show, judging by the shots, explosions, sirens, and general rough-and-tumble that reached Mr. Strang's ears. "Now ye've nabbed the dirthy spalpeen," he heard his landlady cry out in a rich brogue. "Give it to him good. Bite the rogue's ear off!"

The front doorbell rasped loudly. Mrs. Mackey's reluctant footsteps as she left her beloved TV were followed by the sounds of the bolt being pulled back and the door creaking open on unoiled hinges.

"Detective Roberts," cooed Mrs. Mackey. "An' what brings Aldershot's foinest out on a night like this?" A mumble of male voices, then: "Take off them wet coats, the both uv ye. His Lordship's up in his room."

Heavy footsteps on the stairs were followed by a knock at Mr. Strang's door.

"Come in!"

Paul Roberts was the first to enter. The bulky detective and the diminutive teacher had a profound respect for one another. Mr. Strang had given unofficial assistance on a number of Roberts' cases, and the teacher's intuitive logic was an appreciated complement to the detective's dogged police work.

The man who came in behind Roberts was a stranger to Mr. Strang. He was of medium height, and his close-cropped hair was slightly mussed. In dress and demeanor, he was the very model of a conservative businessman. In a crowd of commuters, he would have been almost invisible.

The stranger sank down into the room's easy chair, and Roberts perched on the edge of the bed.

"Mr. Strang, meet Michael Marcos," said Roberts. "Mike's with the F.B.I. We're working together on a—well, on a problem."

"Grasping at straws is more like it," growled Marcos.

"The F.B.I., eh?" Mr. Strang took his pipe from the table. "Tell me, Mr. Marcos, have I been caught double parking again?" He lit the pipe and puffed clouds of pungent smoke into the still air. "Or do you suspect me of cheating Mrs. Mackey out of her rent?"

Marcos' face might have been carved of granite. "Eugene Allerdyce," he said in a flat voice. "What can you tell me about him?"

Mr. Strang turned to Roberts with a chuckle. "Your friend doesn't waste any time on the social niceties, Paul." Then he scratched his head. "Eugene Allerdyce," he said. "I had him as a student, but that was nine or ten years ago. He went into politics, I believe. I see his name in the newspaper from time to time. Why do you ask?"

"Never mind that. What do you remember about him?"

"Mr. Marcos," Mr. Strang said, every inch the stern teacher, "I have no way of knowing whether your churlish manner is inborn or simply assumed for my benefit. In either case, it doesn't impress me. If you want information from me, I suggest you begin treating me as a sapient adult, old enough to be your father, rather than as a backward child. You might begin by telling me what in blazes is going on here."

Roberts hid a grin behind his hand.

"I don't think we can—" began Marcos, and at the same time Roberts said, "Eugene Allerdyce was kidnapped two days ago."

Marcos let out a long breath. "Paul," he said softly, "I don't think it was wise to reveal that information."

"We're here to pick Mr. Strang's brain," Roberts replied. "How's he going to know what sort of information we're looking for unless we let him in on the full story?"

"But he's not a trained investigator—"

"Oh?" Mr. Strang peered at Marcos over the top of his glasses. "Well, how's this for detective work, Mr. Marcos? Allerdyce was kidnapped, but you haven't made the news public as yet. The kidnappers are demanding a ransom, which the powers-that-be are unwilling to pay. You don't know where Allerdyce is being held, but you have a clue as to his whereabouts. The clue makes no sense to you, and you're looking for something—anything—in his past life that would give it meaning. Right so far?"

Marcos gave Roberts a look that would etch glass. "Paul, have you been talking to this guy?"

"I have no data about the kidnapping," snapped Mr. Strang, "except what I've heard from you."

"Then how did you know about the ransom?"

"Ransom is a usual element in any kidnapping. And if you'd been willing to pay it, Allerdyce would probably be free by now."

"But the clue. How'd you know about that?"

"By your presence here, Mr. Marcos. In your own words, you're grasping at straws. You come to me to seek information about a man I haven't seen in ten years. For background? You could get that anywhere, without paying me a visit on a stormy evening. So you're on a fishing expedition. You're contacting everyone who ever knew Allerdyce—no matter how slightly. Therefore, there's a clue, a clue that's still something of a mystery."

Roberts grinned at the somewhat flustered Marcos. "Satisfied, Mike? Now why don't you lay out the whole thing for Mr. Strang?"

"I—okay," said Marcos reluctantly. "Eugene Allerdyce is a personal aide to Governor Hindeman. A brainy kid, young Allerdyce. He's going places in politics."

"All right," said Mr. Strang. "But what about the kidnapping?"

"It happened the day before yesterday. Allerdyce was in Ravensport, laying the groundwork for a new poverty program there. A program, I might add, that will cost four million dollars to implement."

"Can we get to the kidnapping itself?" asked Mr. Strang with a sigh.

"He was taken right out of his hotel room. From what we can make out, at least two men came into the room sometime around nine in the evening. They held Allerdyce there for three or four hours."

"How do you know that?"

"The ashtrays were full of two kinds of cigarette butts, and Allerdyce doesn't smoke. We figure the men were waiting for the other people on the floor to go to sleep, so the halls would be clear. Then they went out the back way, taking Allerdyce with them."

"No witnesses, I suppose?"

"None. But yesterday morning the governor's office got

a phone call. It was Allerdyce himself, obviously pretty scared. He said he'd been grabbed by a group calling itself the Alliance for Liberty and Peace—ALP, for short."

"ALP," mused Mr. Strang. "That's a new one."

"A bunch of cuckoo terrorists," said Marcos. "They want peace like a drowning man wants a lead weight, and liberty to them means no laws or rules of any kind. No police, no firemen, no schools, no government. Just everybody doing their own thing, and if someone gets hurt in the process— well, that's just too bad."

"I see. But what about the phone call to the governor?"

"ALP wants two million bucks—half of the poverty grant—to release Allerdyce. Naturally, Governor Hindeman's not going to pay. It would be political suicide for him to give in to their demands. On the other hand, he's going all out to see if Allerdyce can be rescued."

"So the F.B.I. and the state and local police have been alerted," said the teacher. "But so far word has been kept from the public, right?"

"That's about the size of it."

"And the clue?" asked Mr. Strang.

Marcos opened his briefcase and took out a single sheet of paper. "This is a copy of what the police found on the floor of Allerdyce's room after the kidnapping. It's in his own handwriting, and either the ALP members overlooked it or they didn't think it was important enough to take with them. But we think—we hope—that, during the hours Allerdyce was held captive in his room, he heard his captors say where they were going to be taking him, and he wrote this to tip us off. Here, have a look."

The copy was of a piece of paper wrinkled and streaked with dirt. On one side were several penciled lines of writing. Mr. Strang squinted through his glasses as he read:

1. Midday (4)
2. A Japanese car—a plaything, perhaps? (7)
3. Belief, doctrine, or principle (5)

Scrawled across the bottom of the page was what appeared to be a signature: **Vic Pate**.

"Vic is short for Victor," said Marcos, "and 'pate' means head. Maybe, just maybe, Allerdyce was trying to tell us that, if we use our heads, we'll come out of this as winners." He shrugged. "On the other hand, maybe he was just doodling, and the thing isn't a message at all."

"Uh-huh," replied Mr. Strang absently. He took a small notepad from his pocket, flipped it open, and began printing with his blue pencil.

"It's a message, all right," he said finally. "No question about it. Allerdyce put it in this form to make his kidnappers think he was just scribbling random words to kill time."

"You sound pretty sure of yourself," said Marcos.

"It's strange what you remember about students," Mr. Strang replied. "Eugene Allerdyce was only average in science, but he loved the English language. Words were playthings to him. Many times he'd try out word games and puzzles on me, to lure me away from the subject of the day's lesson. Frankly, I allowed him to succeed far too often."

"What's that got to do with—?"

"Anagrams," Mr. Strang went on, oblivious of the interruption. "You shift the letters of a word or phrase to construct new words or phrases. I remember that Eugene once rearranged the letters of my name—Leonard Strang—to come up with 'Grand Lone Star.' I never thought to ask if he felt movies should be made of my lessons or if he was suggesting I move to Texas."

"So you're saying he was leaving behind a message?"

"Well," said the teacher, "the name Vic Pate is an anagram for 'captive.' Coincidence? Doubtful. Eugene was tipping you off as to his situation. By inference, the rest of the message must be a clue to his whereabouts."

"Y'know," said Roberts, peering at the paper over Mr. Strang's shoulder, "those three numbered things look like crossword-puzzle definitions."

"We've considered that," said Marcos. "And the number in parentheses after each of them gives the number of letters in the answer. So 'midday' is 'noon'—four letters. And 'belief, doctrine, or principle' is 'tenet.' But that second one has got us going around in circles."

"Oh?" Mr. Strang's eyebrows arched. "How many kinds of Japanese cars can there be?"

"Not many," answered Marcos. "And 'Toyota' makes a certain amount of sense, since a toy is a plaything. Except—"

"—except 'Toyota' only has six letters," said Mr. Strang.

"Yes," replied Marcos with a shake of his head. "So maybe Allerdyce made a mistake. Even if he did mean six letters and 'Toyota' is what he wanted us to see, what have we got? 'Noon,' 'Toyota,' and 'tenet'—where does that get us?"

"Not very far," the teacher agreed. "But you're holding back on me, aren't you, Mr. Marcos?"

"Holding back? What do you mean?"

"The city of Ravensport must have thousands of buildings where Eugene Allerdyce could be hidden from sight.

And if ALP took him out of the city, the possibilities would be endless. It would be impossible for Eugene to have indicated a specific hiding place under those circumstances. No, the location of his prison must be limited to a fixed number of places. And I suspect he'd be fairly sure the police would know about them. Mr. Marcos, does ALP have hideouts you're familiar with?"

Marcos frowned. "You told me he was sharp," he said to Roberts, reaching into his briefcase. "If what I'm about to show you gets out, Mr. Strang, the Bureau will have my head on a plate. Understood?"

"Understood," said the teacher solemnly.

Marcos passed him a second sheet of paper. On it were five names and addresses:

```
Ralph Depta, 35 Rachel Boulevard
Mrs. Minnie Feingold, 81-45 Main Street
J.F. Greer, 2591 S. Bayliss Parkway (Apt. 4-B)
Otto Kapak, 904 Cade Lane
Franz Menisch, 786 Singer Street
```

"These are places in Ravensport we've identified as ALP hideouts," Marcos said. "We got the list from an informant, and ALP doesn't know we have it. But it's available to the governor, and therefore it's possible Allerdyce might have seen it."

"So you think Eugene is being held at one of these five locations?"

"We're pretty sure of it. Why would ALP risk leaving the city with so many hideouts available close at hand?"

"Then couldn't a series of raids be organized? If all those addresses were hit at once—"

Marcos shook his head. "Impossible. In the first place, we simply don't have enough trained men to raid all five places and ensure Allerdyce's safety. And even more important, ALP would just love to have us come down on four innocent locations with guns and tear gas. The propaganda value would be worth more to them than the amount of ransom they're asking."

"I see," said the teacher with a frown. "You can't attempt a rescue until you know for sure where Eugene is being held."

"That's about right," replied Marcos. "And you can bet the message Allerdyce left isn't a crossword puzzle, even though it looks like one. We ran 'noon' and 'tenet' and every make of Japanese car through a computer, and nothing."

"Perhaps Eugene was using spoonerisms."

"Spoon—what?"

"A spoonerism is a transposing of sounds between words, like 'blushing crow' for 'crushing blow' or 'the Navy gave the king a twenty-one-sun galoot.' They're named for the late Dean Spooner of New College, Oxford, who legend has it, used to make such verbal errors quite frequently."

"I'm just a detective," said Roberts, "not a college professor."

"Ellery Queen used spoonerisms in one of his short stories," Mr. Strang responded. "It's called 'My Queer Dean.' I'll find you a copy, if you'd like."

"Spoonerism, huh?" muttered Marcos. "So 'Vic Pate' would become 'Pick Vate'? Not helpful, Mr. Strang. Got any other ideas?"

"Well, Eugene was addicted to puns. 'Show me a country where the people ride around in shrimp-colored automobiles, and I'll show you a pink car nation,' that kind of thing. But it doesn't seem to apply here, does it?"

Roberts and Marcos shook their heads.

"Then there are the punctuation tricks," said the teacher.

"Come again?"

Mr. Strang printed a few words in his notebook and showed them to Roberts:

City Property
No Parking
Permitted

"What does that mean to you, Paul?"

"It means that, if you leave your car there, somebody's going to hang a ticket on it."

Mr. Strang used his pencil to jot a few additional marks on the page, then returned the notebook to Roberts. "And now?" he asked.

Roberts smiled as he read the modified notice:

City Property?
No! Parking
Permitted!

"Mr. Strang," said Marcos, "Allerdyce's note includes three periods, three sets of parentheses, one question mark, one dash, and three commas. We can juggle all that around as much as we want, but we still come up empty. How many of these word gimmicks are there, anyway?"

"Dozens, I'm afraid. There's alliteration and synecdoche

and hyperbole and onomatopoeia and—"

"What you're saying is, we could be here for a week messing around with the words in Allerdyce's note—and we just haven't got the time."

"How long do we—?"

"We have to print the governor's answer to ALP's demands in the newspaper the day after tomorrow," Roberts told him.

"Look, Mr. Strang." Marcos put the papers back into his briefcase and closed it. "We've got another call to make this evening. We're checking in with everybody who ever knew Allerdyce, hoping someone will come up with something useful. You've been very cooperative with this business about Allerdyce's word puzzles, but it's not working out. Thanks for your time."

After Roberts and Marcos left, the science teacher was in no mood to continue marking papers. He got very little sleep that night.

The following morning, his car refused to start, and he had to walk to Aldershot High School. By the beginning of first period, when it was time to meet his eleventh-grade physics class, the crusty old man was in an absolutely vile frame of mind.

The science room was set up for an experiment. A heavy metal ball about four inches in diameter hung in the air a foot above the floor, suspended from a twelve-foot length of cord. The other end of the cord was tied to a small ring mounted in the room's high ceiling.

"Today," the teacher snapped peevishly, "we are going to consider the pendulum. It was Galileo who was credited with the discovery that a pendulum will oscillate in a given period of time, regardless of the arc of its swing. We are now going to put that theory to the test. Observe carefully what you see, and record everything in your notebooks. Donald Frazer, you'll assist me, so you'll be closest to the experiment and won't miss anything. You desperately need an A for this marking period."

There were a few titters around the room. Then a plump boy in the front row got up. "Yes, Mr. Strang," he said.

"Take the ball to the side wall. Stand on a chair, if you need to."

Donald grasped the metal ball and walked it over to the wall.

"Good. Now I'm going to start this metronome. Donald, you'll release the ball at the first tick. Ready?"

Donald nodded.

Tick! went the metronome.

Donald opened his hand. The ball swept across the width of the room, slowing and finally stopping inches short of a window.

Tick!

The ball made its return journey.

Tick!

The students were fascinated. As time went by, the arc through which the ball swung became shorter and shorter. But still the pendulum and the metronome kept pace with each other.

Tick!

No one noticed that Mr. Strang seemed to have become hypnotized by the ball as it swung from side to side in front of him. Right to left, left to right...

Midday—noon—

Tick!

Japanese car—Toyota—only six letters—

Tick!

Belief, doctrine, or principle—tenet—

Tick!

You need an A desperately—

Tick!

Japanese car—no, *a* Japanese car—

Tick!

"That's it!" Mr. Strang's shout reverberated in the hushed silence of the room. "That's what Eugene was trying to tell us!"

"Don't you feel well, Mr. Strang?"

With an effort, the teacher averted his eyes from the swinging ball.

"You were staring so hard at the pendulum," said a girl on the other side of the demonstration table. "Like the whole class had just disappeared or something. Do you want me to get the nurse?"

"No, no, Cathy, that won't be necessary. Just sit quietly with the others. You'll have to excuse me for a moment, though. I have to make a phone call."

When Mr. Strang dialed the F.B.I. office in Ravensport, he was told that Special Agent Marcos was out and couldn't be reached for the rest of the day. Mr. Strang had a few rather harsh words for the person who'd answered the phone, and Mike Marcos returned the teacher's call in less than five minutes.

And Mr. Strang told him in which house Eugene Allerdyce was being held captive.

Just before noon that day, a man in the uniform of the U.S. Postal Service knocked at the front door of 904 Cade Lane in Ravensport.

"Yes?" called a woman's voice from behind the door.

"Registered letter, ma'am. You'll have to sign for it."

At the sound of a key being turned in the locked door, the postman adjusted the bag on his shoulder. At this signal, a gardener working nearby reached into the rear of his pickup truck and pulled out the high-powered rifle concealed there. He leaped over the fence and ran toward the adjacent house.

A similarly equipped garbage man approached the other side of the house, while two telephone linemen covered the rear door.

When the front door opened, the woman who stood there did not receive the letter she had been promised. Instead, she found herself looking down the muzzle of a .38 Police Special revolver.

"Police, ma'am," said the postman sharply. "We have a warrant—"

"Harry! George!" yelled the woman. "It's the fuzz! Go down and—"

Her voice was drowned out by the sound of shattering glass as the other men outside punched through the first-floor windows with the butts of their rifles. "Freeze, you two!" shouted the gardener to the two men who were scuttling toward a doorway near the kitchen. For a moment it seemed as if they might make a break for it. But then they saw the guns poking in through the windows and thought better of it.

At the same time, the garbage man broke the glass of a cellar window. He saw another man seated against the far wall.

"Come here!" the garbage man called into the dimly lit basement. "Come over here and let me take a look at you!"

"I—I can't," said the man in a hoarse whisper.

"Why can't you?"

"Because they've got me chained to the wall."

And then, realizing that he was safe, Eugene Allerdyce broke down.

For the second time in as many days, there was a tapping at the door of Mr. Strang's room.

"Come in, Paul," called the teacher.

Paul Roberts stood in the doorway, his bulk almost concealing the light from the hall beyond. "How in blazes did you know it was me, Mr. Strang?"

"The F.B.I. would have gotten in touch with you sometime this afternoon about the rescue of Eugene Allerdyce. Your shift ends at four. You went home, had a beer, and ate supper. After supper, maybe another beer. But all the time, two things were going through your mind."

"Yes?" said Roberts with a grin. "And what were they?"

"First, you were wondering what was in Eugene Allerdyce's puzzle that told me the right house to raid. The F.B.I. didn't tell you, or you wouldn't be here now."

"Okay," said Roberts. "And what was the second thing?"

"You didn't want to give me the satisfaction of asking me to explain. Otherwise, you'd have been here earlier."

"You're right," said Roberts sheepishly. "All through the early news, I told myself there was no way I was coming over here. But Bobbi kept saying, 'Go, have him fill you in. Otherwise, you won't get any sleep tonight.' So here I am. Okay, so now that I've eaten crow, tell me: what was the clue in Allerdyce's puzzle?"

"The answer, Paul, is in two parts. Once I discovered the first, the second was obvious."

"I'll bite: what was the first part?"

"That crossword definition, the one about the Japanese car."

"What about it?"

"It read 'A Japanese car—a plaything, perhaps?' Why was the article 'a' included there, but not in the third definition? Because the 'a' is part of the definition. So the answer is not simply 'Toyota' but 'a Toyota.' And that's seven letters, as specified."

"I still don't get it," said Roberts.

"Well, what do we have now? 'Noon,' 'a Toyota,' and 'tenet.' And there you have it!"

"Have what?" asked Roberts.

"They're all palindromes, Paul. I didn't realize it until I saw a pendulum swinging in my class this morning. The same movement, left to right and right to left."

"But what are palo—pal—what you said?"

"Look at the answer to the first definition: 'noon.' If you read it left to right, the direction in which the English language is read, it's spelled N-O-O-N. Now read in the opposite direction, from right to left."

"N-O-O-N, exactly the same!"

"Right, and that's what makes it a palindrome: the letters read the same from back to front as they do from front to back. And the same applies to 'a Toyota' and 'tenet,' which are also palindromes."

The teacher took a notebook from the table and leafed

through it. "There are longer palindromes Eugene might have used," he said. "Like this one I found in the library: 'Doc, note, I dissent. A fast never prevents a fatness. I diet on cod.' That has fifty-one letters, but it's a perfect palindrome. To some people, it might even make sense."

"But how do those whatever-you-call-thems tell you it was the house on Cade Lane where—"

"Eugene Allerdyce might have clued us to one palindrome by accident," the teacher said. "But three in a row? Too much of a coincidence. No, he used the palindromes for a purpose. And when I remembered Kapak's name on that list of ALP hideouts—"

"Otto Kapak!"

"Both the first name and the last name are palindromes. To someone as fond of word puzzles as Eugene Allerdyce is, the chance to leave a palindromic clue was irresistible. I called Marcos, he accepted my solution—and the rest, as they say, is history."

Roberts sat on the edge of the bed, shaking his head. "I don't know, Mr. Strang," he said. "This time, everything turned out okay. I mean, we got Allerdyce back safely and all. But terrorist groups? Kidnapping of public figures? I can't help wishing I was back in the old days, when police work was a lot less complicated. Give me a good old-fashioned bank robbery any day."

"But Paul," said Mr. Strang, rising and placing a hand on the detective's shoulder. "Are we not drawn onward, we few, drawn onward to new era?"

Roberts looked at the teacher oddly. "Who are you trying to be, the Old Philosopher?"

"As philosophy, that last question of mine is pointless, Paul." Mr. Strang tented his fingertips and looked innocently at the ceiling. "But as a palindrome? It's perfect!"

MR. STRANG AND THE LOST SHIP

While nobody can deny the scenic beauty of New England's rocky coast, the snowfall in mid-winter can be abundant. This was one factor that Mr. Strang, Aldershot High School's gnome-like science teacher, failed to take into consideration when he agreed to spend a long weekend in February at Ye Chandler's Inne in the little fishing village of Pixley's Cove.

The invitation had been extended by Edward Hotchkiss, the Inne's owner and a former college classmate of Mr. Strang's. "It's as balmy as spring, and almost no snow on the ground," was how Hotchkiss put it during their phone conversation. "C'mon up to our rock-strewn coast. Things are kind of slow here, so we'll have plenty of time to talk over the old days, and you can get some sightseeing in. The room and grub's on me."

The bus had arrived in Pixley's Cove late Thursday evening—or extremely early Friday morning, to be more exact. Once in his room, Mr. Strang collapsed on the bed as if poleaxed and slept for ten hours. It was during that period of time that the skies unleashed the full fury of winter, dropping some twenty-four inches of snow on the area.

Now it was Sunday morning, and Mr. Strang had a severe case of cabin fever. Oh, the roads had been plowed, and there was no question that he'd be able to catch his bus back to Aldershot at four that afternoon. It was just that there was nothing to *do*, no place to go, nothing to occupy his mind. The stony fields and scenic beauty of the area were covered by a thick blanket of white, most of the shops—except for the grocery and hardware stores—were closed for the season, and the local movie theater was featuring a monument to cinematic tastelessness titled *Disco Zombie*. Books were scarce, those available being two syrupy romance novels, a half-dozen tales involving the Five Little Peppers, and a volume on how to repair one's own plumbing.

Cataloguing the good times they'd had in college and bringing each other up to date had taken Hotchkiss and Mr. Strang some three hours on Friday afternoon. Since that time, only one form of entertainment had been available to them: checkers.

Mr. Strang, more used to chess, played hard and diligently. But he was no match for his host, and, at a nickel a game, the teacher now owed Hotchkiss a dollar and twenty cents.

"Eddie," he said, when once again the last of his pieces had been taken from the board, "you are an exemplary inn-keeper, and I am an absolute churl of a guest. If I so much as *see* another checker, I shall froth at the mouth, I shall swing from the lighting fixtures, I shall dance the gavotte in the rooms of your guests, wearing nothing but my un-derwear and a seductive smile. I've got to find some other kind of activity, something to occupy my mind and body. Something to *do*!"

"Hmmm." Hotchkiss chewed the stem of his pipe and mulled the problem over in his mind. "Well, there's—no, I guess you wouldn't want to—"

"I have seven ... long ... hours ... before my bus leaves," replied Mr. Strang ponderously. "*Anything*, Eddie."

"Our village museum," Hotchkiss said with his Yankee twang. "It ain't much, but, you being a teacher and all, you might find it interesting."

"Lead me to it!" Already the teacher was reaching for his overcoat and boots.

"Hold on a bit. The museum don't actually open till April. But I'll call Miz Quinn, she's in charge of it. Mayor Blore, too. He's right proud of the place, and he'll want to come down and show you around."

Mr. Strang froze, with one arm jammed into the sleeve of his coat. "You mean the museum will be opened up just for me?"

"Yep. Oh, Miz Quinn and Artis Blore'll be glad to do it. It'll give 'em something to keep their minds occupied. Time hangs heavy around here in the middle o' winter."

"Yes, I've noticed that."

Hotchkiss seemed not to catch the irony of this remark.

Ten minutes later, the teacher was standing on the front steps of the clapboard house that housed the Pixley's Cove Museum. He beat his gloved hands together to generate some warmth, while Ruth Quinn, a rather plump woman in her mid-forties, removed a key from her purse. On the plowed sidewalk, Artis Blore implored Miss Quinn to hurry, before they all turned to icicles.

The interior of the building was only minimally heated, just enough to prevent the pipes from freezing. "We'd best keep our coats on," said Blore, and Mr. Strang was glad to oblige.

In the center of the quaint museum's main room was a model, some four feet square, covered with sheets of clear plastic. It showed an area of land and some tiny buildings, each with one side cut away to reveal its interior.

"That's the old Armell Glass Works," Ruth Quinn began. "Of course, it's only an approximation, because nobody knows—"

"I'll explain, Miss Quinn, if you don't mind," said Blore officiously. "The Armell Glass Works, Mr. Strang, was the first industry in Pixley's Cove. It was started in the mid-eighteenth-century by the Bradwick brothers, Armand and Ellis—whence the name 'Armell.' It apparently fell to ruin sometime around 1800. We can't be more certain of the date because—"

"The fact of the matter is," Ruth Quinn cut in, "nobody knows where in town the Glass Works is—that is, *was*—located. When the old village building was torn down, we found lots of paperwork—bills of lading, pay records, and such. But none of it told where the Works actually *stood*."

Mr. Strang's face took on an impish grin. "Perhaps it never existed at all," he said slyly. "Maybe somebody faked all those documents to confuse future generations."

"Oh, it existed, all right," said Blore seriously. "We've even got a sample of their work." He strode toward the wall opposite the front door. "It's over here, an item that was actually made at the Glass Works. It's an excellent example of—*yeee!*"

At the sound of Mayor Blore's scream, Ruth ran to him, with Mr. Strang on her heels. The mayor had one hand over his eyes; the other pointed to a small display stand. "Look! Look there!" he said, in what seemed to be sheer panic. "What do you see?"

"A little wooden stand with a bottle resting on it," said the teacher.

"Go—go on."

"The top of the bottle's capped with cord tied in some kind of complicated knot, and there's nothing inside the bottle. Well, a bit of clay, perhaps. Or putty."

"What else?" demanded Blore in a shaky voice.

"That's all."

"'That's all', he says. That *can't* be all!" Moaning, Blore lowered his hand from his eyes. "It's gone. But it *can't* be gone."

Mr. Strang turned to Ruth. "Is he always like this? Or is there really something wrong?"

"Something is very definitely wrong," she replied. "When we closed the museum last fall, that bottle had a ship in it!"

For a moment, Mr. Strang just stared at her in amazement. "A—a *what*?" he finally asked.

"A ship—a model, with masts and sails and all that. The

kind they put in bottles. Only it seems to have disappeared."

Mr. Strang peered into the bottle, where the waves of a green putty sea surged in neat rows, as if the ship had sunk beneath them, never to be seen again. "Kind of sailed off into the sunset, you mean?"

"This is no time for comedy!" snapped Blore. "I'm just thankful that whoever did this didn't take the bottle, too."

"It must be hard enough getting a ship *into* a bottle," said Ruth slowly. "But how on earth do you get one *out*, especially though that narrow neck?"

In spite of the evident consternation of Ruth Quinn and Artis Blore, Mr. Strang could have hugged them both. For here was a problem, something to put his mind to. For the first time in two days, he found himself hoping that the bus that would take him home might be a bit late.

"Perhaps I can help," he said diffidently.

"Oh," Ruth began, "I don't think—"

"We'll take any help we can get," said Blore, firmly overruling the museum's curator.

"Very well. Now, what is there about this bottle that's so all-fired important? Ships in bottles aren't exactly a rarity, especially in New England."

Blore reeled his way to a chair and motioned Ruth and Mr. Strang into others. "It all has to do with the Armell Glass Works," he said, mopping a suddenly sweaty brow with a handkerchief. "We know it existed. We just don't know where. When we find the location, the village board and the Chamber of Commerce plan to reconstruct it, just as it was two hundred years ago. That'll make quite a tourist attraction. In fact, we've offered a substantial reward to anyone who can pinpoint the original location. And whoever owns that land will get a pretty penny for it, I can tell you!"

"I see," said the teacher. "And the bottle?"

"I can help you there," said Ruth. "The Glass Works, according to the records we found, produced primarily crown glass, made by blowing a bubble of heated glass and then spinning it at the end of a rod, so it formed a big disc, sometimes as big as fifty inches in diameter. When the glass cooled, the disc was cut into windowpanes. Armell glass was well suited for that purpose, since it was almost clear, with only a slight bluish tinge—as you can see from that bottle."

"So the Glass Works also made bottles?" asked the teacher.

Ruth shook her head. "Not during the regular workday. But when the day ended, there was usually some molten glass left in the crucible. 'Off-hand' glass, it was called. And that became the property of the gaffer."

"The what?"

"A master glass blower was called a gaffer," she replied with a smile. "And the gaffer at the Armell Works—his name was Noah Sterner—made these bottles from leftover glass. The few that remain intact are quite famous and rather valuable. Here in Pixley's Cove—where the bottles came from in the first place—we only have this one example."

"The bottle was found by a farm boy during spring plowing," added Blore. "I convinced him to donate it to the museum, and we thought it would be of interest—and point up the seafaring history of the Cove—if there was a ship inside. So Chris Wayde stuck one in there, gratis." Blore winked at Mr. Strang. "For the good of the village, you know."

Ruth Quinn walked back to where the bottle lay on its wooden stand. "That's what's so odd about this theft, Mr. Strang. Who'd want the ship, even if he *did* figure out how to get it out of the bottle? The bottle itself is far more valuable than what was inside it.

"Look here," she went on, as Mr. Strang walked up beside her. "See the pontil mark on the bottom of the bottle? That's where it was broken away from the shaping rod. And there on the neck is an *S* worked into the glass—Noah Sterner's initial. Every bottle is different. And it's their differences that make them valuable."

"But what happened to the ship?" groaned Blore. "And how—and why—was it taken out of the bottle in the first place?"

"If I'm to have any hope of figuring that out," said Mr. Strang, shivering, "I've got to have someplace warm to think." He tapped a gnarled finger against his brow. "Cold shrinks the brain cells. That's a well-known fact."

"Perhaps, instead of going back to the Inne," said Ruth, "you'd like to come to my house for tea. I'd be glad of someone new to talk to. The townspeople have heard my gossip and I've heard theirs a thousand times. We'll be properly chaperoned: I live with my father. Let me apologize for him in advance. He's rather—well, eccentric."

"He's crazy as a hoot owl," said Blore. "But Mr. Strang, do you really think you can find out how the ship got out of the bottle?"

The teacher shrugged. "I can try, Mr. Blore. At least that'll be more interesting than"—he screwed up his face distastefully—"playing checkers."

On the way to Ruth Quinn's house, Mr. Strang asked if they could stop off to see Chris Wayde. A young giant of a man, Wayde ran the Pixley's Cove Gift Shoppe and spent the off-season whittling grizzled seamen and carving sperm whales and clipper ships on bookends, trivets, cutting boards, and other objects for the summer tourist trade.

"There's not much to putting a ship in a bottle," Wayde told the teacher. "It takes more care than knowledge. The trick is to hinge the mast and spars so they fold down against the deck. There's a thread running from the stern to the top of each mast and from there through a hole in the bowsprit. Once the ship's embedded in its sea of putty, you pull the thread, and everything comes up into place. The thread's glued to the bowsprit, and the excess is cut off with a razor blade on a thin stick after the glue dries. The work's more tedious than anything else."

"And how would you go about getting the ship *out*, once it's in there?" asked Mr. Strang.

Wayde scratched his head. "That would be hard," he said, "unless you smashed it to pieces, and even that would be difficult without breaking the bottle. Who'd want to do such a thing, anyway?"

The teacher shook his head. "How much do you normally charge for a ship in a bottle, Chris?"

"Oh, mebbe twenty-five or thirty dollars. 'Course, I tell my friends that if they bring the bottle—full—we'll empty it together, and then I'll do the job for nothing ... soon as I can see clear enough to find the neck. One or two of 'em has took me up on it, but those were losing propositions for me. Takes me five or six hours to do a good job."

A short time later, Ruth Quinn and Mr. Strang were back in her old black coupe, basking in the warm blast from the heater. Ruth pulled into the driveway of a gaunt frame house, and Mr. Strang marveled at the size of the three huge boulders that seemed to be erupting from the snow-covered front yard.

They entered the kitchen through the back door and stamped the snow from their feet. A door at the other end of the room burst open, and a man appeared there. He was older than Mr. Strang, with only a few wisps of iron-gray hair on his head. He wore bedroom slippers and wrinkled wool trousers, and the upper part of his body was clad only in bright-red long-armed underwear. In one of the man's fists was a battered cane, which he brandished like a club.

"Ruth?" the man demanded in a cracked voice, "is that critter with you?"

"Yes, Daddy." She shook her head in amused annoyance. "This is Mr. Strang, and he's our guest."

"How do, young fella." And Mr. Quinn pumped the teacher's hand vigorously. Mr. Strang was thoroughly charmed. It had been years—decades—since he'd last been called a "young fella."

Ruth made tea, and she and Mr. Strang sat at the kitchen table to drink it. Mr. Quinn disappeared into the living room, where—from the roar of gunshots and the clatter of horses' hooves—a cowboy movie was playing on television.

"Daddy's always been a little—well, *odd*," Ruth told the teacher. "And the stroke he had a few years back didn't help any. The winters are hard for him. He likes to keep occupied, but there's not much for him to do."

"He keeps busy in the summers, though?"

"Yes, his current project is digging a root cellar in the sand bank out behind the house. Of course, we don't have a garden—too many rocks for that—so there's nothing to put *into* a root cellar, once we have one. On the other hand, whenever Daddy digs, the sand just runs right back into the hole, so I expect he'll never get it done. But it keeps him active."

Mr. Strang leaned back in his chair and laughed heartily. Sisyphus's rock was nothing compared to digging a hole in shifting sand.

"You have a nice house," he said, by way of conversation.

Ruth shook her head. "We have a horrid house, Mr. Strang. Why Daddy and I moved out here, I'll never know. The other one was much prettier."

"The other one?"

"Yes, you saw it this morning. The village took it over for the museum. Artis Blore went on about how it was our civic duty to give the place up, so the museum could get started, and the board gave us this one in exchange. They also gave me the curator's job to kind of sweeten the deal. But I don't know if we should have agreed." She sighed.

"It's lonely out here, especially for Daddy. In town, he could walk to the stores and see all his friends. But now—"

And then she brightened. "Perhaps one of these days we'll do some traveling. I'd like that. I've never been more than a hundred miles away from this town in my life. But there's no sense burdening you with my troubles. What about the ship? Any idea who took it out of the bottle—and how—and why?"

"Not a one," the teacher said. "I'm far too relaxed for thinking. A warm house on a cold day, pleasant companionship, a delicious cup of tea—what more could someone my age ask of life?"

*

It was after one when Ruth Quinn dropped Mr. Strang back at Ye Chandler's Inne. "Lunch time's over, Leonard!" yelled Hotchkiss from the kitchen. "But you can make your own from what's in the fridge, if you like."

As the teacher went through the swinging doors into the huge kitchen, he saw his host up to his flour-dusted elbows in the process of making apple pies. "Ten at a time, Eddie?" he asked in surprise.

"Yep. I'm expecting a few tour buses to stop by here this evening on their way back from the ski slopes. Feed 'em plenty, and they're happy. And when they're happy, they tip well." Hotchkiss plied his rolling pin expertly, thinning out the top crusts that would cover the pans filled with apples, sugar, and spices.

"Except for what looks like about fifteen pounds of rolled roast," said Mr. Strang, peering into the depths of the refrigerator, "there's not much here."

"Fry yourself an egg," replied Hotchkiss. "There must be a couple left in the carton."

"Just one, and I'll take it—but soft boiled."

"Suit yourself. The pot's on the rack there, and the egg timer's on the stove."

The teacher brought water to a boil while Hotchkiss flipped the top crusts over his pies with a feather-light touch. Mr. Strang eased the egg into the boiled water and turned the timer upside down. Tiny grains of sand began trickling through its neck.

"One for you." Hotchkiss pricked a little floral design into one of the piecrusts with a fork. "And one for you." A few flicks of the fork, and a bloom and leaves appeared, as if by magic, on another crust. "And one for *you.*"

For a moment, Mr. Strang watched in amusement, then returned his attention to the egg timer.

There was something....

He stared blankly at the wall, deep in thought.

"Leonard?" From somewhere, a voice impinged on his consciousness. "Leonard, if you don't get that pot off the stove right quick, it's gonna boil dry. As it is, your egg'll be hard as a rock."

"I know," he said softly. "I know how it happened."

"So do I," snapped Hotchkiss. "You fell asleep at the switch, that's how it happened."

"No, the ship, the bottle." And suddenly Mr. Strang was alert. "What time is it, Eddie?"

"Nearly two. You got plenty of time before—"

"No, I haven't. Where's your phone book? Quick!"

He was able to get in touch with Ruth Quinn immediately and make his request. But Mayor Blore was out, and it took his secretary a few minutes to locate him. Finally, the little group met outside the Pixley's Cove Museum, just as it had that morning. The single difference was that now, at Mr. Strang's insistence, old Mr. Quinn had accompanied his daughter.

Once inside the museum, Mr. Strang saw that Ruth, her father, and Blore were seated comfortably—at least as comfortably as the chill air permitted. Then, despite the cold, Mr. Strang removed his overcoat. In a gesture that would have been familiar to thousands of present and former students of Aldershot High School, he whipped off his black-rimmed glasses, polished them on his none-too-clean necktie, and stowed them in a jacket pocket. He peered down at the three, now every inch the teacher.

"Do you know, Mr. Strang?" asked Blore eagerly. "Do you know what happened to the ship?"

"Mr. Blore," came the rather imperious reply, "I'm pressed for time, as I have to catch a bus in"—he glanced at his watch—"exactly one hour. So please let me handle this my own way."

Blore sank back in his seat in uncharacteristic silence.

"There are two facets to the problem of the ship that left its bottle," said Mr. Strang, as if he were speaking to a room full of teenaged students. "One is the disappearance of the ship itself. The other has to do with the Armell Glass Works. Surprisingly, the two are related."

Ruth Quinn opened her mouth to speak, then thought better of it.

"First," the teacher continued, "the ship. Its bottle was not broken, nor were there even the tiniest scraps of wood inside to indicate that the ship was smashed to pieces in order to get it out."

"So it was removed whole!" said Blore. "I knew it!"

"It was not, Mr. Blore, I'm sure of it. For I saw something here this morning whose significance I didn't comprehend until I watched Ed Hotchkiss making indentations in piecrusts at the Inne, just after lunch."

"What was it?" asked Ruth Quinn.

"I saw a piece of putty inside the bottle. It was shaped into waves to look like water."

"It's *supposed* to look like water," said Blore.

"Yes, but the point is, it *isn't* water. Take a ship out of water, and its place will immediately be filled by the water left behind. But take a ship—however small—out of putty, and the depression its hull had made *in* the putty will remain. And yet there is no depression in the putty in the bottle!"

Blore scuttled to where the bottle sat on its stand and examined it closely. "You're right," he said. "But what does that mean, Mr. Strang?"

"Unless we accept the absurd idea that, having removed the ship, the thief took the time to remodel the putty into waves, it means that the bottle on the stand is *not* the one the ship was in."

It took some moments for this to sink in. And then Blore made a sound like a deflating tire. "You mean there's another Armell bottle besides this one?"

"That's precisely what I mean, Mr. Blore. Far from removing the ship from its bottle, your thief took the original bottle with the ship still inside, leaving this replacement bottle in its place. Compared to removing a ship under full sail *from* a bottle, putting a little putty *into* a bottle and shaping it into waves with a long thin stick would be child's play."

"But who did it?" cried Ruth.

"Oh, my dear." Mr. Strang shook his head. "That *you* should ask such a question. Mayor Blore, I assume this building is secure? Nobody can get in when the doors are locked?"

"Only by breaking a window."

"But no windows were broken. The thief, therefore, must have had a key. And who *has* the keys to this building, Mayor?"

"There are only two keys. I have one, and Ruth—" Blore spun to stare at the curator. "You!" he said, astounded. "It had to be you!"

For a moment, Ruth Quinn tried to stare him down. Then she turned away, her face reddening, tears springing to her eyes.

"Yes," Mr. Strang went on, "sometime between the autumn closing and now, Ruth, you came in here, carrying the second bottle in a bag or large purse. With no one about, it was easy to make the substitution. I suspect the original bottle is at your house right now."

Ruth Quinn sat tight-lipped, gazing straight ahead.

"But why, Ruth?" asked Blore. "Why would you do a thing like that, even if you *did* have an extra bottle?"

The silence was overwhelming.

Old Mr. Quinn patted his daughter's hand.

And then Mr. Strang spoke again.

"Mayor Blore," he said, "you have a way of getting something for nothing. The farm boy who brought you the bottle was persuaded to hand it over without payment. Chris Wayde spent hours putting the ship into the bottle, and you convinced him that it was his civic duty to donate his time. And, years ago, you talked Ruth and her father into giving up this lovely house in the center of town for a much less suitable place on the outskirts. You must have a golden tongue, sir."

"Why, thank you, Mr. Strang. I—"

"But perhaps later, once the glow of civic pride had faded, isn't it possible that one or two of your 'contributors' might have felt that, however legal the process by which it was done, you had cheated them?"

"Well, I suppose—"

"*You* feel that way, don't you, Ruth?"

With a proud toss of her head, Ruth Quinn nodded her agreement.

"What it comes down to, Mr. Blore, is that, after what you did to Ruth and her father, they wanted to make you sweat a little. So Ruth switched bottles. But she made a mistake."

"I sure did!" snapped Ruth. "If it weren't for Mr. Strang wanting to see the museum, Artis, you wouldn't have known about the different bottle until next spring, when we reopened. I was sure you'd see in a minute that a substitution had been made: those bottles are different as night and day, if you know what to look for. But you, you big lummox, you thought it was the same bottle, except with the ship missing. I had to go along with you, or you might have suspected me."

"Even if I *had* noticed the change," Blore sputtered, "what then?"

"You might have got to wondering where the other bottle came from," cackled old Mr. Quinn. "Then, after letting you stew in your own juice for a week or so, we'd have told you."

"Where *did* the other bottle come from?" asked Blore.

"It was found," said Mr. Strang, "exactly where you'd *expect* such an object to be found: on the site of the old Armell Glass Works."

Blore looked as if he'd been hit with a brick. "You—you mean the Quinns found the Armell Works?"

"They did. Or, more accurately, you and the town fathers *gave* it to them. And I imagine you'll have to pay a pretty penny to get it back, to use your own words. Enough, I expect, so that Ruth and her father will be able to take that trip they've been longing for."

"You mean it's on her property?" Blore asked in a halting voice. "The property the village deeded to her?"

"Correct at last, Mayor."

"But that was our secret, Daddy's and mine," said Ruth, clasping her father's hand tightly. "How did you find out, Mr. Strang?"

The teacher smiled at her. "My dear, a second bottle appeared mysteriously. Your father spends his spare time digging in a sand pit. Ruth, it occurred to me that, in this boulder-infested area, sand is a rather rare commodity. Yet it's the one thing the Armell Works *had* to have—for sand is the chief ingredient in the making of glass. Where better to build the Works than in the middle of a sand bank?"

Mr. Strang spread his hands wide. "Once I was reminded by the sight of sand trickling through an egg timer, the evidence was too compelling to ignore."

"We—that is, Daddy—discovered the Works last summer while he was digging his root cellar," said Ruth. "The place must have burned down. All that's left of the original structure is some charred beams. But there's some brick-work, and some huge kettles, and—"

"The original furnaces and crucibles," breathed Blore. "An incredible find!"

"Yes, and you'll pay through the nose, if you want them!" snapped Ruth. "If you don't, I'll find someone else who will."

"But you did steal the bottle, Ruth," said Blore smoothly. "And to avoid prosecution, I imagine you'll—"

"As curator of the Museum, I have the right to store the exhibits wherever I wish. The ship in a bottle is available whenever it's asked for."

"But, Ruth, think how grateful the village would be if you would see your way clear to return the land to us for— oh, some nominal fee. We'll have a plaque with your name on it, and—"

"Mr. Blore?" said Ruth in her most ladylike voice.

"Yes?"

"You can stick it in your ear!"

Mr. Strang put on his overcoat. "I have a bus to catch," he announced, flicking his left sleeve to expose his wrist-watch. "*Drosophila!* Ruth! Ruth, I need your help!"

"What is it, Mr. Strang?"

"My bus leaves in ten minutes, and I have to pick up my suitcase at the Inne. Can you give me a lift? If I get stuck here and have to play one more game of checkers with Eddie Hotchkiss, my brain will turn into a mothball. A ride, Ruth, quick!"

MR. STRANG TAKES A PARTNER

"Would you be Mr. Strang, now?"

Mr. Strang looked up from the heap of chemical-stained glassware on the demonstration table at the front of his classroom. It was nearly four-thirty, and he still had to wash the lab apparatus—"scrubbing the pots," he called it. This late in the day, he was in no mood to face some overbearing parent bent on turning an offspring's C- into an A by dint of paternal persuasion.

A glance at the figure in the doorway calmed his fears. The slender man who stood there might have been taken for a small boy, but for a face seamed with creases that were accentuated by a broad smile. He stood scarcely five feet tall, and his unruly shock of red hair was tinged here and there with wisps of gray. All in all, he put Mr. Strang in mind of a well-dressed leprechaun.

"Yes, I'm Leonard Strang." The science teacher wiped his damp palms on the lapels of his jacket and shook the hand the little man extended.

"Corcoran's the name, Wesley Corcoran."

"Patty's father?"

"Yas. As a matter of fact, Patricia's the reason I've come calling."

"She's doing quite well in biology and—"

"Tush, man, it's not Patricia's schooling I want to see you about."

"Then—?"

"Mr. Strang, did you not tell my daughter's class that any problem can be solved, if all the evidence is available and it's approached in the proper manner?"

Mr. Strang felt his face redden. "Well, I—"

"Furthermore, I understand you're quite the one for figuring things out. Not just science stuff, neither, but all sorts of puzzles and things."

"Mr. Corcoran, it's really quite late, and I have to—"

"Ah, you force my hand. I was saving this to show you at a more opportune time, but before you can get a man's help, you must first get his attention, as the woman said while bashing her husband's head with a rolling pin."

Corcoran reached into a jacket pocket and brought out what appeared to be a folded sheet of paper from a yellow legal pad. "Would you just take a few seconds to read this?"

The teacher unfolded the paper. The penciled words on it were written in a quavery hand. It appeared to be a poem of some kind.

> WHY work at conundrums, faithful Wes?
>   To seek your fortune, no more and no less.
> Now, having answered WHY, I leave to you
>   To find the WHAT, WHEN, WHERE, and WHO.
> All answers lie beneath my roofing tiles
>   And in Alaska's literary isles.
> The one you seek's a truly Nob'l man.
>   Now solve my word game—if you can.

"What say you, Mr. Strang?" asked Corcoran, when the teacher had finished reading. "Shall I go now and leave you in peace?"

A grin spread across Mr. Strang's face as he saw the impish gleam in Corcoran's eyes. "You old fraud!" the teacher exclaimed. "Patty *told* you I could never turn down a good puzzle. What's this all about? Nothing criminal, I trust?"

Corcoran shook his head. "More in the financial field. So what do you gather from the poem? About the person who wrote it, I mean?"

"Hmm." The teacher ran gnarled fingers through his sparse crop of hair. "I can't make much sense of the poem itself. But the writer—that's something else again. He's quite wealthy but in poor health. He's fairly intelligent, and either his background or his interests—or both—run to the newspaper business."

"Ah, ha!" Corcoran gave Mr. Strang's back a congratulatory pat. "You're just the man for me, sir. How'd you know all them things from just those few lines?"

"Well," Mr. Strang replied, "the hand that wrote this trembled, and I surmise that was due to illness. As to his wealth, not only does he mention a fortune, but he also refers to his 'roofing tiles.' Yes, the phrase does make the line rhyme properly, but it's also suggestive of enough money to afford something better than the usual asphalt shingles. The newspaper business? Well, every cub reporter learns early on that *who, what, when, where,* and *why* are the elements of a good news story. The intelligence is obvious—he wrote the poem, didn't he?"

The teacher sat at his desk. "Now that I've told you what I get from it, Mr. Corcoran, it's back to you. What *is* this all about? Who wrote it? And why?"

"The lines were written," answered Corcoran, "by Rutherford Pyle."

Mr. Strang recognized the name. "He died last week, right here in Aldershot. His heart, wasn't it? A pity: Pyle did incredible things with the English language. He was one of the most persuasive writers I've ever read."

A smile spread across Corcoran's face. "So you know a bit about our Mr. Pyle, then?"

"More than a bit. He was a Horatio Alger hero come to life. A newspaper delivery boy at twelve. Fifteen years later, he owned a paper out in the Midwest, and ten years after that he had four more. Ran them all himself, wrote a lot of the copy and editorials, said what he thought regardless of outside pressure, and the devil take the hindmost."

"That was a long time back," sighed Corcoran. "Those were the good old days, Mr. Strang, and I was at his side through them all. My job was to sort of look after Mr. Pyle and do whatever little tasks he set for me. He said I was his good-luck charm. But old age creeps up on us all. And when he had them two heart attacks—near five years ago, they were—he took the big house here in Aldershot to be near his daughter and her husband. Me and my own daughter Patricia—my wife, her mother, died long since, God rest her soul—lived there with him. The attacks weakened him something terrible. A short walk about the house once a day was the best he could manage. But I saw to it that the chores got done—and in return, Mr. Corcoran gave me an education like none other in the world."

"An education?" asked Mr. Strang. "What do you mean?"

"Mr. Pyle has—had—a library that fills near half the main floor of the house. He was weak of body, but his mind stayed quick as ever. Having naught to occupy himself, he decided to educate me far beyond the six years of public school I had as a boy. I resisted, at first, but later on the problems got to be kind of fun."

"Problems?"

"Yes, sir. He'd pretend like I was a reporter and he was sending me out to get a story. Only the place I'd go to get it was downstairs in the library. And heaven help me if I didn't have the who, what, when, where, and why of it by the time I returned."

"Just how did that work?" asked Mr. Strang.

"Well, I remember one time when he set me the task of finding two words that sounded the same but had opposite meanings. To find 'em, I had to read the dictionary, learning new words by the score."

"And what were the two words?"

"I found quite a few pairs. Take *raise* and *raze*, for example—to build up, and to tear down. Y'see, that was the cleverness of it. To solve Mr Pyle's problems, I had to do a tremendous amount of reading. I daresay there's few books in that vast library of his what ain't got my thumb smudges on 'em. I'd have to find out everything there was to know about famous characters in literature—Uriah Heep, for instance—and report back as if the character was a living person. Or there'd be a *place* I was to research, right down to knowing how much it would cost to fly there. And all the time I was learnin' and learnin', and me not even knowin' it. Because of Mr. Pyle's kindness, I'll vow there's many a college professor I could give a run for his money. It's *because* Mr. Pyle was so good to me that I know he wouldn't—he couldn't—"

"Couldn't what, Mr. Corcoran?"

"Well, Mr. Pyle up and died, you see, and now my Patricia and me are out on our own, without enough money between us to buy a decent meal. That's not how he would have wanted it."

"But surely there's a will," said the teacher.

"There is. It leaves everything to his daughter. He died too soon, Mr. Strang. Too soon."

"Too soon? I don't understand."

"Well, sir, over the past few months, Mr. Pyle began talking with me about how things was going to be after he died. His estate and all. He was beginning to have intimations of his mortality, don't you see? I was not mentioned in his will, as he didn't want his daughter and me arguing over who was to get what. But several weeks ago, he told me he'd put some money aside, so me and Patricia would be taken care of after he passed away."

"I'm still puzzled. Why not take that money and—?"

"He didn't put the money in a bank or anything like that, see? No, he concealed it somewhere in the house. And then he set me one last problem. I was to be a reporter again and use the clues he'd give me—'leads,' he called them—to track down where the money was stashed. If I couldn't find it within a month, he said he'd reveal the hiding place. It was so foolish to do the thing that way, but he had few things to occupy his mind by then. And before the month had ended, he was—"

"Is that what this is all about?" asked Mr. Strang. "Hidden in that big house there's money Rutherford Pyle meant you and Patricia to have?"

"That's it, Mr. Strang," Corcoran replied. "Somewhere in the house—probably in the library itself, I'll wager—is the fortune mentioned in the poem. But before I could give the place a proper search, the lawyers for the estate told me I had to get out. The house is locked up tight, and Patricia and I are living in a single room with barely enough ready cash to pay this week's rent."

"Hmmm." Mr. Strang toyed with his acid-stained necktie. "You know, Mr. Corcoran, legally you haven't a leg to stand on. If Pyle left everything to his daughter, you can't claim a dime based on some vague promise he made."

"That's true, sir. But the daughter—Laura Aikens is her married name—has given me a bit of hope. She knows the high regard her father had for me. She says if Mr. Pyle meant for me to have something, I shall have it."

"Then why not just go back and search until you find the money?"

"That won't do. I showed Mrs. Aikens the poem and the rest, but she's not convinced it was anything but the meanderings of an old man. The only way I can claim what's due me, she says, is to prove to her that the clues make some sense—and then go into the house and straight to the hiding place. She'll not allow any hunting expeditions, with me claimin' any cash I might happen upon."

"I see," said Mr. Strang. "So that's the problem, then. You have to prove to Laura Aikens' satisfaction that a hiding place exists and then locate it, without *any* margin for error."

"That's it, indeed," replied Corcoran. "And it must be done within the next four days, as, after that, Mr. and Mrs. Aikens are moving away, leaving the house locked up tight with only a caretaker to have access. I despaired of havin' any chance at all, until Patricia suggested that you might be able to help."

Mr. Strang rubbed his hands together briskly. "Challenge accepted, Mr. Corcoran." He spread the wrinkled yellow paper on his desk. "Now, let's have a look at the rest of it. You've mentioned 'clues'—plural—as well as 'the poem and the rest.' What 'rest," Mr. Corcoran? What other leads did Mr. Pyle provide?"

Again Corcoran reached into a pocket. This time, he pulled out four white index cards. "I'm afraid you'll find these as confusing as the poem itself."

There were words written on each card in the same spidery handwriting as the poem. Mr. Strang peered through his black-rimmed glasses at the top one:

> Bobby writes to a rodent.
> WHO have plans turned to dust at 39 and 40?

The next message was equally obscure:

> Fight him for a nation!
> WHAT are the fruits of Julie's labors?

The third didn't help much, either:

> Bill's Dickey Three emotes, beginning one and one.
> WHEN is the season of low spirits?

And finally:

> Public Enemy Number One begins to Nod.
> WHERE is the marked man's newfound land?

Mr. Strang stared long and hard at the four cards. "Nothing," he said finally. "Let's look at the poem again."

He tapped the yellow paper with a gnarled finger. "The WHY is given here," he said. "'To seek your fortune, no more and no less.' The WHAT, WHEN, WHERE, and WHO must be connected to the clues on the white cards. But we need to begin with the poem, I'm sure of it."

"Can you find nothing at all?" asked Corcoran anxiously.

"The first part of the poem's clear enough: you're to seek your fortune somewhere in the house, 'beneath my roofing tiles.' It's the next two lines that stump me. What are 'Alaska's literary isles'? And why make a contraction of the word 'noble' and capitalize it?"

"As to the isles," murmured Corcoran, "the only ones I can think of in Alaska are the Aleutians."

"The Aleutians," said Mr. Strang. "Yes, they're well known, and I don't think Pyle would have given you anything *too* obscure. But whoever heard of literary Aleutians?"

"I have!" called a chipper voice from the hallway outside the room.

"What?" cried Mr. Strang and Corcoran together.

A woman's smiling face appeared around the corner of the doorway. It was surmounted by gray hair tied in a large knot at the back, with pencils stuck into the knot like pins in a pincushion.

"Maude Wiggins," bellowed Mr. Strang, "get in here this instant!"

The woman entered the room, cocking her head like an aged sparrow. "Wesley Corcoran, Maude Wiggins," said Mr. Strang. "Maude's our school librarian."

"I've just finished unpacking some reproductions of so-called art masterpieces," she said. "Masterpieces, my foot! Honestly, Leonard, how someone can splash a few daubs of paint on a canvas and sell it for thousands of dollars is beyond me. Anyway, I was passing your room when I heard you say—"

"—literary Aleutians," Mr. Strang said again. "What are they, Maude?"

"It's *allusions*," she said, stressing the pronunciation. "Literary allusions are oblique references to—well, to literature. For example, Leonard, if you were to tell me that age cannot wither me, nor custom stale my infinite variety, I'd know you've been reading Shakespeare's *Antony and Cleopatra,* and then I'd fall swooning into your arms."

"Aleutians, allusions," mused Mr. Strang. "They sound almost the same. Hydrozoa, Maude, I think you've hit on it! That's *just* the sort of linguistic trick Pyle loved to pull. And the last line of the poem even mentions a 'word game.' We didn't catch on because we were reading, not listening. Maude, I love you. You're beautiful. Will you run away with me and live in sin in a thatched hut on the beach?"

And he planted a big kiss on her cheek.

"Leonard Strang," she spluttered, "at your age, sinning means grabbing fifteen extra minutes of sleep on a school morning."

"I'm only two years older than you, Maude."

She made a mock slap at his face. "And you're no gentleman, either!"

By the desk, Corcoran shook his head in confusion. "I don't get it," he said. "What's going on here?"

"I was about to ask the same question," said Maude.

"'All answers lie beneath my roofing tiles'—that is, in the house," explained Mr. Strang, his hands trembling with excitement. "'And in Alaska's literary isles'—meaning in literary allusions. The WHAT, WHEN, WHERE, and WHO questions all have their answers in the Pyle library. And when we find the answers, they'll lead us to the fortune."

"I don't know what this is all about," said Maude, "but if you need a library, mine's available. And this sounds much more exciting than going home and cleaning my oven. So I demand to join you, with full partnership privileges. After all, if it wasn't for me, you two would still be freezing in Alaska."

"We're delighted to have you," said Mr. Strang gallantly. "Tell me, partner, do you think our beloved principal would be annoyed if we spent a few hours in the school library?"

"I think Mr. Guthrey would have a fit," replied Maude. "Everyone's supposed to be out of the building by five o'clock. But it's his blood pressure, not mine. Come on, I have a key." She sighed melodramatically. "Just my luck: the first time in twenty-five years a man—*two* men!—want to spend an evening with me, and all we're going to do is look at books."

Once they were seated at one of the library's long tables, Mr. Strang filled Maude in on Corcoran's problem. Then the three of them huddled over the four index cards.

"Which one are you wrestling with?" Mr. Strang asked Corcoran, after thirty minutes of fruitless endeavor.

"The one about 'Public Enemy Number One,'" was the reply. "All I can think of is James Cagney in the movie."

"I'm working on 'Bill's Dicky,'" said Maude. "Isn't that just too cute for words? To my way of thinking, the person who invented diminutives of names should be drawn and quartered. 'Bill's Dicky,' indeed. How would you like to be called 'Lenny' Strang, Leonard? Why can't this be 'William's Richard'—"

And then there was a silence, as Maude and Mr. Strang stared at each other, followed by a wild scrambling as they both raced to the far end of the room.

Maude, being more familiar with the arrangement of the library, was the first to reach the proper place. She removed a book from the shelf, riffled through its pages for a few moments, then pointed to a line of type.

"Got it," murmured Mr. Strang. "So we know the WHEN." And he jotted something down on a notepad.

"Now that we've got the hang of it," said Maude, "it shouldn't take long to figure out the other cards. Let me try my hand at WHO."

WHO came easily. WHAT and WHERE required a bit more thought, and there were several unproductive searches through the library's stacks. But in another hour, Mr. Strang and Maude were sure they knew the identity of Rutherford Pyle's "Nob'l man," and they were reasonably certain of the location of Wesley Corcoran's promised fortune in the Pyle mansion.

Still, they put their theory to Corcoran himself with some misgivings. "We're only going to get one chance," Mr. Strang said. "If we're wrong, it's goodbye, fortune."

"In for a penny, in for a pound," said Corcoran blithely. "Your ideas sound grand to me. If they don't work out, at least we had our try. I'll not hold hard luck against either of you. And now I guess it's time to make an appointment with Mrs. Aikens."

She was perhaps fifty years old. Her bearing was queenly as she approached the throne-like chair in the center of the room, and she carried a long cigarette holder in her right hand like a royal scepter. Before sitting, she turned in a full circle, studying the shelves of books that covered all four walls from floor to ceiling. The Pyle mansion's library was huge, larger even than the one at Aldershot High.

It has to be huge, thought Mr. Strang, *to contain a presence as commanding as Mrs. Laura Aikens.*

"Mr. Corcoran, Mr. Strang, Miss Wiggins," she said, settling into the chair's depths with great aplomb, "welcome to my father's house. You have told me, Mr. Corcoran, that my father wished you to have a token of gratitude for your years of service. It is my further understanding that Mr. Strang and Miss Wiggins are assisting you—your paladins, so to speak."

"Yes, Mrs. Aikens." Corcoran's voice was little more than a hoarse whisper.

"Very well," she went on. "I will not stand in the way of any wishes my father had concerning the disposition of his estate, and I reject any petty legal arguments concerning the propriety of those wishes. Quite simply, Mr. Corcoran: if Father wished you to have something, you shall have it.

"But I won't have a clever opportunist sullying my father's memory by trying to gain by trickery that which is not his. So the ground rules, if you will, are simple. You must convince me that the 'clues' of which you have spoken came from my father. You must further convince me that those clues lead to a specific spot in this house. And, finally, you must go to that spot and find something of real or sentimental value to you. If those three conditions are met, I will give you that which you claim as soon as the will is probated. Is that understood?"

"Y-yes, Mrs. Aikens," sputtered Corcoran.

"Then you may begin."

Mr. Strang and Maude Wiggins whispered together for a few seconds. Then the librarian shook her head firmly and backed toward the far wall. Mr. Strang approached the throne, reached into his pocket, and removed the poem and the four white cards.

"I've been elected to do the talking," he said. "So, first, I—we—ask you to look at this sheet of notepaper and these cards. Are they in your father's handwriting?"

She examined the five documents intently. Finally, she nodded. "Yes, my father wrote these."

"First condition met, then," the teacher stated. "For these are the clues he gave to Wesley Corcoran."

For the first time, a bit of a smile played about Mrs. Aiken's lips. "Go on."

"The fifth line of the poem tells us that the fortune is in this house—and also in 'Alaska's literary isles.' Mr. Corcoran and I took that to mean the Aleutians and, by extension, the literary Aleutians. But we give Miss Wiggins full marks for realizing that your father was obliquely referring to literary *allusions.*"

Mrs. Aikens' smile grew larger. "I will grant—reluctantly, Mr. Strang—that the pun in the phrase 'literary Aleutians' is one that my father was not only capable of but would have delighted in."

"Therefore," the teacher continued, "the WHAT, WHEN, WHERE, and WHO cards must contain literary references."

"Must they? You'll have to convince me."

"I hope to do exactly that. Each card first makes a cryptic statement and then asks a question. This seems to indicate that the statement is a clue to the corresponding question's answer. Would you agree?"

Mrs. Aikens remained impassive. "Go on."

"Our first break came on the 'Bill's Dicky' card, when Maude—Miss Wiggins—objected to the diminutive names and substituted the full ones. When that was done, the line read: 'William's Richard Three emotes, beginning one and one.'"

"Oh!" Laura Aikens clapped her hands in delight. The childish gesture was so out of character that Mr. Strang stared in astonishment.

"William Shakespeare's *Richard III,*" she cried. "Of course!"

The teacher breathed a sigh of relief. It seemed that the woman's second condition—that she could be convinced the cards indeed held clues—would be met more easily than he'd feared.

"And Scene *One* of Act *One,*" he said, stressing the numbers, "begins with Richard saying, 'Now is the winter of our discontent made glorious summer by this sun of York.' So, Mrs. Aikens, when is 'the season of low spirits?'"

"It must be 'the winter of our discontent.'"

"Good." Mr. Strang felt himself on firm ground now, and Laura Aikens seemed as pleased as any schoolgirl to have given a correct answer. "Now let's try the WHO card."

"Bobby," mused Mrs. Aikens. "So that's Robert, which might be Robert Browning or Robert Burns or Robert Louis—"

"I was at a loss on that one," Mr. Strang interrupted, "until Maude bailed me out. It seems that one of Robert Burns' best-known poems is titled 'To a Mouse.' And line thirty-nine of that poem, continuing on to line forty, is"—he consulted his notepad—"'The best laid schemes o' mice and men gang aft a-gley.' So, if 'a-gley' means *wrong,* then who 'have plans turned to dust'?"

"Mice and men?" replied Laura Aikens.

"Right," said the teacher. "Now, third, let's consider 'Public Enemy Number One.' This one took us a bit longer. But it occurred to me that the words 'begins to' might mean 'starts toward.' I also got to wondering if 'Number One' might mean, not 'the most dangerous,' but 'the first in time.' Public enemies of importance are usually killers, and the Number One killer, who was 'marked' by the Lord for his crime, was—?"

Laura Aikens arched her eyebrows. "You mean Cain? From the Bible?"

"I do. And note the capitalization of 'Nod.' The Bible tells us, in Genesis 4:16, that 'Cain went out from the presence of the Lord, and dwelt in the land of Nod—"

"Which is why it's capitalized!" exclaimed Laura.

"—on the east of Eden,'" Mr. Strang concluded.

"Then the answer to WHERE would be 'east of Eden'!" By now, Laura Aikens was enjoying herself enormously. "But there's still WHAT. 'Fight him for a nation.' That doesn't make sense. Who's Julie? Julius? Julian?"

"Maude, you figured this one out all by yourself," said Mr. Strang. "So you should do the honors, if you please."

"Well," the librarian began, with unaccustomed timidity, "I couldn't think of a pun for 'fight,' so I started substituting words that have about the same meaning: 'war,' 'brawl,' 'quarrel,' and so on. And then I hit on 'battle.'"

"Battle him for a nation," said Laura slowly. "I don't— oh, but, yes, I do! 'Him' and 'hymn'—again, they sound the same, but they're different words. 'Fight him for a nation' is 'The Battle Hymn of the Republic'!"

"—which was written by Julia Ward Howe," Mr. Strang chimed in. "And if you remember the first few lines, you'll get the 'fruits' of Julia's—or Julie's—'labors.'"

Laura began humming softly. "Da-da, da-da, da-*dah*-dah ... 'where the grapes of wrath are stored.' The fruits are the grapes of wrath, then, aren't they?"

Mr. Strang nodded. "So now we have all four questions answered. WHO is 'mice and men.' WHAT is 'the grapes of wrath.' WHEN is 'the winter of our discontent.' And, finally, WHERE is 'east of Eden.'"

Suddenly, Laura Aikens seemed to change again before their eyes. Gone was the schoolgirl, happy to be answering her teacher correctly. Instead, there again sat the imperious queen of the Rutherford Pyle estate on her throne. "This has all been very interesting," she proclaimed. "But I don't see how the literary allusions you've mentioned lead to any kind of hiding place."

At that, Maude Wiggins marched up to the huge chair, her eyes flashing. "Where," she demanded, "did your father keep his copies of the works of John Steinbeck?"

"John Steinbeck? But—"

"Yes, Mrs. Aikens," said Mr. Strang, "John Steinbeck. The author of *Of Mice and Men, The Grapes of Wrath, The Winter of Our Discontent*, and *East of Eden*. Four books, each taking its title from a literary allusion."

"But I always considered Steinbeck a rather *earthly* author. Why would father refer to him as noble?"

"Not 'noble,' Mrs. Aikens. N-O-B-apostrophe-L. Or, if we consider the capital N and replace the missing vowel indicated by the apostrophe, 'Nobel.' Were you aware that, in 1962, John Steinbeck won the Nobel Prize for Literature?"

Slowly, Laura Aikens lowered her head.

And then something shook her body, once, then again.

She was laughing.

"Father's word-play," she giggled. "It goes on, even after his death. There, Mr. Corcoran, on one of those shelves by the fireplace. There's where you'll find the Steinbeck books."

Corcoran approached the shelf. "There are four of them here," he said. "The very four we want."

He drew one of the books from the shelf and peered closely at its cover. Then he sniffed it. "Not a first edition," he said. "It's too new, worth perhaps fifteen dollars at most. I'm afraid we lose, Mr. Strang. Miss Wiggins, I'm sorry to have troubled you."

He held the book loosely by its spine, and Mr. Strang saw tears welling in his eyes. "He forgot about Patricia and me," Corcoran murmured sadly.

And then something appeared from between the pages of the book and fluttered to the floor. It was followed by a second fluttering. They appeared to be slips of green paper.

Maude scooped one of them up and examined it front and back. "It's a thousand-dollar bill," she whispered.

But already Mr. Strang had snatched the book from Corcoran's hands and was shaking it vigorously. Bills dropped from between the pages like green snow.

The second book revealed a similar cache.

And the third.

And the fourth.

A hundred bills in all, hidden away between the pages of the four Steinbeck volumes.

"One hundred thousand dollars!" gasped Cororan, scarcely able to believe it. "Oh, thank you, Mr. Strang! And you, Miss Wiggins! And you, Mrs. Aikens!"

"I won't be able to let you take the money until the will's

been probated," said Laura Aikens. "It's part of the estate, and the lawyers will have to know about it. But as soon as everything is settled, I'll send you a check, Mr. Corcoran. And in the meantime, if you need a little something to tide you over, I'll be happy to—"

"I'm sure that won't be necessary," said Mr. Strang. "Once this story hits the newspapers, Mr. Corcoran's credit will be excellent."

"A hundred thousand dollars," sighed Maude. "Leonard, on the strength of our success, I think you ought to take me out to dinner. Le Chateau Brun, perhaps? Or the Aldershot Inn?"

"Dinner sounds fine," the teacher replied. "But it's Wesley Corcoran who gets the money, not me. And it's a week to payday. So will it be your place or mine?"

MR. STRANG STUDIES EXHIBIT A

"A single superclue that allows the Great Detective to show his genius and crack the case might make for interesting detective fiction," Paul Roberts said, "but in real life it's plain hard work by the police acting as a team, wearing out shoe leather and following up every lead, no matter how slim, that gets the crime solved."

Mr. Strang mopped the sweat from his face with a handkerchief. Although the day was a scorcher even for August, it had been necessary for the gnomelike science teacher to take time out from preparing his curriculum for the upcoming school year to shop for a belated birthday gift for his nephew, a mere lad of forty-seven. Many of the shops in downtown Aldershot were air-conditioned, but the streets themselves were a fiery furnace. And, since he had to pass the Municipal Building on his walk home, Mr. Strang had decided to seek respite from the blistering sun by visiting Roberts in the detective squadroom on the second floor. Now, predictably, the talk had turned to crime and detection, subjects on which the teacher and his friend held firm if divergent views.

"But, Paul," said Mr. Strang, fanning himself with a blank arrest report, "don't you policemen speak of getting 'a break' in a case? What's that, if not some single fact that changes your perception of the whole problem?"

"Those so-called breaks happen because we *make* 'em happen. We get out there on the street and talk to people. We sift and analyze every fact, no matter how unimportant it seems. We work like dogs to crack our cases. It's only in fiction that a detective solves a murder by noticing that Lord Twiddle is using a different brand of toothpaste." Roberts wiped a damp shirtsleeve across his forehead. "How about a can of soda, Mr. Strang? We've got some in the fridge."

"Sounds good. But even in real life, Paul, there must be crimes that are solved by taking a single object or event and inferring—"

The teacher paused and stared past Roberts, who had opened the door of the small refrigerator in the corner of the squadroom. "What in blazes is *that*?"

"Soda," said Roberts, holding up a frosty green can. "Didn't you say you wanted one?"

"I mean that other thing. The obelisk."

"This?" Roberts took a square-based object about eighteen inches long from the fridge. Each of its flat sides had a slight inward slant, and the top was shaped like a tiny pyramid. It resembled an eighteen-inch replica of the Washington Monument, constructed of galvanized sheet steel. "It's a candle."

"A what?"

"A hand-poured candle, still in its metal mold. And it's also a murder weapon. It'll be Exhibit A when Harry Robeling goes on trial next month."

"But why is it in—?"

"It's evidence. Normally we'd keep it in the property room in the basement, but in this weather that place is hotter'n a two-dollar pistol. The DA asked if he could store it in our refrigerator, so it won't melt. Have a look. The lab boys are done with it, so there's no risk of contamination. Here, take it."

Mr. Strang accepted the wax-filled mold and almost dropped it—it was heavier than it looked. A wick spouted from the pointed top, and the base was a flat four-inch square of white wax. "Quite a weapon," he said. "It'd make a wicked club."

Roberts nodded. "Harry Robeling crushed Kirk Dansker's skull with it. Open-and-shut case, the trial's just a formality. But, hey!" He snapped his fingers. "This is a good example of what I was talking about, how the police work as a team. You've read about the Dansker murder, haven't you? There wasn't an awful lot about it at the time, but now, with the trial coming up, the papers are having a field day."

Mr. Strang shook his head. "I've been out of state most of the summer, visiting friends. And since returning I've had little time for the news. Why don't you tell me about it?"

Roberts relaxed in his chair and took a long swig of soda. "It happened last fall—the night of October second, or maybe early morning on the third. But the real start was a week or so before that, when Catherine Dansker got a note from her husband, saying he was coming home."

"Slower, Paul," said Mr. Strang. "Who's Catherine Dansker? And why is it important that her husband was coming home? Don't *most* husbands do that from time to time?"

Roberts smiled. "Catherine Dansker lives over in the Mill Valley section of town. Ten years ago, she and her husband Kirk bought a house there—really not much more than a shack. Kirk did odd jobs, and Catherine did craft work at home that she sold to stores, mostly for the Christmas season—candles, mainly. The family somehow managed to make ends meet. And then, three years ago, Kirk Dansker up and left."

"I see. But he was murdered, so I suppose he *did* return?"

"Like I said, Catherine got a letter from him about a week before the murder. He had a new job down south somewhere, he said, and he wanted to pick up some tools from the house. He said he'd drop by around midnight on October second, just long enough to get the tools, and then he'd be off again. But the thought of Kirk's return scared Catherine silly. She had no desire to come face to face with the husband who'd deserted her. She contacted some friends— George and Jean Greenwald, who live on the next block. They offered to let Catherine spend the night at their place. On the day before her husband was expected, she turned on some lights, unlocked the door, and left a note for Kirk to take whatever he needed but be gone by morning. Then George picked her up from her workshop at the back of the house on his way home from work."

"And I assume," said Mr. Strang, "that death prevented Mr. Dansker's departure."

"Right. Enter the villain of the piece: Harry Robeling. Harry lives next door to the Dansker house, and after Kirk moved out Harry figured that Catherine was ripe for the picking. You should see Robeling, Mr. Strang. What a creep: dirty, bad teeth, breath that would kill a cow, a mind like an open sewer. But he somehow thinks he's God's gift to the female sex. I guess Catherine had to put up with him, since he did occasional repairs around her house. For my money, she'd have been better off doing the work herself or leaving it undone. There's no way she should have gotten herself indebted to that hunk of sludge. But I guess he started calling on her pretty regular, like they were lovers."

"The murder, Paul," Mr. Strang reminded him. "Can we get to the murder?"

"Sure. Next morning, after spending the night at the Greenwalds', Catherine Dansker returned to her house, hoping to find that her husband had come and gone. Well, Kirk had come, all right, but he hadn't gone. When Catherine entered the house, she found his body in the workshop in back, where she made her candles. The side of his skull was crushed. And next to the body was *that* candle, still in its mold. It was pretty obvious to the lab boys that it had been used as a club. There was hair and blood and even bits of bone on it, all now neatly scaped into little envelopes for presentation in court."

"But how did you come to the conclusion that Harry Robeling was the killer?"

"Well, we found several sets of his fingerprints in the living room—which Catherine Dansker had just recently cleaned. No other prints at all, just his."

"Was there anything else?"

"Yep. Catherine Dansker had one piece of valuable jewelry, a gold necklace with a small emerald in it. It had been her mother's, and even when money was tight she never sold it. When she called in the discovery of Kirk's body, she was asked if anything was missing, and she looked around and saw that the necklace was gone.

"We've got a set procedure for locating stolen goods. We put out a bulletin to every pawnshop for miles around, saying we're looking for this and that. And guess what? Six weeks after the murder, Harry walked into a shop over in Holtsville and tried to pawn Catherine's necklace. The proprietor called us, and we picked Harry up while he was still in the shop. You know what he told us? Get this: he denied coming anywhere near the Dansker house on the night of the murder. He said he *found* the necklace hanging on the front doorknob of his own place. Did you ever hear such a yarn?

"So here's the way the case shapes up. Late at night on October second, Harry looks over and sees lights still on in the Dansker house. *Aha,* he thinks, *Catherine's having a little trouble getting to sleep.* So he goes over, planning on 'relaxing' her a bit, not knowing she's at the Greenwalds' and the house is empty. When he gets there and opens the unlocked door, there's nobody home. He goes in, pokes around, spots the necklace, and grabs it, figuring nobody'll be the wiser.

"But just about then, Kirk Dansker walks in to fetch his tools. He sees Harry Robeling with the necklace. Robeling runs back to the workshop to get away, Kirk follows, and Robeling beans him with the candle and goes home with the necklace. Like I said, open and shut.

"But the whole point, Mr. Strang, is that even a case as simple and straightforward as this one took a lot of teamwork and attention to detail to get it ready to be presented in court. Dobbs and I interviewed Catherine Dansker four times to make sure her story was coherent. We had to question the Greenwalds. A couple of guys from Homicide interrogated Robeling for days. His lawyer objected to every question, and naturally Robeling lied through his teeth. Then there was the pawnshop bulletin to get ready and distribute. Hundreds of hours put in by the uniformed patrol-men. Reports and more reports on everything.

"Teamwork and attention to detail, Mr. Strang. And that's why Harry Robeling's going to be found guilty next month."

"You seem pretty sure of that." Mr. Strang tossed off the last of his soda. "But the case is still a little unclear in my mind, Paul. Let's start with the Greenwalds. You interviewed them. How did they react when Catherine Dansker first contacted them?"

Roberts reached into a desk drawer and took out a folder with a thick sheaf of official reports. He glanced through them before answering. "Well, they were surprised when Mrs. Dansker asked them, they said, but they were happy to offer her a place to stay for the night. After work, George Greenwald stopped by the workshop to pick her up and—huh, here's a funny thing. Kind of ironic, really."

"What is?"

"When George came by to pick Catherine up, he watched her take a panful of melted wax from the stove and pour it into that candle mold. She filled it right up to the top. Greenwald said he even remembered a little wax dribbling down the outside of the mold. Catherine told him she wanted the wax to cool overnight, so she could decorate the candle the next day. Imagine that: Greenwald actually *saw* the murder weapon being made."

"Anything else?"

"Not much. Catherine was a perfect guest. The Greenwalds wanted to put her in the guest room upstairs, but she insisted that was too much bother and used the living-room couch. An argument almost started over that, but Catherine ultimately got her way."

"I see. You mentioned that, in your investigation, you found Harry Robeling's fingerprints in the Dansker living room. What's the significance of that? Wouldn't you *expect* to find them there, since he was a frequent visitor?"

Roberts shook his head. "Like I said, Catherine spent several hours cleaning that room just before Greenwald picked her up. Any prints that were there previously would have been wiped away. But during the investigation the fingerprint crew found Robeling's prints on the lamp, an ashtray, and the polished wood arms of the easy chair. No other prints—just Harry Robeling's. It's pretty clear that, when he entered the house that night, he sat down for a while and handled some things in the living room—*after* Catherine had done her cleaning. Police teamwork again, Mr. Strang.

No miracle clues, just doing things by the book."

"Uh huh," replied the teacher absently. "One last question, Paul, just to get things straight in my mind. You mentioned the Dansker 'family,' and that word implies children. If it was just the two of them, you would have said 'Mr. and Mrs.' or used their given names. Did the Danskers have children?"

"That has *nothing* to do with the case, Mr. Strang."

"It's a simple question. *Did* the Danskers have children?"

Roberts sighed. "They had a little girl, but for Pete's sake, don't let on to Catherine Dansker that I told you this."

"Why not? What happened?"

"That's the reason Kirk Dansker left. One day, Catherine was melting down a big pot of candle wax on her stove in the workshop. Her attention was distracted, and the kid—who was just a toddler—managed to reach the pot's handle. She pulled the whole thing over, and the hot wax burned her horribly. She died the next day, in the hospital.

"Kirk never got over it, and he blamed his wife. According to the neighbors, they screamed at one another for two weeks. Then Kirk took off, leaving Catherine alone. But that was three years ago." Roberts stared ruefully into space. "I didn't mean for this to come out. I just wanted to show you how police teamwork solved the case—and I think I've made my point."

Mr. Strang leaned across the desk and spoke in a confidential tone. "I don't think you fully comprehend the point you've made, Paul."

"What do you mean?"

"You have a solid case here."

"Of course we have. When Robeling goes to trial—"

"But it's not against Harry Robeling."

"You're not saying—"

"I am saying. On the basis of what you've told me—and you've gone into quite some detail—I'm saying I'm convinced that Catherine Dansker killed her husband."

Roberts groaned in exasperation. "But she was at the Greenwalds'. And the fingerprints in the living room were Robeling's, not hers. And Robeling had the necklace. You expect me to believe he found it hanging on his doorknob, the way he said, do you?"

"Why not?"

"Okay, okay." Roberts got to his feet, stomped angrily to the refrigerator, and took out another can of soda. "Fine, Mr. Hotshot Teacher who's smarter than the whole Aldershot Police Department. How do you figure?"

"First," said Mr. Strang, "let's consider why she might do such a terrible thing. Here we have a woman whose husband is convinced her negligence killed their child. Perhaps she was afraid of how the little girl's death would affect Kirk. As the months went by and the situation preyed on his mind, might he not one day return with revenge in his heart? Was picking up his tools simply an excuse to gain entrance to the house, where he could get his hands on Catherine?

"And maybe Catherine never forgave her husband for deserting her because of an accident that could have happened to anyone. Might *she* seek revenge for such a slight? We don't know. But it's certainly possible that Catherine felt terrible guilt—and the embodiment of that guilt was her husband, who had cruelly accused her and then abandoned her. Perhaps she sought expiation in his death.

"Fear? Revenge? Guilt? Or a combination of all three? Yes, Catherine Dansker might well wish her husband dead."

"But that's not *evidence*, Mr. Strang. Remember the fingerprints!"

"Ah, yes, those telltale fingerprints of Harry Robeling's. Paul, you told me that Catherine cleaned the living room just before Greenwald got there. And the way you said it disturbed me. You asserted it as an absolute fact. But you weren't there. The only way you could have gotten that information was by questioning Mrs. Dansker."

Roberts' face reddened. "Sure, she told us," he snapped. "But—"

"But I don't think she told you the truth. If I'm correct, Catherine Dansker cleaned the room, all right, but she did it several hours—or even *days*—beforehand. And, after she cleaned, she talked Harry Robeling into paying her one of his visits. From what you've told me about him, that wouldn't have been difficult. He came into the living room, sat in the chair, rested his hands on its arms, touched other objects as well. Meanwhile, Catherine took great pains to touch nothing, so only Robeling's prints would be found in the room."

Mr. Strang settled back in his own chair. "Once Robeling left, the living room was off limits to everyone—even Catherine herself. That wouldn't have been hard: Robeling seems to have been the only outsider who entered the house regularly. George Greenwald picked Catherine up from her workshop in the back of the house—and I suspect she insisted on that. She didn't want Greenwald anywhere near the living room."

"All very neat," said Roberts, his voice tired, "and very wrong. You're forgetting that Catherine was at the Greenwalds' house the night of the murder. Or were they in on the plot, too?"

Mr. Strang shook his head. "No, they only provided her with an alibi. I was struck by Catherine's insistence that she sleep on the living-room couch when the guest room had been offered. Why make a point of such a simple thing? I don't think Catherine was worried in the least about inconveniencing her hosts. But anyone staying in the guest room who wanted to leave the house late at night would presumably have to descend a flight of stairs and then roam about the ground floor before getting to a door. The living room, on the other hand, must have been near the front door, which could easily be unlocked on her way out and then relocked on her return. In short, Catherine chose the couch so as not to awaken the Greenwalds when she left to return to her own house.

"Once home, Catherine went to her workshop and stayed there, knowing that, when Kirk arrived, *he* would go there."

"Oh?" said the detective, his voice dripping with sarcasm. "Well, for your information, the door to the cellar—where Kirk's tools were kept—is just inside the front door. And, since the workshop's at the rear of the house, there'd be no reason for him to go anywhere near it."

"Let's say she found some way to lure him back there. And, when he got there, she struck him down with the candle. Afterwards, she took the necklace to Robeling's house and hung it on the doorknob, knowing full well the story would sound ridiculous when Harry told it to the police. Then she went back to the Greenwalds'.

"Harry found the necklace the next day. He didn't know who owned it, but it was obviously valuable. I'm sure he wasn't about to let on to anyone that he had it. Still, he waited a few weeks to see if anyone claimed it or advertised for it. When the owner didn't turn up, he tried to pawn it—and you caught him. End of story, and Catherine walks away free and clear. And yet she's the one who killed Kirk Dansker."

For a long moment, Roberts stared at his desk, and there was no sound in the squadroom except the whirring of the electric fan near the window.

"You're pretty positive about this, aren't you?" he said at last.

"Yes, I am."

"But *why*? I'll grant you that, if we didn't have so much evidence against Robeling, Catherine could—and I only say *could*—have murdered her husband in the way you said. Maybe she *could* have gotten him back to the workshop, where she could club him to death. But what makes you so sure she *did*?"

"Now we come full circle," said the teacher. "At the beginning of our conversation, we talked about the idea of a single all-important clue on which an entire case might pivot, and this case *has* such a clue. Barring some fact of which I'm not aware, that clue will put Catherine Dansker on trial as surely as it will free Harry Robeling."

"And what clue is that?"

"You have it right here," Mr. Strang replied. "The candle, of course. The murder weapon."

"The candle? But how—?"

"Paul, according to George Greenwald, Catherine Dansker filled the candle mold with melted wax just before she left the house with him. 'She filled it right up to the top.' Those, according to you, were his words. Then she left the house and didn't return until the following day, when she discovered her husband's body."

"That's right."

"That's *wrong,* because the base of the candle is absolutely flat."

"So what?"

"When molten candle wax solidifies, it shrinks considerably. Normally, the hardening wax will cling to the sides of the mold and shrink away from the areas where no metal touches it—in this case, the base. To completely fill a mold as big as this one, it'd be necessary to make several pourings, letting each one cool completely before making the next one."

"I don't—"

"If Catherine Dansker made this candle in a single pouring, the hardening wax—contracting as it set—would have left a large depression or 'socket' at the base of the candle. But the base is flat. This mold would have to have been filled *several* times, the wax cooling and shrinking each time, to result in a flat base."

"Maybe Robeling—or Kirk—"

"Ridiculous! What reason would *they* have for melting and pouring candle wax?"

"Well, what reason did *Catherine* have?"

"Catherine went back to her house that evening to kill her husband. She squirreled herself away in her workshop some time before he was scheduled to arrive. But she needed something—some bait—to get Kirk away from the front of the house, where anything she did to him might be seen by a neighbor. It was then that she melted the wax, using it to complete the candle she'd begun earlier that day.

"Sometime in the early morning hours, Kirk Dansker came up the front walk and entered the house. His plan was to collect his tools from the basement and leave. But then he noticed something—something that brought back all the horror of the tragic death of his child. And, because of that, he was drawn back to the workshop like a moth to a flame."

"What was it?" asked Roberts.

"The stench of hot candle wax, which must have permeated the entire house, the same odor he associated with the day his child pulled the pot off the stove. He ran to the workshop to see why that awful smell should be there in the middle of the night—and his wife struck him down."

There was another long silence as Roberts stared at his desk and doodled on a report form with a ballpoint pen. "You—you're sure about the wax shrinking?" he finally asked.

"Try it for yourself. You don't need a candle mold and special wax. A tin can and a block of paraffin will do. Any molded candle—especially one as massive as this one—must be poured several times to fill it up."

"Oh, boy," Roberts sighed. Several minutes ticked by on the wall clock as the detective turned the problem over in his mind. At last a series of odd sounds came from his parted lips.

He was laughing.

"Wait until I dump this in Jerry Partinger's lap," he chortled. "He'll have a fit."

He picked up the telephone and dialed a single digit. "Get me the DA's office," he muttered into the receiver. "Hello, Jerry? Paul Roberts. Look, I'm sitting here talking with a gentleman—a school teacher, if you must know, and—yeah, Jerry, I know you're busy, but you better get over here and talk with him yourself before the Robeling case goes to trial. You see, there's this one clue, and it's got me looking at the case from a whole new angle. Hello, Jerry? Jerry?"

MR. STRANG AND THE PURLOINED MEMO

The end of the school day was only minutes away, and Mr. Strang had just polished off the last of a set of general-science lab notes he was correcting when he heard a tapping at the door of the faculty lounge. "Yes?" the gnomelike teacher called imperiously. "What is it?"

He fully expected a student aide to peer fearfully around the half-open door and blurt out some message, then quickly pull the door closed. The Aldershot High School faculty lounge was the last bastion of teacher privilege in the entire building. Students were barred from entering it under all circumstances, and Mr. Strang fully intended to keep it that way.

The man who entered was wearing a dark-blue overcoat, unbuttoned, and a suit with a matching vest. His hair was tinged with gray, and his face had a deep tan that, during this winter season, bespoke a recent trip to a warmer climate. "They told me in the office I'd find you here," he said. "Do you remember me, Mr. Strang?"

The teacher shook hands tentatively. "I don't believe I—"

"It's been twenty-five years," the man replied, "but maybe I can refresh your memory. Think of sketches of Sherlock Holmes drawn in the margins of my lab reports, a quote from Agatha Christie that began my paper on alkaloid poisons, and the Ellery Queen paperback you found me reading behind my open textbook."

"Charlie!" cried Mr. Strang, with a broad smile of recognition. "Charlie Unsinger, as I live and breathe." And then the teacher shook his head ruefully. "You know, with all the time you spent reading detective stories when you should have been studying, you almost failed chemistry."

"Yeah, you pointed that out about every other day," Unsinger replied. "But I also remember you were almost as interested in crime fiction as I was."

"For me, it was just a hobby."

"How about that time I came to see you after school, and you thought I wanted extra help—"

"—but all you wanted was to talk about Poe's 'The Purloined Letter.' You'd just read it in English class."

"It was my theory," said Unsinger with mock pomposity, "that such a thing could never happen in real life, that a thorough search by trained police detectives would have been *bound* to discover the missing letter."

"While I, on the other hand, held that the method employed by the evil Minister D___ to conceal the letter might *well* have confounded Police Prefect G___ and his men ... or a modern-day police force, for that matter. Charlie, it's been a quarter of a century, but I'm prepared to continue our debate, if you still feel—"

Unsinger shook his head ruefully. "I concede defeat, Mr. Strang," he said. "But I've got a *real* one for you."

"A real what?"

"A real purloined-letter problem. And I want you to make like C. Auguste Dupin and solve it for me."

"Me? But—"

"Mr. Strang, even as a kid I was amazed at how you could take a bunch of odd facts and make them add up to some logical conclusion. And now—well, my purloined letter isn't anywhere near as glamorous as the one in Poe's story, but all the elements are there. For reasons I'm sure you'll understand when I tell you about it, we haven't wanted to bring in the regular police."

"We?"

"Daley Electronics, the company I work for, out at the edge of town."

"Computers?" Mr. Strang's eyebrows shot upward. "I can remember a time when you had trouble passing elementary algebra."

"Math isn't all that important in my job," said Unsinger. "I'm in charge of plant security. Mostly we just keep a close watch on workers and material in sensitive areas. Nothing much in the way of mystery—until this thing came up, two days ago. My men and I are stumped, and on turning the problem over in my mind I began to see similarities to the Poe story. Then I remembered our talk. Look, Mr. Strang, I know it's late, and I'm sure you want to be getting home, but my future with the company depends on getting this thing solved, so—well, I thought the time had come for extraordinary measures."

"And I'm the extraordinary measures?" Mr. Strang smiled. "All right, Charlie, sit down and tell me all about it. I don't know how much help I'll be, but I'm glad to listen."

Unsinger dropped heavily onto a straight-backed chair. "The letter in this case is an interoffice memo," he began. "It's a single piece of paper, with a diagram and a few equations on it."

"What makes it so all-fired important?"

"It's connected to a new miniaturization process we're working on. If it pans out, we'll be able to take a computer that's now as big as a TV set and reduce it to the size of a pack of cigarettes. Every computer company in the world is working on the same thing. Information any one of those competing companies comes up with would be extremely valuable to all the others. It isn't necessary to have the whole process. Any part of it might save weeks or even months of experimentation. And getting your product onto the market first could mean *millions* of dollars."

"I see. And I assume that this memo was somehow stolen—and you're afraid that whoever has it will sell it to one of your competitors."

Unsinger nodded. "The memo was in an 'Eyes Only' folder. Two days ago, it was passed along to one of our engineers, Warren Kirby. That was okay, because Kirby has clearance to see such material. But then the fool went and got a cup of coffee, leaving the folder out in plain sight."

"And it was gone when he returned, is that it?"

"The folder was still there, but the memo had been removed."

"Charlie, excuse my ignorance, but wouldn't it be a simple matter to ascertain who was near Mr. Kirby's desk while he was away and—"

"Hell, we *know* who took it—he was seen by one of my men."

Mr. Strang looked at Unsinger blankly. "I take it you haven't yet told me the whole story," he said.

Unsinger nodded. "It was a guy on the maintenance crew, Philip Holtz. According to my man, he walked by Kirby's desk, paused for about one second, and zingo—he scooped up the memo and jammed it into his pocket."

"Why wasn't he apprehended immediately?"

Unsinger's face reddened beneath its tan. "I'm afraid that was my fault. The security guard kept an eye on Holtz and called me on the interoffice phone for instructions. It occurred to me that, if we let Holtz think he'd gotten away with it, we might also be able to nab the person he was going to sell the memo to. So I told the guard not to grab Holtz, but to keep a close watch on him—and to carefully examine anything he handled.

"Well, an hour later it was quitting time. We're sure that, when Holtz left the plant, he still had the memo on him. Beatty, the guard, is a good man—he wouldn't make a mistake about something this important.

"I had two men tail Holtz home. He lives in a rooming house about four blocks from the plant. On the way there, he didn't stop for a beer, or to talk with anyone, and he didn't go near a trashcan. He didn't drop anything, either. He went straight home and directly up to his room. One of my men kept an eye on his closed door, and the other made arrangements with the landlady to rent the vacant room right across the hall from Holtz. So the point is, Mr. Strang, that Holtz had the memo when he went into his room. And we're sure he didn't come out again. I was called and went over there myself to keep an eye on the situation.

"About ten o'clock that evening, with Holtz still in his room, I began to get a little nervous, so I phoned our company president for instructions. He about hit the ceiling. He told me I had no business letting the memo out of the building, regardless of the circumstances. I was to bust in on Holtz immediately, get the memo, and deliver it to the president at home personally.

"When the boss speaks, Mr. Strang, I listen. So my men and I went across the hall and knocked on Holtz's door. When he answered and I explained how things were, he started yelling the whole thing was a setup just to get him fired. He insisted on a search—right then, on the spot."

"I take it the search was reasonably thorough," said Mr. Strang with a grin.

"Thorough? I'll say it was. We took Holtz to the room we'd rented and started in on him. First his clothes: shoe heels, jacket lining, pants cuffs, the works. Then we searched Holtz himself. Hair, mouth, in between his fingers and toes—you name it, we looked there. He didn't have the memo on him, that's for sure."

"A question, Charlie. Before you knocked on Holtz's door, did he have any inkling you were in the house?"

Unsinger shook his head. "He wouldn't have had any reason to swallow the memo or flush it down the john, if that's what you're getting at."

"I see. Go on."

"We left the other man to guard Holtz, and Beatty and I started in on his room. A crummy place, if you know what I mean: torn wallpaper, big cracks in the ceilings and walls, only two frosted bulbs working in the ceiling fixture, cigarette burns on the furniture, carpet worn almost through. And Holtz's style of living was just as sloppy. Unmade bed, empty beer cans lying around, sections of the newspaper all over."

"I get the picture," said Mr. Strang. "About how big would you say the room was?"

"Maybe fifteen feet square, including a little bathroom and a closet. One corner had a refrigerator and a hotplate. A bed, a dresser, three tables, a straight chair, and an easy chair. That's it.

"Anyway, we started with the junk on the floor. I got a can opener and took the tops off all the beer cans to make sure he hadn't stuck the memo inside one of them, and Beatty looked at each page of the newspaper separately. Nothing. When we were done, we carried out enough stuff to fill a garbage can.

"Then we checked the usual hiding places. His clothes, the inside of the closet, the dresser drawers, the kitchen cabinets. The fridge, the medicine chest, inside the toilet tank, the bathroom and kitchen drains. It occurred to us that he might have tossed the memo out the window, but no dice. All storm windows, fastened on the outside.

"It was late by then, and we were getting tired, so I sealed the room, put a guard on the door, and sent Holtz to a hotel with a man to look after him. Then I went home to get whatever sleep I could under the circumstances.

"The next day—yesterday—Beatty and I were back on the job. We didn't settle for just *tapping* the furniture, like Poe's policeman. We tore open cushions and bed pillows and the mattress and pawed through the stuffing. Anything made of tube steel, we reamed coat hangers through. If there was a joint in the wood, we broke it open and looked inside. After we hauled all *that* stuff out, there wasn't much left but the bare walls."

"Your methods sound drastic," observed the teacher. "That memo must be extremely valuable."

"It is," Unsinger assured him. "Besides, the stuff we took apart in his room couldn't have been worth fifty bucks all told. Replacing it will be no problem. Anyway, by yesterday evening we were down to taking the plates off the light switches and looking inside. We probed every pipe going or coming through the floor. We tore off all the wallpaper and examined every square foot of it. We didn't call it quits until two in the morning."

There was a wild look in Unsinger's eyes as he stared at the gnomelike teacher. "And we didn't find the memo, Mr. Strang," he moaned. "It's *got* to be there, but it wasn't."

Mr. Strang considered the problem for several moments. "Charlie," he said finally, "if you think I can be of any help to you, I'll be happy to try. But I must say, it sounds as if you've covered everything. Have you considered the possibility that the memo simply isn't there, that Holtz either hid it somewhere else or never stole it in the first place?"

Unsinger shook his head positively. "I trained the security team myself," he said. "They see what they say they see, and they report it properly. If one of them says Holtz took the memo, he took it. And if they say he brought it into his room, that's where it has to be. I'd stake my life on it." He sighed. "In fact, I already have."

"What's that supposed to mean?"

"If I don't find the memo, Holtz will sue me for everything I own, except my underwear. False arrest, illegal detention, you name it. He might even get to keep his job. And who knows what he'll steal from Daley Electronics next?"

"A good point." Mr. Strang glanced at his watch. "It's getting on for dinner time, and I'm hungry. Suppose we grab a bite somewhere, and afterward we can visit Holtz's rooming house?"

"Sure thing. How does the Aldershot Inn grab you?"

"Well—expensive."

"I'm buying. Their desserts are out of this world. That what keeps me going back." Unsinger paused. "The condemned man ate a hearty meal," he concluded wryly.

Dinner was excellent. Mr. Strang felt a bit foolish wearing a plastic bib, but he attacked his lobster—which seemed large enough to endanger small boats—with gusto. When they finished their main courses, Unsinger whispered in the waiter's ear.

Shortly thereafter, the waiter returned, carrying what appeared to be a melon—whole and uncut—on a silver tray.

"What's that?" asked the teacher.

"Dessert," replied Unsinger with a grin. "You're gonna love it."

"I don't know, Charlie. Melon doesn't really—"

"Watch." Unsinger gripped the top of the melon with both hands and lifted. The top came away, leaving the scooped-out lower half, which was filled with a mixture of fruit, ices, and thick syrups in all the colors of the rainbow. "Dig in," he ordered. "It's delicious."

"Amazing, Charlie," said the teacher. "You know, I would have sworn that was an uncut melon. I never suspected it was—it was—"

Unsinger looked across the table in concern. Mr. Strang was staring fixedly at the melon, as if it had exerted some hypnotic effect on him.

"Hey, are you all right?"

"What?" Mr. Strang shook his head, startled back to reality. "Oh, yes, I'm fine. Just fine."

"If you're sick or something, maybe I'd better take you home."

"Not at all. Let's tackle this dessert and then get a move on."

"But—"

"Eat, Charlie. Eat!"

*

Fifteen minutes later, on the way to Holtz's rooming house, Mr. Strang asked Unsinger to stop at an all-night grocery store. Unsinger waited at the wheel while he went in. He returned carrying a brown paper bag holding something that seemed to be about the size of a pint carton of milk.

Maybe the old boy has an ulcer, Unsinger thought.

All the way to the rooming house, Mr. Strang held the bag clutched to his chest.

When the landlady let them in, she asked Unsinger irritably when he'd be finished with "this searching business." Unsinger muttered something noncommittal and led Mr. Strang up to the second floor.

Outside the first door on the right stood a uniformed guard with DALEY ELECTRONICS SECURITY stitched across his shirt pocket.

"He's with me," Unsinger told the guard, reaching for the doorknob.

The teacher grasped his wrist lightly. "Hold on, Charlie. I'd like to go in alone. You wait out here."

"But I don't see—"

"Indulge me. I had a brainstorm back at the restaurant. If I'm right, you'll know very shortly. If I'm wrong, I'd like to be alone when I fall flat on my face."

"Okay, Mr. Strang. Let him in, Jake."

The paper bag in his hand, Mr. Strang entered the room and shut the door behind him.

Two minutes passed.

Three.

Then the door opened, and the teacher stuck his head out. "There's no furniture in here," he said.

"I told you, we ripped it all apart and carted it away with the rubbish."

"I need a chair."

"Mr. Strang, are you just going to sit in there and—oh, all right. Get him a chair, Jake."

Jake brought a straight-backed chair and handed it over. The door closed again. Another minute passed. The teacher had been alone in the room for nearly five minutes when—

"What was that?" cried Unsinger.

"I dunno," replied Jake. "It sounded like a gun with a silencer on it."

Unsinger tried the door, but the teacher had locked it.

"Mr. Strang!" he cried in alarm. "Are you all right?"

"Just fine, Charlie," came the teacher's quiet reassurance. "Would you do me a favor?"

"What do you need?"

"Could you bring Mr. Holtz here? I'd like to talk with him face to face."

"Why the blazes would you—?" And then Unsinger shrugged. "No problem. He's being very cooperative. I guess he figures that'll help his case when he hauls me into court. Jake, go to the hotel and bring Holtz back with you."

Unsinger rattled the doorknob again. "Will you let me in now, Mr. Strang?"

"Not yet. The first person I want to see coming through the door is Mr. Holtz."

Philip Holtz arrived some ten minutes later, closely watched by Jake. A thin redhead with a crop of freckles across the bridge of his nose, he greeted Unsinger with calm self-control. "Finished tearing up my room, have you?"

"Where you're going, Holtz," Unsinger replied, "all the furniture's bolted to the floor."

"I doubt that. When this is over, I'll be able to afford the best money can buy, courtesy of Daley Electronics. You're going to pay for what you're doing to me, Unsinger."

"Maybe. But first there's a man who'd like to talk to you." Unsinger rapped on the door. "Mr. Strang? He's here."

"Send him in, Charlie, by all means."

There was the sound of the bolt being drawn back, and the door opened.

Holtz walked into the room. Except for the light coming in from the hallway, it was inky black.

"Come in, Mr. Holtz," Mr. Strang said from the darkness. "You, too, Charlie. And close the door behind you."

"Put on a light," Holtz said.

"I like the darkness," the teacher replied. "Tell me, Mr. Holtz, do you still maintain that you had nothing to do with removing the missing memo from Mr. Kirby's desk at the plant?"

"You, too?" snapped Holtz. "Man, by the time this is over, I'll be suing half the village of Aldershot. But, for the record, no, I didn't take nothing from the plant."

"Charlie, are you there?"

"I'm here."

"I have a theory. I believe that lies told in darkness cannot survive the light. What say you, Mr. Holtz? Could you look me straight in the eye and still claim innocence?"

"I don't even know where you're *standing*," growled Holtz.

"Then by all means, let there be light!"

There was a *click*, and both Holtz and Unsinger squinted against the sudden glare. Holtz looked wildly about the room, which appeared to have taken a bomb blast. Paper was torn from the walls, pipes hung loosely from the bathroom sink, and there wasn't a stick of furniture to be seen except the straight-backed chair on the far side of the room, in which the teacher sat gazing fixedly at the maintenance man.

"Now then, Holtz," Mr. Strang barked. "Tell me again. Tell me you had nothing to do with stealing the memo. But only if it's the truth."

Holtz jerked his head around as if expecting help to arrive through the window or out of the walls themselves.

"The truth, Holtz," Mr. Strang repeated. "Perhaps a court of law will take a voluntary confession into account. But you must give it *now*."

Holtz lowered his head and stared at the floor.

"Get on with it, Holtz," ordered Mr. Strang.

The redheaded man drew a long breath. "It was me that stole the memo out of the folder on Mr. Kirby's desk," he said.

Only then did Mr. Strang reach into a pocket of his jacket, remove a much-folded piece of paper, and hand it to Unsinger.

"Is this what you're looking for?" he asked blithely.

It was.

Later that evening, after the recovered memo had been dispatched to the president of Daley Electronics, Mr. Strang and Charles Unsinger lounged in a rear booth at King George's Arms, a self-styled English pub in downtown Aldershot.

"I hope none of my students sees me here," said the teacher. "Even in these enlightened times, it's not considered seemly for a teacher to be spotted in a place like this." He sipped at a glass of white wine.

Unsinger was working on his second double scotch. "Okay, Mr. Strang," he said, "you've had your fun playing the man of mystery. Now how come you could find that memo when we couldn't?"

"Because," Mr. Strang replied, "as in Poe's 'Purloined Letter,' your search didn't take into account the manner in which the document was hidden."

"Don't go telling me the place he hid it was too obvious."

"No, the place where it was hidden was far from obvious."

"We skinned that room down to the bare walls."

Mr. Strang sucked at his unlit pipe. "To say the memo was hidden is to imply the existence of a hiding place—a receptacle of some kind, a box or a niche in the wall or any place that could *contain* a single sheet of paper. The question, then, is: why did you overlook such a receptacle?"

"Okay, why did we?"

"I suppose it's a matter of two qualities. One I'll call 'wholeness,' for lack of a better term, and the second is 'place.'"

"Come again?"

"Let's take 'wholeness' first. There are certain things we expect to have a quality of being *whole*, Charlie—that is to say, incapable of being penetrated. If one grants the wholeness of such an object, one would likely ignore it in a search. Let me give you an example from Poe himself. Do you remember how Prefect G___ mentioned removing the table tops?"

Unsinger nodded. "He wanted to see if the tops of the table's legs had been bored out to make a place to hide the letter."

"Yes, but never once did it occur to G___ that the letter might have been hidden *in the table top itself.*"

"Huh?"

"It wouldn't be hard to get a cabinetmaker to take a table top apart and gouge out a space within one of the inner boards. Once the letter was inserted in that space and the table reassembled and varnished, I daresay Prefect G___ would never have tumbled to the hiding place. You see, Charlie, even though it's usually made up of several layers of wood, a table top is *expected* to be solid. That's the quality I call 'wholeness.'"

"But we smashed all the furniture into kindling."

"I mention the table only as an example. Here's another. Suppose you'd opened the refrigerator in Holtz's room and found an egg. And suppose you picked up the egg and found it to be the proper weight and density, and you observed that the shell was apparently intact, with no holes—no matter how tiny—punched into it. Would it occur to you to actually *break* the egg in order to assure yourself it didn't contain the memo you were looking for?"

"I guess not. But there weren't any eggs in—"

"The egg is just another example. But a man who developed a method of puncturing an egg and sealing it again in a way that couldn't be detected would have found a perfect hiding place for a small object—at least until his secret came out."

"Mr. Strang, this is silly. You can't—"

"Not so silly, as you'll understand in a moment. But I also mentioned the quality of 'place.' By that I mean that an object is situated where it would normally be found. Take that egg. If you found it in the middle of the living-room carpet, say—out of its proper setting—your suspicions might be aroused, no matter what the egg looked or felt like.

"There's a children's game, Charlie, called Huckle-Buckle-Beanstalk, which is sometimes played in our elementary schools on rainy days. Very simply, an object—a thimble, perhaps—is given to one child to hide, while the rest have their eyes closed. The one doing the hiding must place the object in plain sight. At a signal, the others open their eyes and search for it. The first one to locate the object hides it for the next round of the game.

"A novice will hide the thimble in some out-of-the-way corner, perhaps at the base of a cupboard, where it can only be seen from certain parts of the room. This idea, however, has already occurred to the more experienced players, and those nooks and crannies are the first to be investigated.

"The really skillful players use a much better tactic. The thimble might be laid beside a pincushion on the teacher's desk or worn on a finger. The searchers accept the premise that a thimble *belongs* with needles and pins or on a finger, so their eyes pass right over it without really seeing it.

"Just one final illustration. Consider a log, three feet long and a foot in diameter. If it's found in a bathtub during an official search, it would be a suspicious object. Such a log would be examined, x-rayed, even chopped apart to see if it might contain the thing being looked for. But put the same log in a fireplace, and the chances are good that nobody'd look at it twice. The log in the fireplace has the virtues of both 'wholeness' and 'place.'"

"But what's all this got to do with Holtz's room?" asked Unsinger. "There aren't any eggs or thimbles or three-foot logs in it."

"The answer came to me earlier this evening, when I saw that melon. It was in its proper place—at our table at the Aldershot Inn. And it seemed to me to be perfectly solid. Without you there to show me otherwise, I'd have gone to my grave swearing it was whole."

Unsinger finished his drink. "Maybe it's the booze, Mr. Strang, but I still don't get it."

"Think, man, think! You burst in on Holtz at ten o'clock in the evening. You searched his room until all hours. And the following day you were there until two in the morning. You needed something to make those searches, Charlie—something that clearly indicates there was one part of the room you never considered."

"We needed," Unsinger began eagerly. Then he slumped in his chair. "What did we need?"

"You needed *light*! And you told me that only two bulbs in the ceiling fixture were operating. Clearly, then, one or more were not."

"You mean the memo was inside one of the dud bulbs?"

"Exactly! Holtz probably prepared his gimmick long before he actually stole the paper. He might have cut the bulb with a glass cutter, or sometimes the glass comes loose from the metal screw socket all by itself. When he got home with the memo, he wrapped it around the filament rod that sticks up from the bulb's base, fixed it in place with a rubber band, then glued the bulb over it, probably using one of those space-age adhesives that will stick *anything* together. Since the bulb was frosted, you'd have no way of knowing anything was inside it without actually breaking it."

"Breaking it," mused Unsinger. "So *that* was the sound I heard when you were in—"

"Right. I'd brought my own replacements from the grocery store."

"So when you turned on the lights—"

The teacher nodded. "Holtz saw that all the bulbs were now working. That was a pretty good indication that his hiding place had been discovered. The jig was up, and he knew it. End of story."

Unsinger shook his head. "Who'd ever think of looking inside a light bulb? Especially one that didn't work. But there it was, sitting in its socket the whole time."

"The requirements of both 'wholeness' and 'place' were satisfied, so there was really very little reason for you to even *consider* looking there. But, Charlie," the teacher smiled, "if I'm to be *whole* for school tomorrow, I'd better be getting back to my *place*."

As they left the pub, one final question occurred to Unsinger. "The chair," he said. "Why did you insist on my getting you a chair?"

"To stand on," said Mr. Strang, "in order to reach the bulb. We short people have our problems, too, you know."

AFTERWORD
by James Brittain

Among the memories I have of my father as a writer is his pounding away on a typewriter as I was in bed in the next room. And pounding it was: he had one of the first Royal portable typewriters, old enough to have seen service during the Second World War. It was a thing of rods and levers, with the action visible as the keys were pushed down, far better than the mechanical toys I had. To a curious boy like me, it was a sore temptation, but certainly off limits!

The action of the keys was such that the darkness of the character was dependent on the force with which a key was struck. My father would make old-fashioned carbon copies by using two sheets of paper (or sometimes more!) with a sheet of carbon paper between. He had to hit the keys hard enough to make an impression on the bottom sheet. I remember falling asleep to the rapid-fi re thudding of that venerable Royal.

From that machine came all the characters you've met in this book—the administrators, students, and faculty of Aldershot High—and all the people in his other stories as well. I'm glad that fans will have this opportunity to renew their acquaintance with my father's work, and I hope that new readers will discover him as well.

James Brittain
September 2021

A WILLIAM BRITTAIN CHECKLIST

The "Man Who Read" series (11 stories, all first published in
Ellery Queen's Mystery Magazine, all reprinted in *The Man Who
Read Mysteries: The Short Fiction of William Brittain*)

• The Man Who Read John Dickson Carr	(12/65)
• The Man Who Read Ellery Queen	(12/65)
• The Man Who Didn't Read	(05/66)
• The Woman Who Read Rex Stout	(07/66)
• The Boy Who Read Agatha Christie	(12/66)
• The Man Who Read Sir Arthur Conan Doyle	(08/68)
• The Man Who Read G. K. Chesterton	(04/73)
• The Man Who Read Dashiell Hammett	(05/74)
• The Man Who Read Georges Simenon	(01/75)
• The Girl Who Read John Creasey	(03/75)
• The Men Who Read Isaac Asimov	(05/78)

The "Mr. Strang" series (32 stories, all first published in EQMM;
those with an asterisk were reprinted in *The Man Who Read
Mysteries: The Short Fiction of William Brittain*, and the rest are
reprinted here)

• Mr. Strang Gives a Lecture	(03/67)*
• Mr. Strang Performs an Experiment	(06/67)*
• Mr. Strang Finds the Answers	(11/67)
• Mr. Strang Sees a Play	(03/68)
• Mr. Strang Takes a Field Trip	(12/68)*
• Mr. Strang Pulls a Switch	(06/69)
• Mr. Strang Takes a Hand	(04/70)
• Mr. Strang Lifts a Glass	(05/71)
• Mr. Strang Finds an Angle	(06/71)
• Mr. Strang Hunts a Bear	(11/71)
• Mr. Strang Checks a Record	(02/72)
• Mr. Strang Finds a Car	(07/72)
• Mr. Strang Versus the Snowman	(12/72)*
• Mr. Strang Examines a Legend	(02/73)
• Mr. Strang Invents a Strange Device	(06/73)
• Mr. Strang Follows Through	(09/73)
• Mr. Strang Discovers a Bug	(12/73)
• Mr. Strang Under Arrest	(02/74)
• Mr. Strang and the Cat Lady	(05/75)

- **Mr. Strang Picks Up the Pieces**   **(09/75)**
- **Mr. Strang, Armchair Detective**   **(12/75)***
- **Mr. Strang Battles a Deadline**   **(06/76)**
- **Mr. Strang Accepts a Challenge**   **(11/76)**
- **Mr. Strang Buys a Big H**   **(04/78)**
- **Mr. Strang Unlocks a Door**   **(06/81)**
- **Mr. Strang Interprets a Picture**   **(08/81)***
- **Mr. Strang Grasps at Straws**   **(11/81)**
- **Mr. Strang and the Lost Ship**   **(06/82)**
- **Mr. Strang Takes a Partner**   **(Mid-July/82)**
- **Mr. Strang Studies Exhibit A**   **(10/82)**
- **Mr. Strang and the Purloined Memo**   **(02/83)**
- **Mr. Strang Takes a Tour**   **(Mid-July/83)***

The Standalone Stories (29 stories, all in *Alfred Hitchcock's Mystery Magazine* unless otherwise noted, and all forthcoming in *The Man Who Wrote Mysteries: The Rest of Brittain,* to be published by Crippen & Landru in 2024)

- **Joshua**   **(10/64)**
- **Mr. Lightning** (as by "James Knox")   **(07/66, EQMM)**
- **The Zaretski Chain**   **(06/68, EQMM)**
- **The Last Word** (as by "James Knox")   **(06/68, EQMM)**
- **The Second Sign in the Melon Patch**   **(01/69, EQMM)**
- **That Day on the Knob**   **(09/69, EQMM)**
- **Hand**   **(10/69)**
- **Just About Average**   **(06/70)**
- **Falling Object**   **(02/71, EQMM)**
- **A Gallon of Gas**   **(04/71)**
- **The Driver**   **(01/72)**
- **Wynken, Blynken and Nod**   **(04/72, EQMM)**
- **The Artificial Liar**   **(04/72)**
- **The Sonic Boomer**   **(02/73)**
- **The Scarab Ring**   **(05/73)**
- **A State of Preparedness**   **(09/73)**
- **The Button**   **(10/73)**
- **The Platt Avenue Irregulars**   **(11/73)**
- **He Can't Die Screaming**   **(02/74)**
- **Waiting for Harry**   **(03/74)**
- **The Impossible Footprint**   **(11/74)**
- **I'm Back, Little Sister**   **(12/74)**
- **Aunt Abigail's Wall Safe**   **(05/75)**
- **Yellowbelly**   **(10/75)**
- **Historical Errors**   **(02/76)**
- **A Private Little War**   **(05/76)**
- **One Big Happy Family**   **(09/76)**
- **The Second Reason**   **(02/77, EQMM)**

• **The Ferret Man**   (Spring-Summer/77, *Antæus*)

The Children's Books

- *All The Money In The World* (1979)
- *Devil's Donkey* (1981)
- *Sherlock Holmes, Master Detective* (1982)
- *The Wish Giver: Three Tales of Coven Tree* (1983)
- *Who Knew There'd Be Ghosts?* (1985)
- *Dr. Dredd's Wagon of Wonders* (1987)
- *The Fantastic Freshman* (1988)
- *My Buddy, the King* (1989)
- *Professor Popkin's Prodigious Polish: A Tale of Coven Tree* (1990)
- *Wings* (1991)
- *The Ghost from Beneath the Sea* (1992)
- *The Mystery of the Several Sevens* (1994)
- *Shape-Changer* (1994)
- *The Wizards and the Monster* (1994)

ACKNOWLEDGMENTS

Once again, my thanks to Ginny Brittain and Susan Brittain Gawley, William Brittain's widow and daughter, for their friendship, encouragement, and support—and, this time around, thanks also to Bill and Ginny's son, James.

Once again, my eternal gratitude to the late Frederic Dannay and Eleanor Sullivan, the first and second editors-in-chief of *Ellery Queen's Mystery Magazine*, who gave each of the stories included in this volume its original publication.

Once again, I am indebted to Jeff Marks and Doug Greene of Crippen & Landru for all they do, and especially for their desire to re-introduce Bill Brittain's work to today's readers.

Once again, a tip of the fedora to Arthur Vidro for tracking down and transcribing several of the stories—and, this time, to Kevin O'Hagen of the Northern Virginia Community College libraries for his assistance in locating several others.

Most of all, my thanks, love and respect to Bill Brittain for writing these wonderful tales—which gave me many hours of enjoyment when I read them on their original publication and did so yet again when I reread them during the preparation of this collection—and for the many kindnesses he and Ginny showed me when I was a lad. This book is not just a companion piece to *The Man Who Read Mysteries*. It's also another expression of my appreciation, Bill, for your talent, and for your and Ginny's and Sue's and James's friendship.

Josh Pachter
October 2021

THE MAN WHO SOLVED MYSTERIES

The Man Who Solved Mysteries by William Brittain is printed on 60 pound paper, and is designed by Jeffrey Marks using InDesign. The type is Bookman Old Style, a serif typeface which evolved from Old Style Antique during the 19th century. The printing and binding is by Southern Ohio Printing for the hard cover and the trade paperback version. Clothbound book binding is from Cincinnati Bindery. The book was published in January 2022 by Crippen & Landru Publishers, Inc., Cincinnati, OH.

Crippen & Landru, Publishers
P. O. Box 532057
Cincinnati, OH 45253
Web: www.Crippenlandru.Com
E-mail: info@crippenlandru.Com

Since 1994, Crippen & Landru has published more than 100 first editions of short-story collections by important detective and mystery writers.

This is the best edited, most attractively packaged line of mystery books introduced in this decade. The books are equally valuable to collectors and readers. [Mystery Scene Magazine]

The specialty publisher with the most star-studded list is Crippen & Landru, which has produced short story collections by some of the biggest names in contemporary crime fiction. [Ellery Queen's Mystery Magazine]

God bless Crippen & Landru. [The Strand Magazine]

A monument in the making is appearing year by year from Crippen & Landru, a small press devoted exclusively to publishing the criminous short story. [Alfred Hitchcock's Mystery Magazine]

Lost Classic Publications

Challenge the Impossible: The Impossible Files of Dr. Sam Hawthorne by Edward D. Hoch. Full cloth in dust jacket, signed and numbered by the publisher, $45.00. Trade softcover, $19.00.

Nothing Is Impossible: Further Problems of Dr. Sam Hawthorne by Edward D. Hoch.
Dr. Sam Hawthorne, a New England country doctor in the first half of the twentieth century, was constantly faced by murders in locked rooms and impossible disappearances. *Nothing Is Impossible* contains fifteen of Dr. Sam's most extraordinary cases. Full cloth in dust jacket, signed and numbered by the publisher, $45.00. Trade softcover, $19.00.

Chain of Witnesses; The Cases of Miss Phipps by Phyllis Bentley, edited by Marvin Lachman. Lost Classics Series. A critic writes, "stylistically, [Bentley's] stories ... share a quiet humor and misleading simplicity of statement with the works of Christie .... Her work [is] informed and consistent with the classic traditions of the mystery." Full cloth in dust jacket, $29.00. Trade softcover, $19.00.

Swords, Sandals And Sirens by Marilyn Todd.
Murder, conmen, elephants. Who knew ancient times could be such fun? Many of the stories feature Claudia Seferius, the super-bitch heroine of Marilyn Todd's critically acclaimed mystery series set in ancient rome. Others feature Cleopatra, the olympian gods, and high priestess Ilion blackmailed to work with Sparta's feared secret police. Full cloth in dust jacket, signed and numbered by the author, $45.00. Trade softcover, $19.00.

The Puzzles of Peter Duluth by Patrick Quentin. Lost Classics Series.
Anthony Boucher wrote: "Quentin is particularly noted for the enviable polish and grace which make him one of the leading American fabricants of the murderous comedy of manners; but this surface smoothness conceals intricate and meticulous plot construction as faultless as that of Agatha Christie." Full cloth in dust jacket, $29.00. Trade softcover, $19.00.

Hunt in the Dark by Q. Patrick, Lost Classics Series. Full cloth in dust jacket, $29.00. Trade softcover, $19.00.

All But Impossible: The Impossible Files of Dr. Sam Hawthorne by Edward D. Hoch. Full cloth in dust jacket, signed and numbered by the publisher, $45.00. Trade softcover, $19.00.

Sequel to Murder by Anthony Gilbert, edited by John Cooper. Full cloth in dust jacket, $29.00. Trade softcover, $19.00.

Hildegarde Withers: Final Riddles? by Stuart Palmer with an introduction by Steven Saylor. Full cloth in dust jacket, $29.00. Trade softcover, $19.00

Shooting Script by William Link and Richard Levinson, edited by Joseph Goodrich. Full cloth in dust jacket, signed and numbered by the families, $47.00. Trade softcover, $22.00.

Subscriptions

Subscribers agree to purchase each forthcoming publication, either the Regular Series or the Lost Classics or (preferably) both. Collectors can thereby guarantee receiving limited editions, and readers won't miss any favorite stories.

Subscribers receive a discount of 20% off the list price (and the same discount on our backlist) and a specially commissioned short story by a major writer in a deluxe edition as a gift at the end of the year.

The point for us is that, since customers don't pick and choose which books they want, we have a guaranteed sale even before the book is published, and that allows us to be more imaginative in choosing short story collections to issue.

That's worth the 20% discount for us. Sign up now and start saving. Email us at orders@crippenlandru.com or visit our website at www.crippenlandru.com on our subscription page.